When the World Shook

When the World Shook

Being an Account of the Great Adventure of Bastin, Bickley and Arbuthnot

BY

H. RIDER HAGGARD

GYAN

Published by

GYAN

Gyan Publishing House
5, Ansari Road
Daryaganj, New Delhi-110002
Phone: 011-47034999, 9811692060
E-mail: books@gyanbooks.com

Distribution Network
gyanbooks.com
India, USA, Canada, UK, Australia

ISBN: 978-81-212-8444-8 (HB)
First Published, 1919

2nd Impression 2024

Printed at: Gyan Press, Delhi.

WHEN THE WORLD SHOOK
Author: H. RIDER HAGGARD

WHEN THE WORLD SHOOK

"Daughter, lead these strangers to me; I would speak with them." (*See page 210.*)

When the World Shook

Being an Account of the Great Adventure
of Bastin, Bickley and Arbuthnot

BY

H. RIDER HAGGARD

LONGMANS, GREEN AND CO.
FOURTH AVENUE & 30TH STREET, NEW YORK
1919

DEDICATION

Ditchingham, 1918.

My dear Curzon,

More than thirty years ago you tried to protect me, then a stranger to you, from one of the falsest and most malignant accusations ever made against a writer.

So complete was your exposure of the methods of those at work to blacken a person whom they knew to be innocent, that, as you will remember, they refused to publish your analysis which destroyed their charges and, incidentally, revealed their motives.

Although for this reason vindication came otherwise, your kindness is one that I have never forgotten, since, whatever the immediate issue of any effort, in the end it is the intention that avails.

Therefore in gratitude and memory I ask you to accept this romance, as I know that you do not disdain the study of romance in the intervals of your Imperial work.

The application of its parable to our state and possibilities —beneath or beyond these glimpses of the moon—I leave to your discernment.

Believe me,
Ever sincerely yours,
H. RIDER HAGGARD.

To
The Earl Curzon of Kedleston, K.G.

CONTENTS

Contents

WHEN THE WORLD SHOOK

CHAPTER I

ARBUTHNOT DESCRIBES HIMSELF

I SUPPOSE that I, Humphrey Arbuthnot, should begin this history in which Destiny has caused me to play so prominent a part, with some short account of myself and of my circumstances.

I was born forty years ago in this very Devonshire village in which I write, but not in the same house. Now I live in the Priory, an ancient place and a fine one in its way, with its panelled rooms, its beautiful gardens where, in this mild climate, in addition to our own, flourish so many plants which one would only expect to find in countries that lie nearer to the sun, and its green, undulating park studded with great timber trees. The view, too, is perfect; behind and around the rich Devonshire landscape with its hills and valleys and its scarped faces of red sandstone, and at a distance in front, the sea. There are little towns quite near too, that live for the most part on visitors, but these are so hidden away by the contours of the ground that from the Priory one cannot see them. Such is Fulcombe where I live, though for obvious reasons I do not give it its real name.

Many years ago my father, the Rev. Humphrey Arbuthnot, whose only child I am, after whom also I am named Humphrey, was the vicar of this place with which our family is said to have some rather vague hereditary connection. If so, it was severed in the Carolian times because my ancestors fought on the side of Parliament.

My father was a recluse, and a widower, for my mother, a Scotswoman, died at or shortly after my birth. Being very High Church for those days he was not popular with the family that owned the Priory before me. Indeed its head, a somewhat vulgar person of the name of Enfield who had made money in trade, almost persecuted him, as he was in a position to do, being the local magnate and the owner of the rectorial tithes.

I mention this fact because owing to it as a boy I made up my mind that one day I would buy that place and sit in his seat, a wild enough idea at the time. Yet it became engrained in me, as do such aspirations of our youth, and when the opportunity arose in after years I carried it out. Poor old Enfield! He fell on evil fortunes, for in trying to bolster up a favourite son who was a gambler, a spendthrift, and an ungrateful scamp, in the end he was practically ruined and when the bad times came, was forced to sell the Fulcombe estate. I think of him kindly now, for after all he was good to me and gave me many a day's shooting and leave to fish for trout in the river.

By the poor people, however, of all the district round, for the parish itself is very small, my father was much beloved, although he did practise confession, wear vestments and set lighted candles on the altar, and was even said to have openly expressed the wish, to which however he never attained, that he could see a censer swinging in the chancel. Indeed the church which, as monks built it, is very large and fine, was always full on Sundays, though many of the worshippers came from far away, some of them doubtless out of curiosity because of its papistical repute, also because, in a learned fashion, my father's preaching was very good indeed.

For my part I feel that I owe much to these High-Church views. They opened certain doors to me and taught me something of the mysteries which lie at the back of all religions and therefore have their home in the inspired soul of man whence religions are born. Only the pity is that in ninety-nine cases out of a hundred he never discovers, never even guesses at that entombed aspiration, never sinks a shaft down on to this secret but most precious vein of ore.

I have said that my father was learned; but this is a mild description, for never did I know anyone quite so learned. He was one of those men who is so good all round that he became pre-eminent in nothing. A classic of the first water, a very respectable mathematician, an expert in theology, a student of sundry foreign languages and literature in his lighter moments, an inquirer into sociology, a theoretical musician though his playing of the organ excruciated most people because it was too correct, a really first-class authority upon flint instruments and the best grower of garden vegetables in the county, also of apples—such were some of his attainments. That was what made his sermons so popular, since at times one or the other of these subjects would break out into them, his theory being that God spoke to us through all of these things.

But if I began to drift into an analysis of my father's abilities, I should never stop. It would take a book to describe them. And yet mark this, with them all his name is as dead to the world to-day as though he had never been. Light reflected from a hundred facets dissipates itself in space and is lost; that concentrated in one tremendous ray pierces to the stars.

Now I am going to be frank about myself, for without frankness what is the value of such a record as this? Then it becomes simply another convention, or rather conventional method of expressing the octoroon kind of truths with which the highly civilised races feed themselves, as fastidious ladies eat cakes and bread from which all but the smallest particle of nourishment has been extracted.

The fact is, therefore, that I inherited most of my father's abilities, except his love for flint instruments which always bored me to distraction, because although they are by association really the most human of things, somehow to me they never convey any idea of humanity. In addition I have a practical side which he lacked; had he possessed it surely he must have become an archbishop instead of dying the vicar of an unknown parish. Also I have a spiritual sense, mayhap mystical would be a better term, which with all this religion was missing from my father's nature.

For I think that notwithstanding his charity and devotion he never quite got away from the shell of things, never cracked it and set his teeth in the kernel which alone can feed our souls. His keen intellect, to take an example, recognised every one of the difficulties of our faith and flashed hither and thither in the darkness, seeking explanation, seeking light, trying to reconcile, to explain. He was not great enough to put all this aside and go straight to the informing Soul beneath that strives to express itself everywhere, even through those husks which are called the World, the Flesh and the Devil, and as yet does not always quite succeed.

It is this boggling over exteriors, this peering into pitfalls, this desire to prove that what such senses as we have tell us is impossible, is in fact possible, which causes the overthrow of many an earnest, seeking heart and renders its work, conducted on false lines, quite nugatory. These *will* trust to themselves and their own intelligence and not be content to spring from the cliffs of human experience into the everlasting arms of that Infinite which are stretched out to receive them and to give them rest and the keys of knowledge. When will man learn what was taught to him of old, that faith is the only plank wherewith he can float upon this sea and that his miserable works avail him nothing; also that it is a plank made of many sorts of wood, perhaps to suit our different weights?

So to be honest, in a sense I believe myself to be my father's superior, and I know that he agreed with me. Perhaps this is owing to the blood of my Scotch mother which mixed well with his own; perhaps because the essential spirit given to me, though cast in his mould, was in fact quite different—or of another alloy. Do we, I wonder, really understand that there are millions and billions of these alloys, so many indeed that Nature, or whatever is behind Nature, never uses the same twice over? That is why no two human beings are or ever will be quite identical. Their flesh, the body of their humiliation, is identical in all, any chemist will prove it to you, but that which animates the flesh is distinct and different because it comes from the home of that infinite variety which is necessary to the ultimate evolution of the good and bad that we symbolise as heaven and hell.

Further, I had and to a certain extent still have another advantage over my father, which certainly came to me from my mother, who was, as I judge from all descriptions and such likenesses as remain of her, an extremely handsome woman. I was born much better looking. He was small and dark, a little man with deep-set eyes and beetling brows. I am also dark, but tall above the average, and well made. I do not know that I need say more about my personal appearance, to me not a very attractive subject, but the fact remains that they called me "handsome Humphrey" at the University, and I was the captain of my college boat and won many prizes at athletic sports when I had time to train for them.

Until I went up to Oxford my father educated me, partly because he knew that he could do it better than anyone else, and partly to save school expenses. The experiment was very successful, as my love of all outdoor sports and of any small hazardous adventure that came to my hand, also of associating with fisherfolk whom the dangers of the deep make men among men, saved me from becoming a milksop. For the rest I learned more from my father, whom I always desired to please because I loved him, than I should have done at the best and most costly of schools. This was shown when at last I went to college with a scholarship, for there I did very well indeed, as search would still reveal.

Here I had better set out some of my shortcomings, which in their sum have made a failure of me. Yes, a failure in the highest sense, though I trust what Stevenson calls "a faithful failure." These have their root in fastidiousness and that lack of perseverance, which really means a lack of faith, again using the word in its higher and wider sense. For if one had real faith one would always persevere, knowing that in every work undertaken with high aim, there is an element of nobility, however humble and unrecognised that work may seem to be. God after all is the God of Work, it is written large upon the face of the Universe. I will not expand upon the thought; it would lead me too far afield, but those who have understanding will know what I mean.

As regards what I interpret as fastidiousness, this is not very easy to express. Perhaps a definition will help. I am like a man with an over-developed sense of smell, who when walking through a foreign city, however clean and well kept, can always catch the evil savours that are inseparable from such cities. More, his keen perception of them interferes with all other perceptions and spoils his walks. The result is that in after years, whenever he thinks of that beautiful city, he remembers, not its historic buildings or its wide boulevards, or whatever it has to boast, but rather its ancient, fish-like smell. At least he remembers that first owing to this defect in his temperament.

So it is with everything. A lovely woman is spoiled for such a one because she eats too much or has too high a voice; he does not care for his shooting because the scenery is flat, or for his fishing because the gnats bite as well as the trout. In short he is out of tune with the world as it is. Moreover, this is a quality which, where it exists, cannot be overcome; it affects day-labourers as well as gentlemen at large. It is bred in the bone.

Probably the second failure-breeding fault, lack of perseverance, has its roots in the first, at any rate in my case. At least on leaving college with some reputation, I was called to the Bar where, owing to certain solicitor and other connections, I had a good opening. Also, owing to the excellence of my memory and powers of work, I began very well, making money even during my first year. Then, as it happened, a certain case came my way and, my leader falling ill suddenly after it was opened, was left in my hands. The man whose cause I was pleading was, I think, one of the biggest scoundrels it is possible to conceive. It was a will case and if he won, the effect would be to beggar two most estimable middle-aged women who were justly entitled to the property, to which end personally I am convinced he had committed forgery; the perjury that accompanied it I do not even mention.

Well, he did win, thanks to me, and the estimable middle-aged ladies were beggared, and as I heard afterwards, driven to such extremities that one of them died of her misery and the other became a lodging-house keeper. The details do not matter, but I may explain that these ladies were unattractive in appearance and manner and broke down beneath my cross-examination which made them appear to be telling falsehoods, whereas they were only completely confused. Further, I invented an ingenious theory of the facts which, although the judge regarded it with suspicion, convinced an unusually stupid jury who gave me their verdict.

Everybody congratulated me and at the time I was triumphant, especially as my leader had declared that our case was impossible. Afterwards, however, my conscience smote me sorely, so much so that arguing from the false premise of this business, I came to the conclusion that the practice of the Law was not suited to an honest man. I did not take the large view that such matters average themselves up and that if I had done harm in this instance, I might live to do good in many others, and perhaps become a just judge, even a great judge. Here I may mention that in after years, when I grew rich, I rescued that surviving old lady from her lodging-house, although to this day she does not know the name of her anonymous friend. So by degrees, without saying anything, for I kept on my chambers, I slipped out of practice, to the great disappointment of everybody connected with me, and took to authorship.

A marvel came to pass, my first book was an enormous success. The whole world talked of it. A leading journal, delighted to have discovered someone, wrote it up; other journals followed suit to be in the movement. One of them, I remember, which had already dismissed it with three or four sneering lines, came out with a second and two-column notice. It sold like wildfire and I suppose had some merits, for it is still read, though few know that I wrote it, since fortunately it was published under a pseudonym.

Again I was much elated and set to work to write another and, as I believe, a much better book. But jealousies had been excited by this leaping into fame of a totally unknown person, which were, moreover, accentuated through a foolish article that I published in answer to some criticisms, wherein I spoke my mind with an insane freedom and biting sarcasm. Indeed I was even mad enough to quote names and to give the example of the very powerful journal which at first carped at my work and then gushed over it when it became the fashion. All of this made me many bitter enemies, as I found out when my next book appeared.

It was torn to shreds, it was reviled as subversive of morality and religion, good arrows in those days. It was called puerile, half-educated stuff—I half-educated! More, an utterly false charge of plagiarism was cooked up against me and so well and venomously run that vast numbers of people concluded that I was a thief of the lowest order. Lastly, my father, from whom the secret could no longer be kept, sternly disapproved of both these books which I admit were written from a very radical and somewhat anti-church point of view. The result was our first quarrel and before it was made up, he died suddenly.

Now again fastidiousness and my lack of perseverance did their work, and solemnly I swore that I would never write another book, an oath which I have kept till this moment, at least so far as publication is concerned, and now break only because I consider it my duty so to do and am not animated by any pecuniary object.

Thus came to an end my second attempt at carving out a career. By now I had grown savage and cynical, rather revengeful also, I fear. Knowing myself to possess considerable abilities in sundry directions, I sat down, as it were, to think things over and digest my past experiences. Then it was that the truth of a very ancient adage struck upon my mind, namely, that money is power. Had I sufficient money I could laugh at unjust critics for example; indeed they or their papers would scarcely dare to criticise me for fear lest it should be in my power to do them a bad turn. Again I could follow my own ideas in life and perhaps work good in the world, and live in such surroundings as commended themselves to me. It was as clear as daylight, but—how to make the money?

I had some capital as the result of my father's death, about £8,000 in all, plus a little more that my two books had brought in. In what way could I employ it to the best advantage? I remembered that a cousin of my father and therefore my own, was a successful stockbroker, also that there had been some affection between them. I went to him, he was a good, easy-natured man who was frankly glad to see me, and offered to put £5,000 into his business, for I was not minded to risk everything I had, if he would give me a share in the profits. He laughed heartily at my audacity.

"Why, my boy," he said, "being totally inexperienced at this game, you might lose us more than that in a month. But I like your courage, I like your courage, and the truth is that I do want help. I will think it over and write to you."

He thought it over and in the end offered to try me for a year at a fixed salary with a promise of some kind of a partnership if I suited him. Meanwhile my £5,000 remained in my pocket.

I accepted, not without reluctance since with the impatience of youth I wanted everything at once. I worked hard in that office and soon mastered the business, for my knowledge of figures—I had taken a first-class mathematical degree at college—came to my aid, as in a way did my acquaintance with Law and Literature. Moreover I had a certain aptitude for what is called high finance. Further, Fortune, as usual, showed me a favourable face.

In one year I got the partnership with a small share in the large profits of the business. In two the partner above me retired, and I took his place with a third share of the firm. In three my cousin, satisfied that it was in able hands, began to cease his attendance at the office and betook himself to gardening which was his hobby. In four I paid him out altogether, although to do this I had to borrow money on our credit, for by agreement the title of the firm was continued. Then came that extraordinary time of boom which many will remember to their cost. I made a bold stroke and won.

On a certain Saturday when the books were made up, I found that after discharging all liabilities, I should not be worth more than £20,000. On the following Saturday but two when the books were made up, I was worth £153,000! *L'appétit vient en mangeant.* It seemed nothing to me when so many were worth millions.

For the next year I worked as few have done, and when I struck a balance at the end of it, I found that on the most conservative estimate I was the owner of a million and a half in hard cash, or its equivalent. I was so tired out that I remember this discovery did not excite me at all. I felt utterly weary of all wealth-hunting and of the City and its ways. Moreover my old fastidiousness and lack of perseverance re-asserted themselves. I reflected, rather late in the day perhaps, on the ruin that this speculation was bringing to thousands, of which some lamentable instances had recently come to my notice, and once more considered whether it were a suitable career for an upright man. I had wealth; why should I not take it and enjoy life?

Also—and here my business acumen came in, I was sure that these times could not last. It is easy to make money on a rising market, but when it is falling the matter is very different. In five minutes I made up my mind. I sent for my junior partners, for I had taken in two, and told them that I intended to retire at once. They were dismayed both at my loss, for really *I* was the firm, and because, as they pointed out, if I withdrew all my capital, there would not be sufficient left to enable them to carry on.

One of them, a blunt and honest man, said to my face that it would be dishonourable of me to do so. I was inclined to answer him sharply, then remembered that his words were true.

"Very well," I said, "I will leave you £600,000 on which you shall pay me five per cent. interest, but no share of the profits."

On these terms we dissolved the partnership and in a year they had lost the £600,000, for the slump came with a vengeance. It saved them, however, and to-day they are earning a reasonable income. But I have never asked them for that £600,000.

CHAPTER II

BASTIN AND BICKLEY

BEHOLD me once more a man without an occupation, but now the possessor of about £900,000. It was a very considerable fortune, if not a large one in England; nothing like the millions of which I had dreamed, but still enough. To make the most of it and to be sure that it remained, I invested it very well, mostly in large mortgages at four per cent. which, if the security is good, do not depreciate in capital value. Never again did I touch a single speculative stock, who desired to think no more about money. It was at this time that I bought the Fulcombe property. It cost me about £120,000 of my capital, or with alterations, repairs, etc., say £150,000, on which sum it may pay a net two and a half per cent., not more.

This £3,700 odd I have always devoted to the upkeep of the place, which is therefore in first-rate order. The rest I live on, or save.

These arrangements, with the beautifying and furnishing of the house and the restoration of the church in memory of my father, occupied and amused me for a year or so, but when they were finished time began to hang heavy on my hands. What was the use of possessing about £20,000 a year when there was nothing upon which it could be spent? For after all my own wants were few and simple and the acquisition of valuable pictures and costly furniture is limited by space.

Oh! in my small way I was like the weary King

Ecclesiast. For I too made me great works and had possessions of great and small cattle (I tried farming and lost money over it!) and gathered me silver and gold and the peculiar treasure of kings, which I presume means whatever a man in authority chiefly desires, and so forth. But "behold all was vanity and vexation of spirit, and there was no profit under the sun."

So, notwithstanding my wealth and health and the deference which is the rich man's portion, especially when the limit of his riches is not known, it came about that I too "hated life," and this when I was not much over thirty. I did not know what to do; for Society as the word is generally understood, I had no taste; it bored me; horse-racing and cards I loathed, who had already gambled too much on a big scale. The killing of creatures under the name of sport palled upon me, indeed I began to doubt if it were right, while the office of a junior county magistrate in a place where there was no crime, only occupied me an hour or two a month.

Lastly my neighbours were few and with all due deference to them, extremely dull. At least I could not understand them because in them there did not seem to be anything to understand, and I am quite certain that they did not understand me. More, when they came to learn that I was radical in my views and had written certain "dreadful" and somewhat socialistic books in the form of fiction, they both feared and mistrusted me as an enemy to their particular section of the race. As I had not married and showed no inclination to do so, their womenkind also, out of their intimate knowledge, proclaimed that I led an immoral life, though a little reflection would have shown them that there was no one in the neighbourhood which for a time I seldom left, who could possibly have tempted an educated creature to such courses.

Terrible is the lot of a man who, while still young and possessing the intellect necessary to achievement, is deprived of all ambition. And I had none at all. I did not even wish to purchase a peerage or a baronetcy in this fashion or in that, and, as in my father's case, my tastes were so many and so catholic that I could not lose myself in any one of them. They never became more than diversions to me. A hobby is only really amusing when it becomes an obsession.

At length my lonesome friendliness oppressed me so much that I took steps to mitigate it. In my college life I had two particular friends whom I think I must have selected because they were so absolutely different from myself.

They were named Bastin and Bickley. Bastin—Basil was his Christian name—was an uncouth, shock-headed, flat-footed person of large, rugged frame and equally rugged honesty, with a mind almost incredibly simple. Nothing surprised him because he lacked the faculty of surprise. He was like that kind of fish which lies at the bottom of the sea and takes every kind of food into its great maw without distinguishing its flavour. Metaphorically speaking, heavenly manna and decayed cabbage were just the same to Bastin. He was not fastidious and both were mental pabulum—of a sort—together with whatever lay between these extremes. Yet he was good, so painfully good that one felt that without exertion to himself he had booked a first-class ticket straight to Heaven; indeed that his guardian angel had tied it round his neck at birth lest he should lose it, already numbered and dated like an identification disc.

I am bound to add that Bastin never went wrong because he never felt the slightest temptation to do so. This I suppose constitutes real virtue, since, in view of certain Bible sayings, the person who is tempted and would like to yield to the temptation, is equally a sinner with the person who does yield. To be truly good one should be too good to be tempted, or too weak to make the effort worth the tempter's while—in short not deserving of his powder and shot.

I need hardly add that Bastin went into the Church; indeed, he could not have gone anywhere else; it absorbed him naturally, as doubtless Heaven will do in due course. Only I think it likely that until they get to know him he will bore the angels so much that they will continually move him up higher. Also if they have any susceptibilities left, probably he will tread upon their toes—an art in which I never knew his equal. However, I always loved Bastin, perhaps because no one else did, a fact of which he remained totally unconscious, or perhaps because of his brutal way of telling one what he conceived to be the truth, which, as he had less imagination than a dormouse, generally it was not. For if the truth is a jewel, it is one coloured and veiled by many different lights and atmospheres.

It only remains to add that he was learned in his theological fashion and that among his further peculiarities were the slow, monotonous voice in which he uttered his views in long sentences, and his total indifference to adverse argument however sound and convincing.

My other friend, Bickley, was a person of a quite different character. Like Bastin, he was learned, but his tendencies faced another way. If Bastin's omnivorous throat could swallow a camel, especially a theological camel, Bickley's would strain at the smallest gnat, especially a theological gnat. The very best and most upright of men, yet he believed in nothing that he could not taste, see or handle. He was convinced, for instance, that man is a brute-descended accident and no more, that what we call the soul or the mind is produced by a certain action of the grey matter of the brain; that everything apparently inexplicable has a perfectly mundane explanation, if only one could find it; that miracles certainly never did happen, and never will; that all religions are the fruit of human hopes and fears and the most convincing proof of human weakness; that notwithstanding our infinite variations we are the subjects of Nature's single law and the victims of blind, black and brutal chance.

Such was Bickley with his clever, well-cut face that always reminded me of a cameo, and thoughtful brow; his strong, capable hands and his rather steely mouth, the mere set of which suggested controversy of an uncompromising kind. Naturally as the Church had claimed Bastin, so medicine claimed Bickley.

Now as it happened the man who succeeded my father as vicar of Fulcombe was given a better living and went away shortly after I had purchased the place and with it the advowson. Just at this time also I received a letter written in the large, sprawling hand of Bastin from whom I had not heard for years. It went straight to the point, saying that he, Bastin, had seen in a Church paper that the last incumbent had resigned the living of Fulcombe which was in my gift. He would therefore be obliged if I would give it to him as the place he was at in Yorkshire did not suit his wife's health.

Here I may state that afterwards I learned that what did not suit Mrs. Bastin was the organist, who was pretty. She was by nature a woman with a temperament so insanely jealous that actually she managed to be suspicious of Bastin, whom she had captured in an unguarded moment when he was thinking of something else and who would as soon have thought of even looking at any woman as he would of worshipping Baal. As a matter of fact it took him months to know one female from another. Except as possible providers of subscriptions and props of Mothers' Meetings, women had no interest for him.

To return—with that engaging honesty which I have mentioned—Bastin's letter went on to set out all his own disabilities, which, he added, would probably render him unsuitable for the place he desired to fill. He was a High Churchman, a fact which would certainly offend many; he had no claims to being a preacher although he was extraordinarily well acquainted with the writings of the Early Fathers. (What on earth had that to do with the question, I wondered.) On the other hand he had generally been considered a good visitor and was fond of walking (he meant to call on distant parishioners, but did not say so).

Then followed a page and a half on the evils of the existing system of the presentation to livings by private persons, ending with the suggestion that I had probably committed a sin in buying this particular advowson in order to increase my local authority, that is, if I had bought it, a point on which he was ignorant. Finally he informed me that as he had to christen a sick baby five miles away on a certain moor and it was too wet for him to ride his bicycle, he must stop. And he stopped.

There was, however, a P.S. to the letter, which ran as follows:

"Someone told me that you were dead a few years ago, and of course it may be another man of the same name who owns Fulcombe. If so, no doubt the Post Office will send back this letter."

That was his only allusion to my humble self in all those diffuse pages. It was a long while since I had received an epistle which made me laugh so much, and of course I gave him the living by return of post, and even informed him that I would increase its stipend to a sum which I considered suitable to the position.

About ten days later I received another letter from Bastin which, as a scrawl on the flap of the envelope informed me, he had carried for a week in his pocket and forgotten to post. Except by inference it returned no thanks for my intended benefits. What it did say, however, was that he thought it wrong of me to have settled a matter of such spiritual importance in so great a hurry, though he had observed that rich men were nearly always selfish where their time was concerned. Moreover, he considered that I ought first to have made inquiries as to his present character and attainments, etc., etc.

To this epistle I replied by telegraph to the effect that I should as soon think of making inquiries about the character of an archangel, or that of one of his High Church saints. This telegram, he told me afterwards, he considered unseemly and even ribald, especially as it had given great offence to the postmaster, who was one of the sidesmen in his church.

Thus it came about that I appointed the Rev. Basil Bastin to the living of Fulcombe, feeling sure that he would provide me with endless amusement and act as a moral tonic and discipline. Also I appreciated the man's blunt candour. In due course he arrived, and I confess that after a few Sundays of experience I began to have doubts as to the wisdom of my choice, glad as I was to see him personally. His sermons at once bored me, and, when they did not send me to sleep, excited in me a desire for debate. How could he be so profoundly acquainted with mysteries before which the world had stood amazed for ages? Was there nothing too hot or too heavy in the spiritual way for him to dismiss in a few blundering and casual words, as he might any ordinary incident of every-day life, I wondered? Also his idea of High Church observances was not mine, or, I imagine, that of anybody else. But I will not attempt to set it out.

His peculiarities, however, were easy to excuse and entirely swallowed up by the innate goodness of his nature which soon made him beloved of everyone in the place, for although he thought that probably most things were sins, I never knew him to discover a sin which he considered to be beyond the reach of forgiveness. Bastin was indeed a most charitable man and in his way wide-minded.

The person whom I could not tolerate, however, was his wife, who, to my fancy, more resembled a vessel, a very unattractive vessel, full of vinegar than a woman. Her name was Sarah and she was small, plain, flat, sandy-haired and odious, quite obsessed, moreover, with her jealousies of the Rev. Basil, at whom it pleased her to suppose that every woman in the countryside under fifty was throwing herself.

Here I will confess that to the best of my ability I took care that they did in outward seeming, that is, whenever she was present, instructing them to sit aside with him in darkened corners, to present him with flowers, and so forth. Several of them easily fell into the humour of the thing, and I have seen him depart from a dinner-party followed by that glowering Sarah, with a handful of rosebuds and violets, to say nothing of the traditional offerings of slippers, embroidered markers and the like. Well, it was my only way of coming even with her, which I think she knew, for she hated me poisonously.

So much for Basil Bastin. Now for Bickley. Him I had met on several occasions since our college days, and after I was settled at the Priory from time to time I asked him to stay with me. At length he came, and I found out that he was not at all comfortable in his London practice which was of a nature uncongenial to him; further, that he did not get on with his partners. Then, after reflection, I made a suggestion to him. I pointed out that, owing to its popularity amongst seaside visitors, the neighbourhood of Fulcombe was a rising one, and that although there were doctors in it, there was no really first-class surgeon for miles.

Now Bickley was a first-class surgeon, having held very high hospital appointments, and indeed still holding them. Why, I asked, should he not come and set up here on his own? I would appoint him doctor to the estate and also give him charge of a cottage hospital which I was endowing, with liberty to build and arrange it as he liked. Further, as I considered that it would be of great advantage to me to have a man of real ability within reach, I would guarantee for three years whatever income he was earning in London.

He thanked me warmly and in the end acted on the idea, with startling results so far as his prospects were concerned. Very soon his really remarkable skill became known and he was earning more money than as an unmarried man he could possibly want. Indeed, scarcely a big operation took place at any town within twenty miles, and even much farther away, at which he was not called in to assist.

Needless to say his advent was a great boon to me, for as he lived in a house I let him quite near by, whenever he had a spare evening he would drop in to dinner, and from our absolutely opposite standpoints we discussed all things human and divine. Thus I was enabled to sharpen my wits upon the hard steel of his clear intellect which was yet, in a sense, so limited.

I must add that I never converted him to my way of thinking and he never converted me to his, any more than he converted Bastin, for whom, queerly enough, he had a liking. They pounded away at each other, Bickley frequently getting the best of it in the argument, and when at last Bastin rose to go, he generally made the same remark. It was:

"It really is sad, my dear Bickley, to find a man of your intellect so utterly wrongheaded and misguided. I have convicted you of error at least half a dozen times, and not to confess it is mere pigheadedness. Good night. I am sure that Sarah will be sitting up for me."

"Silly old idiot!" Bickley would say, shaking his fist after him. "The only way to get him to see the truth would be to saw his head open and pour it in."

Then we would both laugh.

Such were my two most intimate friends, although I admit it was rather like the equator cultivating close relationships with the north and south poles. Certainly Bastin was as far from Bickley as those points of the earth are apart, while I, as it were, sat equally distant between the two. However, we were all very happy together, since in certain characters, there are few things that bind men more closely than profound differences of opinion.

Now I must turn to my more personal affairs. After all, it is impossible for a man to satisfy his soul, if he has anything of the sort about him which in the remotest degree answers to that description, with the husks of wealth, luxury and indolence, supplemented by occasional theological and other arguments between his friends. Becoming profoundly convinced of this truth, I searched round for something to do and, like Noah's dove on the waste of waters, found nothing. Then I asked Bickley and Bastin for their opinions as to my best future course. Bickley proved a barren draw. He rubbed his nose and feebly suggested that I might go in for "research work," which, of course, only represented his own ambitions. I asked him indignantly how I could do such a thing without any scientific qualifications whatever. He admitted the difficulty, but replied that I might endow others who had the qualifications.

"In short, become a milch cow for sucking scientists," I replied, and broke off the conversation.

Bastin's idea was, first, that I should teach in a Sunday School; secondly, that if this career did not satisfy all my aspirations, I might be ordained and become a missionary.

On my rejection of this brilliant advice, he remarked that the only other thing he could think of was that I should get married and have a large family, which might possibly advantage the nation and ultimately enrich the Kingdom of Heaven, though of such things no one could be quite sure. At any rate, he was certain that at present I was in practice neglecting my duty, whatever it might be, and in fact one of those cumberers of the earth who, he observed in the newspaper he took in and read when he had time, were "very happily named—the idle rich."

"Which reminds me," he added, "that the clothing-club finances are in a perfectly scandalous condition; in fact, it is £25 in debt, an amount that as the squire of the parish I consider it incumbent on you to make good, not as a charity but as an obligation."

"Look here, my friend," I said, ignoring all the rest, "will you answer me a plain question? Have you found marriage such a success that you consider it your duty to recommend it to others? And if you have, why have *you* not got the large family of which you speak?"

"Of course not," he replied with his usual frankness. "Indeed, it is in many ways so disagreeable that I am convinced it must be right and for the good of all concerned. As regards the family I am sure I do not know, but Sarah never liked babies, which perhaps has something to do with it."

Then he sighed, adding, "You see, Arbuthnot, we have to take things as we find them in this world and hope for a better."

"Which is just what I am trying to do, you unilluminating old donkey!" I exclaimed, and left him there shaking his head over matters in general, but I think principally over Sarah.

By the way, I think that the villagers recognised this good lady's vinegary nature. At least, they used to call her "Sour Sal."

CHAPTER III

NATALIE

Now what Bastin had said about marriage stuck in my mind as his blundering remarks had a way of doing, perhaps because of the grain of honest truth with which they were often permeated. Probably in my position it was more or less my duty to marry. But here came the rub; I had never experienced any leanings that way. I was as much a man as others, more so than many are, perhaps, and I liked women, but at the same time they repelled me.

My old fastidiousness came in; to my taste there was always something wrong about them. While they attracted one part of my nature they revolted another part, and on the whole I preferred to do without their intimate society, rather than work violence to this second and higher part of me. Moreover, quite at the beginning of my career I had concluded from observation that a man gets on better in life alone, rather than with another to drag at his side, or by whom perhaps he must be dragged. Still true marriage, such as most men and some women have dreamed of in their youth, had always been one of my ideals; indeed it was on and around this vision that I wrote that first book of mine which was so successful. Since I knew this to be unattainable in our imperfect conditions, however, notwithstanding Bastin's strictures, again I dismissed the whole matter from my mind as a vain imagination.

As an alternative I reflected upon a parliamentary career which I was not too old to begin, and even toyed with one or two opportunities that offered themselves, as these do to men of wealth and advanced views. They never came to anything, for in the end I decided that Party politics were so hateful and so dishonest, that I could not bring myself to put my neck beneath their yoke. I was sure that if I tried to do so, I should fail more completely than I had done at the Bar and in Literature. Here, too, I am quite certain that I was right.

The upshot of it all was that I sought refuge in that last expedient of weary Englishmen, travel, not as a globe-trotter, but leisurely and with an inquiring mind, learning much but again finding, like the ancient writer whom I have quoted already, that there is no new thing under the sun; that with certain variations it is the same thing over and over again.

No, I will make an exception, the East did interest me enormously. There it was, at Benares, that I came into touch with certain thinkers who opened my eyes to a great deal. They released some hidden spring in my nature which hitherto had always been striving to break through the crust of our conventions and inherited ideas. I know now that what I was seeking was nothing less than the Infinite; that I had "immortal longings in me." I listened to all their solemn talk of epochs and years measureless to man, and reflected with a thrill that after all man might have his part in every one of them. Yes, that bird of passage as he seemed to be, flying out of darkness into darkness, still he might have spread his wings in the light of other suns millions upon millions of years ago, and might still spread them, grown radiant and glorious, millions upon millions of years hence in a time unborn.

If only I could know the truth. Was Life (according to Bickley) merely a short activity bounded by nothingness before and behind; or (according to Bastin) a conventional golden-harped and haloed immortality, a word of which he did not in the least understand the meaning?

Or was it something quite different from either of these, something vast and splendid beyond the reach of vision, something God-sent, beginning and ending in the Eternal Absolute and at last partaking of His attributes and nature and from æon to æon shot through with His light? And how was the truth to be learned? I asked my Eastern friends, and they talked vaguely of long ascetic preparation, of years upon years of learning, from whom I could not quite discover. I was sure it could not be from them, because clearly they did not know; they only passed on what they had heard elsewhere, when or how they either could not or would not explain. So at length I gave it up, having satisfied myself that all this was but an effort of Oriental imagination called into life by the sweet influences of the Eastern stars.

I gave it up and went away, thinking that I should forget. But I did not forget. I was quick with a new hope, or at any rate with a new aspiration, and that secret child of holy desire grew and grew within my soul, till at length it flashed upon me that this soul of mine was itself the hidden Master from which I must learn my lesson. No wonder that those Eastern friends could not give his name, seeing that whatever they really knew, as distinguished from what they had heard, and it was little enough, each of them had learned from the teaching of his own soul.

Thus, then, I too became a dreamer with only one longing, the longing for wisdom, for that spirit touch which should open my eyes and enable me to see.

Yet now it happened strangely enough that when I seemed within myself to have little further interest in the things of the world, and least of all in women, I, who had taken another guest to dwell with me, those things of the world came back to me and in the shape of Woman the Inevitable. Probably it was so decreed since is it not written that no man can live to himself alone, or lose himself in watching and nurturing the growth of his own soul?

It happened thus. I went to Rome on my way home from India, and stayed there a while. On the day after my arrival I wrote my name in the book of our Minister to Italy at that time, Sir Alfred Upton, not because I wished him to ask me to dinner, but for the reason that I had heard of him as a man of archæological tastes and thought that he might enable me to see things which otherwise I should not see.

As it chanced he knew about me through some of my Devonshire neighbours who were friends of his, and did ask me to dinner on the following night. I accepted and found myself one of a considerable party, some of them distinguished English people who wore Orders, as is customary when one dines with the representative of our Sovereign. Seeing these, and this shows that in the best of us vanity is only latent, for the first time in my life I was sorry that I had none and was only plain Mr. Arbuthnot who, as Sir Alfred explained to me politely, must go in to dinner last, because all the rest had titles, and without even a lady as there was not one to spare.

Nor was my lot bettered when I got there, as I found myself seated between an Italian countess and a Russian prince, neither of whom could talk English, while, alas, I knew no foreign language, not even French in which they addressed me, seeming surprised that I did not understand them. I was humiliated at my own ignorance, although in fact I was not ignorant, only my education had been classical. Indeed I was a good classic and had kept up my knowledge more or less, especially since I became an idle man. In my confusion it occurred to me that the Italian countess might know Latin from which her own language was derived, and addressed her in that tongue. She stared, and Sir Alfred, who was not far off and overheard me (he also knew Latin), burst into laughter and proceeded to explain the joke in a loud voice, first in French and then in English, to the assembled company, who all became infected with merriment and also stared at me as a curiosity.

Then it was that for the first time I saw Natalie, for owing to a mistake of my driver I had arrived rather late and had not been introduced to her. As her father's only daughter, her mother being dead, she was seated at the end of the table behind a fan-like arrangement of white Madonna lilies, and she had bent forward and, like the others, was looking at me, but in such a fashion that her head from that distance seemed as though it were surrounded and crowned with lilies. Indeed the greatest art could not have produced a more beautiful effect which was, however, really one of naked accident.

An angel looking down upon earth through the lilies

of Heaven—that was the rather absurd thought which flashed into my mind. I did not quite realise her face at first except that it seemed to be both dark and fair; as a fact her waving hair which grew rather low upon her forehead, was dark, and her large, soft eyes were grey. I did not know, and to this moment I do not know if she was really beautiful, but certainly the light that shone through those eyes of hers and seemed to be reflected upon her delicate features, was beauty itself. It was like that glowing through a thin vase of the purest alabaster within which a lamp is placed, and I felt this effect to arise from no chance, like that of the lily-setting, but, as it were, from the lamp of the spirit within.

Our eyes met, and I suppose that she saw the wonder and admiration in mine. At any rate her amused smile faded, leaving the face rather serious, though still sweetly serious, and a tinge of colour crept over it as the first hue of dawn creeps into a pearly sky. Then she withdrew herself behind the screen of lilies and for the rest of that dinner which I thought was never coming to an end, practically I saw her no more. Only I noted as she passed out that although not tall, she was rounded and graceful in shape and that her hands were peculiarly delicate.

Afterwards in the drawing-room her father, with whom I had talked at the table, introduced me to her, saying:

"My daughter is the real archæologist, Mr. Arbuthnot, and I think if you ask her, she may be able to help you."

Then he bustled away to speak to some of his important guests, from whom I think he was seeking political information.

"My father exaggerates," she said in a soft and very sympathetic voice, "but perhaps"—and she motioned me to a seat at her side.

Then we talked of the places and things that I more particularly desired to see and, well, the end of it was that I went back to my hotel in love with Natalie, and as she afterwards confessed, she went to bed in love with me.

It was a curious business, more like meeting a very old friend from whom one had been separated by circumstances for a score of years or so than anything else. We were, so to speak, intimate from the first; we knew all about each other, although here and there was something new, something different which we could not remember, lines of thought, veins of memory which we did not possess in common. On one point I am absolutely clear: it was not solely the everyday and ancient appeal of woman to man and man to woman which drew us together, though doubtless this had its part in our attachment as under our human conditions it must do, seeing that it is Nature's bait to ensure the continuance of the race. It was something more, something quite beyond that elementary impulse.

At any rate we loved, and one evening in the shelter of the solemn walls of the great Coliseum at Rome, which at that hour were shut to all except ourselves, we confessed our love. I really think we must have chosen the spot by tacit but mutual consent because we felt it to be fitting. It was so old, so impregnated with every human experience, from the direst crime of the tyrant who thought himself a god, to the sublimest sacrifice of the martyr who already was half a god; with every vice and virtue also which lies between these extremes, that it seemed to be the most fitting altar whereon to offer our hearts and all that caused them to beat, each to the other.

So Natalie and I were betrothed within a month of our first meeting. Within three we were married, for what was there to prevent or delay? Naturally Sir Alfred was delighted, seeing that he possessed but small private resources and I was able to make ample provision for his daughter who had hitherto shown herself somewhat difficult in this business of matrimony and now was bordering on her twenty-seventh year. Everybody was delighted, everything went smoothly as a sledge sliding down a slope of frozen snow and the mists of time hid whatever might be at the end of that slope. Probably a plain; at the worst the upward rise of ordinary life.

That is what we thought, if we thought at all. Certainly we never dreamed of a precipice. Why should we, who were young, by comparison, quite healthy and very rich? Who thinks of precipices under such circumstances, when disaster seems to be eliminated and death is yet a long way off?

And yet we ought to have done so, because we should have known that smooth surfaces without impediment to the runners often end in something of the kind.

I am bound to say that when we returned home to Fulcombe, where of course we met with a great reception, including the ringing (out of tune) of the new peal of bells that I had given to the church, Bastin made haste to point this out.

"Your wife seems a very nice and beautiful lady, Arbuthnot," he reflected aloud after dinner, when Mrs. Bastin, glowering as usual, though what at I do not know, had been escorted from the room by Natalie, "and really, when I come to think of it, you are an unusually fortunate person. You possess a great deal of money, much more than you have any right to, which you seem to have done very little to earn and do not spend quite as I should like you to do, and this nice property, that ought to be owned by a great number of people, as, according to the views you express, I should have thought you would acknowledge, and everything else that a man can want. It is very strange that you should be so favoured and not because of any particular merits of your own which one can see. However, I have no doubt it will all come even in the end and you will get your share of troubles, like others. Perhaps Mrs. Arbuthnot will have no children as there is so much for them to take. Or perhaps you will lose all your money and have to work for your living, which might be good for you. Or," he added, still thinking aloud after his fashion, "perhaps she will die young—she has that kind of face, although, of course, I hope she won't," he added, waking up.

I do not know why, but his wandering words struck me cold; the proverbial funeral bell at the marriage feast was nothing to them. I suppose it was because in a flash of intuition I knew that they would come true and that he was an appointed Cassandra. Perhaps this uncanny knowledge overcame my natural indignation at such super-*gaucherie* of which no one but Bastin could have been capable, and even prevented me from replying at all, so that I merely sat still and looked at him.

But Bickley did reply with some vigour.

"Forgive me for saying so, Bastin," he said, bristling all over as it were, "but your remarks, which may or may not be in accordance with the principles of your religion, seem to me to be in singularly bad taste. They would have turned the stomachs of a gathering of early Christians, who appear to have been the worst mannered people in the world, and at any decent heathen feast your neck would have been wrung as that of a bird of ill omen."

"Why?" asked Bastin blankly. "I only said what I thought to be the truth. The truth is better than what you call good taste."

"Then I will say what I think also to be the truth," replied Bickley, growing furious. "It is that you use your Christianity as a cloak for bad manners. It teaches consideration and sympathy for others of which you seem to have none. Moreover, since you talk of the death of people's wives, I will tell you something about your own, as a doctor, which I can do as I never attended her. It is highly probable, in my opinion, that she will die before Mrs. Arbuthnot, who is quite a healthy person with a good prospect of life."

"Perhaps," said Bastin. "If so, it will be God's will and I shall not complain" (here Bickley snorted), "though I do not see what you can know about it. But why should you cast reflections on the early Christians who were people of strong principle living in rough times, and had to wage war against an established devil-worship? I know you are angry because they smashed up the statues of Venus and so forth, but had I been in their place I should have done the same."

"Of course you would, who doubts it? But as for the early Christians and their iconoclastic performances—well, curse them, that's all!" and he sprang up and left the room.

I followed him.

Let it not be supposed from the above scene that

there was any ill-feeling between Bastin and Bickley. On the contrary they were much attached to each other, and this kind of quarrel meant no more than the strong expression of their individual views to which they were accustomed from their college days. For instance Bastin was always talking about the early Christians and missionaries, while Bickley loathed both, the early Christians because of the destruction which they had wrought in Egypt, Italy, Greece and elsewhere, of all that was beautiful; and the missionaries because, as he said, they were degrading and spoiling the native races and by inducing them to wear clothes, rendering them liable to disease. Bastin would answer that their souls were more important than their bodies, to which Bickley replied that as there was no such thing as a soul except in the stupid imagination of priests, he differed entirely on the point. As it was quite impossible for either to convince the other, there the conversation would end, or drift into something in which they were mutually interested, such as natural history and the hygiene of the neighbourhood.

Here I may state that Bickley's keen professional eye was not mistaken when he diagnosed Mrs. Bastin's state of health as dangerous. As a matter of fact she was suffering from heart disease that a doctor can often recognise by the colour of the lips, etc., which brought about her death under the following circumstances:

Her husband attended some ecclesiastical function at a town over twenty miles away and was to have returned by a train which would have brought him home about five o'clock. As he did not arrive she waited at the station for him until the last train came in about seven o'clock—without the beloved Basil. Then, on a winter's night she tore up to the Priory and begged me to lend her a dog-cart in which to drive to the said town to look for him. I expostulated against the folly of such a proceeding, saying that no doubt Basil was safe enough but had forgotten to telegraph, or thought that he would save the sixpence which the wire cost.

Then it came out, to Natalie's and my intense amusement, that all this was the result of her jealous nature of which I have spoken. She said she had never slept a night away from her husband since they were married and with so many "designing persons" about she could not say what might happen if she did so, especially as he was "such a favourite and so handsome." (Bastin was a fine looking man in his rugged way.)

I suggested that she might have a little confidence in him, to which she replied darkly that she had no confidence in anybody.

The end of it was that I lent her the cart with a fast horse and a good driver, and off she went. Reaching the town in question some two and a half hours later, she searched high and low through wind and sleet, but found no Basil. He, it appeared, had gone on to Exeter, to look at the cathedral where some building was being done, and missing the last train had there slept the night.

About one in the morning, after being nearly locked up as a mad woman, she drove back to the Vicarage, again to find no Basil. Even then she did not go to bed but raged about the house in her wet clothes, until she fell down utterly exhausted. When her husband did return on the following morning, full of information about the cathedral, she was dangerously ill, and actually passed away while uttering a violent tirade against him for his supposed suspicious proceedings.

That was the end of this truly odious British matron.

In after days Bastin, by some peculiar mental process, canonised her in his imagination as a kind of saint. "So loving," he would say, "such a devoted wife! Why, my dear Humphrey, I can assure you that even in the midst of her death-struggle her last thoughts were of me," words that caused Bickley to snort with more than usual vigour, until I kicked him to silence beneath the table.

CHAPTER IV

DEATH AND DEPARTURE

Now I must tell of my own terrible sorrow, which turned my life to bitterness and my hopes to ashes.

Never were a man and a woman happier together than I and Natalie. Mentally, physically, spiritually we were perfectly mated, and we loved each other dearly. Truly we were as one. Yet there was something about her which filled me with vague fears, especially after she found that she was to become a mother. I would talk to her of the child, but she would sigh and shake her head, her eyes filling with tears, and say that we must not count on the continuance of such happiness as ours, for it was too great.

I tried to laugh away her doubts, though whenever I did so I seemed to hear Bastin's slow voice remarking casually that she might die, as he might have commented on the quality of the claret. At last, however, I grew terrified and asked her bluntly what she meant.

"I don't quite know, dearest," she replied, "especially as I am wonderfully well. But—but——"

"But what?" I asked.

"But I think that our companionship is going to be broken for a little while."

"For a little while!" I exclaimed.

"Yes, Humphrey. I think that I shall be taken away from you—you know what I mean," and she nodded towards the churchyard.

"Oh, my God!" I groaned.

"I want to say this," she added quickly, "that if such a thing should happen, as it happens every day, I implore you, dearest Humphrey, not to be too much distressed, since I am sure that you will find me again. No, I can't explain how or when or where, because I do not know. I have prayed for light, but it has not come to me. All I know is that I am not talking of re-union in Mr. Bastin's kind of conventional heaven, which he speaks about as though to reach it one stumbled through darkness for a minute into a fine new house next door, where excellent servants had made everything ready for your arrival and all the lights were turned up. It is something quite different from that and very much more real."

Then she bent down ostensibly to pat the head of a little black cocker spaniel called Tommy which had been given to her as a puppy, a highly intelligent and affectionate animal that we both adored and that loved her as only a dog can love. Really, I knew, it was to hide her tears, and fled from the room lest she should see mine.

As I went I heard the dog whimpering in a peculiar way, as though some sympathetic knowledge had been communicated to its wonderful animal intelligence.

That night I spoke to Bickley about the matter, repeating exactly what had passed. As I expected, he smiled in his grave, rather sarcastic way, and made light of it.

"My dear Humphrey," he said, "don't torment yourself about such fancies. They are of everyday occurrence among women in your wife's condition. Sometimes they take one form, sometimes another. When she has got her baby you will hear no more of them."

I tried to be comforted but in vain.

The days and weeks went by like a long nightmare

and in due course the event happened. Bickley was not attending the case; it was not in his line, he said, and he preferred that where a friend's wife was concerned, somebody else should be called in. So it was put in charge of a very good local man with a large experience in such domestic matters.

How am I to tell of it? Everything went wrong; as for the details, let them be. Ultimately Bickley did operate, and if surpassing skill could have saved her, it would have been done. But the other man had misjudged the conditions; it was too late, nothing could help either mother or child, a little girl who died shortly after she was born but not before she had been christened, also by the name of Natalie.

I was called in to say farewell to my wife and found her radiant, triumphant even in her weakness.

"I know now," she whispered in a faint voice. "I understood as the chloroform passed away, but I cannot tell you. Everything is quite well, my darling. Go where you seem called to go, far away. Oh! the wonderful place in which you will find me, not knowing that you have found me. Good-bye for a little while; only for a little while, my own, my own!"

Then she died. And for a time I too seemed to die, but could not. I buried her and the child here at Fulcombe; or rather I buried their ashes since I could not endure that her beloved body should see corruption.

Afterwards, when all was over, I spoke of these last words of Natalie's with both Bickley and Bastin, for somehow I seemed to wish to learn their separate views.

The latter I may explain, had been present at the end in his spiritual capacity, but I do not think that he in the least understood the nature of the drama which was passing before his eyes. His prayers and the christening absorbed all his attention, and he never was a man who could think of more than one thing at a time.

When I told him exactly what had happened and repeated the words that Natalie spoke, he was much interested in his own nebulous way, and said that it was delightful to meet with an example of a good Christian, such as my wife had been, who actually saw something of Heaven before she had gone there. His own faith was, he thanked God, fairly robust, but still an undoubted occurrence of the sort acted as a refreshment, "like rain on a pasture when it is rather dry, you know," he added, breaking into simile.

I remarked that she had not seemed to speak in the sense he indicated, but appeared to allude to something quite near at hand and more or less immediate.

"I don't know that there is anything nearer at hand than the Hereafter," he answered. "I expect she meant that you will probably soon die and join her in Paradise, if you are worthy to do so. But of course it is not wise to put too much reliance upon words spoken by people at the last, because often they don't quite know what they are saying. Indeed sometimes I think this was so in the case of my own wife, who really seemed to me to talk a good deal of rubbish. Good-bye, I promised to see Widow Jenkins this afternoon about having her varicose veins cut out, and I mustn't stop here wasting time in pleasant conversation. She thinks just as much of her varicose veins as we do of the loss of our wives."

I wonder what Bastin's ideas of *unpleasant* conversation may be, thought I to myself, as I watched him depart already wool-gathering on some other subject, probably the heresy of one of those "early fathers" who occupied most of his thoughts.

Bickley listened to my tale in sympathetic silence, as a doctor does to a patient. When he was obliged to speak, he said that it was interesting as an example of a tendency of certain minds towards romantic vision which sometimes asserts itself, even in the throes of death.

"You know," he added, "that I put faith in none of these things. I wish that I could, but reason and science both show me that they lack foundation. The world on the whole is a sad place, where we arrive through the passions of others implanted in them by Nature, which, although it cares nothing for individual death, is tender towards the impulse of races of every sort to preserve their collective life. Indeed the impulse *is* Nature, or at least its chief manifestation. Consequently, whether we be gnats or elephants, or anything between and beyond, even stars for aught I know, we must make the best of things as they are, taking the good and the evil as they come and getting all we can out of life until it leaves us, after which we need not trouble. You had a good time for a little while and were happy in it; now you are having a bad time and are wretched. Perhaps in the future, when your mental balance has re-asserted itself, you will have other good times in the afternoon of your days, and then follow twilight and the dark. That is all there is to hope for, and we may as well look the thing in the face. Only I confess, my dear fellow, that your experience convinces me that marriage should be avoided at whatever inconvenience. Indeed I have long wondered that anyone can take the responsibility of bringing a child into the world. But probably nobody does in cold blood, except misguided idiots like Bastin," he added. "He would have twenty, had not his luck intervened."

"Then you believe in nothing, Friend," I said.

"Nothing, I am sorry to say, except what I see and my five senses appreciate."

"You reject all possibility of miracle, for instance?"

"That depends on what you mean by miracle. Science shows us all kinds of wonders which our great grandfathers would have called miracles, but these are nothing but laws that we are beginning to understand. Give me an instance."

"Well," I replied at hazard, "if you were assured by someone that a man could live for a thousand years?"

"I should tell him that he was a fool or a liar, that is all. It is impossible."

"Or that the same identity, spirit, animating principle—call it what you will—can flit from body to body, say in successive ages? Or that the dead can communicate with the living?"

"Convince me of any of these things, Arbuthnot, and mind you I desire to be convinced, and I will take back every word I have said and walk through Fulcombe in a white sheet proclaiming myself the fool. Now, I must get off to the Cottage Hospital to cut out Widow Jenkins's varicose veins. They are tangible and real at any rate; about the largest I ever saw, indeed. Give up dreams, old boy, and take to something useful. You might go back to your fiction writing; you seem to have leanings that way, and you know you need not publish the stories, except privately for the edification of your friends."

With this Parthian shaft Bickley took his departure to make a job of Widow Jenkins's legs.

I took his advice. During the next few months I did write something which occupied my thoughts for a while, more or less. It lies in my safe to this minute, for somehow I have never been able to make up my mind to burn what cost me so much physical and mental toil.

When it was finished my melancholy returned to me with added force. Everything in the house took a tongue and cried to me of past days. Its walls echoed a voice that I could never hear again; in the very looking-glasses I saw the reflection of a lost presence. Although I had moved myself for the purposes of sleep to a little room at the further end of the building, footsteps seemed to creep about my bed at night and I heard the rustle of a remembered dress without the door. The place grew hateful to me. I felt that I must get away from it or I should go mad.

One afternoon Bastin arrived carrying a book and in a state of high indignation. This work, written, as he said, by some ribald traveller, grossly traduced the character of missionaries to the South Sea Islands, especially of those of the Society to which he subscribed, and he threw it on the table in his righteous wrath. Bickley picked it up and opened it at a photograph of a very pretty South Sea Island girl clad in a few flowers and nothing else, which he held towards Bastin, saying:

"Is it to this child of Nature that you object? I call her distinctly attractive, though perhaps she does wear her hibiscus blooms with a difference to our women—a little lower down."

"The devil is always attractive," replied Bastin gloomily. "Child of Nature indeed! I call her Child of Sin. That photograph is enough to make my poor Sarah turn in her grave."

"Why?" asked Bickley, "seeing that wide seas roll

between you and this dusky Venus. Also I thought that according to your Hebrew legend sin came in with bark garments."

"You should search the Scriptures, Bickley," I broke in, "and cultivate accuracy. It was fig-leaves that symbolised its arrival. The garments, which I think were of skin, developed later."

"Perhaps," went on Bickley, who had turned the page, "she" (he referred to the late Mrs. Bastin) "would have preferred her thus," and he held up another illustration of the same woman.

In this the native belle appeared after conversion, clad in broken-down stays—I suppose they were stays—out of which she seemed to bulge and flow in every direction, a dirty white dress several sizes too small, a kind of Salvation Army bonnet without a crown and a prayer-book which she held pressed to her middle; the general effect being hideous, and in some curious way, improper.

"Certainly," said Bastin, "though I admit her clothes do not seem to fit and she has not buttoned them up as she ought. But it is not of the pictures so much as of the letterpress with its false and scandalous accusations, that I complain."

"Why do you complain?" asked Bickley. "Probably it is quite true, though that we could never ascertain without visiting the lady's home."

"If I could afford it," exclaimed Bastin with rising anger, "I should like to go there and expose this vile traducer of my cloth."

"So should I," answered Bickley, "and expose these introducers of consumption, measles and other European diseases, to say nothing of gin, among an innocent and Arcadian people."

"How can you call them innocent, Bickley, when they murder and eat missionaries?"

"I dare say we should all eat a missionary, Bastin, if we were hungry enough," was the answer, after which something occurred to change the conversation.

But I kept the book and read it as a neutral observer, and came to the conclusion that these South Sea Islands, a land where it was always afternoon, must be a charming place, in which perhaps the stars of the Tropics and the scent of the flowers might enable one to forget a little, or at least take the edge off memory. Why should I not visit them and escape another long and dreary English winter? No, I could not do so alone. If Bastin and Bickley were there, their eternal arguments might amuse me. Well, why should they not come also? When one has money things can always be arranged.

The idea, which had its root in this absurd conversation, took a curious hold on me. I thought of it all the evening, being alone, and that night it re-arose in my dreams. I dreamed that my lost Natalie appeared to me and showed me a picture. It was of a long, low land, a curving shore of which the ends were out of the picture, whereon grew tall palms, and where great combers broke upon gleaming sand.

Then the picture seemed to become a reality and I saw Natalie herself, strangely changeful in her aspect, strangely varying in face and figure, strangely bright, standing in the mouth of a pass whereof the little bordering cliffs were covered with bushes and low trees, whose green was almost hid in lovely flowers. There in my dream she stood, smiling mysteriously, and stretched out her arms towards me.

As I awoke I seemed to hear her voice, repeating

her dying words: "Go where you seem called to go, far, away. Oh! the wonderful place in which you will find me, not knowing that you have found me."

With some variations this dream visited me twice that night. In the morning I woke up quite determined that I would go to the South Sea Islands, even if I must do so alone. On that same evening Bastin and Bickley dined with me. I said nothing to them about my dream, for Bastin never dreamed and Bickley would have set it down to indigestion. But when the cloth had been cleared away and we were drinking our glass of port—both Bastin and Bickley only took one, the former because he considered port a sinful indulgence of the flesh, the latter because he feared it would give him gout—I remarked casually that they both looked very run down and as though they wanted a rest. They agreed, at least each of them said he had noticed it in the other. Indeed Bastin added that the damp and the cold in the church, in which he held daily services to no congregation except the old woman who cleaned it, had given him rheumatism, which prevented him from sleeping.

"Do call things by their proper names," interrupted Bickley. "I told you yesterday that what you are suffering from is neuritis in your right arm, which will become chronic if you neglect it much longer. I have the same thing myself, so I ought to know, and unless I can stop operating for a while I believe my fingers will become useless. Also something is affecting my sight, overstrain, I suppose, so that I am obliged to wear stronger and stronger glasses. I think I shall have to leave Ogden" (his partner) "in charge for a while, and get away into the sun. There is none here before June."

"I would if I could pay a *locum tenens* and were quite sure it isn't wrong," said Bastin.

"I am glad you both think like that," I remarked, "as I have a suggestion to make to you. I want to go to the South Seas about which we were talking yesterday, to get the thorough change that Bickley has been advising for me, and I should be very grateful if you would both come as my guests. You, Bickley, make so much money out of cutting people about, that you can arrange your own affairs during your absence. But as for you, Bastin, I will see to the wherewithal for the *locum tenens,* and everything else."

"You are very kind," said Bastin, "and certainly I should like to expose that misguided author, who probably published his offensive work without thinking that what he wrote might affect the subscriptions to the missionary societies, also to show Bickley that he is not always right, as he seems to think. But I could never dream of accepting without the full approval of the Bishop."

"You might get that of your nurse also, if she happens to be still alive," mocked Bickley. "As for his Lordship, I don't think he will raise any objection when he sees the certificate I will give you about the state of your health. He is a great believer in me ever since I took that carbuncle out of his neck which he got because he will not eat enough. As for me, I mean to come if only to show you how continually and persistently you are wrong. But, Arbuthnot, how do you mean to go?"

"I don't know. In a mail steamer, I suppose."

"If you can run to it, a yatch would be much better."

"That's a good idea, for one could get out of the beaten tracks and see the places that are never, or seldom, visited. I will make some inquiries. And now, to celebrate the occasion, let us all have another glass of port and drink a toast."

They hesitated and were lost, Bastin murmuring something about doing without his stout next day as a penance. Then they both asked what was the toast, each of them, after thought, suggesting that it should be the utter confusion of the other.

I shook my head, whereon as a result of further cogitation, Bastin submitted that the Unknown would be suitable. Bickley said that he thought this a foolish idea as everything worth knowing was already known, and what was the good of drinking to the rest? A toast to the Truth would be better.

A notion came to me.

"Let us combine them," I said, "and drink to the Unknown Truth."

So we did, though Bastin grumbled that the performance made him feel like Pilate.

"We are all Pilates in our way," I replied with a sigh.

"That is what I think every time I diagnose a case," exclaimed Bickley.

As for me I laughed and for some unknown reason felt happier than I had done for months. Oh! if only the writer of that tourist tale of the South Sea Islands could have guessed what fruit his light-thrown seed would yield to us and to the world!

I made my inquiries through a London agency which hired out yachts or sold them to the idle rich. As I expected, there were plenty to be had, at a price, but wealthy as I was, the figure asked of the buyer of any suitable craft staggered me. In the end, however, I chartered one for six months certain and at so much per month for as long as I liked afterwards. The owners paid insurance and everything else on condition that they appointed the captain and first mate, also the engineer, for this yacht, which was named *Star of the South,* could steam at about ten knots as well as sail.

I know nothing about yachts, and therefore shall not attempt to describe her, further than to say that she was of five hundred and fifty tons burden, very well constructed, and smart to look at, as well she might be, seeing that a deceased millionaire from whose executors I hired her had spent a fortune in building and equipping her in the best possible style. In all, her crew consisted of thirty-two hands. A peculiarity of the vessel was that owing to some fancy of the late owner, the passenger accommodation, which was splendid, lay forward of the bridge, this with the ship's store-rooms, refrigerating chamber, etc., being almost in the bows. It was owing to these arrangements, which were unusual, that the executors found it impossible to sell, and were therefore glad to accept such an offer as mine in order to save expenses. Perhaps they hoped that she might go to the bottom, being heavily insured. If so, the Fates did not disappoint them.

The captain, named Astley, was a jovial person who held every kind of certificate. He seemed so extraordinarily able at his business that personally I suspected him of having made mistakes in the course of his career, not unconnected with the worship of Bacchus. In this I believe I was right; otherwise a man of such attainments would have been commanding something bigger than a private yacht. The first mate, Jacobsen, was a melancholy Dane, a spiritualist who played the concertina, and seemed to be able to do without sleep. The crew were a mixed lot, good men for the most part and quite unobjectionable, more than half of them being Scandinavian. I think that is all I need say about the *Star of the South.*

The arrangement was that the *Star of the South* should proceed through the Straits of Gibraltar to Marseilles, where we would join her, and thence travel via the Suez Canal, to Australia and on to the South Seas, returning home as our fancy or convenience might dictate.

All the first part of the plan we carried out to the letter. Of the remainder I say nothing at present.

The *Star of the South* was amply provided with every kind of store. Among them were medicines and surgical instruments, selected by Bickley, and a case of Bibles and other religious works in sundry languages of the South Seas, selected by Bastin, whose bishop, when he understood the pious objects of his journey, had rather encouraged than hindered his departure on sick leave, and a large number of novels, books of reference, etc., laid in by myself. She duly sailed from the Thames and reached Marseilles after a safe and easy passage, where all three of us boarded her.

I forgot to add that she had another passenger, the little spaniel, Tommy. I had intended to leave him behind, but while I was packing up he followed me about with such evident understanding of my purpose that my heart was touched. When I entered the motor to drive to the station he escaped from the hands of the servant, whimpering, and took refuge on my knee. After this I felt that Destiny intended him to be our companion. Moreover, was he not linked with my dead past, and, had I but known it, with my living future also?

CHAPTER V

THE CYCLONE

WE enjoyed our voyage exceedingly. In Egypt, a land I was glad to revisit, we only stopped a week while the *Star of the South,* which we rejoined at Suez, coaled and went through the Canal. This, however, gave us time to spend a few days in Cairo, visit the Pyramids and Sakkara which Bastin and Bickley had never seen before, and inspect the great Museum. The journey up the Nile was postponed until our return. It was a pleasant break and gave Bickley, a most omnivorous reader who was well acquainted with Egyptian history and theology, the opportunity of trying to prove to Bastin that Christianity was a mere development of the ancient Egyptian faith. The arguments that ensued may be imagined. It never seemed to occur to either of them that all faiths may be and indeed probably are progressive; in short, different rays of light thrown from the various facets of the same crystal, as in turn these are shone upon by the sun of Truth.

Our passage down the Red Sea was cool and agreeable. Thence we shaped our course for Ceylon. Here again we stopped a little while to run up to Kandy and to visit the ruined city of Anarajapura with its great Buddhist topes that once again gave rise to religious argument between my two friends. Leaving Ceylon we struck across the Indian Ocean for Perth in Western Australia.

It was a long voyage, since to save our coal we made

most of it under canvas. However, we were not dull as Captain Astley was a good companion, and even out of the melancholy Dane, Jacobsen, we had entertainment. He insisted on holding séances in the cabin, at which the usual phenomena occurred. The table twisted about, voices were heard and Jacobsen's accordion wailed out tunes above our heads. These happenings drove Bickley to a kind of madness, for here were events which he could not explain. He was convinced that someone was playing tricks upon him, and devised the most elaborate snares to detect the rogue, entirely without result.

First he accused Jacobsen, who was very indignant, and then me, who laughed. In the end Jacobsen and I left the "circle" and the cabin, which was locked behind us; only Bastin and Bickley remaining there in the dark. Presently we heard sounds of altercation, and Bickley emerged looking very red in the face, followed by Bastin, who was saying:

"Can I help it if something pulled your nose and snatched off your eyeglasses, which anyhow are quite useless to you when there is no light? Again, is it possible for me, sitting on the other side of that table, to have placed the concertina on your head and made it play the National Anthem, a thing that I have not the slightest idea how to do?"

"Please do not try to explain," snapped Bickley. "I am perfectly aware that you deceived me somehow, which no doubt you think a good joke."

"My dear fellow," I interrupted, "is it possible to imagine old Basil deceiving anyone?"

"Why not," snorted Bickley, "seeing that he deceives himself from one year's end to the other?"

"I think," said Bastin, "that this is an unholy business and that we are both deceived by the devil. I will have no more to do with it," and he departed to his cabin, probably to say some appropriate prayers.

After this the séances were given up but Jacobsen produced an instrument called a planchette and with difficulty persuaded Bickley to try it, which he did after many precautions. The thing, a heart-shaped piece of wood mounted on wheels and with a pencil stuck at its narrow end, cantered about the sheet of paper on which it was placed, Bickley, whose hands rested upon it, staring at the roof of the cabin. Then it began to scribble and after a while stopped still.

"Will the Doctor look?" said Jacobsen. "Perhaps the spirits have told him something."

"Oh! curse all this silly talk about spirits," exclaimed Bickley, as he arranged his eyeglasses and held up the paper to the light, for it was after dinner.

He stared, then with an exclamation which I will not repeat, and a glance of savage suspicion at the poor Dane and the rest of us, threw it down and left the cabin. I picked it up and next moment was screaming with laughter. There on the top of the sheet was a rough but entirely recognizable portrait of Bickley with the accordion on his head, and underneath, written in a delicate, Italian female hand, absolutely different from his own, were these words taken from one of St. Paul's Epistles—"Oppositions of science falsely so called." Underneath them again in a scrawling, schoolboy fist, very like Bastin's, was inscribed, "Tell us how this is done, you silly doctor, who think yourself so clever."

"It seems that the devil really can quote Scripture," was Bastin's only comment, while Jacobsen stared before him and smiled.

Bickley never alluded to the matter, but for days afterwards I saw him experimenting with paper and chemicals, evidently trying to discover a form of invisible ink which would appear upon the application of the hand. As he never said anything about it, I fear that he failed.

This planchette business had a somewhat curious ending. A few nights later Jacobsen was working it and asked me to put a question. To oblige him I inquired on what day we should reach Fremantle, the port of Perth. It wrote an answer which, I may remark, subsequently proved to be quite correct.

"That is not a good question," said Jacobsen, "since as a sailor I might guess the reply. Try again, Mr. Arbuthnot."

"Will anything remarkable happen on our voyage to the South Seas?" I inquired casually.

The planchette hesitated a while then wrote rapidly and stopped. Jacobsen took up the paper and began to read the answer aloud—"To A, B the D, and B the C, the most remarkable things will happen that have happened to men living in the world."

"That must mean me, Bickley the doctor and Bastin the clergyman," I said, laughing.

Jacobsen paid no attention, for he was reading what followed. As he did so I saw his face turn white and his eyes begin to start from his head. Then suddenly he tore the paper in pieces which he thrust into his pocket. Lifting his great fist he uttered some Danish oath and with a single blow smashed the planchette to fragments, after which he strode away, leaving me astonished and somewhat disturbed. When I met him the next morning I asked him what was on the paper.

"Oh!" he said quietly, "something I should not like you too-proper English gentlemens to see. Something not nice. You understand. Those spirits not always good; they do that kind of thing sometimes. That's why I broke up this planchette."

Then he began to talk of something else and there the matter ended.

I should have said that, principally with a view to putting themselves in a position to confute each other, ever since we had started from Marseilles both Bastin and Bickley spent a number of hours each day in assiduous study of the language of the South Sea Islands. It became a kind of competition between them as to which could learn the most. Now Bastin, although simple and even stupid in some ways, was a good scholar, and as I knew at college, had quite a faculty for acquiring languages in which he had taken high marks at examinations. Bickley, too, was an extraordinarily able person with an excellent memory, especially when he was on his mettle. The result was that before we ever reached a South Sea island they had a good working knowledge of the local tongues.

As it chanced, too, at Perth we picked up a Samoan and his wife who, under some of the "white Australia" regulations, were not allowed to remain in the country and offered to work as servants in return for a passage to Apia where we proposed to call some time or other. With these people Bastin and Bickley talked all day long till really they became fairly proficient in their soft and beautiful dialect. They wished me to learn also, but I said that with two such excellent interpreters and the natives while they remained with us, it seemed quite unnecessary. Still, I picked up a good deal in a quiet way, as much as they did perhaps.

At length, travelling on and on as a voyager to the planet Mars might do, we sighted the low shores of Australia and that same evening were towed, for our coal was quite exhausted, to the wharf at Fremantle. Here we spent a few days exploring the beautiful town of Perth and its neighbourhood where it was very hot just then, and eating peaches and grapes till we made ourselves ill, as a visitor often does who is unaware that fruit should not be taken in quantity in Australia while the sun is high. Then we departed for Melbourne almost before our arrival was generally known, since I did not wish to advertise our presence or the object of our journey.

We crossed the Great Australian Bight, of evil reputation, in the most perfect weather; indeed it might have been a mill pond, and after a short stay at Melbourne, went on to Sydney, where we coaled again and laid in supplies.

Then our real journey began. The plan we laid out was to sail to Suva in Fiji, about 1,700 miles away, and after a stay there, on to Hawaii or the Sandwich Islands, stopping perhaps at the Phœnix Islands and the Central Polynesian Sporades, such as Christmas and Fanning Isles. Then we proposed to turn south again through the Marshall Archipelago and the Caroline Islands, and so on to New Guinea and the Coral Sea. Particularly did we wish to visit Easter Island on account of its marvellous sculptures that are supposed to be the relics of a pre-historic race. In truth, however, we had no fixed plan except to go wherever circumstance and chance might take us. Chance, I may add, or something else, took full advantage of its opportunities.

We came to Suva in safety and spent a while in exploring the beautiful Fiji Isles where both Bastin and Bickley made full inquiries about the work of the missionaries, each of them drawing exactly opposite conclusions from the same set of admitted facts. Thence we steamed to Samoa and put our two natives ashore at Apia, where we procured some coal. We did not stay long enough in these islands to investigate them, however, because persons of experience there assured us from certain familiar signs that one of the terrible hurricanes with which they are afflicted, was due to arrive shortly and that we should do well to put ourselves beyond its reach. So having coaled and watered we departed in a hurry.

Up to this time I should state we had met with the most wonderful good fortune in the matter of weather, so good indeed that never on one occasion since we left Marseilles, had we been obliged to put the fiddles on the tables. With the superstition of a sailor Captain Astley, when I alluded to the matter, shook his head saying that doubtless we should pay for it later on, since "luck never goes all the way" and cyclones were reported to be about.

Here I must tell that after we were clear of Apia, it was discovered that the Danish mate who was believed to be in his cabin unwell from something he had eaten, was missing. The question arose whether we should put back to find him, as we supposed that he had made a trip inland and met with an accident, or been otherwise delayed. I was in favour of doing so though the captain, thinking of the threatened hurricane, shook his head and said that Jacobsen was a queer fellow who might just as well have gone overboard as anywhere else, if he thought he heard "the spirits, of whom he was so fond," calling him. While the matter was still in suspense I happened to go into my own stateroom and there, stuck in the looking-glass, saw an envelope in the Dane's handwriting addressed to myself. On opening it I found another sealed letter, unaddressed, also a note that ran as follows:

"Honoured Sir,

"You will think very badly of me for leaving you, but the enclosed which I implore you not to open until you have seen the last of the *Star of the South*, will explain my reason and I hope clear my reputation. I thank you again and again for all your kindness and pray that the Spirits who rule the world may bless and preserve you, also the Doctor and Mr. Bastin."

This letter, which left the fate of Jacobsen quite unsolved, for it might mean either that he had deserted or drowned himself, I put away with the enclosure in my pocket. Of course there was no obligation on me to refrain from opening the letter, but I shrank from doing so both from some kind of sense of honour and, to tell the truth, for fear of what it might contain. I felt that this would be disagreeable; also, although there was nothing to connect them together, I bethought me of the scene when Jacobsen had smashed the planchette.

On my return to the deck I said nothing whatsoever about the discovery of the letter, but only remarked that on reflection I had changed my mind and agreed with the captain that it would be unwise to attempt to return in order to look for Jacobsen. So the boatswain, a capable individual who had seen better days, was promoted to take his watches and we went on as before. How curiously things come about in the world! For nautical reasons that were explained to me, but which I will not trouble to set down, if indeed I could remember them, I believe that if we had returned to Apia we should have missed the great gale and subsequent cyclone, and with these much else. But it was not so fated.

It was on the fourth day, when we were roughly seven hundred miles or more north of Samoa, that we met the edge of this gale about sundown. The captain put on steam in the hope of pushing through it, but that night we dined for the first time with the fiddles on, and by eleven o'clock it was as much as one could do to stand in the cabin, while the water was washing freely over the deck. Fortunately, however, the wind veered more aft of us, so that by putting about her head a little (seamen must forgive me if I talk of these matters as a landlubber) we ran almost before the wind, though not quite in the direction that we wished to go.

When the light came it was blowing very hard indeed, and the sky was utterly overcast, so that we got no glimpse of the sun, or of the stars on the following night. Unfortunately, there was no moon visible; indeed, if there had been I do not suppose that it would have helped us because of the thick pall of clouds. For quite seventy-two hours we ran on beneath bare poles before that gale. The little vessel behaved splendidly, riding the seas like a duck, but I could see that Captain Astley was growing alarmed. When I said something complimentary to him about the conduct of the *Star of the South,* he replied that she was forging ahead all right, but the question was—where to? He had been unable to take an observation of any sort since we left Samoa; both his patent logs had been carried away, so that now only the compass remained, and he had not the slightest idea where we were in that great ocean studded with atolls and islands.

I asked him whether we could not steam back to our proper course, but he answered that to do so he would have to travel dead in the eye of the gale, and he doubted whether the engines would stand it. Also there was the question of coal to be considered. However, he had kept the fires going and would do what he could if the weather moderated.

That night during dinner which now consisted of tinned foods and whisky and water, for the seas had got to the galley fire, suddenly the gale dropped, whereat we rejoiced exceedingly. The captain came down into the saloon very white and shaken, I thought, and I asked him to have a nip of whisky to warm him up, and to celebrate our good fortune in having run out of the wind. He took the bottle and, to my alarm, poured out a full half tumbler of spirit, which he swallowed undiluted in two or three gulps.

"That's better!" he said with a hoarse laugh. "But man, what is it you are saying about having run out of the wind? Look at the glass!"

"We have," said Bastin, "and it is wonderfully steady. About 29 degrees or a little over, which it has been for the last three days."

Again Astley laughed in a mirthless fashion, as he answered:

"Oh, that thing! That's the passengers' glass. I told the steward to put it out of gear so that you might not be frightened; it is an old trick. Look at this," and he produced one of the portable variety out of his pocket.

We looked, and it stood somewhere between 27 degrees and 28 degrees.

"That's the lowest glass I ever saw in the Polynesian or any other seas during thirty years. It's right, too, for I have tested it by three others," he said.

"What does it mean?" I asked rather anxiously.

"South Sea cyclone of the worst breed," he replied. "That cursed Dane knew it was coming and that's why he left the ship. Pray as you never prayed before," and again he stretched out his hand towards the whisky bottle. But I stepped between him and it, shaking my head. Thereon he laughed for the third time and left the cabin. Though I saw him once or twice afterwards, these were really the last words of intelligible conversation that I ever had with Captain Astley.

"It seems that we are in some danger," said Bastin, in an unmoved kind of way. "I think that was a good idea of the captain's, to put up a petition, I mean, but as Bickley will scarcely care to join in it I will go into the cabin and do so myself."

Bickley snorted, then said:

"Confound that captain! Why did he play such a trick upon us about the barometer? Humphrey, I believe he had been drinking."

"So do I," I said, looking at the whisky bottle. "Otherwise, after taking those precautions to keep us in the dark, he would not have let on like that."

"Well," said Bickley, "he can't get to the liquor, except through this saloon, as it is locked up forward with the other stores."

"That's nothing," I replied, "as doubtless he has a supply of his own; rum, I expect. We must take our chance."

Bickley nodded, and suggested that we should go on deck to see what was happening. So we went. Not a breath of wind was stirring, and even the sea seemed to be settling down a little. At least, so we judged from the motion, for we could not see either it or the sky; everything was as black as pitch. We heard the sailors, however, engaged in rigging guide ropes fore and aft, and battening down the hatches with extra tarpaulins by the light of lanterns. Also they were putting ropes round the boats and doing something to the spars and topmasts.

Presently Bastin joined us, having, I suppose, finished his devotions.

"Really, it is quite pleasant here," he said. "One never knows how disagreeable so much wind is until it stops."

I lit my pipe, making no answer, and the match burned quite steadily there in the open air.

"What is that?" exclaimed Bickley, staring at something which now I saw for the first time. It looked like a line of white approaching through the gloom. With it came a hissing sound, and although there was still no wind, the rigging began to moan mysteriously like a thing in pain. A big drop of water also fell from the skies into my pipe and put it out. Then one of the sailors cried in a hoarse voice:

"Get down below, governors, unless you want to go out to sea!"

"Why?" inquired Bastin.

"Why? Becos the 'urricane is coming, that's all. Coming as though the devil had kicked it out of 'ell."

Bastin seemed inclined to remonstrate at this sort of language, but we pushed him down the companion and followed, propelling the spaniel Tommy in front of us. Next moment I heard the sailors battening the hatch with hurried blows, and when this was done to their satisfaction, heard their feet also as they ran into shelter.

Another instant and we were all lying in a heap on the cabin floor with poor Tommy on top of us. The cyclone had struck the ship! Above the wash of water and the screaming of the gale we heard other mysterious sounds, which doubtless were caused by the yards hitting the seas, for the yacht was lying on her side. I thought that all was over, but presently there came a rending, crashing noise. The masts, or one of them, had gone, and by degrees we righted.

"Near thing!" said Bickley. "Good heavens, what's that?"

I listened, for the electric light had temporarily gone out, owing, I suppose, to the dynamo having stopped for a moment. A most unholy and hollow sound was rising from the cabin floor. It might have been caused by a bullock with its windpipe cut, trying to get its breath and groaning. Then the light came on again and we saw Bastin lying at full length on the carpet.

"He's broken his neck or something," I said.

Bickley crept to him and having looked, sang out:

"It's all right! He's only sea-sick. I thought it would come to that if he drank so much tea."

"Sea-sick," I said faintly—"sea-sick?"

"That's all," said Bickley. "The nerves of the stomach acting on the brain or vice-versa—that is, if Bastin has a brain," he added sotto voce.

"Oh!" groaned the prostrate clergyman. "I wish that I were dead!"

"Don't trouble about that," answered Bickley. "I expect you soon will be. Here, drink some whisky, you donkey."

Bastin sat up and obeyed, out of the bottle, for it was impossible to pour anything into a glass, with results too dreadful to narrate.

"I call that a dirty trick," he said presently, in a feeble voice, glowering at Bickley.

"I expect I shall have to play you a dirtier before long, for you are a pretty bad case, old fellow."

As a matter of fact he had, for once Bastin had begun really we thought that he was going to die. Somehow we got him into his cabin, which opened off the saloon, and as he could drink nothing more, Bickley managed to inject morphia or some other compound into him, which made him insensible for a long while.

"He must be in a poor way," he said, "for the needle went more than a quarter of an inch into him, and he never cried out or stirred. Couldn't help it in that rolling."

But now I could hear the engines working, and I think that the bow of the vessel was got head on to the seas, for instead of rolling we pitched, or rather the ship stood first upon one end and then upon the other. This continued for a while until the first burst of the cyclone had gone by. Then suddenly the engines stopped; I suppose that they had broken down, but I never learned, and we seemed to veer about, nearly sinking in the process, and to run before the hurricane at terrific speed.

"I wonder where we are going to?" I said to Bickley.

"To the land of sleep, Humphrey, I imagine," he replied in a more gentle voice than I had often heard him use, adding: "Good-bye, old boy, we have been real friends, haven't we, notwithstanding my peculiarities? I only wish that I could think that there was anything in Bastin's views. But I can't, I can't. It's good night for us poor creatures!"

CHAPTER VI

LAND

At last the electric light really went out. I had looked at my watch just before this happened and wound it up, which, Bickley remarked, was superfluous and a waste of energy. It then marked 3.20 in the morning. We had wedged Bastin, who was now snoring comfortably, into his berth, with pillows, and managed to tie a cord over him—no, it was a large bath towel, fixing one end of it to the little rack over his bed and the other to its framework. As for ourselves, we lay down on the floor between the table legs, which, of course, were screwed, and the settee, protecting ourselves as best we were able by help of the cushions, etc., between two of which we thrust the terrified Tommy who had been sliding up and down the cabin floor. Thus we remained, expecting death every moment till the light of day, a very dim light, struggling through a port-hole of which the iron cover had somehow been wrenched off. Or perhaps it was never shut, I do not remember.

About this time there came a lull in the hellish, howling hurricane; the fact being, I suppose, that we had reached the centre of the cyclone. I suggested that we should try to go on deck and see what was happening. So we started, only to find the entrance to the companion so faithfully secured that we could not by any means get out. We knocked and shouted, but no one answered. My belief is that at this time everyone on the yacht except ourselves had been washed away and drowned.

Then we returned to the saloon, which, except for a little water trickling about the floor, was marvellously dry, and, being hungry, retrieved some bits of food and buscuit from its corners and ate. At this moment the cyclone began to blow again worse than ever, but it seemed to us, from another direction, and before it sped our poor derelict barque. It blew all day till for my part I grew utterly weary and even longed for the inevitable end. If my views were not quite those of Bastin, certainly they were not those of Bickley. I had believed from my youth up that the individuality of man, the *ego,* so to speak, does not die when life goes out of his poor body, and this faith did not desert me then. Therefore, I wished to have it over and learn what there might be upon the other side.

We could not speak much because of the howling of the wind, but Bickley did manage to shout to me something to the effect that his partners would, in his opinion, make an end of their great practice within two years, which, he added, was a pity. I nodded my head, not caring twopence what happened to Bickley's partners or their business, or to my own property, or to anything else. When death is at hand most of us do not think much of such things because then we realise how small they are. Indeed I was wondering whether within a few minutes or hours I should or should not see Natalie again, and if this were the end to which she had seemed to beckon me in that dream.

On we sped, and on. About four in the afternoon we heard sounds from Bastin's cabin which faintly reminded me of some tune. I crept to the door and listened. Evidently he had awakened and was singing or trying to sing, for music was not one of his strong points, "For those in peril on the sea." Devoutly did I wish that it might be heard. Presently it ceased, so I suppose he went to sleep again.

The darkness gathered once more. Then of a sudden something fearful happened. There were stupendous noises of a kind I had never heard; there were convulsions. It seemed to us that the ship was flung right up into the air a hundred feet or more.

"Tidal wave, I expect," shouted Bickley.

Almost as he spoke she came down with the most appalling crash on to something hard and nearly jarred the senses out of us. Next the saloon was whirling round and round and yet being carried forward, and we felt air blowing upon us. Then our senses left us. As I clasped Tommy to my side, whimpering and licking my face, my last thought was that all was over, and that presently I should learn everything or nothing.

I woke up feeling very bruised and sore and perceived that light was flowing into the saloon. The door was still shut, but it had been wrenched off its hinges, and that was where the light came in; also some of the teak planks of the decking, jagged and splintered, were sticking up through the carpet. The table had broken from its fastenings and lay upon its side. Everything else was one confusion. I looked at Bickley. Apparently he had not awakened. He was stretched out still wedged in with his cushions and bleeding from a wound in his head. I crept to him in terror and listened. He was not dead, for his breathing was regular and natural. The whisky bottle which had been corked was upon the floor unbroken and about a third full. I took a good pull at the spirit; to me it tasted like nectar from the gods.

Then I tried to force some down Bickley's throat but could not, so I poured a little upon the cut on his head. The smart of it woke him in a hurry.

"Where are we now?" he exclaimed. "You don't mean to tell me that Bastin is right after all and that we live again somewhere else? Oh! I could never bear that ignominy."

"I don't know about living somewhere else," I said, "although my opinions on that matter differ from yours. But I do know that you and I are still on earth in what remains of the saloon of the *Star of the South.*"

"Thank God for that! Let's go and look for old Bastin," said Bickley. "I do pray that he is all right also."

"It is most illogical of you, Bickley, and indeed wrong," groaned a deep voice from the other side of the cabin door, "to thank a God in Whom you do not believe, and to talk of praying for one of the worst and most inefficient of His servants when you have no faith in prayer."

"Got you there, my friend," I said.

Bickley murmured something about force of habit, and looked smaller than I had ever seen him do before.

Somehow we forced that door open; it was not easy because it had jammed. Within the cabin, hanging on either side of the bath towel which had stood the strain nobly, something like a damp garment over a linen line, was Bastin most of whose bunk seemed to have disappeared. Yes—Bastin, pale and dishevelled and looking shrunk, with his hair touzled and his beard apparently growing all ways, but still Bastin alive, if very weak.

Bickley ran at him and made a cursory examination with his fingers.

"Nothing broken," he said triumphantly. "He's all right."

"If *you* had hung over a towel for many hours in most violent weather you would not say that," groaned Bastin. "My inside is a pulp. But perhaps you would be kind enough to untie me."

"Bosh!" said Bickley as he obeyed. "All you want is something to eat. Meanwhile, drink this," and he handed him the remains of the whisky.

Bastin swallowed it every drop, murmuring something about taking a little wine for his stomach's sake, "one of the Pauline injunctions, you know," after which he was much more cheerful. Then we hunted about and found some more of the biscuits and other food with which we filled ourselves after a fashion.

"I wonder what has happened," said Bastin. "I suppose that, thanks to the skill of the captain, we have after all reached the haven where we would be."

Here he stopped, rubbed his eyes and looked towards the saloon door which, as I have said, had been wrenched off its hinges, but appeared to have opened wider than when I observed it last. Also Tommy, who was recovering his spirits, uttered a series of low growls.

"It is a most curious thing," he went on, "and I suppose I must be suffering from hallucinations, but I could swear that just now I saw looking through that door the same improper young woman clothed in a few flowers and nothing else, whose photograph in that abominable and libellous book was indirectly the cause of our tempestuous voyage."

"Indeed!" replied Bickley. "Well, so long as she has not got on the broken-down stays and the Salvation Army bonnet without a crown, which you may remember she wore after she had fallen into the hands of your fraternity, I am sure *I* do not mind. In fact I should be delighted to see anything so pleasant."

At this moment a distinct sound of female tittering arose from beyond the door. Tommy barked and Bickley stepped towards it, but I called to him.

"Look out! Where there are women there are sure to be men. Let us be ready against accidents."

So we armed ourselves with pistols, that is Bickley and I did, Bastin being fortified solely with a Bible.

Then we advanced, a remarkable and dilapidated trio, and dragged the door wide. Instantly there was a scurry and we caught sight of women's forms wearing only flowers, and but few of these, running over white sand towards groups of men armed with odd-looking clubs, some of which were fashioned to the shapes of swords and spears. To make an impression I fired two shots with my revolver into the air, whereupon both men and women fled into groves of trees and vanished.

"They don't seem to be accustomed to white people," said Bickley. "Is it possible that we have found a shore upon which no missionary has set a foot?"

"I hope so," said Bastin, "seeing that unworthy as I am, then the opportunities for me would be very great."

We stood still and looked about us. This was what we saw. All the after part of the ship from forward of the bridge had vanished utterly; there was not a trace of it; she had as it were been cut in two. More, we were some considerable distance from the sea which was still raging over a quarter of a mile away where great white combers struck upon a reef and spouted into the air. Behind us was a cliff, apparently of rock but covered with earth and vegetation, and against this cliff, in which the prow of the ship was buried, she, or what remained of her, had come to anchor for the last time.

"You see what has happened," I said. "A great tidal wave has carried us up here and retreated."

"That's it," exclaimed Bickley. "Look at the débris," and he pointed to torn-up palms, bushes and seaweed piled into heaps which still ran salt water; also to a number of dead fish that lay about among them, adding, "Well, we are saved anyhow."

"And yet there are people like you who say that there is no Providence!" ejaculated Bastin.

"I wonder what the views of Captain Astley and the crew are, or rather were, upon that matter," interrupted Bickley.

"I don't know," answered Bastin, looking about him vaguely. "It is true that I can't see any of them, but if they are drowned no doubt it is because their period of usefulness in this world had ended."

"Let's get down and look about us," I remarked, being anxious to avoid further argument.

So we scrambled from the remnant of the ship, like Noah descending out of the ark, as Bastin said, on to the beach beneath, where Tommy rushed to and fro, gambolling for joy. Here we discovered a path which ran diagonally up the side of a cliff which was nowhere more than fifty or sixty feet in height, and possibly had once formed the shore of this land, or perhaps that of a lake. Up this path we went, following the tracks of many human feet, and reaching the crest of the cliff, looked about us, basking as we did so in the beautiful morning sun, for the sky was now clear of clouds and with that last awful effort, which destroyed our ship, the cyclone had passed away.

We were standing on a plain down which ran a little

stream of good water whereof Tommy drank greedily, we following his example. To the right and left of this plain, further than we could see, stretched bushland over which towered many palms, rather ragged now because of the lashing of the gale. Looking inland we perceived that the ground sloped gently downwards, ending at a distance of some miles in a large lake. Far out in this lake something like the top of a mountain of a brown colour rose above the water, and on the edge of it was what from that distance appeared to be a tumbled ruin.

"This is all very interesting," I said to Bickley. "What do you make of it?"

"I don't quite know. At first sight I should say that we are standing on the lip of a crater of some vast extinct volcano. Look how it curves to north and south and at the slope running down to the lake."

I nodded.

"Lucky that the tidal wave did not get over the cliff," I said. "If it had the people here would have all been drowned out. I wonder where they have gone?"

As I spoke Bastin pointed to the edge of the bush some hundreds of yards away, where we perceived brown figures slipping about among the trees. I suggested that we should go back to the mouth of our path, so as to have a line of retreat open in case of necessity, and await events. So we did and there stood still. By degrees the brown figures emerged on to the plain to the number of some hundreds, and we saw that they were both male and female. The women were clothed in nothing except flowers and a little girdle; the men were all armed with wooden weapons and also wore a girdle but no flowers. The children, of whom there were many, were quite naked.

Among these people we observed a tall person

clothed in what seemed to be a magnificent feather cloak, and, walking around and about him, a number of grotesque forms adorned with hideous masks and basket-like head-dresses that were surmounted by plumes.

"The king or chief and his priests or medicine-men! This is splendid," said Bickley triumphantly.

Bastin also contemplated them with enthusiasm as raw material upon which he hoped to get to work.

By degrees and very cautiously they approached us. To our joy, we perceived that behind them walked several young women who bore wooden trays of food or fruit.

"That looks well," I said. "They would not make offerings unless they were friendly."

"The food may be poisoned," remarked Bickley suspiciously.

The crowd advanced, we standing quite still looking as dignified as we could, I as the tallest in the middle, with Tommy sitting at my feet. When they were about five and twenty yards away, however, that wretched little dog caught sight of the masked priests. He growled and then rushed at them barking, his long black ears flapping as he went.

The effect was instantaneous. One and all they turned and fled precipitately, who evidently had never before seen a dog and looked upon it as a deadly creature. Yes, even the tall chief and his masked medicine-men fled like hares pursued by Tommy, who bit one of them in the leg, evoking a terrific howl. I called him back and took him into my arms. Seeing that he was safe for a while the crowd re-formed and once again advanced.

As they came we noted that they were a wonderfully handsome people, tall and straight with regularly shaped features and nothing of the negro about them. Some of the young women might even be called beautiful, though those who were elderly had become corpulent. The feather-clothed chief, however, was much disfigured by a huge growth with a narrow stalk to it that hung from his neck and rested on his shoulder.

"I'll have that off him before he is a week older," said Bickley, surveying this deformity with great professional interest.

On they came, the girls with the platters walking ahead. On one of these were what looked like joints of baked pork, on another some plantains and pear-shaped fruits. They knelt down and offered these to us. We contemplated them for a while. Then Bickley shook his head and began to rub his stomach with appropriate contortions. Clearly they were quick-minded enough for they saw the point. At some words the girls brought the platters to the chief and others, who took from them portions of the food at hazard and ate them to show that it was not poisoned, we watching their throats the while to make sure that it was swallowed. Then they returned again and we took some of the food though only Bickley ate, because, as I pointed out to him, being a doctor who understood the use of antidotes, clearly he should make the experiment. However, nothing happened; indeed he said that it was very good.

After this there came a pause. Then suddenly Bastin took up his parable in the Polynesian tongue which—to a certain extent—he had acquired with so much pains.

"What is this place called?" he asked slowly and distinctly, pausing between each word.

His audience shook their heads and he tried again,

putting the accents on different syllables. Behold! some bright spirit understood him and answered:

"Orofena."

"That means a hill, or an island, or a hill in an island," whispered Bickley to me.

"Who is your God?" asked Bastin again.

The point seemed one upon which they were a little doubtful, but at last the chief answered, "Oro. He who fights."

"In other words, Mars," said Bickley.

"I will give you a better one," said Bastin in the same slow fashion.

Thinking that he referred to himself these children of Nature contemplated his angular form doubtfully and shook their heads. Then for the first time one of the men who was wearing a mask and a wicker crate on his head, spoke in a hollow voice, saying:

"If you try Oro will eat you up."

"Head priest!" said Bickley, nudging me. "Old Bastin had better be careful or he will get his teeth into him and call them Oro's."

Another pause, after which the man in a feather cloak with the growth on his neck that a servant was supporting, said:

"I am Marama, the chief of Orofena. We have never seen men like you before, if you are men. What brought you here and with you that fierce and terrible animal, or evil spirit which makes a noise and bites?"

Now Bickley pretended to consult me who stood brooding and majestic, that is if I can be majestic. I whispered something and he answered:

"The gods of the wind and the sea."

"What nonsense," ejaculated Bastin, "there are no such things."

"Shut up," I said, "we must use similes here," to which he replied:

"I don't like similes that tamper with the truth."

"Remember Neptune and Aeolus," I suggested, and he lapsed into consideration of the point.

"We knew that you were coming," said Marama. "Our doctors told us all about you a moon ago. But we wish that you would come more gently, as you nearly washed away our country."

After looking at me Bickley replied:

"How thankful should you be that in our kindness we have spared you."

"What do you come to do?" inquired Marama again.

After the usual formula of consulting me Bickley answered:

"We come to take that mountain (he meant lump) off your neck and make you beautiful; also to cure all the sickness among your people."

"And I come," broke in Bastin, "to give you new hearts."

These announcements evidently caused great excitement. After consultation Marama answered:

"We do not want new hearts as the old ones are good, but we wish to be rid of lumps and sicknesses. If you can do this we will make you gods and worship you and give you many wives." (Here Bastin held up his hands in horror.) "When will you begin to take away the lumps?"

"To-morrow," said Bickley. "But learn that if you try to harm us we will bring another wave which will drown all your country."

Nobody seemed to doubt our capacities in this direction, but one inquiring spirit in a wicker crate did ask how it came about that if we controlled the ocean we had arrived in half a canoe instead of a whole one.

Bickley replied to the effect that it was because the gods always travelled in half-canoes to show their higher nature, which seemed to satisfy everyone. Then we announced that we had seen enough of them for that day and would retire to think. Meanwhile we should be obliged if they would build us a house and keep us supplied with whatever food they had.

"Do the gods eat?" asked the sceptic again.

"That fellow is a confounded radical," I whispered to Bickley. "Tell him that they do when they come to Orofena."

He did so, whereon the chief said:

"Would the gods like a nice young girl cooked?"

At this point Bastin retired down the path, realising that he had to do with cannibals. We said that we preferred to look at the girls alive and would meet them again to-morrow morning, when we hoped that the house would be ready.

So our first interview with the inhabitants of Orofena came to an end, on which we congratulated ourselves.

On reaching the remains of the *Star of the South* we set to work to take stock of what was left to us. Fortunately it proved to be a very great deal. As I think I mentioned, all the passenger part of the yacht lay forward of the bridge, just in front of which the vessel had been broken in two, almost as cleanly as though she were severed by a gigantic knife. Further our stores were forward and practically everything else that belonged to us, even down to Bickley's instruments and medicines and Bastin's religious works, to say nothing of a great quantity of tinned food and groceries. Lastly on the deck above the saloon had stood two large life-boats. Although these were amply secured at the commencement of the gale one of them, that on the port side, was smashed to smithers; probably some spar had fallen upon it. The starboard boat, however, remained intact and so far as we could judge, seaworthy, although the bulwarks were broken by the waves.

"There's something we can get away in if necessary," I said.

"Where to?" remarked Bastin. "We don't know where we are or if there is any other land within a thousand miles. I think we had better stop here as Providence seems to have intended, especially when there is so much work to my hand."

"Be careful," answered Bickley, "that the work to your hand does not end in the cutting of all our throats. It is an awkward thing interfering with the religion of savages, and I believe that these untutored children of Nature sometimes eat missionaries."

"Yes, I have heard that," said Bastin; "they bake them first as they do pigs. But I don't know that they would care to eat me," and he glanced at his bony limbs, "especially when you are much plumper. Anyhow one can't stop for a risk of that sort."

Deigning no reply, Bickley walked away to fetch some fine fish which had been washed up by the tidal wave and were still flapping about in a little pool of salt water. Then we took counsel as to how to make the best of our circumstances, and as a result set to work to tidy up the saloon and cabins, which was not difficult as what remained of the ship lay on an even keel. Also we got out some necessary stores, including paraffin for the swinging lamps with which the ship was fitted in case of accident to the electric light, candles, and the guns we had brought with us so that they might be handy in the event of attack. This done, by the aid of the tools that were in the storerooms, Bickley, who was an excellent carpenter, repaired the saloon door, all that was necessary to keep us private, as the bulkhead still remained.

"Now," he said triumphantly when he had finished and got the lock and bolts to work to his satisfaction, "we can stand a siege if needed, for as the ship is iron built they can't even burn us out and that teak door would take some forcing. Also we can shore it up."

"How about something to eat? I want my tea," said Bastin.

"Then, my reverend friend," replied Bickley, "take a couple of the fire buckets and fetch some water from the stream. Also collect driftwood of which there is plenty about, clean those fish and grill them over the saloon stove."

"I'll try," said Bastin, "but I never did any cooking before."

"No," replied Bickley, "on second thoughts I will see to that myself, but you can get the fish ready."

So, with due precautions, Bastin and I fetched water from the stream which we found flowed over the edge of the cliff quite close at hand into a beautiful coral basin that might have been designed for a bath of the nymphs. Indeed one at a time, while the other watched, we undressed and plunged into it, and never was a tub more welcome than after our long days of tempest. Then we returned to find that Bickley had already set the table and was engaged in frying the fish very skilfully on the saloon stove, which proved to be well adapted to the purpose. He was cross, however, when he found that we had bathed and that it was now too late for him to do likewise.

While he was cleaning himself as well as he could in his cabin basin and Bastin was boiling the water for tea, suddenly I remembered the letter from the Danish mate Jacobsen. Concluding that it might now be opened as we had certainly parted with most of the *Star of the South* for the last time, I read it. It was as follows:

> "The reason, honoured Sir, that I am leaving the ship is that on the night I tore up the paper, the spirit controlling the planchette wrote these words: 'After leaving Samoa the *Star of the South* will be wrecked in a hurricane and everybody on board drowned except A. B. and B. Get out of her! Get out of her! Don't be a fool, Jacob, unless you want to come over here at once. Take our advice and get out of her and you will live to be old.—SKOLL.'
>
> "Sir, I am not a coward but I know that this will happen, for that spirit which signs itself Skoll never tells a lie. I did try to give the captain a hint to stop at Apia, but he had been drinking and openly cursed me and called me a sneaking cheat. So I am going to run away, of which I am very much ashamed. But I do not wish to be drowned yet as there is a girl whom I want to marry, and my mother I support. You will be safe and I hope you will not think too badly of me.—JACOB JACOBSEN.
>
> "*P.S.*—It is an awful thing to know the future. Never try to learn that."

I gave this letter to Bastin and Bickley to read and asked them what they thought of it.

" Coincidence," said Bickley. " The man is a weak-minded idiot and heard in Samoa that they expected a hurricane."

" I think," chimed in Bastin, " that the devil knows how to look after his own at any rate for a little while. I dare say it would have been much better for him to be drowned."

" At least he is a deserter and failed in his duty. I never wish to hear of him again," I said.

As a matter of fact I never have. But the incident remains quite unexplained either by Bickley or Bastin.

CHAPTER VII

THE OROFENANS

To our shame we had a very pleasant supper that night off the grilled fish, which was excellent, and some tinned meat. I say to our shame, in a sense, for on our companions the sharks were supping and by rights we should have been sunk in woe. I suppose that the sense of our own escape intoxicated us. Also, notwithstanding his joviality, none of us had cared much for the captain, and his policy had been to keep us somewhat apart from the crew, of whom therefore we knew but little. It is true that Bastin held services on Sundays, for such as would attend, and Bickley had doctored a few of them for minor ailments, but there, except for a little casual conversation, our intercourse began and ended.

Now the sad fact is that it is hard to be overwhelmed with grief for those with whom we are not intimate. We were very sorry and that is all that can be said, except that Bastin, being High Church, announced in a matter-of-fact way that he meant to put up some petitions for the welfare of their souls. To this Bickley retorted that from what he had seen of their bodies he was sure they needed them.

Yes, it was a pleasant supper, not made less so by a bottle of champagne which Bickley and I shared. Bastin stuck to his tea, not because he did not like champagne, but because, as he explained, having now come in contact with the heathen it would never do for him to set them an example in the use of spirituous liquors.

"However much we may differ, Bastin, I respect you for that sentiment," commented Bickley.

"I don't know why you should," answered Bastin; "but if so, you might follow my example."

That night we slept like logs, trusting to our teak door which we barricaded, and to Tommy, who was a most excellent watch-dog, to guard us against surprise. At any rate we took the risk. As a matter of fact, nothing happened, though before dawn Tommy did growl a good deal, for I heard him, but as he sank into slumber again on my bed, I did not get up. In the morning I found from fresh footprints that two or three men had been prowling about the ship, though at a little distance.

We rose early, and taking the necessary precautions, bathed in the pool. Then we breakfasted, and having filled every available receptacle with water, which took us a long time as these included a large tank that supplied the bath, so that we might have at least a week's supply in case of siege, we went on deck and debated what we should do. In the end we determined to stop where we were and await events, because, as I pointed out, it was necessary that we should discover whether these natives were hostile or friendly. In the former event we could hold our own on the ship, whereas away from it we must be overwhelmed; in the latter there was always time to move inland.

About ten o'clock when we were seated on stools smoking, with our guns by our side—for here, owing to the overhanging cliff in which it will be remembered the prow of the ship was buried, we could not be reached by missiles thrown from above—we saw numbers of the islanders advancing upon us along the beach on either side. They were preceded as before by women who bore food on platters and in baskets. These people, all talking excitedly and laughing after their fashion, stopped at a distance, so we took no notice of them. Presently Marama, clad in his feather cloak, and again accompanied by priests or medicine-men, appeared walking down the path on the cliff face, and, standing below, made salutations and entered into a conversation with us of which I give the substance—that is, so far as we could understand it.

He reproached us for not having come to him as he expected we would do. We replied that we preferred to remain where we were until we were sure of our greeting and asked him what was the position. He explained that only once before, in the time of his grandfather, had any people reached their shores, also during a great storm as we had done. They were dark-skinned men like themselves, three of them, but whence they came was never known, since they were at once seized and sacrificed to the god Oro, which was the right thing to do in such a case.

We asked whether he would consider it right to sacrifice us. He replied:

Certainly, unless we were too strong, being gods ourselves, or unless an arrangement could be concluded. We asked—what arrangement? He replied that we must make them gifts; also that we must do what we had promised and cure him—the chief—of the disease which had tormented him for years. In that event everything would be at our disposal and we, with all our belongings, should become *taboo,* holy, not to be touched. None would attempt to harm us, nothing should be stolen under penalty of death.

We asked him to come up on the deck with only one companion that his sickness might be ascertained, and after much hesitation he consented to do so. Bickley made an examination of the growth and announced that he believed it could be removed with perfect safety as the attachment to the neck was very slight, but of course there was always a risk. This was explained to him with difficulty, and much talk followed between him and his followers who gathered on the beach beneath the ship. They seemed adverse to the experiment, till Marama grew furious with them and at last burst into tears saying that he could no longer drag this terrible burden about with him, and he touched the growth. He would rather die. Then they gave way.

I will tell the rest as shortly as I can.

A hideous wooden idol was brought on board, wrapped in leaves and feathers, and upon it the chief and his head people swore safety to us whether he lived or died, making us the guests of their land. There were, however, two provisos made, or as such we understood them. These seemed to be that we should offer no insult or injury to their god, and secondly, that we should not set foot on the island in the lake. It was not till afterwards that it occurred to me that this must refer to the mountain top which appeared in the inland sheet of water. To those stipulations we made no answer. Indeed, the Orofenans did all the talking. Finally, they ratified their oaths by a man who, I suppose, was a head priest, cutting his arm and rubbing the blood from it on the lips of the idol; also upon those of the chief. I should add that Bastin had retired as soon as he saw that false god appear, of which I was glad, since I felt sure that he would make a scene.

The operation took place that afternoon and on the ship, for when once Marama had made up his mind to trust us he did so very thoroughly. It was performed on deck in the presence of an awed multitude who watched from the shore, and when they saw Bickley appear in a clean nightshirt and wash his hands, uttered a groan of wonder. Evidently they considered it a magical and religious ceremony; indeed ever afterwards they called Bickley the Great Priest, or sometimes the Great Healer in later days. This was a grievance to Bastin who considered that he had been robbed of his proper title, especially when he learned that among themselves he was only known as "the Bellower," because of the loud voice in which he addressed them. Nor did Bickley particularly appreciate the compliment.

With my help he administered the chloroform, which was done under shelter of a sail for fear lest the people should think that we were smothering their chief. Then the operation went on to a satisfactory conclusion. I omit the details, but an electric battery and a red-hot wire came into play.

"There," said Bickley triumphantly when he had finished tying the vessels and made everything neat and tidy with bandages, "I was afraid he might bleed to death, but I don't think there is any fear of that now, for I have made a real job of it." Then advancing with the horrid tumour in his hands he showed it in triumph to the crowd beneath, who groaned again and threw themselves on to their faces. Doubtless now it is the most sacred relic of Orofena.

When Marama came out of the anæsthetic, Bickley gave him something which sent him to sleep for twelve hours, during all which time his people waited beneath. This was our dangerous period, for our difficulty was to persuade them that he was not dead, although Bickley had assured them that he would sleep for a time while the magic worked. Still, I was very glad when he woke up on the following morning, and two or three of his leading men could see that he was alive. The rest was lengthy but simple, consisting merely in keeping him quiet and on a suitable diet until there was no fear of the wound opening. We achieved it somehow with the help of an intelligent native woman who, I suppose, was one of his wives, and five days later were enabled to present him healed, though rather tottery, to his affectionate subjects.

It was a great scene, which may be imagined. They bore him away in a litter with the native woman to watch him and another to carry the relic preserved in a basket, and us they acclaimed as gods. Thenceforward we had nothing to fear in Orofena—except Bastin, though this we did not know at the time.

All this while we had been living on our ship and growing very bored there, although we employed the empty hours in conversation with selected natives, thereby improving our knowledge of the language. Bickley had the best of it, since already patients began to arrive which occupied him. One of the first was that man whom Tommy had bitten. He was carried to us in an almost comatose state, suffering apparently from the symptoms of snake poisoning.

Afterwards it turned out that he conceived Tommy to be a divine but most venomous lizard that could make a very horrible noise, and began to suffer as one might do from the bite of such a creature. Nothing that Bickley could do was enough to save him and ultimately he died in convulsions, a circumstance that enormously enhanced Tommy's reputation. To tell the truth, we took advantage of it to explain that Tommy was in fact a supernatural animal, a sort of tame demon which only harmed people who had malevolent intentions towards those he served or who tried to steal any of their possessions or to intrude upon them at inconvenient hours, especially in the dark. So terrible was he, indeed, that even the skill of the Great Priest, *i.e.,* Bickley, could not avail to save any whom once he had bitten in his rage. Even to be barked at by him was dangerous and conveyed a curse that might last for generations.

All this we set out when Bastin was not there. He had wandered off, as he said, to look for shells, but as we knew, to practise religious orations in the Polynesian tongue with the waves for audience, as Demosthenes is said to have done to perfect himself as a political orator. Personally I admit that I relied more on the terrors of Tommy to safeguard us from theft and other troubles than I did upon those of the native *taboo* and the priestly oaths.

The end of it all was that we left our ship, having padlocked up the door (the padlock, we explained, was a magical instrument that bit worse than Tommy), and moved inland in a kind of triumphal procession, priests and singers going before (the Orofenans sang extremely well) and minstrels following after playing upon instruments like flutes, while behind came the bearers carrying such goods as we needed. They took us to a beautiful place in a grove of palms on a ridge where grew many breadfruit trees, that commanded a view of the ocean upon one side and of the lake with the strange brown mountain top on the other. Here in the midst of the native gardens we found that a fine house had been built for us of a kind of mud brick and thatched with palm leaves, surrounded by a fenced courtyard of beaten earth and having wide overhanging verandahs; a very comfortable place indeed in that delicious climate.

In it we took up our abode, visiting the ship occasionally to see that all was well there, and awaiting events.

For Bickley these soon began to happen in the shape of an ever-increasing stream of patients. The population of the island was considerable, anything between five and ten thousand, so far as we could judge, and among these of course there were a number of sick. Ophthalmia, for instance, was a prevalent disease, as were the growths such as Marama had suffered from, to say nothing of surgical cases and those resulting from accident or from nervous ailments. With all of these Bickley was called upon to deal, which he did with remarkable success by help of his books on Tropical Diseases and his ample supplies of medical necessaries.

At first he enjoyed it very much, but when we had been established in the house for about three weeks he remarked, after putting in a solid ten hours of work, that for all the holiday he was getting he might as well be back at his old practice, with the difference that there he was earning several thousands a year. Just then a poor woman arrived with a baby in convulsions to whose necessities he was obliged to sacrifice his supper, after which came a man who had fallen from a palm tree and broken his leg.

Nor did I escape, since having somehow or other established a reputation for wisdom, as soon as I had mastered sufficient of the language, every kind of knotty case was laid before me for decision. In short, I became a sort of Chief Justice—not an easy office as it involved the acquirement of the native law which was intricate and peculiar, especially in matrimonial cases.

At these oppressive activities Bastin looked on with a gloomy eye.

"You fellows seem very busy," he said one evening;

"but I can find nothing to do. They don't seem to want me, and merely to set a good example by drinking water or tea while you swallow whisky and their palm wine, or whatever it is, is very negative kind of work, especially as I am getting tired of planting things in the garden and playing policeman round the wreck which nobody goes near. Even Tommy is better off, for at least he can bark and hunt rats."

"You see," said Bickley, "we are following our trades. Arbuthnot is a lawyer and acts as a judge. I am a surgeon and I may add a general—a very general—practitioner and work at medicine in an enormous and much-neglected practice. Therefore, you, being a clergyman, should go and do likewise. There are some ten thousand people here, but I do not observe that as yet you have converted a single one."

Thus spoke Bickley in a light and unguarded moment with his usual object of what is known as "getting a rise" out of Bastin. Little did he guess what he was doing.

Bastin thought a while ponderously, then said:

"It is very strange from what peculiar sources Providence sometimes sends inspirations. If wisdom flows from babes and sucklings, why should it not do so from the well of agnostics and mockers?"

"There is no reason which I can see," scoffed Bickley, "except that as a rule wells do not flow."

"Your jest is ill-timed and I may add foolish," continued Bastin. "What I was about to add was that you have given me an idea, as it was no doubt intended that you should do. I will, metaphorically speaking, gird up my loins and try to bear the light into all this heathen blackness."

"Then it is one of the first you ever had, old fellow. But what's the need of girding up your loins in this hot climate?" inquired Bickley with innocence. "Pyjamas and that white and green umbrella of yours would do just as well."

Bastin vouchsafed no reply and sat for the rest of that evening plunged in deep thought.

On the following morning he approached Marama and asked his leave to teach the people about the gods. The chief readily granted this, thinking, I believe, that he alluded to ourselves, and orders were issued accordingly. They were to the effect that Bastin was to be allowed to go everywhere unmolested and to talk to whom he would about what he would, to which all must listen with respect.

Thus he began his missionary career in Orofena, working at it, good and earnest man that he was, in a way that excited even the admiration of Bickley. He started a school for children, which was held under a fine, spreading tree. These listened well, and being of exceedingly quick intellect soon began to pick up the elements of knowledge. But when he tried to persuade them to clothe their little naked bodies his failure was complete, although after much supplication some of the bigger girls did arrive with a chaplet of flowers—round their necks!

Also he preached to the adults, and here again was very successful in a way, especially after he became more familiar with the language. They listened; to a certain extent they understood; they argued and put to poor Bastin the most awful questions such as the whole Bench of Bishops could not have answered. Still he did answer them somehow, and they politely accepted his interpretation of their theological riddles. I observed that he got on best when he was telling them stories out of the Old Testament, such as the account of the creation of the world and of human beings, also of the Deluge, etc. Indeed one of their elders said—Yes, this was quite true. They had heard it all before from their fathers, and that once the Deluge had taken place round Orofena, swallowing up great countries, but sparing them because they were so good.

Bastin, surprised, asked them who had caused the deluge. They replied, Oro which was the name of their god, Oro who dwelt yonder on the mountain in the lake, and whose representation they worshipped in idols. He said that God dwelt in Heaven, to which they replied with calm certainty:

"No, no, he dwells on the mountain in the lake," which was why they never dared to approach that mountain.

Indeed it was only by giving the name Oro to the Divinity and admitting that He might dwell in the mountain as well as everywhere else, that Bastin was able to make progress. Having conceded this, not without scruples, however, he did make considerable progress, so much, in fact, that I perceived that the priests of Oro were beginning to grow very jealous of him and of his increasing authority with the people. Bastin was naturally triumphant, and even exclaimed exultingly that within a year he would have half of the population baptised.

"Within a year, my dear fellow," said Bickley, "you will have your throat cut as a sacrifice, and probably ours also. It is a pity, too, as within that time I should have stamped out ophthalmia and some other diseases in the island."

Here, leaving Bastin and his good work aside for a while, I will say a little about the country. From information which I gathered on some journeys that I made and by inquiries from the chief Marama, who had become devoted to us, I found that Orofena was quite a large place. In shape the island was circular, a broad band of territory surrounding the great lake of which I have spoken, that in its turn surrounded a smaller island from which rose the mountain top. No other land was known to be near the shores of Orofena, which had never been visited by anyone except the strangers a hundred years ago or so, who were sacrificed and eaten. Most of the island was covered with forest which the inhabitants lacked the energy, and indeed had no tools, to fell. They were an extremely lazy people and would only cultivate enough bananas and other food to satisfy their immediate needs. In truth they lived mostly upon breadfruit and other products of the wild trees.

Thus it came about that in years of scarcity through drought or climatic causes, which prevented the forest trees from bearing, they suffered very much from hunger. In such years hundreds of them would perish and the remainder resorted to the dreadful expedient of cannibalism. Sometimes, too, the shoals of fish avoided their shores, reducing them to great misery. Their only domestic animal was the pig which roamed about half wild and in no great numbers, for they had never taken the trouble to breed it in captivity. Their resources, therefore, were limited, which accounted for the comparative smallness of the population, further reduced as it was by a wicked habit of infanticide practised in order to lighten the burden of bringing up children.

They had no traditions as to how they reached this land, their belief being that they had always been there but that their forefathers were much greater than they. They were poetical, and sang songs in a language which themselves they could not understand; they said that it was the tongue their forefathers had spoken. Also they had several strange customs of which they did not know the origin. My own opinion, which Bickley shared, was that they were in fact a shrunken and deteriorated remnant of some high race now coming to its end through age and inter-breeding. About them indeed, notwithstanding their primitive savagery which in its qualities much resembled that of other Polynesians, there was a very curious air of antiquity. One felt that they had known the older world and its mysteries, though now both were forgotten. Also their language, which in time we came to speak perfectly, was copious, musical, and expressive in its idioms.

One circumstance I must mention. In walking about the country I observed all over it enormous holes, some of them measuring as much as a hundred yards across, with a depth of fifty feet or more, and this not on alluvial lands although there traces of them existed also, but in solid rock. What this rock was I do not know as none of us were geologists, but it seemed to me to partake of the nature of granite. Certainly it was not coral like that on and about the coast, but of a primeval formation.

When I asked Marama what caused these holes, he only shrugged his shoulders and said he did not know, but their fathers had declared that they were made by stones falling from heaven. This, of course, suggested meteorites to my mind. I submitted the idea to Bickley, who, in one of his rare intervals of leisure, came with me to make an examination.

"If they were meteorites," he said, "of which a

shower struck the earth in some past geological age, all life must have been destroyed by them and their remains ought to exist at the bottom of the holes. To me they look more like the effect of high explosives, but that, of course, is impossible, though I don't know what else could have caused such craters."

Then he went back to his work, for nothing that had to do with antiquity interested Bickley very much. The present and its problems were enough for him, he would say, who neither had lived in the past nor expected to have any share in the future.

As I remained curious I made an opportunity to scramble to the bottom of one of these craters, taking with me some of the natives with their wooden tools. Here I found a good deal of soil either washed down from the surface or resulting from the decomposition of the rock, though oddly enough in it nothing grew. I directed them to dig. After a while to my astonishment there appeared a corner of a great worked stone quite unlike that of the crater, indeed it seemed to me to be of marble. Further examination showed that this block was most beautifully carved in bas-relief, apparently with a design of leaves and flowers. In the disturbed soil also I picked up a life-sized marble hand of a woman exquisitely finished and apparently broken from a statue that might have been the work of one of the great Greek sculptors. Moreover, on the third finger of this hand was a representation of a ring whereof, unfortunately, the bezel had been destroyed.

I put the hand in my pocket, but as darkness was coming on, I could not pursue the research and disinter the block. When I wished to return the next day, I was informed politely by Marama that it would not be safe for me to do so as the priests of Oro declared that if I sought to meddle with the "buried things the god would grow angry and bring disaster on me."

When I persisted he said that at least I must go alone since no native would accompany me, and added earnestly that he prayed me not to go. So to my great regret and disappointment I was obliged to give up the idea.

CHAPTER VIII

BASTIN ATTEMPTS THE MARTYR'S CROWN

THAT carved stone and the marble hand took a great hold of my imagination. What did they mean? How could they have come to the bottom of that hole, unless indeed they were part of some building and its ornaments which had been destroyed in the neighbourhood? The stone of which we had only uncovered a corner seemed far too big to have been carried there from any ship; it must have weighed several tons. Besides, ships do not carry such things about the world, and none had visited this island during the last two centuries at any rate, or local tradition would have recorded so wonderful a fact. Were there, then, once edifices covered with elegant carving standing on this place, and were they adorned with lovely statues that would not have disgraced the best period of Greek art? The thing was incredible except on the supposition that these were relics of an utterly lost civilisation.

Bickley was as much puzzled as myself. All he could say was that the world was infinitely old and many things might have happened in it whereof we had no record. Even Bastin was excited for a little while, but as his imagination was represented by zero, all he could say was:

"I suppose someone left them there, and anyhow it doesn't matter much, does it?"

But I, who have certain leanings towards the ancient and mysterious, could not be put off in this fashion. I remembered that unapproachable mountain in the midst of the lake and that on it appeared to be something which looked like ruins as seen from the top of the cliff through glasses. At any rate this was a point that I might clear up.

Saying nothing to anybody, one morning I slipped away and walked to the edge of the lake, a distance of five or six miles over rough country. Having arrived there I perceived that the cone-shaped mountain in the centre, which was about a mile from the lake shore, was much larger than I had thought, quite three hundred feet high indeed, and with a very large circumference. Further, its sides evidently once had been terraced, and it was on one of these broad terraces, half-way up and facing towards the rising sun, that the ruin-like remains were heaped. I examined them through my glasses. Undoubtedly it was a cyclopean ruin built of great blocks of coloured stone which seemed to have been shattered by earthquake or explosion. There were the pillars of a mighty gateway and the remains of walls.

I trembled with excitement as I stared and stared. Could I not get to the place and see for myself? I observed that from the flat bush-clad land at the foot of the mountain, ran out what seemed to be the residue of a stone pier which ended in a large table-topped rock between two and three hundred feet across. But even this was too far to reach by swimming, besides for aught I knew there might be alligators in that lake. I walked up and down its borders, till presently I came to a path which led into a patch of some variety of cotton palm.

Following this path I discovered a boat-house thatched over with palm leaves. Inside it were two good canoes with their paddles, floating and tied to the stumps of trees by fibre ropes. Instantly I made up my mind that I would paddle to the island and investigate. Just as I was about to step into one of the canoes the light was cut off. Looking up I saw that a man was crouching in the door-place of the boat-house in order to enter, and paused guiltily.

"Friend-from-the-Sea" (that was the name that these islanders had given to me), said the voice of Marama, "say—what are you doing here?"

"I am about to take a row on the lake, Chief," I answered carelessly.

"Indeed, Friend. Have we then treated you so badly that you are tired of life?"

"What do you mean?" I asked.

"Come out into the sunlight, Friend, and I will explain to you."

I hesitated till I saw Marama lifting the heavy wooden spear he carried and remembered that I was unarmed. Then I came out.

"What does all this mean, Chief?" I asked angrily when we were clear of the patch of cotton palm.

"I mean, Friend, that you have been very near to making a longer journey than you thought. Have patience now and listen to me. I saw you leaving the village this morning and followed, suspecting your purpose. Yes, I followed alone, saying nothing to the priests of Oro who fortunately were away watching the Bellower for their own reasons. I saw you searching out the secrets of the mountain with those magic tubes that make things big that are small, and things that are far off come near, and I followed you to the canoes."

"All that is plain enough, Marama. But why?"

"Have I not told you, Friend-from-the-Sea, that yonder hill which is called Orofena, whence this island takes its name, is sacred?"

"You said so, but what of it?"

"This: to set foot thereon is to die and, I suppose, great as you are, you, too, can die like others. At least, although I love you, had you not ccme away from that canoe I was about to discover whether this is so."

"Then for what are the canoes used?" I asked with irritation.

"You see that flat rock, Friend, with the hole beyond, which is the mouth of a cave that appeared only in the great storm that brought you to our land? They are used to convey offerings which are laid upon the rock. Beyond it no man may go, and since the beginning no man has ever gone."

"Offerings to whom?"

"To the Oromatuas, the spirits of the great dead who live there."

"Oromatuas? Oro! It is always something to do with Oro. Who and what is Oro?"

"Oro is a god, Friend, though it is true that the priests say that above him there is a greater god called Degai, the Creator, the Fate who made all things and directs all things."

"Very well, but why do you suppose that Oro, the servant of Degai, lives in that mountain? I thought that he lived in a grove yonder where your priests, as I am told, have an image of him."

"I do not know, Friend-from-the-Sea, but so it has been held from the beginning. The image in the grove is only visited by his spirit from time to time. Now, I pray you, come back and before the priests discover that you have been here, and forget that there are any canoes upon this lake."

So, thinking it wisest, I turned the matter with a laugh and walked away with him to the village. On our road I tried to extract some more information but without success. He did not know who built the ruin upon the mountain, or who destroyed it. He did not know how the terraces came there. All he knew was that during the convulsion of Nature which resulted in the tidal wave that had thrown our ship upon the island, the mountain had been seen to quiver like a tree in the wind as though within it great forces were at work. Then it was observed to have risen a good many more feet above the surface of the lake, as might be noted by the water mark upon the shore, and then also the mouth of the cave had appeared. The priests said that all this was because the Oromatuas who dwelt there were stirring, which portended great things. Indeed great things had happened—for had we not arrived in their land?

I thanked him for what he had told me, and, as there was nothing more to be learned, dropped the subject which was never mentioned between us again, at least not for a long while. But in my heart I determined that I would reach that mountain even though to do so I must risk my life. Something seemed to call me to the place; it was as though I were being drawn by a magnet.

As it happened, before so very long I did go to the mountain, not of my own will but because I was obliged. It came about thus. One night I asked Bastin how he was getting on with his missionary work. He replied: Very well indeed, but there was one great obstacle in his path, the idol in the Grove. Were it not for this accursed image he believed that the whole island would become Christian. I asked him to be more plain. He explained that all his work was thwarted by this idol, since his converts declared that they did not dare to be baptised while it sat there in the Grove. If they did, the spirit that was in it would bewitch them and perhaps steal out at night and murder them.

"The spirit being our friends the sorcerers," I suggested.

"That's it, Arbuthnot. Do you know, I believe those devilish men sometimes offer human sacrifices to this satanic fetish, when there is a drought or anything of that sort."

"I can quite believe it," I answered, "but as they will scarcely remove their god and with it their own livelihood and authority, I am afraid that as *we* don't want to be sacrificed, there is nothing to be done."

At this moment I was called away. As I went I heard Bastin muttering something about martyrs, but paid no attention. Little did I guess what was going on in his pious but obstinate mind. In effect it was this—that if no one else would remove that idol he was quite ready to do it himself.

However, he was very cunning over that business, almost Jesuitical indeed. Not one word did he breathe of his dark plans to me, and still less to Bickley. He just went on with his teaching, lamenting from time to time the stumbling-block of the idol and expressing wonder as to how it might be circumvented by a change in the hearts of the islanders, or otherwise. Sad as it is to record, in fact, dear old Bastin went as near to telling a fib in connection with this matter as I suppose he had ever done in his life. It happened thus. One day Bickley's sharp eye caught sight of Bastin walking about with what looked like a bottle of whisky in his pocket.

"Hallo, old fellow," he said, "has the self-denying ordinance broken down? I didn't know that you took pegs on the sly," and he pointed to the bottle.

"If you are insinuating, Bickley, that I absorb spirits surreptitiously, you are more mistaken than usual, which is saying a good deal. This bottle contains, not Scotch whisky but paraffin, although I admit that its label may have misled you, unintentionally, so far as I am concerned."

"What are you going to do with the paraffin?" asked Bickley.

Bastin coloured through his tan and replied awkwardly:

"Paraffin is very good to keep away mosquitoes if one can stand the smell of it upon one's skin. Not that I have brought it here with that sole object. The truth is that I am anxious to experiment with a lamp of my own design made—um—of native wood," and he departed in a hurry.

"When next old Bastin wants to tell a lie," commented Bickley, "he should make up his mind as to what it is to be, and stick to it. I wonder what he is after with that paraffin? Not going to dose any of my patients with it, I hope. He was arguing the other day that it is a great remedy taken internally, being quite unaware that the lamp variety is not used for that purpose."

"Perhaps he means to swallow some himself, just to show that he is right," I suggested.

"The stomach-pump is at hand," said Bickley, and the matter dropped.

Next morning I got up before it was light. Having some elementary knowledge of the main facts of astronomy, which remained with me from boyhood when I had attended lectures on the subject, which I had tried to refresh by help of an encyclopædia I had brought from the ship, I wished to attempt to obtain an idea of our position by help of the stars. In this endeavour, I may say, I failed absolutely, as I did not know how to take a stellar or any other observation.

On my way out of our native house I observed, by the lantern I carried, that the compartment of it occupied by Bastin was empty, and wondered whither he had gone at that hour. On arriving at my observation-post, a rocky eminence on open ground, where, with Tommy at my side, I took my seat with a telescope, I was astonished to see or rather to hear a great number of the natives walking past the base of the mound towards the bush. Then I remembered that some one, Marama, I think, had informed me that there was to be a great sacrifice to Oro at dawn on that day. After this I thought no more of the matter but occupied myself in a futile study of the heavenly bodies. At length the dawn broke and put a period to my labours.

Glancing round me before I descended from the little hill, I saw a flame of light appear suddenly about half a mile or more away among those trees which I knew concealed the image of Oro. On this personally I had never had the curiosity to look, as I knew that it was only a hideous idol stuck over with feathers and other bedizenments. The flame shot suddenly straight into the still air and was followed a few seconds later by the sound of a dull explosion, after which it went out. Also it was followed by something else—a scream of rage from an infuriated mob.

At the foot of the hill I stopped to wonder what these sounds might mean. Then of a sudden appeared Bickley, who had been attending some urgent case, and asked me who was exploding gunpowder. I told him that I had no idea.

"Then I have," he answered. "It is that ass Bastin up to some game. Now I guess why he wanted that paraffin. Listen to the row. What are they after?"

"Sacrificing Bastin, perhaps," I replied, half in jest. "Have you your revolver?"

He nodded. We always wore our pistols if we went out during the dark hours.

"Then perhaps we had better go to see."

We started, and had not covered a hundred yards before a girl, whom I recognised as one of Bastin's converts, came flying towards us and screaming out, "Help! Help! They kill the Bellower with fire! They cook him like a pig!"

"Just what I expected," said Bickley.

Then we ran hard, as evidently there was no time to lose. While we went I extracted from the terrified girl, whom we forced to show us the way, that as the sacrifice was about to be offered Bastin had appeared, and, "making fire," applied it to the god Oro, who instantly burst into flame. Then he ran back, calling out that the devil was dead. As he did so there was a loud explosion and Oro flew into pieces. His burning head went a long way into the air and, falling on to one of the priests, killed him. Thereon the other priests and the people seized the Bellower and made him fast. Now they were engaged in heating an oven in which to put him to cook. When it was ready they would eat him in honour of Oro.

"And serve him right too!" gasped Bickley, who, being stout, was not a good runner. "Why can't he leave other people's gods alone instead of blowing them up with gunpowder?"

"Don't know," I answered. "Hope we shall get there in time!"

"To be cooked and eaten with Bastin!" wheezed Bickley, after which his breath gave out.

As it chanced we did, for these stone ovens take a long time to heat. There by the edge of his fiery grave with his hands and legs bound in palm-fibre shackles, stood Bastin, quite unmoved, smiling indeed, in a sort of seraphic way which irritated us both extremely. Round him danced the infuriated priests of Oro, and round them, shrieking and howling with rage, was most of the population of Orofena. We rushed up so suddenly that none tried to stop us, and took our stand on either side of him, producing our pistols as we did so.

"Thank you for coming," said Bastin in the silence which followed; "though I don't think it is the least use. I cannot recall that any of the early martyrs were ever roasted and eaten, though, of course, throwing them into boiling oil or water was fairly common. I take it that the rite is sacrificial and even in a low sense, sacramental, not merely one of common cannibalism."

I stared at him, and Bickley gasped out:

"If you are to be eaten, what does it matter why you are eaten?"

"Oh!" replied Bastin; "there is all the difference in the world, though it is one that I cannot expect you to appreciate. And now please be quiet as I wish to say my prayers. I imagine that those stones will be hot enough to do their office within twenty minutes or so, which is not very long."

At that moment Marama appeared, evidently in a state of great perturbation. With him were some of the priests or sorcerers who were dancing about as I imagine the priests of Baal must have done, and filled with fury. They rolled their eyes, they stuck out their tongues, they uttered weird cries and shook their wooden knives at the placid Bastin.

"What is the matter?" I asked sternly of the chief.

"This, Friend-from-the-Sea. The Bellower there, when the sacrifice was about to be offered to Oro at the dawn, rushed forward, and having thrust something between the legs of the image of the god, poured yellow water over it, and with fire caused it to burst into fierce flame. Then he ran away and mocked the god who presently, with a loud report, flew into pieces and killed that man. Therefore the Bellower must be sacrificed."

"What to?" I asked. "The image has gone and the piece of it that ascended fell not upon the Bellower, as would have happened if the god had been angry with him, but on one of its own priests, whom it killed. Therefore, having been sacrificed by the god itself, he it is that should be eaten, not the Bellower, who merely did what his Spirit bade him."

This ingenious argument seemed to produce some effect upon Marama, but to the priests it did not at all appeal.

"Eat them all!" these cried. "They are the enemies of Oro and have worked sacrilege!"

Moreover, to judge from their demeanour, the bulk of the people seemed to agree with them. Things began to look very ugly. The priests rushed forward, threatening us with their wooden weapons, and one of them even aimed a blow at Bickley, which only missed him by an inch or two.

"Look here, my friend," called the doctor whose

temper was rising, "you name me the Great Priest or Great Healer, do you not? Well, be careful, lest I should show you that I can kill as well as heal!"

Not in the least intimidated by this threat the man, a great bedizened fellow who literally was foaming at the mouth with rage, rushed forward again, his club raised, apparently with the object of dashing out Bickley's brains.

Suddenly Bickley lifted his revolver and fired. The man, shot through the heart, sprang into the air and fell upon his face—stone dead. There was consternation, for these people had never seen us shoot anything before, and were quite unacquainted with the properties of firearms, which they supposed to be merely instruments for making a noise. They stared, they gasped in fear and astonishment, and then they fled, pursued by Tommy, barking, leaving us alone with the two dead men.

"It was time to teach them a lesson," said Bickley as he replaced the empty cartridge, and, seizing the dead man, rolled him into the burning pit.

"Yes," I answered; "but presently, when they have got over their fright, they will come back to teach *us* one."

Bastin said nothing; he seemed too dazed at the turn events had taken.

"What do you suggest?" asked Bickley.

"Flight," I answered.

"Where to—the ship? We might hold that."

"No; that is what they expect. Look! They are cutting off our road there. To the island in the lake where they dare not follow us, for it is holy ground."

"How are we going to live on the island?" asked Bickley.

"I don't know," I replied; "but I am quite certain that if we stay here we shall die."

"Very well," he said; "let us try it."

While we were speaking I was cutting Bastin's bonds.

"Thank you," he said. "It is a great relief to stretch one's arms after they have been compressed with cords. But at the same time, I do not know that I am really grateful. The martyr's crown was hanging above me, so to speak, and now it has vanished into the pit, like that man whom Bickley murdered."

"Look here," exclaimed the exasperated Bickley, "if you say much more, Bastin, I'll chuck you into the pit too, to look for your martyr's crown, for I think you have done enough mischief for one morning."

"If you are trying to shift the responsibility for that unfortunate man's destruction on to me——"

"Oh! shut it and trot," broke in Bickley. "Those infernal savages are coming with your blessed converts leading the van."

So we "trotted" at no mean pace. As we passed it, Bastin stooped down and picked up the head of the image of Oro, much as Atalanta in Academy pictures is represented as doing to the apples, and bore it away in triumph.

"I know it is scorched," he ejaculated at intervals, "but they might trim it up and stick it on to a new body as the original false god. Now they *can't*, for there's nothing left."

As a matter of fact, we were never in any real danger, for our pursuit was very half-hearted indeed. To begin with, now that their first rage was over, the Orofenans who were fond of us had no particular wish to do us to death, while the ardour of their sorcerers, who wished this very much, had been greatly cooled by the mysterious annihilation of their idol and the violent deaths of two of their companions, which they thought might be reduplicated in their own persons. So it came about that the chase, if noisy, was neither close nor eager.

We reached the edge of the lake where was the boat-house of which I have spoken already, travelling at little more than a walk. Here we made Bastin unfasten the better of the two canoes that by good luck was almost filled with offerings, which doubtless, according to custom, must be made upon the day of this feast to Oro, while we watched against surprise at the boat-house door. When he was ready we slipped in and took our seats, Tommy jumping in after us, and pushed the canoe, now very heavily laden, out into the lake.

Here, at a distance of about forty paces, which we judged to be beyond wooden spear-throw, we rested upon our paddles to see what would happen. All the crowd of islanders had rushed to the lake edge where they stood staring at us stupidly. Bastin, thinking the occasion opportune, lifted the hideous head of the idol which he had carefully washed, and began to preach on the downfall of "the god of the Grove."

This action of his appeared to awake memories or forebodings in the minds of his congregation. Perhaps some ancient prophecy was concerned—I do not know. At any rate, one of the priests shouted something, whereon everybody began to talk at once. Then, stooping down, they threw water from the lake over themselves and rubbed its sand and mud into their hair, all the while making genuflexions towards the mountain in the middle, after which they turned and departed.

"Don't you think we had better go back?" asked Bastin. "Evidently my words have touched them and their minds are melting beneath the light of Truth."

"Oh! by all means," replied Bickley with sarcasm; "for then their spears will touch *us,* and our bodies will soon be melting above the fires of that pit."

"Perhaps you are right," said Bastin; "at least, I admit that you have made matters very difficult by your unjustifiable homicide of that priest who I do not think meant to injure you seriously, and really was not at all a bad fellow, though opinionated in some ways. Also, I do not suppose that anybody is expected, as it were, to run his head into the martyr's crown. When it settles there of itself it is another matter."

"Like a butterfly!" exclaimed the enraged Bickley.

"Yes, if you like to put it that way, though the simile seems a very poor one; like a sunbeam would be better."

Here Bickley gave way with his paddle so vigorously that the canoe was as nearly as possible upset into the lake.

In due course we reached the flat Rock of Offerings, which proved to be quite as wide as a double croquet lawn and much longer.

"What are those?" I asked, pointing to certain knobs on the edge of the rock at a spot where a curved projecting point made a little harbour.

Bickley examined them, and answered:

"I should say that they are the remains of stone mooring-posts worn down by many thousands of years of weather. Yes, look, there is the cut of the cables upon the base of that one, and very big cables they must have been."

We stared at one another—that is, Bickley and I did, for Bastin was still engaged in contemplating the blackened head of the god which he had overthrown.

CHAPTER IX

THE ISLAND IN THE LAKE

We made the canoe fast and landed on the great rock, to perceive that it was really a peninsula. That is to say, it was joined to the main land of the lake island by a broad roadway quite fifty yards across, which appeared to end in the mouth of the cave. On this causeway we noted a very remarkable thing, namely, two grooves separated by an exact distance of nine feet which ran into the mouth of the cave and vanished there.

"Explain!" said Bickley.

"Paths," I said, "worn by countless feet walking on them for thousands of years."

"You should cultivate the art of observation, Arbuthnot. What do you say, Bastin?"

He stared at the grooves through his spectacles, and replied:

"I don't say anything, except that I can't see anybody to make paths here. Indeed, the place seems quite unpopulated, and all the Orofenans told me that they never landed on it because if they did they would die. It is a part of their superstitious nonsense. If you have any idea in your head you had better tell us quickly before we breakfast. I am very hungry."

"You always are," remarked Bickley; "even when most people's appetites might have been affected. Well, I think that this great plateau was once a landing-place for flying machines, and that there is the air-shed or garage."

Bastin stared at him.

"Don't you think we had better breakfast?" he said. "There are two roast pigs in that canoe, and lots of other food, enough to last us a week, I should say. Of course, I understand that the blood you have shed has thrown you off your balance. I believe it has that effect, except on the most hardened. Flying machines were only invented a few years ago by the brothers Wright in America."

"Bastin," said Bickley, "I begin to regret that I did not leave you to take part in another breakfast yonder —I mean as the principal dish."

"It was Providence, not you, who prevented it, Bickley, doubtless because I am unworthy of such a glorious end."

"Then it is lucky that Providence is a good shot with a pistol. Stop talking nonsense and listen. If those were paths worn by feet they would run to the edge of the rock. They do not. They begin there in that gentle depression and slope upwards somewhat steeply. The air machines, which were evidently large, lit in the depression, possibly as a bird does, and then ran on wheels or sledge skids along the grooves to the air-shed in the mountain. Come to the cave and you will see."

"Not till we have breakfast," said Bastin. "I will get out a pig. As a matter of fact, I had no supper last night, as I was taking a class of native boys and making some arrangements of my own."

As for me, I only whistled. It all seemed very feasible. And yet how could such things be?

We unloaded the canoe and ate. Bastin's appetite

was splendid. Indeed, I had to ask him to remember that when this supply was done I did not know where we should find any more.

"Take no thought for the morrow," he replied. "I have no doubt it will come from somewhere," and he helped himself to another chop.

Never had I admired him so much. Not a couple of hours before he was about to be cruelly murdered and eaten. But this did not seem to affect him in the least. Bastin was the only man I have ever known with a really perfect faith. It is a quality worth having and one that makes for happiness. What a great thing not to care whether you are breakfasted on, or breakfast!

"I see that there is lots of driftwood about here," he remarked, "but unfortunately we have no tea, so in this climate it is of little use, unless indeed we can catch some fish and cook them."

"Stop talking about eating and help us to haul up the canoe," said Bickley.

Between the three of us we dragged and carried the canoe a long way from the lake, fearing lest the natives should come and bear it off with our provisions. Then, having given Tommy his breakfast off the scraps, we walked to the cave. I glanced at my companions. Bickley's face was alight with scientific eagerness. Here are not dreams or speculations, but facts to be learned, it seemed to say, and I will learn them. The past is going to show me some of its secrets, to tell me how men of long ago lived and died and how far they had advanced to that point on the road of civilisation at which I stand in my little hour of existence.

That of Bastin was mildly interested, no more. Obviously, with half his mind he was thinking of something else, probably of his converts on the main island

and of the school class fixed for this hour which circumstances prevented him from attending. Indeed, like Lot's wife he was casting glances behind him towards the wicked place from which he had been forced to flee.

Neither the past nor the future had much real interest for Bastin, any more than they had for Bickley, though for different reasons. The former was done with; the latter he was quite content to leave in other hands. If he had any clear idea thereof, probably that undiscovered land appeared to him as a big, pleasant place where are no unbelievers or erroneous doctrines, and all sinners will be sternly repressed, in which, clad in a white surplice with all proper ecclesiastical trappings, he would argue eternally with the Early Fathers and in due course utterly annihilate Bickley, that is in a moral sense. Personally and as a man he was extremely attached to Bickley as a necessary and wrong-headed nuisance to which he had become accustomed.

And I! What did I feel? I do not know; I cannot describe. An extraordinary attraction, a semi-spiritual exaltation, I think. That cave mouth might have been a magnet drawing my soul. With my body I should have been afraid, as I daresay I was, for our circumstances were sufficiently desperate. Here we were, castaways upon an island, probably uncharted, one of thousands in the recesses of a vast ocean, from which we had little chance of escape. More, having offended the religious instincts of the primeval inhabitants of that island, we had been forced to flee to a rocky mountain in the centre of a lake, where, after the food we had brought with us by accident was consumed, we should no doubt be forced to choose between death by starvation, or, if we attempted to retreat, at the hands of justly infuriated savages. Yet these facts did not oppress me, for I was being drawn, drawn to I knew not what, and if it were to doom—well, no matter.

Therefore, none of us cared: Bastin because his faith was equal to any emergency and there was always that white-robed heaven waiting for him beyond which his imagination did not go (I often wondered whether he pictured Mrs. Bastin as also waiting; if so, he never said anything about her); Bickley because as a child of the Present and a servant of knowledge he feared no future, believing it to be for him non-existent, and was careless as to when his strenuous hour of life should end; and I because I felt that yonder lay my true future; yes, and my true past, even though to discover them I must pass through that portal which we know as Death.

We reached the mouth of the cave. It was a vast place; perhaps the arch of it was a hundred feet high, and I could see that once all this arch had been adorned with sculptures. Protected as these were by the overhanging rock, for the sculptured mouth of the cave was cut deep into the mountain face, they were still so worn that it was impossible to discern their details. Time had eaten them away like an acid. But what length of time? I could not guess, but it must have been stupendous to have worked thus upon that hard and sheltered rock.

This came home to me with added force when, from subsequent examination, we learned that the entire mouth of this cave had been sealed up for unnumbered ages. It will be remembered that Marama told me the mountain in the lake had risen much during the frightful cyclone in which we were wrecked, and with it the cave mouth which previously had been invisible. From the markings on the mountain side it was obvious that something of the sort had happened very recently, at any rate on this eastern face. That is, either the flat rock had sunk or the volcano had been thrown upwards.

Once in the far past the cave had been as it was when we found it. Then it had gone down in such a way that the table-rock entirely sealed the entrance. Now this entrance was once more open, and although of course there was a break in them, the grooves of which I have spoken ran on into the cave at only a slightly different level from that at which they lay upon the flat rock. And yet, although they had been thus sheltered by a great stone curtain in front of them, still these sculptures were worn away by the tooth of Time. Of course, however, this may have happened to them *before* they were buried in some ancient cataclysm, to be thus resurrected at the hour of our arrival upon the island.

Without pausing to make any closer examination of these crumbled carvings, we entered the yawning mouth of that great place, following and indeed walking in the deep grooves that I have mentioned. Presently it seemed to open out as a courtyard might at the end of a passage; yes, to open on to some vast place whereof in that gloom we could not see the roof or the limits. All we knew was that it must be enormous—the echoes of our voices and footsteps told us as much, for these seemed to come back to us from high, high above and from far, far away. Bickley and I said nothing; we were too overcome. But Bastin remarked:

"Did you ever go to Olympia? I did once to see a kind of play where the people said nothing, only ran about dressed up. They told me it was religious, the sort of thing a clergyman should study. I didn't think it religious at all. It was all about a nun who had a baby."

"Well, what of it?" snapped Bickley.

"Nothing particular, except that nuns don't have babies, or if they do the fact should not be advertised. But I wasn't thinking of that. I was thinking that this place is like an underground Olympia."

"Oh, be quiet!" I said, for though Bastin's description was not bad, his monotonous, drawling voice jarred on me in that solemnity.

"Be careful where you walk," whispered Bickley, for even he seemed awed, "there may be pits in this floor."

"I wish we had a light," I said, halting.

"If candles are of any use," broke in Bastin, "as it happens I have a packet in my pocket. I took them with me this morning for a certain purpose."

"Not unconnected with the paraffin and the burning of the idol, I suppose?" said Bickley. "Hand them over."

"Yes; if I had been allowed a little more time I intended——"

"Never mind what you intended; we know what you did and that's enough," said Bickley as he snatched the packet from Bastin's hand and proceeded to undo it, adding, "By heaven! I have no matches, nor have you, Arbuthnot!"

"I have a dozen boxes of wax vestas in my other pocket," said Bastin. "You see, they burn so well when you want to get up a fire on a damp idol. As you may have noticed, the dew is very heavy here."

In due course these too were produced. I took possession of them as they were too valuable to be left in the charge of Bastin, and, extracting a box from the packet, lit two of the candles which were of the short thick variety, like those used in carriage-lamps.

Presently they burned up, making two faint stars of light which, however, were not strong enough to show us either the roof or the sides of that vast place. By their aid we pursued our path, still following the grooves till suddenly these came to an end. Now all around us was a flat floor of rock which, as we perceived clearly when we pushed aside the dust that had gathered thickly on it in the course of ages, doubtless from the gradual disintegration of the stony walls, had once been polished till it resembled black marble. Indeed, certain cracks in the floor appeared to have been filled in with some dark-coloured cement. I stood looking at them while Bickley wandered off to the right and a little forward, and presently called to me. I walked to him, Bastin sticking close to me as I had the other candle, as did the little dog, Tommy, who did not like these new surroundings and would not leave my heels.

"Look," said Bickley, holding up his candle, "and tell me—what's that?"

Before me, faintly shown, was some curious structure of gleaming rods made of yellowish metal, which rods appeared to be connected by wires. The structure might have been forty feet high and perhaps a hundred long. Its bottom part was buried in dust.

"What is that?" asked Bickley again.

I made no answer, for I was thinking. Bastin, however, replied:

"It's difficult to be sure in this light, but I should think that it may be the remains of a cage in which some people who lived here kept monkeys, or perhaps it was an aviary. Look at those little ladders for the monkeys to climb by, or possibly for the birds to sit on."

"Are you sure it wasn't tame angels?" asked Bickley.

"What a ridiculous remark! How can you keep an angel in a cage? I——"

"Aeroplane!" I almost whispered to Bickley.

"You've got it!" he answered. "The framework of an aeroplane and a jolly large one, too. Only why hasn't it oxidised?"

"Some indestructible metal," I suggested. "Gold, for instance, does not oxidise."

He nodded and said:

"We shall have to dig it out. The dust is feet thick about it; we can do nothing without spades. Come on."

We went round to the end of the structure, whatever it might be, and presently came to another. Again we went on and came to another, all of them being berthed exactly in line.

"What did I tell you?" said Bickley in a voice of triumph. "A whole garage full, a regular fleet of aeroplanes!"

"That must be nonsense," said Bastin, "for I am quite sure that these Orofenans cannot make such things. Indeed they have no metal, and even cut the throats of pigs with wooden knives."

Now I began to walk forward, bearing to the left so as to regain our former line. We could do nothing with these metal skeletons, and I felt that there must be more to find beyond. Presently I saw something looming ahead of me and quickened my pace, only to recoil. For there, not thirty feet away and perhaps three hundred yards from the mouth of the cave, suddenly appeared what looked like a gigantic man. Tommy saw it also and barked as dogs do when they are frightened, and the sound of his yaps echoed endlessly from every quarter, which scared him to silence. Recovering myself I went forward, for now I guessed the truth. It was not a man but a statue.

The thing stood upon a huge base which lessened by successive steps, eight of them, I think, to its summit. The foot of this base may have been a square of fifty feet or rather more; the real support or pedestal of the statue, however, was only a square of about six feet. The figure itself was little above life-size, or at any rate above our life-size, say seven feet in height. It was very peculiar in sundry ways.

To begin with, nothing of the body was visible, for it was swathed like a corpse. From these wrappings projected one arm, the right, in the hand of which was the likeness of a lighted torch. The head was not veiled. It was that of a man, long-nosed, thin-lipped, stern-visaged; the countenance pervaded by an awful and unutterable calm, as deep as that of Buddha only less benign. On the brow was a wreathed head-dress, not unlike an Eastern turban, from which sprang two little wings resembling in some degree those on the famous Greek head of Hypnos, lord of Sleep. Between the folds of the wrappings on the back sprang two other wings, enormous wings bent like those of a bird about to take flight. Indeed the whole attitude of the figure suggested that it was springing from earth to air. It was executed in black basalt or some stone of the sort, and very highly finished. For instance, on the bare feet and the arm which held the torch could be felt every muscle and even some of the veins. In the same way the details of the skull were perfectly perceptible to the touch, although at first sight not visible on the marble surface. This was ascertained by climbing on the pedestal and feeling the face with our hands.

Here I may say that its modelling as well as that of the feet and the arm filled Bickley, who, of course, was a highly trained anatomist, with absolute amazement. He said that he would never have thought it possible that such accuracy could have been reached by an artist working in so hard a material.

When the others had arrived we studied this relic as closely as our two candles would allow, and in turn expressed our opinions of its significance. Bastin thought that if those things down there were really the remains of aeroplanes, which he did not believe, the statue had something to do with flying, as was shown by the fact that it had wings on its head and shoulders. Also, he added, after examining the face, the head was uncommonly like that of the idol that he had blown up. It had the same long nose and severe shut mouth. If he was right, this was probably another effigy of Oro which we should do well to destroy at once before the islanders came to worship it.

Bickley ground his teeth as he listened to him.

"Destroy that!" he gasped. "Destroy! Oh! you, you—early Christian."

Here I may state that Bastin was quite right, as we proved subsequently when we compared the head of the fetish, which, as it will be remembered, he had brought away with him, with that of the statue. Allowing for an enormous debasement of art, they were essentially identical in the facial characteristics. This would suggest the descent of a tradition through countless generations. Or of course it may have been accidental. I am sure I do not know, but I think it possible that for unknown centuries other old statues may have existed in Orofena from which the idol was copied. Or some daring and impious spirit may have found his way to the cave in past ages and fashioned the local god upon this ancient model.

Bickley was struck at once, as I had been, with the resemblance of the figure to that of the Egyptian Osiris. Of course there were differences. For instance, instead of the crook and the scourge, this divinity held a torch. Again, in place of the crown of Egypt it wore a winged head-dress, though it is true this was not very far removed from the winged disc of that country. The wings that sprang from its shoulders, however, suggested Babylonia rather than Egypt, or the Assyrian bulls that are similarly adorned. All of these symbolical ideas might have been taken from that figure. But what was it? What was it?

In a flash the answer came to me. A representation of the spirit of Death! Neither more nor less. There was the shroud; there the cold, inscrutable countenance suggesting mysteries that it hid. But the torch and the wings? Well, the torch was that which lighted souls to the other world, and on the wings they flew thither. Whoever fashioned that statue hoped for another life, or so I was convinced.

I explained my ideas. Bastin thought them fanciful and preferred his notion of a flying man, since by constitution he was unable to discover anything spiritual in any religion except his own. Bickley agreed that it was probably an allegorical representation of death but sniffed at my interpretation of the wings and the torch, since by constitution he could not believe that the folly of a belief in immortality could have developed so early in the world, that is, among a highly civilised people such as must have produced this statue.

What we could none of us understand was why this ominous image with its dead, cold face should have been placed in an aerodrome, nor in fact did we ever discover. Possibly it was there long before the cave was put to this use. At first the place may have been a temple and have so remained until circumstances forced the worshippers to change their habits, or even their Faith.

We examined this wondrous work and the pedestal on which it stood as closely as we were able by the dim light of our candles. I was anxious to go further and see what lay beyond it; indeed we did walk a few paces, twenty perhaps, onward into the recesses of the cave.

Then Bickley discovered something that looked like the mouth of a well down which he nearly tumbled, and Bastin began to complain that he was hot and very thirsty; also to point out that he wished for no more caves and idols at present.

"Look here, Arbuthnot," said Bickley, "these candles are burning low and we don't want to use up more if we can prevent it, for we may need what we have got very badly later on. Now, according to my pocket compass the mouth of this cave points due east; probably at the beginning it was orientated to the rising sun for purposes of astronomical observation or of worship at certain periods of the year. From the position of the sun when we landed on the rock this morning I imagine that just now it rises almost exactly opposite to the mouth of the cave. If this is so, to-morrow at dawn, for a time at least, the light should penetrate as far as the statue, and perhaps further. What I suggest is that we should wait till then to explore."

I agreed with him, especially as I was feeling tired, being exhausted by wonder, and wanted time to think. So we turned back. As we did so I missed Tommy.

and inquired anxiously where he was, being afraid lest he might have tumbled down the well-like hole.

"He's all right," said Bastin. "I saw him sniffing at the base of that statue. I expect there is a rat in there, or perhaps a snake."

Sure enough when we reached it there was Tommy with his black nose pressed against the lowest of the tiers that formed the base of the statue, and sniffing loudly. Also he was scratching in the dust as a dog does when he has winded a rabbit in a hole. So engrossed was he in this occupation that it was with difficulty that I coaxed him to leave the place.

I did not think much of the incident at that time, but afterwards it came back to me, and I determined to investigate those stones at the first opportunity.

Passing the wrecks of the machines, we emerged on to the causeway without accident. After we had rested and washed we set to work to draw our canoe with its precious burden of food right into the mouth of the cave, where we hid it as well as we could.

This done we went for a walk round the base of the peak. This proved to be a great deal larger than we had imagined, over two miles in circumference indeed. All about it was a belt of fertile land, as I suppose deposited there by the waters of the great lake and resulting from the decay of vegetation. Much of this belt was covered with ancient forest ending in mud flats that appeared to have been thrown up recently, perhaps at the time of the tidal wave which bore us to Orofena. On the higher part of the belt were many of the extraordinary crater-like holes that I have mentioned as being prevalent on the main island; indeed the place had all the appearance of having been subjected to a terrific and continuous bombardment.

When we had completed its circuit we set to work to climb the peak in order to explore the terraces of which I have spoken and the ruins which I had seen through my field-glasses. It was quite true; they were terraces cut with infinite labour out of the solid rock, and on them had once stood a city, now pounded into dust and fragments. We struggled over the broken blocks of stone to what we had taken for a temple, which stood near the lip of the crater, for without doubt this mound was an extinct volcano, or rather its crest. All we could make out when we arrived was that here had once stood some great building, for its courts could still be traced; also there lay about fragments of steps and pillars.

Apparently the latter had once been carved, but the passage of innumerable ages had obliterated the work and we could not turn these great blocks over to discover if any remained beneath. It was as though the god Thor had broken up the edifice with his hammer, or Jove had shattered it with his thunderbolts; nothing else would account for that utter wreck, except, as Bickley remarked significantly, the scientific use of high explosives.

Following the line of what seemed to have been a road, we came to the edge of the volcano and found, as we expected, the usual depression out of which fire and lava had once been cast, as from Hecla or Vesuvius. It was now a lake more than a quarter of a mile across. Indeed it had been thus in the ancient days when the buildings stood upon the terraces, for we saw the remains of steps leading down to the water. Perhaps it had served as the sacred lake of the temple.

We gazed with wonderment and then, wearied out, scrambled back through the ruins, which, by the way, were of a different stone from the lava of the mountain, to the mouth of the great cave.

CHAPTER X

THE DWELLERS IN THE TOMB

By now it was drawing towards sunset, so we made such preparations as we could for the night. One of these was to collect dry driftwood, of which an abundance lay upon the shore, to serve us for firing, though unfortunately we had nothing that we could cook for our meal.

While we were thus engaged we saw a canoe approaching the table-rock and perceived that in it were the chief Marama and a priest. After hovering about for a while they paddled the canoe near enough to allow of conversation which, taking no notice of their presence, we left it to them to begin.

"O, Friend-from-the-Sea," called Marama, addressing myself, "we come to pray you and the Great Healer to return to us to be our guests as before. The people are covered with darkness because of the loss of your wisdom, and the sick cry aloud for the Healer; indeed two of those whom he has cut with knives are dying."

"And what of the Bellower?" I asked, indicating Bastin.

"We should like to see him back also, Friend-from-the-Sea, that we may sacrifice and eat him, who destroyed our god with fire and caused the Healer to kill his priest."

"That is most unjust," exclaimed Bastin. "I deeply regret the blood that was shed on the occasion, unnecessarily as I think."

"Then go and atone for it with your own," said Bickley, "and everybody will be pleased."

Waving to them to be silent, I said:

"Are you mad, Marama, that you should ask us to return to sojourn among people who tried to kill us, merely because the Bellower caused fire to burn an image of wood and its head to fly from its shoulders, just to show you that it had no power to hold itself together, although you call it a god? Not so, we wash our hands of you; we leave you to go your own way while we go ours, till perchance in a day to come, after many misfortunes have overtaken you, you creep about our feet and with prayers and offerings beg us to return."

I paused to observe the effect of my words. It was excellent, for both Marama and the priest wrung their hands and groaned. Then I went on:

"Meanwhile we have something to tell you. We have entered the cave where you said no man might set a foot, and have seen him who sits within, the true god." (Here Bastin tried to interrupt, but was suppressed by Bickley.)

They looked at each other in a frightened way and groaned more loudly than before.

"He sends you a message, which, as he told us of your approach, we came to the shore to deliver to you."

"How can you say that?" began Bastin, but was again violently suppressed by Bickley.

"It is that he, the real Oro, rejoices that the false Oro, whose face is copied from his face, has been destroyed. It is that he commands you day by day to bring food in plenty and lay it upon the Rock of Offerings, not forgetting a supply of fresh fish from the sea, and with it all those things that are stored in the house wherein we, the strangers from the sea, deigned to dwell awhile until we left you because in your wickedness you wished to murder us."

"And if we refuse—what then?" asked the priest, speaking for the first time.

"Then Oro will send death and destruction upon you. Then your food shall fail and you shall perish of sickness and want, and the Oromatuas, the spirits of the great dead, shall haunt you in your sleep, and Oro shall eat up your souls."

At these horrible threats both of them uttered a kind of wail, after which Marama asked:

"And if we consent, what then, Friend-from-the-Sea?"

"Then, perchance," I answered, "in some day to come we may return to you, that I may give you of my wisdom and the Great Healer may cure your sick and the Bellower may lead you through his gate, and in his kindness make you to see with his eyes."

This last clause of my ultimatum did not seem to appeal to the priest, who argued a while with Marama, though what he said we could not hear. In the end he appeared to give way. At any rate Marama called out that all should be done as we wished, and that meanwhile they prayed us to intercede with Oro in the cave, and to keep back the ghosts from haunting them, and to protect them from misfortune. I replied that we would do our best, but could guarantee nothing since their offence was very great.

Then, to show that the conversation was at an end, we walked away with dignity, pushing Bastin in front of us, lest he should spoil the effect by some of his ill-timed and often over-true remarks.

"That's capital," said Bickley, when we were out of

hearing. "The enemy has capitulated. We can stop here as long as we like, provisioned from the mainland, and if for any reason we wish to leave, be sure of our line of retreat."

"I don't know what you call capital," exclaimed Bastin. "It seems to me that all the lies which Arbuthnot has just told are sufficient to bring a judgment upon us. Indeed, I think that I will go back with Marama and explain the truth."

"I never before knew anybody who was so anxious to be cooked and eaten," remarked Bickley. "Moreover, you are too late, for the canoe is a hundred yards away by now, and you shan't have ours. Remember the Pauline maxims, old fellow, which you are so fond of quoting, and be all things to all men, and another that is more modern, that when you are at Rome, you must do as the Romans do; also a third, that necessity has no law, and for the matter of that, a fourth, that all is fair in love and war."

"I am sure, Bickley, that Paul never meant his words to bear the debased sense which you attribute to them——" began Bastin, but at this point I hustled him off to light a fire—a process at which I pointed out he had shown himself an expert.

We slept that night under the overhanging rock just to one side of the cave, not in the mouth, because of the draught which drew in and out of the great place. In that soft and balmy clime this was no hardship, although we lacked blankets. And yet, tired though I was, I could not rest as I should have done. Bastin snored away contentedly, quite unaffected by his escape which to him was merely an incident in the day's work; and so, too, slumbered Bickley, except that he did not snore. But the amazement and the mystery of all that we had discovered and of all that might be left for us to discover, held me back from sleep.

What did it mean? What could it mean? My nerves were taut as harp strings and seemed to vibrate to the touch of invisible fingers, although I could not interpret the music that they made. Once or twice also I thought I heard actual music with my physical ears, and that of a strange quality. Soft and low and dreamful, it appeared to well from the recesses of the vast cave, a wailing song in an unknown tongue from the lips of women, or of a woman, multiplied mysteriously by echoes. This, however, must have been pure fancy, since there was no singer there.

Presently I dozed off, to be awakened by the sudden sound of a great fish leaping in the lake. I sat up and stared, fearing lest it might be the splash of a paddle, for I could not put from my mind the possibility of attack. All I saw, however, was the low line of the distant shore, and above it the bright and setting stars that heralded the coming of the sun. Then I woke the others, and we washed and ate, since once the sun rose time would be precious.

At length it appeared, splendid in a cloudless sky, and, as I had hoped, directly opposite to the mouth of the cave. Taking our candles and some stout pieces of driftwood which, with our knives, we had shaped on the previous evening to serve us as levers and rough shovels, we entered the cave. Bickley and I were filled with excitement and hope of what we knew not, but Bastin showed little enthusiasm for our quest. His heart was with his half-converted savages beyond the lake, and of them, quite rightly I have no doubt, he thought more than he did of all the archæological treasures in the whole earth. Still, he came, bearing the blackened head of Oro with him which, with unconscious humour, he had used as a pillow through the night because, as he said, "it was after all softer than stone." Also, I believe that in his heart he hoped that he might find an opportunity of destroying the bigger and earlier edition of Oro in the cave, before it was discovered by the natives who might wish to make it an object of worship. Tommy came also, with greater alacrity than I expected, since dogs do not as a rule like dark places. When we reached the statue I learned the reason; he remembered the smell he had detected at its base on the previous day, which Bastin supposed to proceed from a rat, and was anxious to continue his investigations.

We went straight to the statue, although Bickley passed the half-buried machines with evident regret. As we had hoped, the strong light of the rising sun fell upon it in a vivid ray, revealing all its wondrous workmanship and the majesty—for no other word describes it—of the somewhat terrifying countenance that appeared above the wrappings of the shroud. Indeed, I was convinced that originally this monument had been placed here in order that on certain days of the year the sun might fall upon it thus, when probably worshippers assembled to adore their hallowed symbol. After all, this was common in ancient days: witness the instance of the awful Three who sit in the deepest recesses of the temple of Abu Simbel, on the Nile.

We gazed and gazed our fill, at least Bickley and I did, for Bastin was occupied in making a careful comparison between the head of his wooden Oro and that of the statue.

"There is no doubt that they are very much alike," he said. "Why, whatever is that dog doing? I think it is going mad," and he pointed to Tommy who was digging furiously at the base of the lowest step, as at home I have seen him do at roots that sheltered a rabbit.

Tommy's energy was so remarkable that at length it seriously attracted our attention. Evidently he meant that it should do so, for occasionally he sprang back to me barking, then returned and sniffed and scratched. Bickley knelt down and smelt at the stone.

"It is an odd thing, Humphrey," he said, "but there is a strange odour here, a very pleasant odour like that of sandal-wood or attar of roses."

"I never heard of a rat that smelt like sandal-wood or attar of roses," said Bastin. "Look out that it isn't a snake."

I knelt down beside Bickley, and in clearing away the deep dust from what seemed to be the bottom of the step, which was perhaps four feet in height, by accident thrust my amateur spade somewhat strongly against its base where it rested upon the rocky floor.

Next moment a wonder came to pass. The whole massive rock began to turn outwards as though upon a pivot! I saw it coming and grabbed Bickley by the collar, dragging him back so that we just rolled clear before the great block, which must have weighed several tons, fell down and crushed us. Tommy saw it too, and fled, though a little late, for the edge of the block caught the tip of his tail and caused him to emit a most piercing howl. But we did not think of Tommy and his woes; we did not think of our own escape or of anything else because of the marvel that appeared to us. Seated there upon the ground, after our backward tumble, we could see into the space which lay behind the fallen step, for there the light of the sun penetrated.

The first idea it gave me was that of the jewelled shrine of some mediæval saint which, by good fortune, had escaped the plunderers; there are still such existing in the world. It shone and glittered, apparently with gold and diamonds, although, as a matter of fact, there were no diamonds, nor was it gold which gleamed, but some ancient metal, or rather amalgam, which is now lost to the world, the same that was used in the tubes of the air-machines. I think that it contained gold, but I do not know. At any rate, it was equally lasting and even more beautiful, though lighter in colour.

For the rest this adorned recess which resembled that of a large funeral vault, occupying the whole space beneath the base of the statue that was supported on its arch, was empty save for two flashing objects that lay side by side but with nearly the whole width of the vault between them.

I pointed at them to Bickley with my finger, for really I could not speak.

"Coffins, by Jove!" he whispered. "Glass or crystal coffins and people in them. Come on!"

A few seconds later we were crawling into that vault while Bastin, still nursing the head of Oro as though it were a baby, stood confused outside muttering something about desecrating hallowed graves.

Just as we reached the interior, owing to the heightening of the sun, the light passed away, leaving us in a kind of twilight. Bickley produced carriage candles from his pocket and fumbled for matches. While he was doing so I noticed two things—firstly, that the place really did smell like a scent-shop, and, secondly, that the coffins seemed to glow with a kind of phosphorescent light of their own, not very strong, but sufficient to reveal their outlines in the gloom. Then the candles burnt up and we saw.

Within the coffin that stood on our left hand as we entered, for this crystal was as transparent as plate glass, lay a most wonderful old man, clad in a gleaming, embroidered robe. His long hair, which was parted in the middle, as we could see beneath the edge of the pearl-sewn and broidered cap he wore, also his beard were snowy white. The man was tall, at least six feet four inches in height, and rather spare. His hands were long and thin, very delicately made, as were his sandalled feet.

But it was his face that fixed our gaze, for it was marvellous, like the face of a god, and, as we noticed at once, with some resemblance to that of the statue above. Thus the brow was broad and massive, the nose straight and long, the mouth stern and clear-cut, while the cheekbones were rather high, and the eyebrows arched. Such are the characteristics of many handsome old men of good blood, and as the mummies of Seti and others show us, such they have been for thousands of years. Only this man differed from all others because of the fearful dignity stamped upon his features. Looking at him I began to think at once of the prophet Elijah as he must have appeared rising to heaven, enhanced by the more earthly glory of Solomon, for although the appearance of these patriarchs is unknown, of them one conceives ideas. Only it seemed probable that Elijah may have looked more benign. Here there was no benignity, only terrible force and infinite wisdom.

Contemplating him I shivered a little and felt thankful that he was dead. For to tell the truth I was afraid of that awesome countenance which, I should add, was of the whiteness of paper, although the cheeks still showed tinges of colour, so perfect was the preservation of the corpse.

I was still gazing at it when Bickley said in a voice of amazement:

"I say, look here, in the other coffin."

I turned, looked, and nearly collapsed on the floor of the vault, since beauty can sometimes strike us like a blow. Oh! there before me lay all loveliness, such loveliness that there burst from my lips an involuntary cry:

"Alas! that she should be dead!"

A young woman, I supposed, at least she looked young, perhaps five or six and twenty years of age, or so I judged. There she lay, her tall and delicate shape half hidden in masses of rich-hued hair in colour of a ruddy blackness. I know not how else to describe it, since never have I seen any of the same tint. Moreover, it shone with a life of its own as though it had been dusted with gold. From between the masses of this hair appeared a face which I can only call divine. There was every beauty that woman can boast, from the curving eyelashes of extraordinary length to the sweet and human mouth. To these charms also were added a wondrous smile and an air of kind dignity, very different from the fierce pride stamped upon the countenance of the old man who was her companion in death.

She was clothed in some close-fitting robe of white broidered with gold; pearls were about her neck, lying far down upon the perfect bosom, a girdle of gold and shining gems encircled her slender waist, and on her little feet were sandals fastened with red stones like rubies. In truth, she was a splendid creature, and yet,

I know not how, her beauty suggested more of the spirit than of the flesh. Indeed, in a way, it was unearthly. My senses were smitten, it pulled at my heart-strings, and yet its unutterable strangeness seemed to awake memories within me, though of what I could not tell. A wild fancy came to me that I must have known this heavenly creature in some past life.

By now Bastin had joined us, and, attracted by my exclamation and by the attitude of Bickley, who was staring down at the coffin with a fixed look upon his face, not unlike that of a pointer when he scents game, he began to contemplate the wonder within it in his slow way.

"Well, I never!" he said. "Do you think the Glittering Lady in there is human?"

"The Glittering Lady is dead, but I suppose that she was human in her life," I answered in an awed whisper.

"Of course she is dead, otherwise she would not be in that glass coffin. I think I should like to read the Burial Service over her, which I daresay was never done when she was put in there."

"How do you know that she is dead?" asked Bickley in a sharp voice and speaking for the first time. "I have seen hundreds of corpses, and mummies too, but never any that looked like these."

I stared at him. It was strange to hear Bickley, the scoffer at miracles, suggesting that this greatest of all miracles might be possible.

"They must have been here a long time," I said, "for although human, they are not, I think, of any people known to the world to-day; their dress, everything, shows it, though perhaps thousands of years ago——" and I stopped.

"Quite so," answered Bickley; "I agree. That is

why I suggest that they may have belonged to a race who knew what we do not, namely, how to suspend animation for great periods of time."

I said no more, nor did Bastin, who was now engaged in studying the old man, and for once, wonderstruck and overcome. Bickley, however, took one of the candles and began to make a close examination of the coffins. So did Tommy, who sniffed along the join of that of the Glittering Lady until his nose reached a certain spot, where it remained, while his black tail began to wag in a delighted fashion. Bickley pushed him away and investigated.

"As I thought," he said—"air-holes. See!"

I looked, and there, bored through the crystal of the coffin in a line with the face of its occupant, were a number of little holes that either by accident or design outlined the shape of a human mouth.

"They are not airtight," murmured Bickley; "and if air can enter, how can dead flesh remain like that for ages?"

Then he continued his search upon the other side.

"The lid of this coffin works on hinges," he said. "Here they are, fashioned of the crystal itself. A living person within could have pulled it down before the senses departed."

"No," I answered; "for look, here is a crystal bolt at the end and it is shot from without."

This puzzled him; then as though struck by an idea, he began to examine the other coffin.

"I've got it!" he exclaimed presently. "The old god in here" (somehow we all thought of this old man as not quite normal) "shut down the Glittering Lady's coffin and bolted it. His own is not bolted, although the bolt exists in the same place. He just got in and pulled down the lid. Oh! what nonsense I am talking —for how can such things be? Let us get out and think."

So we crept from the sepulchre in which the perfumed air had begun to oppress us and sat ourselves down upon the floor of the cave, where for a while we remained silent.

"I am very thirsty," said Bastin presently. "Those smells seem to have dried me up. I am going to get some tea—I mean water, as unfortunately there is no tea," and he set off towards the mouth of the cave.

We followed him, I don't quite know why, except that we wished to breathe freely outside, also we knew that the sepulchre and its contents would be as safe as they had been for—well, how long?

It proved to be a beautiful morning outside. We walked up and down enjoying it sub-consciously, for really our—that is Bickley's and my own—intelligences were concentrated on that sepulchre and its contents. Where Bastin's may have been I do not know, perhaps in a visionary teapot, since I was sure that it would take him a day or two to appreciate the significance of our discoveries. At any rate, he wandered off, making no remarks about them, to drink water, I suppose.

Presently he began to shout to us from the end of the table-rock and we went to see the reason of his noise. It proved to be very satisfactory, for while we were in the cave the Orofenans had brought absolutely everything belonging to us, together with a large supply of food from the main island. Not a single article was missing; even our books, a can with the bottom out, and the broken pieces of a little pocket mirror had been religiously transported, and with these a few articles that had been stolen from us, notably my pocket-knife.

Evidently a great taboo had been laid upon all our possessions. They were now carefully arranged in one of the grooves of the rock that Bickley supposed had been made by the wheels of aeroplanes, which was why we had not seen them at once.

Each of us rushed for what we desired most—Bastin for one of the canisters of tea, I for my diaries, and Bickley for his chest of instruments and medicines. These were removed to the mouth of the cave, and after them the other things and the food; also a bell tent and some camp furniture that we had brought from the ship. Then Bastin made some tea of which he drank four large pannikins, having first said grace over it with unwonted fervour. Nor did we disdain our share of the beverage, although Bickley preferred cocoa and I coffee. Cocoa and coffee we had no time to make then, and in view of that sepulchre in the cave, what had we to do with cocoa and coffee?

So Bickley and I said to each other, and yet presently he changed his mind and in a special metal machine carefully made some extremely strong black coffee which he poured into a thermos flask, previously warmed with hot water, adding thereto about a claret glass of brandy. Also he extracted certain drugs from his medicine-chest, and with them, as I noted, a hypodermic syringe, which he first boiled in a kettle and then shut up in a little tube with a glass stopper.

These preparations finished, he called to Tommy to give him the scraps of our meal. But there was no Tommy. The dog was missing, and though we hunted everywhere we could not find him. Finally we concluded that he had wandered off down the beach on business of his own and would return in due course. We could not bother about Tommy just then.

After making some further preparations and fidgeting about a little, Bickley announced that as we had now some proper paraffin lamps of the powerful sort which are known as "hurricane," he proposed by their aid to carry out further examinations in the cave.

"I think I shall stop where I am," said Bastin, helping himself from the kettle to a fifth pannikin of tea. "Those corpses are very interesting, but I don't see any use in staring at them again at present. One can always do that at any time. I have missed Marama once already by being away in that cave, and I have a lot to say to him about my people; I don't want to be absent in case he should return."

"To wash up the things, I suppose," said Bickley with a sniff; "or perhaps to eat the tea-leaves."

"Well, as a matter of fact, I have noticed that these natives have a peculiar taste for tea-leaves. I think they believe them to be a medicine, but I don't suppose they would come so far for them, though perhaps they might in the hope of getting the head of Oro. Anyhow, I am going to stop here."

"Pray do," said Bickley. "Are you ready, Humphrey?"

I nodded, and he handed to me a felt-covered flask of the non-conducting kind, filled with boiling water, a tin of preserved milk, and a little bottle of meat extract of a most concentrated sort. Then, having lit two of the hurricane lamps and seen that they were full of oil, we started back up the cave.

CHAPTER XI

RESURRECTION

We reached the sepulchre without stopping to look at the parked machines or even the marvellous statue that stood above it, for what did we care about machines or statues now? As we approached we were astonished to hear low and carvernous growlings.

"There is some wild beast in there," said Bickley, halting. "No, by George! it's Tommy. What can the dog be after?"

We peeped in, and there sure enough was Tommy lying on the top of the Glittering Lady's coffin and growling his very best with the hair standing up upon his back. When he saw who it was, however, he jumped off and frisked round, licking my hand.

"That's very strange," I exclaimed.

"Not stranger than everything else," said Bickley.

"What are you going to do?" I asked.

"Open these coffins," he answered, "beginning with that of the old god, since I would rather experiment on him. I expect he will crumble into dust. But if by chance he doesn't I'll jam a little strychnine, mixed with some other drugs, of which you don't know the names, into one of his veins and see if anything happens. If it doesn't, it won't hurt him, and if it does—well, who knows? Now give me a hand."

We went to the left-hand coffin and by inserting the hook on the back of my knife, of which the real use is to pick stones out of horses' hoofs, into one of the little air-holes I have described, managed to raise the heavy crystal lid sufficiently to enable us to force a piece of wood between it and the top. The rest was easy, for the hinges being of crystal had not corroded. In two minutes it was open.

From the chest came an overpowering spicy odour, and with it a veritable breath of warm air before which we recoiled a little. Bickley took a pocket thermometer which he had at hand and glanced at it. It marked a temperature of 82 degrees in the sepulchre. Having noted this, he thrust it into the coffin between the crystal wall and its occupant. Then we went out and waited a little while to give the odours time to dissipate, for they made the head reel.

After five minutes or so we returned and examined the thermometer. It had risen to 98 degrees, the natural temperature of the human body.

"What do you make of that if the man is dead?" he whispered.

I shook my head, and as we had agreed, set to helping him to lift the body from the coffin. It was a good weight, quite eleven stone I should say; moreover, *it was not stiff*, for the hip joints bent. We got it out and laid it on a blanket we had spread on the floor of the sepulchre. Whilst I was thus engaged I saw something that nearly caused me to loose my hold from astonishment. Beneath the head, the centre of the back and the feet were crystal boxes about eight inches square, or rather crystal blocks, for in them I could see no opening, and these boxes emitted a faint phosphorescent light. I touched one of them and found that it was quite warm.

"Great heavens!" I exclaimed, "here's magic."

"There's no such thing," answered Bickley in his

usual formula. Then an explanation seemed to strike him and he added, "Not magic but radium or something of the sort. That's how the temperature was kept up. In sufficient quantity it is practically indestructible, you see. My word! this old gentleman knew a thing or two."

Again we waited a little while to see if the body began to crumble on exposure to the air, I taking the opportunity to make a rough sketch of it in my pocket-book in anticipation of that event. But it did not; it remained quite sound.

"Here goes," said Bickley. "If he should be alive, he will catch cold in his lungs after lying for ages in that baby incubator, as I suppose he has done. So it is now or never."

Then bidding me hold the man's right arm, he took the sterilized syringe which he had prepared, and thrusting the needle into a vein he selected just above the wrist, injected the contents.

"It would have been better over the heart," he whispered, "but I thought I would try the arm first. I don't like risking chills by uncovering him."

I made no answer and again we waited and watched.

"Great heavens, he's stirring!" I gasped presently.

Stirring he was, for his fingers began to move.

Bickley bent down and placed his ear to the heart—I forgot to say that he had tested this before with a stethoscope, but had been unable to detect any movement.

"I believe it is beginning to beat," he said in an awed voice.

Then he applied the stethoscope, and added, "It is, it is!"

Next he took a filament of cotton wool and laid it on the man's lips. Presently it moved; he was breathing, though very faintly. Bickley took more cotton wool and having poured something from his medicine-chest on to it, placed it over the mouth beneath the man's nostrils —I believe it was sal volatile.

Nothing further happened for a little while, and to relieve the strain on my mind I stared absently into the empty coffin. Here I saw what had escaped our notice, two small plates of white metal and cut upon them what I took to be star maps. Beyond these and the glowing boxes which I have mentioned, there was nothing else in the coffin. I had no time to examine them, for at that moment the old man opened his mouth and began to breathe, evidently with some discomfort and effort, as his empty lungs filled themselves with air. Then his eyelids lifted, revealing a wonderful pair of dark glowing eyes beneath. Next he tried to sit up but would have fallen, had not Bickley supported him with his arm.

I do not think he saw Bickley, indeed he shut his eyes again as though the light hurt them, and went into a kind of faint. Then it was that Tommy, who all this while had been watching the proceedings with grave interest, came forward, wagging his tail, and licked the man's face. At the touch of the dog's red tongue, he opened his eyes for the second time. Now he saw—not us but Tommy, for after contemplating him for a few seconds, something like a smile appeared upon his fierce but noble face. More, he lifted his hand and laid it on the dog's head, as though to pat it kindly. Half a minute or so later his awakening senses appreciated our presence. The incipient smile vanished and was replaced by a somewhat terrible frown.

Meanwhile Bickley had poured out some of the hot

coffee laced with brandy into the cup that was screwed on the top of the thermos flask. Advancing to the man whom I supported, he put it to his lips. He tasted and made a wry face, but presently he began to sip, and ultimately swallowed it all. The effect of the stimulant was wonderful, for in a few minutes he came to life completely and was even able to sit up without support.

For quite a long while he gazed at us gravely, taking us in and everything connected with us. For instance, Bickley's medicine-case which lay open showing the little vulcanite tubes, a few instruments and other outfit, engaged his particular attention, and I saw at once that he understood what it was. Thus his arm still smarted where the needle had been driven in and on the blanket lay the syringe. He looked at his arm, then looked at the syringe, and nodded. The paraffin hurricane lamps also seemed to interest and win his approval. We two men, as I thought, attracted him least of all; he just summed us up and our garments, more especially the garments, with a few shrewd glances, and then seemed to turn his thoughts to Tommy, who had seated himself quite contentedly at his side, evidently accepting him as a new addition to our party.

I confess that this behaviour on Tommy's part reassured me not a little. I am a great believer in the instincts of animals, especially of dogs, and I felt certain that if this man had not been in all essentials human like ourselves, Tommy would not have tolerated him. In the same way the sleeper's clear liking for Tommy, at whom he looked much oftener and with greater kindness than he did at us, suggested that there was goodness in him somewhere, since although a dog in its wonderful tolerance may love a bad person in whom it smells out hidden virtue, no really bad person ever loved a dog, or, I may add, a child or a flower.

As a matter of fact, the "old god," as we had christened him while he was in his coffin, during all our association with him, cared infinitely more for Tommy than he did for any of us, a circumstance that ultimately was not without its influence upon our fortunes. But for this there was a reason as we learned afterwards, also he was not really so amiable as I hoped.

When we had looked at each other for a long while the sleeper began to arrange his beard, of which the length seemed to surprise him, especially as Tommy was seated on one end of it. Finding this out and apparently not wishing to disturb Tommy, he gave up the occupation, and after one or two attempts, for his tongue and lips still seemed to be stiff, addressed us in some sonorous and musical language, unlike any that we had ever heard. We shook our heads. Then by an afterthought I said "Good day" to him in the language of the Orofenans. He puzzled over the word as though it were more or less familiar to him, and when I repeated it, gave it back to me with a difference indeed, but in a way which convinced us that he quite understood what I meant. The conversation went no further at the moment because just then some memory seemed to strike him.

He was sitting with his back against the coffin of the Glittering Lady, whom therefore he had not seen. Now he began to turn round, and being too weak to do so, motioned me to help him. I obeyed, while Bickley, guessing his purpose, held up one of the hurricane lamps that he might see better. With a kind of fierce eagerness he surveyed her who lay within the coffin, and after he had done so, uttered a sigh as of intense relief.

Next he pointed to the metal cup out of which he had drunk. Bickley filled it again from the thermos flask, which I observed excited his keen interest, for, having touched the flask with his hand and found that it was cool, he appeared to marvel that the fluid coming from it should be hot and steaming. Presently he smiled as though he had got the clue to the mystery, and swallowed his second drink of coffee and spirit. This done, he motioned to us to lift the lid of the lady's coffin, pointing out a certain catch in the bolts which at first we could not master, for it will be remembered that on this coffin these were shot.

In the end, by pursuing the same methods that we had used in the instance of his own, we raised the coffin lid and once more were driven to retreat from the sepulchre for a while by the overpowering odour like to that of a whole greenhouse full of tuberoses, that flowed out of it, inducing a kind of stupefaction from which even Tommy fled.

When we returned it was to find the man kneeling by the side of the coffin, for as yet he could not stand, with his glowing eyes fixed upon the face of her who slept therein and waving his long arms above her.

"Hypnotic business! Wonder if it will work," whispered Bickley. Then he lifted the syringe and looked inquiringly at the man, who shook his head, and went on with his mesmeric passes.

I crept round him and took my stand by the sleeper's head, that I might watch her face, which was well worth watching, while Bickley, with his medicine at hand, remained near her feet, I think engaged in disinfecting the syringe in some spirit or acid. I believe he was about to make an attempt to use it when suddenly, as though beneath the influence of the hypnotic passes, a change appeared on the Glittering Lady's face. Hitherto, beautiful as it was, it had been a dead face though one of a person who had suddenly been cut off while in full health and vigour a few hours, or at the most a day or so before. Now it began to live again; it was as though the spirit were returning from afar, and not without toil and tribulation.

Expression after expression flitted across the features; indeed these seemed to change so much from moment to moment that they might have belonged to several different individuals, though each was beautiful. The fact of these remarkable changes with the suggestion of multiform personalities which they conveyed impressed both Bickley and myself very much indeed. Then the breast heaved tumultuously; it even appeared to struggle. Next the eyes opened. They were full of wonder, even of fear, but oh! what marvellous eyes. I do not know how to describe them, I cannot even state their exact colour, except that it was dark, something like the blue of sapphires of the deepest tint, and yet not black; large, too, and soft as a deer's. They shut again as though the light hurt them, then once more opened and wandered about, apparently without seeing.

At length they found my face, for I was still bending over her, and, resting there, appeared to take it in by degrees. More, it seemed to touch and stir some human spring in the still-sleeping heart. At least the fear passed from her features and was replaced by a faint smile, such as a patient sometimes gives to one known and well loved, as the effects of chloroform pass away. For a while she looked at me with an earnest, searching gaze, then suddenly, for the first time moving her arms, lifted them and threw them round my neck.

The old man stared, bending his imperial brows into

a little frown, but did nothing. Bickley stared also through his glasses and sniffed as though in disapproval, while I remained quite still, fighting with a wild impulse to kiss her on the lips as one would an awakening and beloved child. I doubt if I could have done so, however, for really I was immovable; my heart seemed to stop and all my muscles to be paralysed.

I do not know for how long this endured, but I do know how it ended. Presently in the intense silence I heard Bastin's heavy voice and looking round, saw his big head projecting into the sepulchre.

"Well, I never!" he said, "you seem to have woke them up with a vengeance. If you begin like *that* with the lady, there will be complications before you have done, Arbuthnot."

Talk of being brought back to earth with a rush! I could have killed Bastin, and Bickley, turning on him like a tiger, told him to be off, find wood and light a large fire in front of the statue. I think he was about to argue when the Ancient gave him a glance of his fierce eyes, which alarmed him, and he departed, bewildered, to return presently with the wood.

But the sound of his voice had broken the spell. The Lady let her arms fall with a start, and shut her eyes again, seeming to faint. Bickley sprang forward with his sal volatile and applied it to her nostrils, the Ancient not interfering, for he seemed to recognise that he had to deal with a man of skill and one who meant well by them.

In the end we brought her round again and, to omit details, Bickley gave her, not coffee and brandy, but a mixture he compounded of hot water, preserved milk and meat essence. The effect of it on her was wonderful, since a few minutes after swallowing it she sat up in the coffin. Then we lifted her from that narrow bed in which she had slept for—ah! how long? and perceived that beneath her also were crystal boxes of the radiant, heat-giving substance. We sat her on the floor of the sepulchre, wrapping her also in a blanket.

Now it was that Tommy, after frisking round her as though in welcome of an old friend, calmly established himself beside her and laid his black head upon her knee. She noted it and smiled for the first time, a marvellously sweet and gentle smile. More, she placed her slender hand upon the dog and stroked him feebly.

Bickley tried to make her drink some more of his mixture, but she refused, motioning him to give it to Tommy. This, however, he would not do because there was but one cup. Presently both of the sleepers began to shiver, which caused Bickley anxiety. Abusing Bastin beneath his breath for being so long with the fire, he drew the blankets closer about them.

Then an idea came to him and he examined the glowing boxes in the coffin. They were loose, being merely set in prepared cavities in the crystal. Wrapping our handkerchiefs about his hand, he took them out and placed them around the wakened patients, a proceeding of which the Ancient nodded approval. Just then, too, Bastin returned with his first load of firewood, and soon we had a merry blaze going just outside the sepulchre. I saw that they observed the lighting of this fire by means of a match with much interest.

Now they grew warm again, as indeed we did also—too warm. Then in my turn I had an idea. I knew that by now the sun would be beating hotly against the rock of the mount, and suggested to Bickley, that, if possible, the best thing we could do would be to get them into its life-giving rays. He agreed, if we could make them understand and they were able to walk. So I tried. First I directed the Ancient's attention to the mouth of the cave which at this distance showed as a white circle of light. He looked at it and then at me with grave inquiry. I made motions to suggest that he should proceed there, repeating the word "Sun" in the Orofenan tongue. He understood at once, though whether he read my mind rather than what I said I am not sure. Apparently the Glittering Lady understood also and seemed to be most anxious to go. Only she looked rather pitifully at her feet and shook her head. This decided me.

I do not know if I have mentioned anywhere that I am a tall man and very muscular. She was tall, also, but as I judged not so very heavy after her long fast. At any rate I felt quite certain that I could carry her for that distance. Stooping down, I lifted her up, signing to her to put her arms round my neck, which she did. Then calling to Bickley and Bastin to bring along the Ancient between them, with some difficulty I struggled out of the sepulchre, and started down the cave. She was more heavy than I thought, and yet I could have wished the journey longer. To begin with she seemed quite trustful and happy in my arms, where she lay with her head against my shoulder, smiling a little as a child might do, especially when I had to stop and throw her long hair round my neck like a muffler, to prevent it from trailing in the dust.

A bundle of lavender, or a truss of new-mown hay, could not have been more sweet to carry and there was something electric about the touch of her, which went through and through me. Very soon it was over, and we were out of the cave into the full glory of the tropical sun. At first, that her eyes might become accustomed to its light and her awakened body to its heat, I set her down where shadow fell from the overhanging rock, in a canvas deck chair that had been brought by Marama with the other things, throwing the rug about her to protect her from such wind as there was. She nestled gratefully into the soft seat and shut her eyes, for the motion had tired her. I noted, however, that she drew in the sweet air with long breaths.

Then I turned to observe the arrival of the Ancient, who was being borne between Bickley and Bastin in what children know as a dandy-chair, which is formed by two people crossing their hands in a peculiar fashion. It says much for the tremendous dignity of his presence that even thus, with one arm round the neck of Bickley and the other round that of Bastin, and his long white beard falling almost to the ground, he still looked most imposing.

Unfortunately, however, just as they were emerging from the cave, Bastin, always the most awkward of creatures, managed to leave hold with one hand, so that his passenger nearly came to the ground. Never shall I forget the look that he gave him. Indeed, I think that from this moment he hated Bastin. Bickley he respected as a man of intelligence and learning, although in comparison with his own, the latter was infantile and crude; me he tolerated and even liked; but Bastin he detested. The only one of our party for whom he felt anything approaching real affection was the spaniel Tommy.

We set him down, fortunately uninjured, on some rugs, and also in the shadow. Then, after a little while, we moved both of them into the sun. It was quite curious to see them expand there. As Bickley said, what happened to them might well be compared to the development of a butterfly which has just broken from the living grave of its chrysalis and crept into the full, hot radiance of the light. Its crinkled wings unfold, their brilliant tints develop; in an hour or two it is perfect, glorious, prepared for life and flight, a new creature.

So it was with this pair, from moment to moment they gathered strength and vigour. Near-by to them, as is happened, stood a large basket of the luscious native fruits brought that morning by the Orofenans, and at these the Lady looked with longing. With Bickley's permission, I offered them to her and to the Ancient, first peeling them with my fingers. They ate of them greedily, a full meal, and would have gone on had not the stern Bickley, fearing untoward consequences, removed the basket. Again the results were wonderful, for half an hour afterwards they seemed to be quite strong. With my assistance the Glittering Lady, as I still call her, for at that time I did not know her name, rose from the chair, and, leaning on me, tottered a few steps forward. Then she stood looking at the sky and all the lovely panorama of nature beneath, and stretching out her arms as though in worship. Oh! how beautiful she seemed with the sunlight shining on her heavenly face!

Now for the first time I heard her voice. It was soft and deep, yet in it was a curious bell-like tone that seemed to vibrate like the sound of chimes heard from far away. Never have I listened to such another voice. She pointed to the sun whereof the light turned her radiant hair and garments to a kind of golden glory, and called it by some name that I could not understand. I shook my head, whereon she gave it a different name taken, I suppose, from another language. Again I shook my head and she tried a third time. To my delight this word was practically the same that the Orofenans used for "sun."

"Yes," I said, speaking very slowly, "so it is called by the people of this land."

She understood, for she answered in much the same language:

"What, then, do you call it?"

"Sun in the English tongue," I replied.

"Sun. English," she repeated after me, then added, "How are you named, Wanderer?"

"Humphrey," I answered.

"Hum—fe—ry!" she said as though she were learning the word, "and those?"

"Bastin and Bickley," I replied.

Over these patronymics she shook her head; as yet they were too much for her.

"How are you named, Sleeper?" I asked.

"Yva," she answered.

"A beautiful name for one who is beautiful," I declared with enthusiasm, of course always in the rich Orofenan dialect which by now I could talk well enough.

She repeated the words once or twice, then of a sudden caught their meaning, for she smiled and even coloured, saying hastily with a wave of her hand towards the Ancient who stood at a distance between Bastin and Bickley, "My father, Oro; great man; great king; great god!"

At this information I started, for it was startling to learn that here was the original Oro, who was still worshipped by the Orofenans, although of his actual existence they had known nothing for uncounted time. Also I was glad to learn that he was her father and not her old husband, for to me that would have been horrible, a desecration too deep for words.

"How long did you sleep, Yva?" I asked, pointing towards the sepulchre in the cave.

After a little thought she understood and shook her head hopelessly, then by an afterthought, she said,

"Stars tell Oro to-night."

So Oro was an astronomer as well as a king and a god. I had guessed as much from those plates in the coffin which seemed to have stars engraved on them.

At this point our conversation came to an end, for the Ancient himself approached, leaning on the arm of Bickley who was engaged in an animated argument with Bastin.

"For Heaven's sake!" said Bickley, "keep your theology to yourself at present. If you upset the old fellow and put him in a temper he may die."

"If a man tells me that he is a god it is my duty to tell him that he is a liar," replied Bastin obstinately.

"Which you did, Bastin, only fortunately he did not understand you. But for your own sake I advise you not to take liberties. He is not one, I think, with whom it is wise to trifle. I think he seems thirsty. Go and get some water from the rain pool, not from the lake."

Bastin departed and presently returned with an aluminium jug full of pure water and a glass. Bickley poured some of it into a glass and handed it to Yva who bent her head in thanks. Then she did a curious thing. Having first lifted the glass with both hands to the sky and held it so for a few seconds, she turned and with an obeisance poured a little of it on the ground before her father's feet.

A libation, thought I to myself, and evidently Bastin agreed with me, for I heard him mutter,

"I believe she is making a heathen offering."

Doubtless we were right, for Oro accepted the homage by a little motion of the head. After this, at a sign from him she drank the water. Then the glass was refilled and handed to Oro who also held it towards the sky. He, however, made no libation but drank at once, two tumblers of it in rapid succession.

By now the direct sunlight was passing from the mouth of the cave, and though it was hot enough, both of them shivered a little. They spoke together in some language of which we could not understand a word, as though they were debating what their course of action should be. The dispute was long and earnest. Had we known what was passing, which I learned afterwards, it would have made us sufficiently anxious, for the point at issue was nothing less than whether we should or should not be forthwith destroyed—an end, it appears, that Oro was quite capable of bringing about if he so pleased. Yva, however, had very clear views of her own on the matter and, as I gather, even dared to threaten that she would protect us by the use of certain powers at her command, though what these were I do not know.

While the event hung doubtful Tommy, who was growing bored with these long proceedings, picked up a bough still covered with flowers which, after their pretty fashion, the Orofenans had placed on the top of one of the baskets of food. This small bough he brought and laid at the feet of Oro, no doubt in the hope that he would throw it for him to fetch, a game in which the dog delighted. For some reason Oro saw an omen in this simple canine performance, or he may have thought that the dog was making an offering to him, for he put his thin hand to his brow and thought a while, then motioned to Bastin to pick up the bough and give it to him.

Next he spoke to his daughter as though assenting to something, for I saw her sigh in relief. No wonder, for he was conveying his decision to spare our lives and admit us to their fellowship.

After this again they talked, but in quite a different tone and manner. Then the Glittering Lady said to me in her slow and archaic Orofenan:

"We go to rest. You must not follow. We come back perhaps to-night, perhaps next night. We are quite safe. You are quite safe under the beard of Oro. Spirit of Oro watch you. You understand?"

I said I understood, whereon she answered:

"Good-bye, O Humfe-ry."

"Good-bye, O Yva," I replied, bowing.

Thereon they turned and refusing all assistance from us, vanished into the darkness of the cave leaning upon each other and walking slowly.

CHAPTER XII

TWO HUNDRED AND FIFTY THOUSAND YEARS!

"You seem to have made the best of your time, old fellow," said Bickley in rather a sour voice.

"I never knew people begin to call each other by their Christian names so soon," added Bastin, looking at me with a suspicious eye.

"I know no other," I said.

"Perhaps not, but at any rate *you* have another, though you don't seem to have told it to her. Anyway, I am glad they are gone, for I was getting tired of being ordered by everybody to carry about wood and water for them. Also I am terribly hungry as I can't eat before it is light. They have taken most of the best fruit to which I was looking forward, but thank goodness they do not seem to care for pork."

"So am I," said Bickley, who really looked exhausted. "Get the food, there's a good fellow. We'll talk afterwards."

When we had eaten, somewhat silently, I asked Bickley what he made of the business; also whither he thought the sleepers had gone.

"I think I can answer the last question," interrupted Bastin. "I expect it is to a place well known to students of the Bible which even Bickley mentions sometimes when he is angry. At any rate, they seem to be very fond of heat, for they wouldn't part from it even in their coffins, and you will admit that they are not quite natural, although that Glittering Lady is so attractive as regards her exterior."

Bickley waved these remarks aside and addressed himself to me.

"I don't know what to think of it," he said; "but as the experience is not natural and everything in the Universe, so far as we know it, has a natural explanation, I am inclined to the belief that we are suffering from hallucinations, which in their way are also quite natural. It does not seem possible that two people can really have been asleep for an unknown length of time enclosed in vessels of glass or crystal, kept warm by radium or some such substance, and then emerge from them comparatively strong and well. It is contrary to natural law."

"How about microbes?" I asked. "They are said to last practically for ever, and they are living things. So in their case your natural law breaks down."

"That is true," he answered. "Some microbes in a sealed tube and under certain conditions do appear to possess indefinite powers of life. Also radium has an indefinite life, but that is a mineral. Only these people are not microbes nor are they minerals. Also, experience tells us that they could not have lived for more than a few months at the outside in such circumstances as we seemed to find them."

"Then what do you suggest?"

"I suggest that we did not really find them at all; that we have all been dreaming. You know that there are certain gases which produce illusions, laughing gas is one of them, and that these gases are sometimes met with in caves. Now there were very peculiar odours in that place under the statue, which may have worked upon our imaginations in some such way. Otherwise we are up against a miracle, and, as you know, I do not believe in miracles."

"*I* do," said Bastin calmly. "You'll find all about it in the Bible if you will only take the trouble to read. Why do you talk such rubbish about gases?"

"Because only gas, or something of the sort, could have made us imagine them."

"Nonsense, Bickley! Those people were here right enough. Didn't they eat our fruit and drink the water I brought them without ever saying thank you? Only, they are not human. They are evil spirits, and for my part I don't want to see any more of them, though I have no doubt Arbuthnot does, as that Glittering Lady threw her arms round his neck when she woke up, and already he is calling her by her Christian name, if the word Christian can be used in connection with her. The old fellow had the impudence to tell us that he was a god, and it is remarkable that he should have called himself Oro, seeing that the devil they worship on the island is also called Oro and the place itself is named Orofena."

"As to where they have gone," continued Bickley, taking no notice of Bastin, "I really don't know. My expectation is, however, that when we go to look to-morrow morning—and I suggest that we should not do so before then in order that we may give our minds time to clear—we shall find that sepulchre place quite empty, even perhaps without the crystal coffins we have imagined to stand there."

"Perhaps we shall find that there isn't a cave at all and that we are not sitting on a flat rock outside of it," suggested Bastin with heavy sarcasm, adding, "You are clever in your way, Bickley, but you can talk more rubbish than any man I ever knew."

"They told us they would come back to-night or to-morrow," I said. "If they do, what will you say then, Bickley?"

"I will wait till they come to answer that question. Now let us go for a walk and try to change our thoughts. We are all over-strained and scarcely know what we are saying."

"One more question," I said as we rose to start. "Did Tommy suffer from hallucinations as well as ourselves?"

"Why not?" answered Bickley. "He is an animal just as we are, or perhaps we thought we saw Tommy do the things he did."

"When you found that basket of fruit, Bastin, which the natives brought over in the canoe, was there a bough covered with red flowers lying on the top of it?"

"Yes, Arbuthnot, one bough only; I threw it down on the rock as it got in the way when I was carrying the basket."

"Which flowering bough we all thought we saw the Sleeper Oro carry away after Tommy had brought it to him."

"Yes; he made me pick it up and give it to him," said Bastin.

"Well, if we did not see this it should still be lying on the rock, as there has been no wind and there are no animals here to carry it away. You will admit that, Bickley?"

He nodded.

"Then if it has gone you will admit also that the presumption is that we saw what we thought we did see?"

"I do not know how that conclusion can be avoided,

at any rate so far as the incident of the bough is concerned," replied Bickley with caution.

Then, without more words, we started to look. At the spot where the bough should have been, there was no bough, but on the rock lay several of the red flowers, bitten off, I suppose, by Tommy while he was carrying it. Nor was this all. I think I have mentioned that the Glittering Lady wore sandals which were fastened with red studs that looked like rubies or carbuncles. On the rock lay one of these studs. I picked it up and we examined it. It had been sewn to the sandal-strap with golden thread or silk. Some of this substance hung from the hole drilled in the stone which served for an eye. It was as rotten as tinder, apparently with extreme age. Moreover, the hard gem itself was pitted as though the passage of time had taken effect upon it, though this may have been caused by other agencies, such as the action of the radium rays. I smiled at Bickley who looked disconcerted and even sad. In a way it is painful to see the effect upon an able and earnest man of the upsetting of his lifelong theories.

We went for our walk, keeping to the flat lands at the foot of the volcano cone, for we seemed to have had enough of wonders and to desire to reassure ourselves, as it were, by the study of natural and familiar things. As it chanced, too, we were rewarded by sundry useful discoveries. Thus we found a place where the bread-tree and other fruits, most of them now ripe, grew in abundance, as did the yam. Also, we came to an inlet that we noticed was crowded with large and beautiful fish from the lake, which seemed to find it a favourite spot. Perhaps this was because a little stream of excellent water ran in here, overflowing from the great pool or mere which filled the crater above.

At these finds we rejoiced greatly, for now we knew that we need not fear starvation even should our supply of food from the main island be cut off. Indeed, by help of some palm-leaf stalks which we wove together roughly, Bastin, who was rather clever at this kind of thing, managed to trap four fish weighing two or three pounds apiece, wading into the water to do so. It was curious to observe with what ease he adapted himself to the manners and customs of primeval man, so much so, indeed, that Bickley remarked that if he could believe in re-incarnation, he would be absolutely certain that Bastin was a troglodyte in his last sojourn on the earth.

However this might be, Bastin's primeval instincts and abilities were of the utmost service to us. Before we had been many days on that island he had built us a kind of native hut or house roofed with palm leaves in which, until provided with a better, as happened afterwards, we ate and he and Bickley slept, leaving the tent to me. Moreover, he wove a net of palm fibre with which he caught abundance of fish, and made fishing-lines of the same material (fortunately we had some hooks) which he baited with freshwater mussels and the insides of fish. By means of these he secured some veritable monsters of the carp species that proved most excellent eating. His greatest triumph, however, was a decoy which he constructed of boughs, wherein he trapped a number of waterfowl. So that soon we kept a very good table of a sort, especially after he had learned how to cook our food upon the native plan by means of hot stones. This suited us admirably, as it enabled Bickley and myself to devote all our time to archæological and other studies which did not greatly interest Bastin.

By the time that we got back to camp it was drawing

towards evening, so we cooked our food and ate, and then, thoroughly exhausted, made ourselves as comfortable as we could and went to sleep. Even our marvellous experiences could not keep Bickley and myself from sleeping, and on Bastin such things had no effect. He accepted them and that was all, much more readily than we did, indeed. Triple-armed as he was in the mail of a child-like faith, he snapped his fingers at evil spirits which he supposed the Sleepers to be, and at everything else that other men might dread.

Now, as I have mentioned, after our talk with Marama, although we did not think it wise to adventure ourselves among them again at present, we had lost all fear of the Orofenans. In this attitude, so far as Marama himself and the majority of his people were concerned, we were quite justified, for they were our warm friends. But in the case of the sorcerers, the priests and all their rascally and superstitious brotherhood, we were by no means justified. They had not forgiven Bastin his sacrilege or for his undermining of their authority by the preaching of new doctrines which, if adopted, would destroy them as a hierarchy. Nor had they forgiven Bickley for shooting one of their number, or any of us for our escape from the vengeance of their god.

So it came about that they made a plot to seize us all and hale us off to be sacrificed to a substituted image of Oro, which by now they had set up. They knew exactly where we slept upon the rock; indeed, our fire showed it to them and so far they were not afraid to venture, since here they had been accustomed for generations to lay their offerings to the god of the Mountain. Secretly on the previous night, without the knowledge of Marama, they had carried two more canoes to the borders of the lake. Now on this night, just as the moon was setting about three in the morning, they made their attack, twenty-one men in all, for the three canoes were large, relying on the following darkness to get us away and convey us to the place of sacrifice to be offered up at dawn and before Marama could interfere.

The first we knew of the matter, for most foolishly we had neglected to keep a watch, was the unpleasant sensation of brawny savages kneeling on us and trussing us up with palm-fibre ropes. Also they thrust handfuls of dry grass into our mouths to prevent us from calling out, although as air came through the interstices of the grass, we did not suffocate. The thing was so well done that we never struck a blow in self-defence, and although we had our pistols at hand, much less could we fire a shot. Of course, we struggled as well as we were able, but it was quite useless; in three minutes we were as helpless as calves in a net and like calves were being conveyed to the butcher. Bastin managed to get the gag out of his mouth for a few seconds, and I heard him say in his slow, heavy voice:

"This, Bickley, is what comes of trafficking with evil spirits in museum cases——" There his speech stopped, for the grass wad was jammed down his throat again, but distinctly I heard the inarticulate Bickley snort as he conceived the repartee he was unable to utter. As for myself, I reflected that the business served us right for not keeping a watch, and abandoned the issue to fate.

Still, to confess the truth, I was infinitely more sorry to die than I should have been forty-eight hours earlier. This is a dull and in most ways a dreadful world, one, if we could only summon the courage, that some of us would be glad to leave in search of new adventures. But here a great and unprecedented adventure had begun to befall me, and before its mystery was solved, before even I could formulate a theory concerning it, my body must be destroyed, and my intelligence that was caged therein, sent far afield; or, if Bickley were right, eclipsed. It seemed so sad just when the impossible, like an unguessed wandering moon, had risen over the grey flats of the ascertained and made them shine with hope and wonder.

They carried us off to the canoes, not too gently; indeed, I heard the bony frame of Bastin bump into the bottom of one of them and reflected, not without venom, that it served him right as he was the fount and origin of our woes. Two stinking magicians, wearing on their heads undress editions of their court cages, since these were too cumbersome for active work of the sort, and painted all over with various pigments, were just about to swing me after him into the same, or another canoe, when something happened. I did not know what it was, but as a result, my captors left hold of me so that I fell to the rock, lying upon my back.

Then, within my line of vision, which, it must be remembered, was limited because I could not lift my head, appeared the upper part of the tall person of the Ancient who said that he was named Oro. I could only see him down to his middle, but I noted vaguely that he seemed to be much changed. For instance, he wore a different coloured dress, or rather robe; this time it was dark blue, which caused me to wonder where on earth it came from. Also, his tremendous beard had been trimmed and dressed, and on his head there was a simple black cap, strangely quilted, which looked as though it were made of velvet. Moreover, his face had plumped out. He still looked ancient, it is true, and unutterably wise, but now he resembled an antique youth, so great were his energy and vigour. Also, his dark and glowing eyes shone with a fearful intensity. In short, he seemed impressive and terrible almost beyond imagining.

He looked about him slowly, then asked in a deep, cold voice, speaking in the Orofenan tongue:

"What do you, slaves?"

No one seemed able to answer, they were too horror-stricken at this sudden vision of their fabled god, whose fierce features of wood had become flesh; they only turned to fly. He waved his thin hand and they came to a standstill, like animals which have reached the end of their tether and are checked by the chains that bind them. There they stood in all sorts of postures, immovable and looking extremely ridiculous in their paint and feathers, with dread unutterable stamped upon their evil faces.

The Sleeper spoke again:

"You would murder as did your forefathers, O children of snakes and hogs fashioned in the shape of men. You would sacrifice those who dwell in my shadow to satisfy your hate because they are wiser than you. Come hither thou," and he beckoned with a bony finger to the chief magician.

The man advanced towards him in short jumps, as a mechanical toy might do, and stood before him, his miniature crate and feathers all awry and the sweat of terror melting the paint in streaks upon his face.

"Look into the eyes of Oro, O worshipper of Oro," said the Sleeper, and he obeyed, his own eyes starting out of his head.

"Receive the curse of Oro," said the Ancient again.

Then followed a terrible spectacle. The man went

raving mad. He bounded into the air to a height inconceivable. He threw himself upon the ground and rolled upon the rock. He rose again and staggered round and round, tearing pieces out of his arms with his teeth. He yelled hideously like one possessed. He grovelled, beating his forehead against the rock. Then he sat up, slowly choked and—died.

His companions seemed to catch the infection of death as terrified savages often do. They too performed dreadful antics, all except three of them who stood paralysed. They rushed about battering each other with their fists and wooden weapons, looking like devils from hell in their hideous painted attire. They grappled and fought furiously. They separated and plunged into the lake, where with a last grimace they sank like stones.

It seemed to last a long while, but I think that as a matter of fact within five minutes it was over; they were all dead. Only the three paralysed ones remained standing and rolling their eyes.

The Sleeper beckoned to them with his thin finger, and they walked forward in step like soldiers.

"Lift that man from the boat," he said, pointing to Bastin, "cut his bonds and those of the others."

They obeyed with a wonderful alacrity. In a minute we stood at liberty and were pulling the grass gags from our mouths. The Ancient pointed to the head magician who lay dead upon the rock, his hideous, contorted countenance staring open-eyed at heaven.

"Take that sorcerer and show him to the other sorcerers yonder," he said, "and tell them where your fellows are if they would find them. Know by these signs that the Oro, god of the Mountain, who has slept awhile, is awake, and ill will it go with them who question his power or dare to try to harm those who dwell in his house. Bring food day by day and await commands. Begone!"

The dreadful-looking body was bundled into one of the canoes, that out of which Bastin had emerged. A rower sprang into each of them and presently was paddling as he had never done before. As the setting moon vanished, they vanished with it, and once more there was a great silence.

"I am going to find my boots," said Bastin. "This rock is hard and I hurt my feet kicking at those poor fellows who appear to have come to a bad end, how, I do not exactly understand. Personally, I think that more allowances should have been made for them, as I hope will be the case elsewhere, since after all they only acted according to their lights."

"Curse their lights!" ejaculated Bickley, feeling his throat which was bruised. "I'm glad they are out."

Bastin limped away in search of his boots, but Bickley and I stood where we were contemplating the awakened Sleeper. All recollection of the recent tumultuous scene seemed to have passed from his mind, for he was engaged in a study of the heavens. They were wonderfully brilliant now that the moon was down, brilliant as they only can be in the tropics when the sky is clear.

Something caused me to look round, and there, coming towards us, was she who said her name was Yva. Evidently all her weakness had departed also, for now she needed no support, but walked with a peculiar gliding motion that reminded me of a swan floating forward on the water. Well had we named her the Glittering Lady, for in the starlight literally she seemed to glitter. I suppose the effect came from her golden raiment, which, however, I noticed, as in her father's case, was not the same that she had worn in the coffin; also from her hair that seemed to give out a light of its own. At least, she shimmered as she came, her tall shape swaying at every step like a willow in the wind. She drew near, and I saw that her face, too, had filled out and now was that of one in perfect health and vigour, while her eyes shone softly and seemed wondrous large.

In her hands she carried those two plates of metal which I had seen lying in the coffin of the Sleeper Oro. These she gave to him, then fell back out of his hearing —if it were ever possible to do this, a point on which I am not sure—and began to talk to me. I noted at once that in the few hours during which she was absent, her knowledge of the Orofenan tongue seemed to have improved greatly as though she had drunk deeply from some hidden fount of memory. Now she spoke it with readiness, as Oro had done when he addressed the sorcerers, although many of the words she used were not known to me, and the general form of her language appeared archaic, as for instance that of Spenser is compared with modern English. When she saw I did not comprehend her, however, she would stop and cast her sentences in a different shape, till at length I caught her meaning. Now I give the substance of what she said.

"You are safe," she began, glancing first at the palm ropes that lay upon the rock and then at my wrists, one of which was cut.

"Yes, Lady Yva, thanks to your father."

"You should say thanks to me. My father was thinking of other things, but I was thinking of you strangers, and from where I was I saw those wicked ones coming to kill you."

"Oh! from the top of the mountain, I suppose."

She shook her head and smiled but vouchsafed no further explanation, unless her following words can be so called. These were:

"I can see otherwise than with my eyes, if I choose." A statement that caused Bickley, who was listening, to mutter:

"Impossible! What the deuce can she mean? Telepathy, perhaps."

"I saw," she continued, "and told the Lord, my father. He came forth. Did he kill them? I did not look to learn."

"Yes. They lie in the lake, all except three whom he sent away as messengers."

"I thought so. Death is terrible, O Humphrey, but it is a sword which those who rule must use to smite the wicked and the savage."

Not wishing to pursue this subject, I asked her what her father was doing with the metal plates.

"He reads the stars," she answered, "to learn how long we have been asleep. Before we went to sleep he made two pictures of them, as they were then and as they should be at the time he had set for our awakening."

"We set that time," interrupted Bickley.

"Not so, O Bickley," she answered, smiling again. "In the divine Oro's head was the time set. You were the hand that executed his decree."

When Bickley heard this I really thought he would have burst. However, he controlled himself nobly, being anxious to hear the end of this mysterious fib.

ORO'S CHART OF THE STARS MADE BY HIM ABOUT 250,000 YEARS AGO

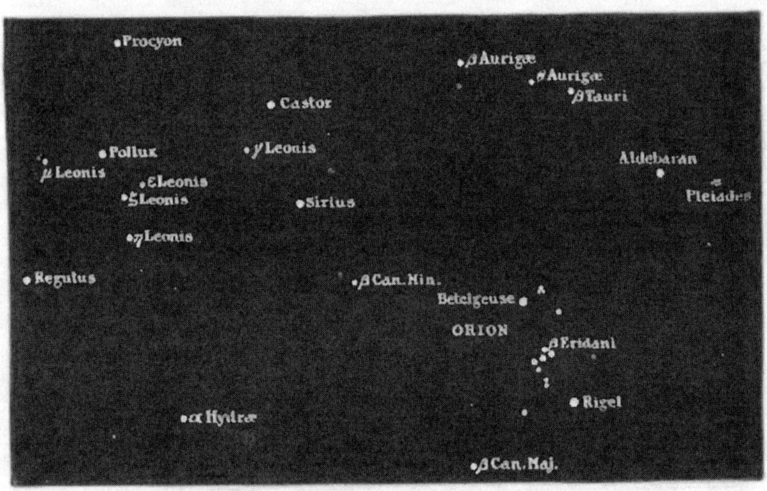

KEY CHART TO THE ABOVE

ORO'S CHART OF THE STARS AS HE CALCULATED THAT THEY WOULD APPEAR AT HIS AWAKENING

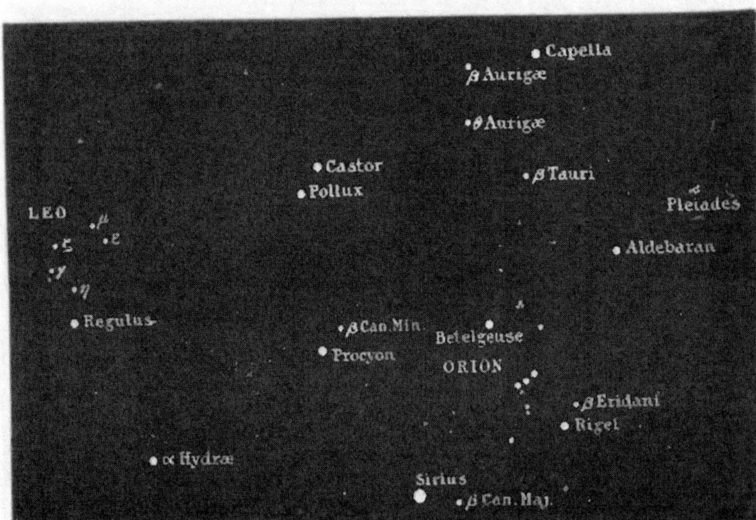

KEY CHART TO THE ABOVE

"How long was the time that the lord Oro set apart for sleep?" I asked.

She paused as though puzzled to find words to express her meaning, then held up her hands and said:

"Ten," nodding at her fingers. By second thoughts she took Bickley's hands, not mine, and counted his ten fingers.

"Ten years," said Bickley. "Well, of course, it is impossible, but perhaps——" and he paused.

"Ten tens," she went on with a deepening smile, "one hundred."

"O!" said Bickley.

"Ten hundreds, one thousand."

"I say!" said Bickley.

"Ten times ten thousand, one hundred thousand."

Bickley became silent.

"Twice one hundred thousand and half a hundred thousand, two hundred and fifty thousand years. *That* was the space of time which the lord Oro, my father, set for our sleep. Whether it has been fulfilled he will know presently when he has read the book of the stars and made comparison of it with what he wrote before we laid us down to rest," and she pointed to the metal plates which the Ancient was studying.

Bickley walked away, making sounds as though he were going to be ill and looking so absurd in his indignation that I nearly laughed. The Lady Yva actually did laugh, and very musical was that laugh.

"He does not believe," she said. "He is so clever he knows everything. But two hundred and fifty thousand years ago we should have thought him quite stupid. Then we could read the stars and calculate their movements for ever."

"So can we," I answered, rather nettled.

"I am glad, O Humphrey, since you will be able to show my father if in one of them he is wrong."

Secretly I hoped that this task would not be laid on me. Indeed, I thought it well to change the subject for the edification of Bickley who had recovered and was drawn back by his eager curiosity. Just then, too, Bastin joined us, happy in his regained boots.

"You tell us, Lady Yva," I said, "that you slept, or should have slept for two hundred and fifty thousand years." Here Bastin opened his eyes. "If that was so, where was your mind all this time?"

"If by my mind you mean spirit, O Humphrey, I have to answer that at present I do not know for certain. I think, however, that it dwelt elsewhere, perhaps in other bodies on the earth, or some different earth. At least, I know that my heart is very full of memories which as yet I cannot unroll and read."

"Great heavens, this is madness!" said Bickley.

"In the great heavens," she answered slowly, "there are many things which you, poor man, would think to be madness, but yet are truth and perfect wisdom. These things, or some of them, soon I shall hope to show you."

"Do if you can," said Bickley.

"Why not?" interrupted Bastin. "I think the lady's remarks quite reasonable. It seems to me highly improbable if really she has slept for two hundred and fifty thousand years, which, of course, I can't decide, that an immortal spirit would be allowed to remain idle for so long. That would be wallowing in a bed of idleness and shirking its duty which is to do its work. Also, as she tells you, Bickley, you are not half so clever as you think you are in your silly scepticism, and I have no doubt that there are many things in other worlds which would expose your ignorance, if only you could see them."

At this moment Oro turned and called his daughter. She went at once, saying:

"Come, strangers, and you shall learn."

So we followed her.

"Daughter," he said, speaking in Orofenan, I think that we might understand, "ask these strangers to bring one of those lamps of theirs that by the light of it I may study these writings."

"Perhaps this may serve," said Bickley, suddenly producing an electric torch from his pocket and flashing it into his face. It was his form of repartee for all he had suffered at the hands of this incomprehensible pair. Let me say at once that it was singularly successful. Perhaps the wisdom of the ages in which Oro flourished had overlooked so small a matter as electric torches, or perhaps he did not expect to meet with them in these degenerate days. At any rate for the first and last time in my intercourse with him I saw the god, or lord—the native word bears either meaning—Oro genuinely astonished. He started and stepped back, and for a moment or two seemed a little frightened. Then muttering something as to the cleverness of this light-producing instrument, he motioned to his daughter to take it from Bickley and hold it in a certain position. She obeyed, and in its illumination he began to study the engraved plates, holding one of them in either hand.

After a while he gave me one of the plates to hold, and with his disengaged hand pointed successively to the constellation of Orion, to the stars Castor, Pollux, Aldebaran, Rigel, the Pleiades, Sirius and others which with my very limited knowledge I could not recognise offhand. Then on the plate which I held, he showed us those same stars and constellations, checking them one by one.

Then he remarked very quietly that all was in order, and handing the plate he held to Yva, said:

"The calculations made so long ago are correct, nor have the stars varied in their proper motions during what is after all but an hour of time. If you, Stranger, who, I understand, are named Humphrey, should be, as I gather, a heaven-master, naturally you will ask me how I could fix an exact date by the stars without an error of, let us say, from five to ten thousand years. I answer you that by the proper motion of the stars alone it would have been difficult. Therefore I remember that in order to be exact, I calculated the future conjunctions of those two planets," and he pointed to Saturn and Jupiter. "Finding that one of these occurred near yonder star," and he indicated the bright orb, Spica, "at a certain time, I determined that then I would awake. Behold! There are the stars as I engraved them from my foreknowledge, upon this chart, and there those two great planets hang in conjunction. Daughter Yva, my wisdom has not failed me. This world of ours has travelled round the sun neither less nor more than two hundred and fifty thousand times since we laid ourselves down to sleep. It is written here, and yonder," and he pointed, first to the engraved plates and then to the vast expanse of the starlit heavens.

Awe fell on me; I think that even Bickley and Bastin were awed, at any rate for the moment. It was a terrible thing to look on a being, to all appearance more or less human, who alleged that he had been asleep for two hundred and fifty thousand years, and proceeded to prove it by certain ancient star charts. Of course at the time I could not check those charts, lacking the necessary knowledge, but I have done so since and found that they are quite accurate. However this made no difference, since the circumstances and something in his manner convinced me that he spoke the absolute truth.

He and his daughter had been asleep for two hundred and fifty thousand years. Oh! Heavens, *for two hundred and fifty thousand years!*

CHAPTER XIII

ORO SPEAKS AND BASTIN ARGUES

THE reader of what I have written, should there ever be such a person, may find the record marvellous, and therefore rashly conclude that because it is beyond experience, it could not be. It is not a wise deduction, as I think Bickley would admit to-day, because without doubt many things are which surpass our extremely limited experience. However, those who draw the veil from the Unknown and reveal the New, must expect incredulity, and accept it without grumbling. Was that not the fate, for instance, of those who in the Middle Ages, a few hundred years ago, discovered, or rather re-discovered the mighty movements of those constellations which served Oro for an almanac?

But the point I want to make is that if the sceptic plays a Bickleyan part as regards what has been written, it seems probable that his attitude will be accentuated as regards that which it still remains for me to write. If so, I cannot help it, and must decline entirely to water down or doctor facts and thus pander to his prejudice and ignorance. For my part I cannot attempt to explain these occurrences; I only know that they happened and that I set down what I saw, heard and felt, neither more nor less.

Immediately after Oro had triumphantly vindicated his stellar calculations he turned and departed into the cave, followed by his daughter, waving to us to remain where we were. As she passed us, however, the Glittering Lady whispered—this time to Bastin—that he would see them again in a few hours, adding:

"We have much to learn and I hope that then you who, I understand, are a priest, will begin to teach us of your religion and other matters."

Bastin was so astonished that he could make no reply, but when they had gone he said:

"Which of you told her that I was a priest?"

We shook our heads for neither of us could remember having done so.

"Well, I did not," continued Bastin, "since at present I have found no opportunity of saying a word in season. So I suppose she must have gathered it from my attire, though as a matter of fact I haven't been wearing a collar, and those men who wanted to cook me, pulled off my white tie and I didn't think it worth while dirtying a clean one."

"If," said Bickley, "you imagine that you look like the minister of any religion ancient or modern in a grubby flannel shirt, a battered sun-helmet, a torn green and white umbrella and a pair of ragged duck trousers, you are mistaken, Bastin, that is all."

"I admit that the costume is not appropriate, Bickley, but how otherwise could she have learned the truth?"

"These people seem to have ways of learning a good many things. But in your case, Bastin, the cause is clear enough. You have been walking about with the head of that idol and always keep it close to you. No doubt they believe that you are a priest of the worship of the god of the Grove—Baal, you know, or something of that sort."

When he heard this Bastin's face became a perfect

picture. Never before did I see it so full of horror struggling with indignation.

"I must undeceive them without a moment's delay," he said, and was starting for the cave when we caught his arms and held him.

"Better wait till they come back, old fellow," I said, laughing. "If you disobey that Lord Oro you may meet with another experience in the sacrifice line."

"Perhaps you are right, Arbuthnot. I will occupy the interval in preparing a suitable address."

"Much better occupy it in preparing breakfast," said Bickley. "I have always noticed that you are at your best extempore."

In the end he did prepare breakfast though in a *distrait* fashion; indeed I found him beginning to make tea in the frying-pan. Bastin felt that his opportunity had arrived, and was making ready to rise to the occasion.

Also we felt, all three of us, that we were extremely shabby-looking objects, and though none of us said so, each did his best to improve his personal appearance. First of all Bickley cut Bastin's and my hair, after which I did him the same service. Then Bickley who was normally clean shaven, set to work to remove a beard of about a week's growth, and I who wore one of the pointed variety, trimmed up mine as best I could with the help of a hand-glass. Bastin, too, performed on his which was of the square and rather ragged type, wisely rejecting Bickley's advice to shave it off altogether, offered, I felt convinced, because he felt that the result on Bastin would be too hideous for words. After this we cut our nails, cleaned our teeth and bathed; I even caught Bickley applying hair tonic from his dressing case in secret, behind a projecting rock, and borrowed some myself. He gave it me on condition that I did not mention its existence to Bastin who, he remarked, would certainly use the lot and make himself smell horrible.

Next we found clean ducks among our store of spare clothes, for the Orofenans had brought these with our other possessions, and put them on, even adding silk cumberbunds and neckties. My tie I fastened with a pin that I had obtained in Egypt. It was a tiny gold statuette of very fine and early workmanship, of the god Osiris, wearing the crown of the Upper Land with the uræus crest, and holding in his hands, which projected from the mummy wrappings, the emblems of the crook, the scourge and the *crux ansata,* or Sign of Life.

Bastin, for his part, arrayed himself in full clerical costume, black coat and trousers, white tie and stick-up clergyman's collar which, as he remarked, made him feel extremely hot in that climate, and were unsuitable to domestic duties, such as washing-up. I offered to hold his coat while he did this office and told him he looked very nice indeed.

"Beautiful!" remarked Bickley, "but why don't you put on your surplice and biretta?" (Being very High-Church Bastin did wear a biretta on festival Sundays at home.) "There would be no mistake about you then."

"I do not think it would be suitable," replied Bastin whose sense of humour was undeveloped. "There is no service to be performed at present and no church, though perhaps that cave——" and he stopped.

When we had finished these vain adornments and Bastin had put away the things and tidied up, we sat down, rather at a loose end. We should have liked to walk but refrained from doing so for fear lest we might dirty our clean clothes. So we just sat and thought. At least Bickley thought, and so did I for a while until I gave it up. What was the use of thinking, seeing that we were face to face with circumstances which baffled reason and beggared all recorded human experience? What Bastin did I am sure I do not know, but I think from the expression of his countenance that he was engaged in composing sermons for the benefit of Oro and the Glittering Lady.

One diversion we did have. About eleven o'clock a canoe came from the main island laden with provisions and paddled by Marama and two of his people. We seized our weapons, remembering our experiences of the night, but Marama waved a bough in token of peace. So, carrying our revolvers, we went to the rock edge to meet him. He crept ashore and, chief though he was, prostrated himself upon his face before us, which told me that he had heard of the fate of the sorcerers. His apologies were abject. He explained that he had no part in the outrage of the attack, and besought us to intercede on behalf of him and his people with the awakened god of the Mountain whom he looked for with a terrified air.

We consoled him as well as we could, and told him that he had best be gone before the god of the Mountain appeared, and perhaps treated him as he had done the sorcerers. In his name, however, we commanded Marama to bring materials and build us a proper house upon the rock, also to be sure to keep up a regular and ample supply of provisions. If he did these things, and anything else we might from time to time command, we said that perhaps his life and those of his people would be spared. This, however, after the evil behaviour of some of them of course we could not guarantee.

Marama departed so thoroughly frightened that he even forgot to make any inquiries as to who this god of the Mountain might be, or where he came from, or whither he was going. Of course, the place had been sacred among his people from the beginning, whenever that may have been, but that its sacredness should materialise into an active god who brought sorcerers of the highest reputation to a most unpleasant end, just because they wished to translate their preaching into practice, was another matter. It was not to be explained even by the fact of which he himself had informed me, that during the dreadful storm of some months before, the cave mouth which previously was not visible on the volcano, had suddenly been lifted up above the level of the Rock of Offerings, although, of course, all religious and instructed persons would have expected something peculiar to happen after this event.

Such I knew were his thoughts, but, as I have said, he was too frightened and too hurried to express them in questions that I should have found it extremely difficult to answer. As it was he departed quite uncertain as to whether one of us was not the real "god of the Mountain," who had power to bring hideous death upon his molesters. After all, what had he to go on to the contrary, except the word of three priests who were so terrified that they could give no coherent account of what had happened? Of these events, it was true, there was evidence in the twisted carcass of their lamented high sorcerer, and, for the matter of that, of certain corpses which he had seen, that lay in shallow water at the bottom of the lake. Beyond all was vague, and in his heart I am sure that Marama believed that Bastin was the real "god of the Mountain." Naturally, he would desire to work vengeance on those who tried to sacrifice and eat him. Moreover, had he not destroyed the image of the god of the Grove and borne away its head whence he had sucked magic and power?

Thus argued Marama, disbelieving the tale of the frightened sorcerers, for he admitted as much to me in after days.

Marama departed in a great hurry, fearing lest the "god of the Mountain," or Bastin, whose new and splendid garb he regarded with much suspicion, might develop some evil energy against him. Then we went back to our camp, leaving the industrious Bastin, animated by a suggestion from Bickley that the fruit and food might spoil if left in the sun, to carry it into the shade of the cave. Owing to the terrors of the Orofenans the supply was so large that to do this he must make no fewer than seven journeys, which he did with great good will since Bastin loved physical exercise. The result on his clerical garments, however, was disastrous. His white tie went awry, squashed fruit and roast pig gravy ran down his waistcoat and trousers, and his high collar melted into limp crinkles in the moisture engendered by the tropical heat. Only his long coat escaped, since that Bickley kindly carried for him.

It was just as he arrived with the seventh load in this extremely dishevelled condition that Oro and his daughter emerged from the cave. Indeed Bastin, who, being shortsighted, always wore spectacles that, owing to his heated state were covered with mist, not seeing that dignitary, dumped down the last basket on to his toes, exclaiming:

"There, you lazy beggar, I told you I would bring it all, and I have."

In fact he thought he was addressing Bickley and playing off on him a troglodytic practical joke.

Oro, however, who at his age did not appreciate jokes, resented it and was about to do something unpleasant when with extraordinary tact his daughter remarked:

"Bastin the priest makes you offerings. Thank him, O Lord my father."

So Oro thanked him, not too cordially for evidently he still had feeling in his toes, and once more Bastin escaped. Becoming aware of his error, he began to apologise profusely in English, while the lady Yva studied him carefully.

"Is that the costume of the priests of your religion, O Bastin?" she asked, surveying his dishevelled form. "If so, you were better without it."

Then Bastin retired to straighten his tie, and grabbing his coat from Bickley, who handed it to him with a malicious smile, forced his perspiring arms into it in a peculiarly awkward and elephantine fashion.

Meanwhile Bickley and I produced two camp chairs which we had made ready, and on these the wondrous pair seated themselves side by side.

"We have come to learn," said Oro. "Teach!"

"Not so, Father," interrupted Yva, who, I noted, was clothed in yet a third costume, though whence these came I could not imagine. "First I would ask a question. Whence are you, Strangers, and how came you here?"

"We are from the country called England and a great storm shipwrecked us here; that, I think, which raised the mouth of the cave above the level of this rock," I answered.

"The time appointed having come when it should be raised," said Oro as though to himself.

"Where is England?" asked Yva.

Now among the books we had with us was a pocket atlas, quite a good one of its sort. By way of answer I opened it at the map of the world and showed her England. Also I showed, to within a thousand miles or so, that spot on the earth's surface where we spoke together.

The sight of this atlas excited the pair greatly. They had not the slightest difficulty in understanding everything about it and the shape of the world with its division into hemispheres seemed to be quite familiar to them. What appeared chiefly to interest them, and especially Oro, were the relative areas and positions of land and sea.

"Of this, Strangers," he said, pointing to the map, "I shall have much to say to you when I have studied the pictures of your book and compared them with others of my own."

"So he has got maps," said Bickley in English, "as well as star charts. I wonder where he keeps them."

"With his clothes, I expect," suggested Bastin.

Meanwhile Oro had hidden the atlas in his ample robe and motioned to his daughter to proceed.

"Why do you come here from England so far away?" the Lady Yva asked, a question to which each of us had an answer.

"To see new countries," I said.

"Because the cyclone brought us," said Bickley.

"To convert the heathen to my own Christian religion," said Bastin, which was not strictly true.

It was on this last reply that she fixed.

"What does your religion teach?" she asked.

"It teaches that those who accept it and obey its commands will live again after death for ever in a better world where is neither sorrow nor sin," he answered.

When he heard this saying I saw Oro start as though struck by a new thought and look at Bastin with a curious intentness.

"Who are the heathen?" Yva asked again after a pause, for she also seemed to be impressed.

"All who do not agree with Bastin's spiritual views," answered Bickley.

"Those who, whether from lack of instruction or from hardness of heart, do not follow the true faith. For instance, I suppose that your father and you are heathen," replied Bastin stoutly.

This seemed to astonish them, but presently Yva caught his meaning and smiled, while Oro said:

"Of this great matter of faith we will talk later. It is an old question in the world."

"Why," went on Yva, "if you wished to travel so far did you come in a ship that so easily is wrecked? Why did you not journey through the air, or better still, pass through space, leaving your bodies asleep, as, being instructed, doubtless you can do?"

"As regards your first question," I answered, "there are no aircraft known that can make so long a journey."

"And as regards the second," broke in Bickley, "we did not do so because it is impossible for men to transfer themselves to other places through space either with or without their bodies."

At this information the Glittering Lady lifted her arched eyebrows and smiled a little, while Oro said:

"I perceive that the new world has advanced but a little way on the road of knowledge."

Fearing that Bastin was about to commence an argument, I began to ask questions in my turn.

"Lord Oro and Lady Yva," I said, "we have told you something of ourselves and will tell you more when you desire it. But pardon us if first we pray you to tell us what we burn to know. Who are you? Of what race and country? And how came it that we found you sleeping yonder?"

"If it be your pleasure, answer, my Father," said Yva.

Oro thought a moment, then replied in a calm voice:

"I am a king who once ruled most of the world as it was in my day, though it is true that much of it rebelled against me, my councillors and servants. Therefore I destroyed the world as it was then, save only certain portions whence life might spread to the new countries that I raised up. Having done this I put myself and my daughter to sleep for a space of two hundred and fifty thousand years, that there might be time for fresh civilisations to arise. Now I begin to think that I did not allot a sufficiency of ages, since I perceive from what you tell me, that the learning of the new races is as yet but small."

Bickley and I looked at each other and were silent. Mentally we had collapsed. Who could begin to discuss statements built upon such a foundation of gigantic and paralysing falsehoods?

Well, Bastin could for one. With no more surprise in his voice than if he were talking about last night's dinner, he said:

"There must be a mistake somewhere, or perhaps I

misunderstand you. It is obvious that you, being a man, could not have destroyed the world. That could only be done by the Power which made it and you."

I trembled for the results of Bastin's methods of setting out the truth. To my astonishment, however, Oro replied:

"You speak wisely, Priest, but the Power you name may use instruments to accomplish its decrees. I am such an instrument."

"Quite so," said Bastin, "just like anybody else. You have more knowledge of the truth than I thought. But pray, how did you destroy the world?"

"Using my wisdom to direct the forces that are at work in the heart of this great globe, I drowned it with a deluge, causing one part to sink and another to rise, also changes of climate which completed the work."

"That's quite right," exclaimed Bastin delightedly. "We know all about the Deluge, only *you* are not mentioned in connection with the matter. A man, Noah, had to do with it when he was six hundred years old."

"Six hundred?" said Oro. "That is not very old. I myself had seen more than a thousand years when I lay down to sleep."

"A thousand!" remarked Bastin, mildly interested. "That is unusual, though some of these mighty men of renown we know lived over nine hundred."

Here Bickley snorted and exclaimed:

"Nine hundred moons," he means.

"I did not know Noah," went on Oro. "Perhaps he lived after my time and caused some other local deluge. Is there anything else you wish to ask me before I leave you that I may study this map-writing?"

"Yes," said Bastin. "Why were you allowed to drown your world?"

"Because it was evil, Priest, and disobeyed me and the Power I serve."

"Oh! thank you," said Bastin, "that fits in exactly. It was just the same in Noah's time."

"I pray that it is not just the same now," said Oro, rising. "To-morrow we will return, or if I do not who have much that I must do, the lady my daughter will return and speak with you further."

He departed into the cave, Yva following at a little distance.

I accompanied her as far as the mouth of the cave, as did Tommy, who all this time had been sitting contentedly upon the hem of her gorgeous robe, quite careless of its immemorial age, if it was immemorial and not woven yesterday, a point on which I had no information.

"Lady Yva," I said, "did I rightly understand the Lord Oro to say that he was a thousand years old?"

"Yes, O Humphrey, and really he is more, or so I think."

"Then are you a thousand years old also?" I asked, aghast.

"No, no," she replied, shaking her head, "I am young, quite young, for I do not count my time of sleep."

"Certainly you look it," I said. "But what, Lady Yva, do you mean by young?"

She answered my question by another.

"What age are your women when they are as I am?"

"None of our women were ever quite like you, Lady Yva. Yet, say from twenty-five to thirty years of age."

"Ah! I have been counting and now I remember. When my father sent me to sleep I was twenty-seven years old. No, I will not deceive you, I was twenty-seven years and three moons." Then, saying something to the effect that she would return, she departed, laughing a little in a mischievous way, and, although I did not observe this till afterwards, Tommy departed with her.

When I repeated what she had said to Bastin and Bickley, who were standing at a distance straining their ears and somewhat aggrieved, the former remarked:

"If she is twenty-seven her father must have married late in life, though of course it may have been a long while before he had children."

Then Bickley, who had been suppressing himself all this while, went off like a bomb.

"Do you tell us, Bastin," he asked, "that you believe one word of all this ghastly rubbish? I mean as to that antique charlatan being a thousand years old and having caused the Flood and the rest?"

"If you ask me, Bickley, I see no particular reason to doubt it at present. A person who can go to sleep in a glass coffin kept warm by a pocketful of radium together with very accurate maps of the constellations at the time he wakes up, can, I imagine, do most things."

"Even cause the Deluge," jeered Bickley.

"I don't know about *the* Deluge, but perhaps he may have been permitted to cause *a* deluge. Why not? You can't look at things from far enough off, Bickley. And if something seems big to you, you conclude that therefore it is impossible. The same Power which gives you skill to succeed in an operation, that hitherto was held impracticable, as I know you have done once or twice, may have given that old fellow power to cause a deluge. You should measure the universe and its possibilities by worlds and not by acres, Bickley."

"And believe, I suppose, that a man can live a

thousand years, whereas we know well that he cannot live more than about a hundred."

"You don't *know* anything of the sort, Bickley. All you know is that over the brief period of history with which we are acquainted, say ten thousand years at most, men have only lived to about a hundred. But the very rocks which you are so fond of talking about, tell us that even this planet is millions upon millions of years of age. Who knows then but that at some time in its history, men did not live for a thousand years, and that lost civilisations did not exist of which this Oro and his daughter may be two survivors?"

"There is no proof of anything of the sort," said Bickley.

"I don't know about proof, as you understand it, though I have read in Plato of a continent called Atlantis that was submerged, according to the story of old Egyptians priests. But personally I have every proof, for it is all written down in the Bible at which you turn up your nose, and I am very glad that I have been lucky enough to come across this unexpected confirmation of the story. Not that it matters much, since I should have learned all about it when it pleases Providence to remove me to a better world, which in our circumstances may happen any day. Now I must change my clothes before I see to the cooking and other things."

"I am bound to admit," said Bickley, looking after him, "that old Bastin is not so stupid as he seems. From his point of view the arguments he advances are quite logical. Moreover I think he is right when he says that we look at things through the wrong end of the telescope. After all the universe is very big and who knows what may happen there? Who knows even what may have happened on this little earth during the æons of its existence, whenever its balance chanced to shift, as the Ice Ages show us it has often done? Still I believe that old Oro to be a Prince of Liars."

"That remains to be proved," I answered cautiously. "All I know is that he is a wonderfully learned person of most remarkable appearance, and that his daughter is the loveliest creature I ever saw."

"There I agree," said Bickley decidedly, "and as brilliant as she is lovely. If she belongs to a past civilisation, it is a pity that it ever became extinct. Now let's go and have a nap. Bastin will call us when supper is ready."

CHAPTER XIV

THE UNDER-WORLD

THAT night we slept well and without fear, being quite certain that after their previous experience the Orofenans would make no further attempts upon us. Indeed our only anxiety was for Tommy, whom we could not find when the time came to give him his supper. Bastin, however, seemed to remember having seen him following the Glittering Lady into the cave. This, of course, was possible, as certainly he had taken an enormous fancy to her and sat himself down as close to her as he could on every occasion. He even seemed to like the ancient Oro, and was not afraid to jump up and plant his dirty paws upon that terrific person's gorgeous robe. Moreover Oro liked him, for several times I observed him pat the dog upon the head; as I think I have said, the only human touch that I had perceived about him. So we gave up searching and calling in the hope that he was safe with our supernatural friends.

The next morning quite early the Lady Yva appeared alone; no, not alone, for with her came our lost Tommy looking extremely spry and well at ease. The faithless little wretch just greeted us in a casual fashion and then went and sat by Yva. In fact when the awkward Bastin managed to stumble over the end of her dress Tommy growled at him and showed his teeth. Moreover the dog was changed. He was blessed with a shiny black coat, but now this coat sparkled in the sunlight, like the Lady Yva's hair.

"The Glittering Lady is all very well, but I'm not sure that I care for a glittering dog. It doesn't look quite natural," said Bastin, contemplating him.

"Why does Tommy shine, Lady?" I asked.

"Because I washed him in certain waters that we have, so that now he looks beautiful and smells sweet," she answered, laughing.

It was true, the dog did smell sweet, which I may add had not always been the case with him, especially when there were dead fish about. Also he appeared to have been fed, for he turned up his nose at the bits we had saved for his breakfast.

"He has drunk of the Life-water," explained Yva, "and will want no food for two days."

Bickley pricked up his ears at this statement and looked incredulous.

"You do not believe, O Bickley," she said, studying him gravely. "Indeed, you believe nothing. You think my father and I tell you many lies. Bastin there, he believes all. Humphrey? He is not sure; he thinks to himself, I will wait and find out whether or no these funny people cheat me."

Bickley coloured and made some remark about things which were contrary to experience, also that Tommy in a general way was rather a greedy little dog.

"You, too, like to eat, Bickley" (this was true, he had an excellent appetite), "but when you have drunk the Life-water you will care much less."

"I am glad to hear it," interrupted Bastin, "for Bickley wants a lot of cooking done, and I find it tedious."

"You eat also, Lady," said Bickley.

"Yes, I eat sometimes because I like it, but I can go weeks and not eat, when I have the Life-water. Just now, after so long a sleep, I am hungry. Please give me some of that fruit. No, not the flesh, flesh I hate."

We handed it to her. She took two plantains, peeled and ate them with extraordinary grace. Indeed she reminded me, I do not know why, of some lovely butterfly drawing its food from a flower.

While she ate she observed us closely; nothing seemed to escape the quick glances of those beautiful eyes. Presently she said:

"What, O Humphrey, is that with which you fasten your neckdress?" and she pointed to the little gold statue of Osiris that I used as a pin.

I told her that it was a statuette of a god named Osiris and very, very ancient, probably quite five thousand years old, a statement at which she smiled a little; also that it came from Egypt.

"Ah!" she answered, "is it so? I asked because we have figures that are very like to that one, and they also hold in their hands a staff surmounted by a loop. They are figures of Sleep's brother—Death."

"So is this," I said. "Among the Egyptians Osiris was the god of Death."

She nodded and replied that doubtless the symbol had come down to them.

"One day you shall take me to see this land which you call so very old. Or I will take you, which would be quicker," she added.

We all bowed and said we should be delighted. Even Bastin appeared anxious to revisit Egypt in such company, though when he was there it seemed to bore him. But what she meant about taking us I could not guess. Nor had we time to ask her, for she went on, watching our faces as she spoke.

"The Lord Oro sends you a message, Strangers. He asks whether it is your wish to see where we dwell. He adds that you are not to come if you do not desire, or if you fear danger."

We all answered that there was nothing we should like better, but Bastin added that he had already seen the tomb.

"Do you think, Bastin, that we live in a tomb because we slept there for a while, awaiting the advent of you wanderers at the appointed hour?"

"I don't see where else it could be, unless it is further down that cave," said Bastin. "The top of the mountain would not be convenient as a residence."

"It has not been convenient for many an age, for reasons that I will show you. Think now, before you come. You have naught to fear from us, and I believe that no harm will happen to you. But you will see many strange things that will anger Bickley because he cannot understand them, and perhaps will weary Bastin because his heart turns from what is wondrous and ancient. Only Humphrey will rejoice in them because the doors of his soul are open and he longs—what do you long for, Humphrey?"

"That which I have lost and fear I shall never find again," I answered boldly.

"I know that you have lost many things—last night, for instance, you lost Tommy, and when he slept with me he told me much about you and—others."

"This is ridiculous," broke in Bastin. "Can a dog talk?"

"Everything can talk, if you understand its language, Bastin. But keep a good heart, Humphrey, for the bold seeker finds in the end. Oh! foolish man, do you not understand that all is yours if you have but the soul to conceive and the will to grasp? All, all, below, between, above! Even I know that, I who have so much to learn."

So she spoke and became suddenly magnificent. Her face which had been but that of a super-lovely woman, took on grandeur. Her bosom swelled; her presence radiated some subtle power, much as her hair radiated light.

In a moment it was gone and she was smiling and jesting.

"Will you come, Strangers, where Tommy was not afraid to go, down to the Under-world? Or will you stay here in the sun? Perhaps you will do better to stay here in the sun, for the Under-world has terrors for weak hearts that were born but yesterday, and feeble feet may stumble in the dark."

"I shall take my electric torch," said Bastin with decision, "and I advise you fellows to do the same. I always hated cellars, and the catacombs at Rome are worse, though full of sacred interest."

Then we started, Tommy frisking on ahead in a most provoking way as though he were bored by a visit to a strange house and going home, and Yva gliding forward with a smile upon her face that was half mystic and half mischievous. We passed the remains of the machines, and Bickley asked her what they were.

"Carriages in which once we travelled through the skies, until we found a better way, and that the uninstructed used till the end," she answered carelessly, leaving me wondering what on earth she meant.

We came to the statue and the sepulchre beneath without trouble, for the glint of her hair, and I may add of Tommy's back, were quite sufficient to guide us through the gloom. The crystal coffins were still there, for Bastin flashed his torch and we saw them, but the boxes of radium had gone.

"Let that light die," she said to Bastin. "Humphrey, give me your right hand and give your left to Bickley. Let Bastin cling to him and fear nothing."

We passed to the end of the tomb and stood against what appeared to be a rock wall, all close together, as she directed.

"Fear nothing," she said again, but next second I was never more full of fear in my life, for we were whirling downwards at a speed that would have made an American elevator attendant turn pale.

"Don't choke me," I heard Bickley say to Bastin, and the latter's murmured reply of:

"I never could bear these moving staircases and tube-lifts. They always make me feel sick."

I admit that for my part I also felt rather sick and clung tightly to the hand of the Glittering Lady. She, however, placed her other hand upon my shoulder, saying in a low voice:

"Did I not tell you to have no fear?"

Then I felt comforted, for somehow I knew that it was not her desire to harm and much less to destroy me. Also Tommy was seated quite at his ease with his head resting against my leg, and his absence of alarm was reassuring. The only stoic of the party was Bickley. I have no doubt that he was quite as frightened as we were, but rather than show it he would have died.

"I presume this machinery is pneumatic," he began when suddenly and without shock, we arrived at the end of our journey. How far we had fallen I am sure I do not know, but I should judge from the awful speed at which we travelled, that it must have been several thousand feet, probably four or five.

"Everything seems steady now," remarked Bastin, "so I suppose this luggage lift has stopped. The odd thing is that I can't see anything of it. There ought to be a shaft, but we seem to be standing on a level floor."

"The odd thing is," said Bickley, "that we can see at all. Where the devil does the light come from thousands of feet underground?"

"I don't know," answered Bastin, "unless there is natural gas here, as I am told there is at a town called Medicine Hat in Canada."

"Natural gas be blowed," said Bickley. "It is more like moonlight magnified ten times."

So it was. The whole place was filled with a soft radiance, equal to that of the sun at noon, but gentler and without heat.

"Where does it come from?" I whispered to Yva.

"Oh!" she replied, as I thought evasively. "It is the light of the Under-world which we know how to use. The earth is full of light, which is not wonderful, is it, seeing that its heart is fire? Now look about you."

I looked and leant on her harder than ever, since amazement made me weak. We were in some vast place whereof the roof seemed almost as far off as the sky at night. At least all that I could make out was a dim and distant arch which might have been one of cloud. For the rest, in every direction stretched vastness, illuminated far as the eye could reach by the soft light of which I have spoken, that is, probably for several miles. But this vastness was not empty. On the contrary it was occupied by a great city. There were streets much wider than Piccadilly, all bordered by houses, though these, I observed, were roofless, very fine houses, some of them, built of white stone or marble. There were roadways and pavements worn by the passage of feet. There, farther on, were market-places or public squares, and there, lastly, was a huge central enclosure one or two hundred acres in extent, which was filled with majestic buildings that looked like palaces, or town-halls; and, in the midst of them all, a vast temple with courts and a central dome. For here, notwithstanding the lack of necessity, its builders seemed to have adhered to the Over-world tradition, and had roofed their fane.

And now came the terror. All of this enormous city was *dead.* Had it stood upon the moon it could not have been more dead. None paced its streets; none looked from its window-places. None trafficked in its markets, none worshipped in its temple. Swept, garnished, lighted, practically untouched by the hand of Time, here where no rains fell and no winds blew, it was yet a howling wilderness. For what wilderness is there to equal that which once has been the busy haunt of men? Let those who have stood among the buried cities of Central Asia, or of Anarajapura in Ceylon, or even amid the ruins of Salamis on the coast of Cyprus, answer the question. But here was something infinitely more awful. A huge human haunt in the bowels of the earth utterly devoid of human beings, and yet as perfect as on the day when these ceased to be.

"I do not care for underground localities," remarked Bastin, his gruff voice echoing strangely in that terrible silence, "but it does seem a pity that all these fine buildings should be wasted. I suppose their inhabitants left them in search of fresh air."

"Why did they leave them?" I asked of Yva.

"Because death took them," she answered solemnly. "Even those who live a thousand years die at last, and if they have no children, with them dies the race."

"Then were you the last of your people?" I asked.

"Inquire of my father," she replied, and led the way through the massive arch of a great building.

It led into a walled courtyard in the centre of which was a plain cupola of marble with a gate of some pale metal that looked like platinum mixed with gold. This gate stood open. Within it was the statue of a woman beautifully executed in white marble and set in a niche of some black stone. The figure was draped as though to conceal the shape, and the face was stern and majestic rather than beautiful. The eyes of the statue were cunningly made of some enamel which gave them a strange and lifelike appearance. They stared upwards as though looking away from the earth and its concerns. The arms were outstretched. In the right hand was a cup of black marble, in the left a similar cup of white marble. From each of these cups trickled a thin stream of sparkling water, which two streams met and mingled at a distance of about three feet beneath the cups. Then they fell into a metal basin which, although it must have been quite a foot thick, was cut right through by their constant impact, and apparently vanished down some pipe beneath. Out of this metal basin Tommy, who gambolled into the place ahead of us, began to drink in a greedy and demonstrative fashion.

"The Life-water?" I said, looking at our guide.

She nodded and asked in her turn:

"What is the statue and what does it signify, Humphrey?"

I hesitated, but Bastin answered:

"Just a rather ugly woman who hid up her figure because it was bad. Probably she was a relation of the artist who wished to have her likeness done and sat for nothing."

"The goddess of Health," suggested Bickley. "Her

proportions are perfect; a robust, a thoroughly normal woman."

"Now, Humphrey," said Yva.

I stared at the work and had not an idea. Then it flashed on me with such suddenness and certainty that I am convinced the answer to the riddle was passed to me from her and did not originate in my own mind.

"It seems quite easy," I said in a superior tone. "The figure symbolises Life and is draped because we only see the face of Life, the rest is hidden. The arms are bare because Life is real and active. One cup is black and one is white because Life brings both good and evil gifts; that is why the streams mingle, to be lost beneath in the darkness of death. The features are stern and even terrifying rather than lovely, because such is the aspect of Life. The eyes look upward and far away from present things, because the real life is not here."

"Of course one may say anything," said Bastin, "but I don't understand all that."

"Imagination goes a long way," broke in Bickley, who was vexed that he had not thought of this interpretation himself. But Yva said:

"I begin to think that you are quite clever, Humphrey. I wonder whence the truth came to you, for such is the meaning of the figure and the cups. Had I told it to you myself, it could not have been better said," and she glanced at me out of the corners of her eyes. "Now, Strangers, will you drink? Once that gate was guarded, and only at a great price or as a great reward were certain of the Highest Blood given the freedom of this fountain which might touch no common lips. Indeed it was one of the causes of our last war, for all the world which was, desired this water which now is lapped by a stranger's hound."

"I suppose there is nothing medicinal in it?" said Bastin. "Once when I was very thirsty, I made a mistake and drank three tumblers of something of the sort in the dark, thinking that it was Apollinaris, and I don't want to do it again."

"Just the sort of thing you would do," said Bickley. "But, Lady Yva, what are the properties of this water?"

"It is very health-giving," she answered, "and if drunk continually, not less than once each thirty days, it wards off sickness, lessens hunger and postpones death for many, many years. That is why those of the High Blood endured so long and became the rulers of the world, and that, as I have said, is the greatest of the reasons why the peoples who dwelt in the ancient outer countries and never wished to die, made war upon them, to win this secret fountain. Have no fear, O Bastin, for see, I will pledge you in this water."

Then she lifted a strange-looking, shallow, metal cup whereof the handles were formed of twisted serpents, that lay in the basin, filled it from the trickling stream, bowed to us and drank. But as she drank I noted with a thrill of joy that her eyes were fixed on mine as though it were me she pledged and me alone. Again she filled the cup with the sparkling water, for it did sparkle, like that French liqueur in which are mingled little flakes of gold, and handed it to me.

I bowed to her and drank. I suppose the fluid was water, but to me it tasted more like strong champagne, dashed with Château Yquem. It was delicious. More, its effects were distinctly peculiar. Something quick and subtle ran through my veins; something that for a few moments seemed to burn away the obscureness which blurs our thought. I began to understand several problems that had puzzled me, and then lost their explanations in the midst of light, inner light, I mean. Moreover, of a sudden it seemed to me as though a window had been opened in the heart of that Glittering Lady who stood beside me. At least I knew that it was full of wonderful knowledge, wonderful memories and wonderful hopes, and that in the latter two of these I had some part; what part I could not tell. Also I knew that my heart was open to her and that she saw in it something which caused her to marvel and to sigh.

In a few seconds, thirty perhaps, all this was gone. Nothing remained except that I felt extremely strong and well, happier, too, than I had been for years. Mutely I asked her for more of the water, but she shook her head and, taking the cup from me, filled it again and gave it to Bickley, who drank. He flushed, seemed to lose the self-control which was his very strong characteristic, and said in a rather thick voice:

"Curious! but I do not think at this moment there is any operation that has ever been attempted which I could not tackle single-handed and with success."

Then he was silent, and Bastin's turn came. He drank rather noisily, after his fashion, and began:

"My dear young lady, I think the time has come when I should expound to you——" Here he broke off and commenced singing very badly, for his voice was somewhat raucous:

> From Greenland's icy mountains,
> From India's coral strand,
> Where Afric's sunny fountains
> Roll down their golden sand.

Ceasing from melody, he added:

"I determined that I would drink nothing intoxicating while I was on this island that I might be a shining light in a dark place, and now I fear that quite unwittingly I have broken what I look upon as a promise."

Then he, too, grew silent.

"Come," said Yva, "my father, the Lord Oro, awaits you."

We crossed the court of the Water of Life and mounted steps that led to a wide and impressive portico, Tommy frisking ahead of us in a most excited way for a dog of his experience. Evidently the water had produced its effect upon him as well as upon his masters. This portico was in a solemn style of architecture which I cannot describe, because it differed from any other that I know. It was not Egyptian and not Greek, although its solidity reminded me of the former, and the beauty and grace of some of the columns, of the latter. The profuseness and rather grotesque character of the carvings suggested the ruins of Mexico and Yucatan, and the enormous size of the blocks of stone, those of Peru and Baalbec. In short, all the known forms of ancient architecture might have found their inspiration here, and the general effect was tremendous.

"The palace of the King," said Yva, "whereof we approach the great hall."

We entered through mighty metal doors, one of which stood ajar, into a vestibule which from certain indications I gathered had once been a guard, or perhaps an assembly-room. It was about forty feet deep by a hundred wide. Thence she led us through a smaller door into the hall itself. It was a vast place without columns, for there was no roof to support. The walls of marble or limestone were sculptured like those of Egyptian temples, apparently with battle scenes, though of this I am not sure for I did not go near to them. Except for a broad avenue along the middle, up which we walked, the area was filled with marble benches that would, I presume, have accommodated several thousand people. But they were empty—empty, and oh! the loneliness of it all.

Far away at the head of the hall was a dais enclosed, and, as it were, roofed in by a towering structure that mingled grace and majesty to a wonderful degree. It was modelled on the pattern of a huge shell. The base of the shell was the platform; behind were the ribs, and above, the overhanging lip of the shell. On this platform was a throne of silvery metal. It was supported on the arched coils of snakes, whereof the tails formed the back and the heads the arms of the throne.

On this throne, arrayed in gorgeous robes, sat the Lord Oro, his white beard flowing over them, and a jewelled cap upon his head. In front of him was a low table on which lay graven sheets of metal, and among them a large ball of crystal.

There he sat, solemn and silent in the midst of this awful solitude, looking in very truth like a god, as we conceive such a being to appear. Small as he was in that huge expanse of buildings, he seemed yet to dominate it, in a sense to fill the emptiness which was accentuated by his presence. I know that the sight of him filled me with true fear which it had never done in the light of day, not even when he arose from his crystal coffin. Now for the first time I felt as though I were really in the presence of a Being Supernatural. Doubtless the surroundings heightened this impression. What were these mighty edifices in the bowels of the world? When came this wondrous, all-pervading and translucent light, whereof we could see no origin? Whither had vanished those who had reared and inhabited them?

How did it happen that of them all, this man, if he were a man; and this lovely woman at my side, who, if I might trust my senses and instincts, was certainly a woman, alone survived of their departed multitudes?

The thing was crushing. I looked at Bickley for encouragement, but got none, for he only shook his head. Even Bastin, now that the first effects of the Life-water had departed, seemed overwhelmed, and muttered something about the halls of Hades.

Only the little dog Tommy remained quite cheerful. He trotted down the hall, jumped on to the dais and sat himself comfortably at the feet of its occupant.

"I greet you," Oro said in his slow, resonant voice. "Daughter, lead these strangers to me; I would speak with them."

CHAPTER XV

ORO IN HIS HOUSE

WE climbed on to the dais by some marble steps, and sat ourselves down in four curious chairs of metal that were more or less copied from that which served Oro as a throne; at least the arms ended in graven heads of snakes. These chairs were so comfortable that I concluded the seats were fixed on springs, also we noticed that they were beautifully polished.

"I wonder how they keep everything so clean," said Bastin as we mounted the dais. "In this big place it must take a lot of housemaids, though I don't see any. But perhaps there is no dust here."

I shrugged my shoulders while we seated ourselves, the Lady Yva and I on Oro's right, Bickley and Bastin on his left, as he indicated by pointing with his finger.

"What say you of this city?" Oro asked after a while of me.

"We do not know what to say," I replied. "It amazes us. In our world there is nothing like to it."

"Perchance there will be in the future when the nations grow more skilled in the arts of war," said Oro darkly.

"Be pleased, Lord Oro," I went on, "if it is your will, to tell us why the people who built this place chose to live in the bowels of the earth instead of upon its surface."

"They did not choose; it was forced upon them,"

was the answer. "This is a city of refuge that they occupied in time of war, not because they hated the sun. In time of peace and before the Barbarians dared to attack them, they dwelt in the city Pani which signifies Above. You may have noted some of its remaining ruins on the mount and throughout the island. The rest of them are now beneath the sea. But when trouble came and the foe rained fire on them from the air, they retreated to this town, Nyo, which signifies Beneath."

"And then?"

"And then they died. The Water of Life may prolong life, but it cannot make women bear children. That they will only do beneath the blue of heaven, not deep in the belly of the world where Nature never designed that they should dwell. How would the voices of children sound in such halls as these? Tell me, you, Bickley, who are a physician."

"I cannot. I cannot imagine children in such a place, and if born here they would die," said Bickley.

Oro nodded.

"They did die, and if they went above to Pani they were murdered. So soon the habit of birth was lost and the Sons of Wisdom perished one by one. Yes, they who ruled the world and by tens of thousands of years of toil had gathered into their bosoms all the secrets of the world, perished, till only a few, and among them I and this daughter of mine, were left."

"And then?"

"Then, Humphrey, having power so to do, I did what long I had threatened, and unchained the forces that work at the world's heart, and destroyed them who were my enemies and evil, so that they perished by millions, and with them all their works. Afterwards we slept, leaving the others, our subjects who had not the secret of this Sleep, to die, as doubtless they did in the course of Nature or by the hand of the foe. The rest you know."

"Can such a thing happen again?" asked Bickley in a voice that did not hide his disbelief.

"Why do you question me, Bickley, you who believe nothing of what I tell you, and therefore make wrath? Still I will say this, that what I caused to happen I can cause once more—only once, I think—as perchance you shall learn before all is done. Now, since you do not believe, I will tell you no more of our mysteries, no, not whence this light comes nor what are the properties of the Water of Life, both of which you long to know, nor how to preserve the vital spark of Being in the grave of dreamless sleep, like a live jewel in a casket of dead stone, nor aught else. As to these matters, Daughter, I bid you also to be silent, since Bickley mocks at us. Yes, with all this around him, he who saw us rise from the coffins, still mocks at us in his heart. Therefore let him, this little man of a little day, when his few years are done go to the tomb in ignorance, and his companions with him, they who might have been as wise as I am."

Thus Oro spoke in a voice of icy rage, his deep eyes glowing like coals. Hearing him I cursed Bickley in my heart for I was sure that once spoken, his decree was like to that of the Medes and Persians and could not be altered. Bickley, however, was not in the least dismayed. Indeed he argued the point. He told Oro straight out that he would not believe in the impossible until it had been shown to him to be possible, and that the law of Nature never had been and never could be violated. It was no answer, he said, to show him wonders without explaining their cause, since all that he seemed to see might be but mental illusions produced he knew not how.

Oro listened patiently, then answered:

"Good. So be it, they are illusions. I am an illusion; those savages who died upon the rock will tell you so. This fair woman before you is an illusion; Humphrey, I am sure, knows it as you will also before you have done with her. These halls are illusions. Live on in your illusions, O little man of science, who because you see the face of things, think that you know the body and the heart, and can read the soul at work within. You are a worthy child of tens of thousands of your breed who were before you and are now forgotten."

Bickley looked up to answer, then changed his mind and was silent, thinking further argument dangerous, and Oro went on:

"Now I differ from you, Bickley, in this way. I who have more wisdom in my finger-point than you with all the physicians of your world added to you, have in your brains and bodies, yet desire to learn from those who can give me knowledge. I understand from your words to my daughter that you, Bastin, teach a faith that is new to me, and that this faith tells of life eternal for the children of earth. Is it so?"

"It is," said Bastin eagerly. "I will set out——"

Oro cut him short with a wave of the hand.

"Not now in the presence of Bickley who doubtless disbelieves your faith, as he does all else, holding it, with justice or without, to be but another illusion. Yet you shall teach me and on it I will form my own judgment."

"I shall be delighted," said Bastin. Then a doubt struck him, and he added: "But why do you wish to learn? Not that you may make a mock of my religion, is it?"

"I mock at no man's belief, because I think that what men believe is true—for them. I will tell you why I wish to hear of yours, since I never hide the truth. I who am so wise and old, yet must die; though that time may be far away, still I must die, for such is the lot of man born of woman. And I do not desire to die. Therefore I shall rejoice to learn of any faith that promises to the children of earth a life eternal beyond the earth. To-morrow you shall begin to teach me. Now leave me, Strangers, for I have much to do," and he waved his hand towards the table.

We rose and bowed, wondering what he could have to do down in this luminous hole, he who had been for so many thousands of years out of touch with the world. It occurred to me, however, that during this long period he might have got in touch with other worlds, indeed he looked like it.

"Wait," he said, "I have something to tell you. I have been studying this book of writings, or world pictures," and he pointed to my atlas which, as I now observed for the first time, was also lying upon the table. "It interests me much. Your country is small, very small. When I caused it to be raised up I think that it was larger, but since then that seas have flowed in."

Here Bickley groaned aloud.

"This one is much greater," went on Oro, casting a glance at Bickley that must have penetrated him like a searchlight. Then he opened the map of Europe and with his finger indicated Germany and Austria-Hungary. "I know nothing of the peoples of these lands," he added, "but as you belong to one of them and are my guests, I trust that yours may succeed in the war."

"What war?" we asked with one voice.

"Since Bickley is so clever, surely he should know better than an illusion such as I. All I can tell you is that I have learned that there is war between this country and that," and he pointed to Great Britain and to Germany upon the map; "also between others."

"It is quite possible," I said, remembering many things. "But how do you know?"

"If I told you, Humphrey, Bickley would not believe, so I will not tell. Perhaps I saw it in that crystal, as did the necromancers of the early world. Or perhaps the crystal serves some different purpose and I saw it otherwise—with my soul. At least what I say is true."

"Then who will win?" asked Bastin.

"I cannot read the future, Preacher. If I could, should I ask you to expound to me your religion which probably is of no more worth than a score of others I have studied, just because it tells of the future? If I could read the future I should be a god instead of only an earth-lord."

"Your daughter called you a god and you said that you knew we were coming to wake you up, which is reading the future," answered Bastin.

"Every father is a god to his daughter, or should be; also in my day millions named me a god because I saw further and struck harder than they could. As for the rest, it came to me in a vision. Oh! Bickley, if you were wiser than you think you are, you would know that all things to come are born elsewhere and travel hither like the light from stars. Sometimes they come faster before their day into a single mind, and that is what men call prophecy. But this is a gift which cannot be commanded, even by me. Also I did not know that *you* would come. I knew only that we should awaken and by the help of men, for if none had been present at that destined hour we must have died for lack of warmth and sustenance."

"I deny your hypothesis *in toto,*" exclaimed Bickley, but nobody paid any attention to him.

"My father," said Yva, rising and bowing before him with her swan-like grace, "I have noted your commands. But do you permit that I show the temple to these strangers, also something of our past?"

"Yes, yes," he said. "It will save much talk in a savage tongue that is difficult to me. But bring them here no more without my command, save Bastin only. When the sun is four hours high in the upper world, let him come to-morrow to teach me, and afterwards if so I desire. Or if he wills, he can sleep here."

"I think I would rather not," said Bastin hurriedly. "I make no pretence to being particular, but this place does not appeal to me as a bedroom. There are degrees in the pleasures of solitude and, in short, I will not disturb your privacy at night."

Oro waved his hand and we departed down that awful and most dreary hall.

"I hope you will spend a pleasant time here, Bastin," I said, looking back from the doorway at its cold, illuminated vastness.

"I don't expect to," he answered, "but duty is duty, and if I can drag that old sinner back from the pit that awaits him, it will be worth doing. Only I have my doubts about him. To me he seems to bear a strong family resemblance to Beelzebub, and he's a bad companion week in and week out."

We went through the portico, Yva leading us, and

passed the fountain of Life-water, of which she cautioned us to drink no more at present, and to prevent him from doing so, dragged Tommy past it by his collar. Bickley, however, lingered under pretence of making a further examination of the statue. As I had seen him emptying into his pocket the contents of a corked bottle of quinine tabloids which he always carried with him, I guessed very well that his object was to procure a sample of this water for future analysis. Of course I said nothing, and Yva and Bastin took no note of what he was doing.

When we were clear of the palace, of which we had only seen one hall, we walked across an open space made unutterably dreary by the absence of any vegetation or other sign of life, towards a huge building of glorious proportions that was constructed of black stone or marble. It is impossible for me to give any idea of the frightful solemnity of this doomed edifice, for as I think I have said, it alone had a roof, standing there in the midst of that brilliant, unvarying and most unnatural illumination which came from nowhere and yet was everywhere. Thus, when one lifted a foot, there it was between the sole of the boot and the floor, or to express it better, the boot threw no shadow. I think this absence of shadows was perhaps the most terrifying circumstance connected with that universal and pervading light. Through it we walked on to the temple. We passed three courts, pillared all of them, and came to the building which was larger than St. Paul's in London. We entered through huge doors which still stood open, and presently found ourselves beneath the towering dome. There were no windows, why should there be in a place that was full of light? There was no ornamentation, there was nothing except black walls. And yet the general effect was magnificent in its majestic grace.

"In this place," said Yva, and her sweet voice went whispering round the walls and the arching dome, "were buried the Kings of the Sons of Wisdom. They lie beneath, each in his sepulchre. Its entrance is yonder," and she pointed to what seemed to be a chapel on the right. "Would you wish to see them?"

"Somehow I don't care to," said Bastin. "The place is dreary enough as it is without the company of a lot of dead kings."

"I should like to dissect one of them, but I suppose that would not be allowed," said Bickley.

"No," she answered. "I think that the Lord Oro would not wish you to cut up his forefathers."

"When you and he went to sleep, why did you not choose the family vault?" asked Bastin.

"Would you have found us there?" she queried by way of answer. Then, understanding that the invitation was refused by general consent, though personally I should have liked to accept it, and have never ceased regretting that I did not, she moved towards a colossal object which stood beneath the centre of the dome.

On a stepped base, not very different from that in the cave but much larger, sat a figure, draped in a cloak on which was graved a number of stars, doubtless to symbolise the heavens. The fastening of the cloak was shaped like the crescent moon, and the footstool on which rested the figure's feet was fashioned to suggest the orb of the sun. This was of gold or some such metal, the only spot of brightness in all that temple. It was impossible to say whether the figure were male or female, for the cloak falling in long, straight folds hid its outlines. Nor did the head tell us, for the hair also was hidden beneath the mantle and the face might have been that of either man or woman. It was terrible in its solemnity and calm, and its expression was as remote and mystic as that of Buddha, only more stern. Also without doubt it was blind; it was impossible to mistake the sightlessness of those staring orbs. Across the knees lay a naked sword and beneath the cloak the arms were hidden. In its complete simplicity the thing was marvellous.

On either side upon the pedestal knelt a figure of the size of life. One was an old and withered man with death stamped upon his face; the other was a beautiful, naked woman, her hands clasped in the attitude of prayer and with vague terror written on her vivid features.

Such was this glorious group of which the meaning could not be mistaken. It was Fate throned upon the sun, wearing the constellations as his garment, armed with the sword of Destiny and worshipped by Life and Death. This interpretation I set out to the others.

Yva knelt before the statue for a little while, bowing her head in prayer, and really I felt inclined to follow her example, though in the end I compromised, as did Bickley, by taking off my hat, which, like the others, I still wore from force of habit, though in this place none were needed. Only Bastin remained covered.

"Behold the god of my people," said Yva. "Have you no reverence for it, O Bastin?"

"Not much," he answered, "except as a work of art. You see I worship Fate's Master. I might add that *your* god doesn't seem to have done much for you, Lady Yva, as out of all your greatness there's nothing left but two people and a lot of old walls and caves."

At first she was inclined to be angry, for I saw her start. Then her mood changed, and she said with a sigh:

"Fate's Master! Where does He dwell?"

"Here amongst other places," said Bastin. "I'll soon explain that to you."

"I thank you," she replied gravely. "But why have you not explained it to Bickley?" Then waving her hand to show that she wished for no answer, she went on:

"Friends, would you wish to learn something of the history of my people?"

"Very much," said the irrepressible Bastin, "but I would rather the lecture took place in the open air."

"That is not possible," she answered. "It must be here and now, or not at all. Come, stand by me. Be silent and do not move. I am about to set loose forces that are dangerous if disturbed."

CHAPTER XVI

VISIONS OF THE PAST

SHE led us to the back of the statue and pointed to each of us where we should remain. Then she took her place at right angles to us, as a showman might do, and for a while stood immovable. Watching her face, once more I saw it, and indeed all her body, informed with that strange air of power, and noted that her eyes flashed and that her hair grew even more brilliant than was common, as though some abnormal strength were flowing through it and her. Presently she spoke, saying:

"I shall show you first our people in the day of their glory. Look in front of you."

We looked and by degrees the vast space of the apse before us became alive with forms. At first these were vague and shadowy, not to be separated or distinguished. Then they became so real that until he was reproved by a kick, Tommy growled at them and threatened to break out into one of his peals of barking.

A wonderful scene appeared. There was a palace of white marble and in front of it a great courtyard upon which the sun beat vividly. At the foot of the steps of the palace, beneath a silken awning, sat a king enthroned, a crown upon his head and wearing glorious robes. In his hand was a jewelled sceptre. He was a noble-looking man of middle age and about him were gathered the glittering officers of his court. Fair women fanned him and to right and left, but a little behind, sat other fair and jewelled women who, I suppose, were his wives or daughters.

"One of the Kings of the Children of Wisdom new-crowned, receives the homage of the world," said Yva.

As she spoke there appeared, walking in front of the throne one by one, other kings, for all were crowned and bore sceptres. At the foot of the throne each of them kneeled and kissed the foot of him who sat thereon, as he did so laying down his sceptre which at a sign he lifted again and passed away. Of these kings there must have been quite fifty, men of all colours and of various types, white men, black men, yellow men, red men.

Then came their ministers bearing gifts, apparently of gold and jewels, which were piled on trays in front of the throne. I remember noting an incident. An old fellow with a lame leg stumbled and upset his tray, so that the contents rolled hither and thither. His attempts to recover them were ludicrous and caused the monarch on the throne to relax from his dignity and smile. I mention this to show that what we witnessed was no set scene but apparently a living piece of the past. Had it been so the absurdity of the bedizened old man tumbling down in the midst of the gorgeous pageant would certainly have been omitted.

No, it must be life, real life, something that had happened, and the same may be said of what followed. For instance, there was what we call a review. Infantry marched, some of them armed with swords and spears, though these I took to be an ornamental bodyguard, and others with tubes like savage blowpipes of which I could not guess the use. There were no cannon, but carriages came by loaded with bags that had spouts to them. Probably these were charged with poisonous gases. There were some cavalry also, mounted on a different stamp of horse from ours, thicker set and nearer the ground, but with arched necks and fiery eyes and, I should say, very strong. These again, I take it, were ornamental. Then came other men upon a long machine, slung in pairs in armoured sacks, out of which only their heads and arms projected. This machine, which resembled an elongated bicycle, went by at a tremendous rate, though whence its motive power came did not appear. It carried twenty pairs of men, each of whom held in his hand some small but doubtless deadly weapon, that in appearance resembled an orange. Other similar machines which followed carried from forty to a hundred pairs of men.

The marvel of the piece, however, were the aircraft. These came by in great numbers. Sometimes they flew in flocks like wild geese, sometimes singly, sometimes in line and sometimes in ordered squadrons, with outpost and officer ships and an exact distance kept between craft and craft. None of them seemed to be very large or to carry more than four or five men, but they were extraordinarily swift and as agile as swallows. Moreover they flew as birds do by beating their wings, but again we could not guess whence came their motive power.

The review vanished, and next appeared a scene of festivity in a huge, illuminated hall. The Great King sat upon a dais and behind him was that statue of Fate, or one very similar to it, beneath which we stood. Below him in the hall were the feasters seated at long tables, clad in the various costumes of their countries. He rose and, turning, knelt before the statue of Fate. Indeed he prostrated himself thrice in prayer. Then taking his seat again, he lifted a cup of wine and pledged that vast company. They drank back to him and prostrated themselves before him as he had done before the image of Fate. Only I noted that certain men clad in sacerdotal garments not at all unlike those which are worn in the Greek Church to-day, remained standing.

Now all this exhibition of terrestrial pomp faded. The next scene was simple, that of the death-bed of this same king—we knew him by his wizened features. There he lay, terribly old and dying. Physicians, women, courtiers, all were there watching the end. The tableau vanished and in place of it appeared that of the youthful successor amidst cheering crowds, with joy breaking through the clouds of simulated grief upon his face. It vanished also.

"Thus did great king succeed great king for ages upon ages," said Yva. "There were eighty of them and the average of their reigns was 700 years. They ruled the earth as it was in those days. They gathered up learning, they wielded power, their wealth was boundless. They nurtured the arts, they discovered secrets. They had intercourse with the stars; they were as gods. But like the gods they grew jealous. They and their councillors became a race apart who alone had the secret of long life. The rest of the world and the commonplace people about them suffered and died. They of the Household of Wisdom lived on in pomp for generations till the earth was mad with envy of them.

"Fewer and fewer grew the divine race of the Sons of Wisdom since children are not given to the aged and to those of an ancient, outworn blood. Then the World said:

"'They are great but they are not many; let us make an end of them by numbers and take their place and power and drink of their Life-water, that they will not give to us. If myriads of us perish by their arts, what does it matter, since we are countless?' So the World made war upon the Sons of Wisdom. See!"

Again a picture formed. The sky was full of aircraft which rained down fire like flashes of lightning upon cities beneath. From these cities leapt up other fires that destroyed the swift-travelling things above, so that they fell in numbers like gnats burned by a lamp. Still more and more of them came till the cities crumbled away and the flashes that darted from them ceased to rush upwards. The Sons of Wisdom were driven from the face of the earth.

Again the scene changed. Now it showed this subterranean hall in which we stood. There was pomp here, yet it was but a shadow of that which had been in the earlier days upon the face of the earth. Courtiers moved about the palace and there were people in the radiant streets and the houses, for most of them were occupied, but rarely did the vision show children coming through their gates.

Of a sudden this scene shifted. Now we saw that same hall in which we had visited Oro not an hour before. There he sat, yes, Oro himself, upon the dais beneath the overhanging marble shell. Round him were some ancient councillors. In the body of the hall on either side of the dais were men in military array, guards without doubt though their only weapon was a black rod not unlike a ruler, if indeed it were a weapon and not a badge of office.

Yva, whose face had suddenly grown strange and fixed, began to detail to us what was passing in this scene, in a curious monotone such as a person might use who was repeating something learned by heart. This was the substance of what she said:

"The case of the Sons of Wisdom is desperate. But few of them are left. Like other men they need food which is hard to come by, since the foe holds the upper earth and that which their doctors can make here in the Shades does not satisfy them, even though they drink the Life-water. They die and die. There comes an embassy from the High King of the confederated Nations to talk of terms of peace. See, it enters."

As she spoke, up the hall advanced the embassy. At the head of it walked a young man, tall, dark, handsome and commanding, whose aspect seemed in some way to be familiar to me. He was richly clothed in a purple cloak and wore upon his head a golden circlet that suggested royal rank. Those who followed him were mostly old men who had the astute faces of diplomatists, but a few seemed to be generals. Yva continued in her monotonous voice:

"Comes the son of the King of the confederated Nations, the Prince who will be king. He bows before the Lord Oro. He says 'Great and Ancient Monarch of the divine blood, Heaven-born One, your strait, and that of those who remain to you, is sore. Yet on behalf of the Nations I am sent to offer terms of peace, but this I may only do in the presence of your child who is your heiress and the Queen-to-be of the Sons of Wisdom.'"

Here, in the picture, Oro waved his hand and from behind the marble shell appeared Yva herself, gloriously apparelled, wearing royal ornaments and with her train held by waiting ladies. She bowed to the Prince and his company and they bowed back to her. More, we saw a glance of recognition pass between her and the Prince.

Now the real Yva by our side pointed to the shadow

Yva of the vision or the picture, whichever it might be called, a strange thing to see her do, and went on:

"The daughter of the Lord Oro comes. The Prince of the Nations salutes her. He says that the great war has endured for hundreds of years between the Children of Wisdom fighting for absolute rule and the common people of the earth fighting for liberty. In that war many millions of the Sons of the Nations had perished, brought to their death by fearful arts, by wizardries and by plagues sown among them by the Sons of Wisdom. Yet they were winning, for the glorious cities of the Sons of Wisdom were destroyed and those who remained of them were driven to dwell in the caves of the earth where with all their strength and magic they could not increase, but faded like flowers in the dark.

"The Lord Oro asks what are the terms of peace proposed by the Nations. The Prince answers that they are these: That the Sons of Wisdom shall teach all their wisdom to the wise men among the Nations. That they shall give them to drink of the Life-water, so that their length of days also may be increased. That they shall cease to destroy them by sickness and their mastery of the forces which are hid in the womb of the world. If they will do these things, then the Nations on their part will cease from war, will rebuild the cities they have destroyed by means of their flying ships that rain down death, and will agree that the Lord Oro and his seed shall rule them for ever as the King of kings.

"The Lord Oro asks if that be all. The Prince answers that it is not all. He says that when he dwelt a hostage at the court of the Sons of Wisdom he and the divine Lady, the daughter of the Lord Oro, and his only living child, learned to love each other. He demands, and the Nations demand, that she shall be given to him to wife, that in a day to come he may rule with her and their children after them.

"See!" went on Yva in her chanting, dreamy voice, "the Lord Oro asks his daughter if this be true. She says," here the real Yva at my side turned and looked me straight in the eyes, "that it is true; that she loves the Prince of the Nations and that if she lives a million years she will wed no other man, since she who is her father's slave in all else is still the mistress of herself, as has ever been the right of her royal mothers.

"See again! The Lord Oro, the divine King, the Ancient, grows wroth. He says that it is enough and more than enough that the Barbarians should ask to eat of the bread of hidden learning and to drink of the Life-water of the Sons of Wisdom, gifts that were given to them of old by Heaven whence they sprang in the beginning. But that one of them, however highly placed, should dare to ask to mix his blood with that of the divine Lady, the Heiress, the Queen of the Earth to be, and claim to share her imperial throne that had been held by her pure race from age to age, was an insult that could only be purged by death. Sooner would he give his daughter in marriage to an ape than to a child of the Barbarians who had worked on them so many woes and striven to break the golden fetters of their rule.

"Look again!" continued Yva. "The Lord Oro, the divine, grows angrier still" (which in truth he did, for never did I see such dreadful rage as that which the picture revealed in him). "He warns, he threatens. He says that hitherto out of gentle love and pity he has held his hand; that he has strength at his command which will slay them, not by millions in slow war, but by tens of millions at one blow; that will blot them and their peoples from the face of earth and that will cause the deep seas to roll where now their pleasant lands are fruitful in the sun. They shrink before his fury; behold, their knees tremble because they know that he has this power. He mocks them, does the Lord Oro. He asks for their submission here and now, and that in the name of the Nations they should take the great oath which may not be broken, swearing to cease from war upon the Sons of Wisdom and to obey them in all things to the ends of the earth. Some of the ambassadors would yield. They look about them like wild things that are trapped. But madness takes the Prince. He cries that the oath of an ape is of no account, but that he will tear up the Children of Wisdom as an ape tears leaves, and afterwards take the divine Lady to be his wife.

"Look on the Lord Oro!" continued the living Yva, "his wrath leaves him. He grows cold and smiles. His daughter throws herself upon her knees and pleads with him. He thrusts her away. She would spring to the side of the Prince; he commands his councillors to hold her. She cries to the Prince that she loves him and him only, and that in a day to come him she will wed and no other. He thanks her, saying that as it is with her, so it is with him, and that because of his love he fears nothing. She swoons. The Lord Oro motions with his hand to the guard. They lift their death-rods. Fire leaps from them. The Prince and his companions, all save those who were afraid and would have sworn the oath, twist and writhe. They turn black; they die. The Lord Oro commands those who are left to enter their flying ships and bear to the Nations of the Earth tidings of what befalls those who dare to defy and insult him; to warn them also to eat and drink and be merry while they may, since for their wickedness they are about to perish."

The scene faded and there followed another which really I cannot describe. It represented some vast underground place and what appeared to be a huge mountain of iron clothed in light, literally a thing like an alp, rocking and spinning down a declivity, which farther on separated into two branches because of a huge razor-edge precipice that rose between. There in the middle of this vast space with the dazzling mountain whirling towards him, stood Oro encased in some transparent armour, as though to keep off heat, and with him his daughter who under his direction was handling something in the rock behind her. Then there was a blinding flash and everything vanished. All of this picture passed so swiftly that we could not grasp its details; only a general impression remained.

"The Lord Oro, using the strength that is in the world whereof he alone has the secret, changes the world's balance causing that which was land to become sea and that which was sea to become land," said Yva in her chanting, unnatural voice.

Another scene of stupendous and changing awfulness. Countries were sinking, cities crashing down, volcanoes were spouting fire; the end of the earth seemed to be at hand. We could see human beings running to and fro in thousands like ants. Then in huge waves hundreds and hundreds of feet high, the ocean flowed in and all was troubled, yeasty sea.

"Oro carries out his threat to destroy the Nations who had rebelled against him," said Yva. "Much of the world sinks beneath the waves, but in place of it other lands arise above the waves, to be inhabited by the seed of those who remain living in those portions of the Earth that the deluge spared."

This horrible vision passed and was succeeded by one more, that of Oro standing in the sepulchre of the cave by the side of the crystal coffin which contained what appeared to be the body of his daughter. He gazed at her, then drank some potion and laid himself down in the companion coffin, that in which we had found him.

All vanished away and Yva, appearing to wake from some kind of a trance, smiled, and in her natural voice asked if we had seen enough.

"Quite," I answered in a tone that caused her to say:

"I wonder what you have seen, Humphrey. Myself I do not know, since it is through me that you see at all and when you see I am in you who see."

"Indeed," I replied. "Well, I will tell you about it later."

"Thank you so much," exclaimed Bastin, recovering suddenly from his amazement. "I have heard a great deal of these moving-picture shows which are becoming so popular, but have always avoided attending them because their influence on the young is supposed to be doubtful, and a priest must set a good example to his congregation. Now I see that they can have a distinct educational value, even if it is presented in the form of romance."

"How is it done?" asked Bickley, almost fiercely.

"I do not altogether know," she answered. "This I do know, however, that everything which has happened on this world can be seen from moment to moment at some point in the depths of space, for thither the sun's light takes it. There, too, it can be caught and thence in an instant returned to earth again, to be reflected in the mirror of the present by those who know how that mirror should be held. Ask me no more; one so wise as you, O Bickley, can solve such problems for himself."

"If you don't mind, Lady Yva," said Bastin, "I think I should like to get out of this place, interesting as it is. I have food to cook up above and lots of things to attend to, especially as I understand I am to come back here to-morrow. Would you mind showing me the way to that lift or moving staircase?"

"Come," she said, smiling.

So we went past the image of Fate, out of the temple, down the vast and lonely streets so unnaturally illuminated, to the place where we had first found ourselves on arrival in the depths. There we stood.

A moment later and we were whirling up as we had whirled down. I suppose that Yva came with us though I never saw her do so, and the odd thing was that when we arrived in the sepulchre, she seemed already to be standing there waiting to direct us.

"Really," remarked Bastin, "this is exactly like Maskelyne and Cook. Did you ever see their performance, Bickley? If so, it must have given you lots to explain for quite a long while."

"Jugglery never appealed to me, whether in London or in Orofena," replied Bickley in a sour voice as he extracted from his pocket an end of candle to which he set light.

"What is jugglery?" asked Bastin, and they departed arguing, leaving me alone with Yva in the sepulchre.

"What have I seen?" I asked her.

"I do not know, Humphrey. Everyone sees different things, but perhaps something of the truth."

"I hope not, Yva, for amongst other things I seemed to see you swear yourself to a man for ever."

"Yes, and this I did. What of it?"

"Only that it might be hard for another man."

"Yes, for another man it might be hard. You were once married, were you not, Humphrey, to a wife who died?"

"Yes, I was married."

"And did you not swear to that wife that you would never look in love upon another woman?"

"I did," I answered in a shamed voice. "But how do you know? I never told you so."

"Oh! I know you and therefore guessed."

"Well, what of it, Yva?"

"Nothing, except that you must find your wife before you love again, and before I love again I must find him whom I wish to be my husband."

"How can that happen," I asked, "when both are dead?"

"How did all that you have seen to-day in Nyo happen?" she replied, laughing softly. "Perhaps you are very blind, Humphrey, or perhaps we both are blind. If so, mayhap light will come to us. Meanwhile do not be sad. To-morrow I will meet you and you shall teach me—your English tougue, Humphrey, and other things."

"Then let it be in the sunlight, Yva. I do not love those darksome halls of Nyo that glow like something dead."

"It is fitting, for are they not dead?" she answered, with a little laugh. "So be it. Bastin shall teach my father down below, since sun and shade are the same to him who only thinks of his religion, and you shall teach me up above."

"I am not so certain about Bastin and of what he thinks," I said doubtfully. "Also will the Lord Oro permit you to come?"

"Yes, for in such matters I rule myself. Also," she added meaningly, "he remembers my oath that I will wed no man—save one who is dead. Now farewell a while and bid Bastin be here when the sun is three hours high, not before or after."

Then I left her.

CHAPTER XVII

YVA EXPLAINS

WHEN I reached the rock I was pleased to find Marama and about twenty of his people engaged in erecting the house that we had ordered them to build for our accommodation. Indeed, it was nearly finished, since house-building in Orofena is a simple business. The framework of poles let into palm trunks, since they could not be driven into the rock, had been put together on the further shore and towed over bodily by canoes. The overhanging rock formed one side of the house; the ends were of palm leaves tied to the poles, and the roof was of the same material. The other side was left open for the present, which in that equable and balmy clime was no disadvantage. The whole edifice was about thirty feet long by fifteen deep and divided into two portions, one for sleeping and one for living, by a palm leaf partition. Really, it was quite a comfortable abode, cool and rainproof, especially after Bastin had built his hut in which to cook.

Marama and his people were very humble in their demeanour and implored us to visit them on the main island. I answered that perhaps we would later on, as we wished to procure certain things from the wreck. Also, he requested Bastin to continue his ministrations as the latter greatly desired to do. But to this proposal I would not allow him to give any direct answer at the moment. Indeed, I dared not do so until I was sure of Oro's approval.

Towards evening they departed in their canoes, leaving behind them the usual ample store of provisions.

We cooked our meal as usual, only to discover that what Yva had said about the Life-water was quite true, since we had but little appetite for solid food, though this returned upon the following day. The same thing happened upon every occasion after drinking of that water which certainly was a most invigorating fluid. Never for years had any of us felt so well as it caused us to do.

So we lit our pipes and talked about our experiences, though of these, indeed, we scarcely knew what to say. Bastin accepted them as something out of the common, of course, but as facts which admitted of no discussion. After all, he said, the Old Testament told much the same story of people called the Sons of God who lived very long lives and ran after the daughters of men whom they should have left alone, and thus became the progenitors of a remarkable race. Of this race, he presumed that Oro and his daughter were survivors, especially as they spoke of their family as "Heaven born." How they came to survive was more than he could understand and really scarcely worth bothering over, since there they were.

It was the same about the Deluge, continued Bastin, although naturally Oro spoke falsely, or, at any rate, grossly exaggerated, when he declared that he had caused this catastrophe, unless indeed he was talking about a totally different deluge, though even then *he* could not have brought it about. It was curious, however, that the people drowned were said to have been wicked, and Oro had the same opinion about those whom he claimed to have drowned, though for the matter of that, he could not conceive anyone more wicked than Oro himself. On his own showing he was a most revengeful person and one who declined to agree to a quite suitable alliance, apparently desired by both parties, merely because it offended his family pride. No, on reflection he might be unjust to Oro in this particular, since *he* never told that story; it was only shown in some pictures which very likely were just made up to astonish us. Meanwhile, it was his business to preach to this old sinner down in that hole, and he confessed honestly that he did not like the job. Still, it must be done, so with our leave he would go apart and seek inspiration, which at present seemed to be quite lacking.

Thus declaimed Bastin and departed.

"Don't you tell your opinion about the Deluge or he may cause another just to show that you are wrong," called Bickley after him.

"I can't help that," answered Bastin. "Certainly I shall not hide the truth to save Oro's feelings, if he has got any. If he revenges himself upon us in any way, we must just put up with it like other martyrs."

"I haven't the slightest ambition to be a martyr," said Bickley.

"No," shouted Bastin from a little distance, "I am quite aware of that, as you have often said so before. Therefore, if you become one, I am sorry to say that I do not see how you can expect any benefit. You would only be like a man who puts a sovereign into the offertory bag in mistake for a shilling. The extra nineteen shillings will do him no good at all, since in his heart he regrets the error and wishes that he could have them back."

Then he departed, leaving me laughing. But Bickley did not laugh.

"Arbuthnot," he said, "I have come to the conclusion that I have gone quite mad. I beg you if I should show signs of homicidal mania, which I feel developing in me where Bastin is concerned, or of other abnormal violence, that you will take whatever steps you consider necessary, even to putting me out of the way if that is imperative."

"What do you mean?" I asked. "You seem sane enough."

"Sane, when I believe that I have seen and experienced a great number of things which I know it to be quite impossible that I should have seen or experienced. The only explanation is that I am suffering from delusions."

"Then is Bastin suffering from delusions, too?"

"Certainly, but that is nothing new in his case."

"I don't agree with you, Bickley—about Bastin, I mean. I am by no means certain that he is not the wisest of the three of us. He has a faith and he sticks to it, as millions have done before him, and that is better than making spiritual experiments, as I am sorry to say I do, or rejecting things because one cannot understand them, as you do, which is only a form of intellectual vanity."

"I won't argue the matter, Arbuthnot; it is of no use. I repeat that I am mad, and Bastin is mad."

"How about me? I also saw and experienced these things. Am I mad, too?"

"You ought to be, Arbuthnot. If it isn't enough to drive a man mad when he sees himself exactly reproduced in an utterly impossible moving-picture show exhibited by an utterly impossible young woman in an utterly impossible underground city, then I don't know what is."

"What do you mean?" I asked, starting.

"Mean? Well, if you didn't notice it, there's hope for you."

"Notice what?"

"All that envoy scene. There, as I thought, appeared Yva. Do you admit that?"

"Of course; there could be no mistake on that point."

"Very well. Then according to my version there came a man, still young, dressed in outlandish clothes, who made propositions of peace and wanted to marry Yva, who wanted to marry him. Is that right?"

"Absolutely."

"Well, and didn't you recognise the man?"

"No; I only noticed that he was a fine-looking fellow whose appearance reminded me of someone."

"I suppose it must be true," mused Bickley, "that we do not know ourselves."

"So the old Greek thought, since he urged that this should be our special study. 'Know thyself,' you remember."

"I meant physically, not intellectually. Arbuthnot, do you mean to tell me that you did not recognise your own double in that man? Shave off your beard and put on his clothes and no one could distinguish you apart."

I sprang up, dropping my pipe.

"Now you mention it," I said slowly, "I suppose there was a resemblance. I didn't look at him very much; I was studying the simulacrum of Yva. Also, you know it is some time since—I mean, there are no pier-glasses in Orofena."

"The man was *you,*" went on Bickley with conviction. "If I were superstitious I should think it a queer sort of omen. But as I am not, I know that I must be mad."

"Why? After all, an ancient man and a modern man might resemble each other."

"There are degrees in resemblance," said Bickley with one of his contemptuous snorts. "It won't do, Humphrey, my boy," he added. "I can only think of one possible explanation—outside of the obvious one of madness."

"What is that?"

"The Glittering Lady produced what Bastin called that cinematograph show in some way or other, did she not? She said that in order to do this she loosed some hidden forces. I suggest that she did nothing of the sort."

"Then whence did the pictures come and why?"

"From her own brain, in order to impress us with a cock-and-bull, fairy-book story. If this were so she would quite naturally fill the rôle of the lover of the piece with the last man who had happened to impress her. Hence the resemblance."

"You presuppose a great deal, Bickley, including supernatural cunning and unexampled hypnotic influence. I don't know, first, why she should be so anxious to add another impression to the many we have received in this place; and, secondly, if she was, how she managed to mesmerise three average but totally different men into seeing the same things. *My* explanation is that you were deceived as to the likeness, which, mind you, I did not recognise; nor, apparently, did Bastin."

"Bastin never recognises anything. But if you are in doubt, ask Yva herself. She ought to know. Now I'm off to try to analyse that confounded Life-water, which I suspect is of the ordinary spring variety, lightened up with natural carbonic acid gas and possibly not uninfluenced by radium. The trouble is that here I can only apply some very elementary tests."

So he went also, in an opposite direction to Bastin, and I was left alone with Tommy, who annoyed me much by attempting continually to wander off into the cave, whence I must recall him. I suppose that my experiences of the day, reviewed beneath the sweet influences of the wonderful tropical night, affected me. At any rate, that mystical side of my nature, to which I think I alluded at the beginning of this record, sprang into active and, in a sense, unholy life. The normal vanished, the abnormal took possession, and that is unholy to most of us creatures of habit and tradition, at any rate, if we are British. I lost my footing on the world; my spirit began to wander in strange places; of course, always supposing that we have a spirit, which Bickley would deny.

I gave up reason; I surrendered myself to unreason; it is a not unpleasant process, occasionally. Supposing now that all we see and accept is but the merest fragment of the truth, or perhaps only a refraction thereof? Supposing that we do live again and again, and that our animating principle, whatever it might be, does inhabit various bodies, which, naturally enough, it would shape to its own taste and likeness? Would that taste and likeness vary so very much over, let us say, a million years or so, which, after all, is but an hour, or a minute, in the æons of Eternity?

On this hypothesis, which is so wild that one begins to suspect that it may be true, was it impossible that I and that murdered man of the far past were in fact identical? If the woman were the same, preserved across the gulf in some unknown fashion, why should not her lover be the same? What did I say—her lover? Was I her lover? No, I was the lover of one who had died—my lost wife. Well, if I had died and lived again, why should not—why should not that Sleeper—have lived again during her long sleep? Through all those years the spirit must have had some home, and, if so, in what shapes did it live? There were points, similarities, which rushed in upon me—oh! it was ridiculous. Bickley was right. We were all mad!

There was another thing. Oro had declared that we were at war with Germany. If this were so, how could he know it? Such knowledge would presume powers of telepathy or vision beyond those given to man. I could not believe that he possessed these; as Bickley said, it would be past experience. Yet it was most strange that he who was uninformed as to our national history and dangers, should have hit upon a country with which we might well have been plunged into sudden struggle. Here again I was bewildered and overcome. My brain rocked. I would seek sleep, and in it escape, or at any rate rest from all these mysteries.

On the following morning we despatched Bastin to keep his rendezvous in the sepulchre at the proper time. Had we not done so I felt sure that he would have forgotten it, for on this occasion he was for once an unwilling missioner. He tried to persuade one of us to come with him—even Bickley would have been welcome; but we both declared that we could not dream of interfering in such a professional matter; also that our presence was forbidden, and would certainly distract the attention of his pupil.

"What you mean," said the gloomy Bastin, "is that

you intend to enjoy yourselves up here in the female companionship of the Glittering Lady whilst I sit thousands of feet underground attempting to lighten the darkness of a violent old sinner whom I suspect of being in league with Satan."

"With whom you should be proud to break a lance," said Bickley.

"So I am, in the daylight. For instance, when he uses *your* mouth to advance his arguments. Bickley, but this is another matter. However, if I do not appear again you will know that I died in a good cause, and, I hope, try to recover my remains and give them decent burial. Also, you might inform the Bishop of how I came to my end, this is, if you ever get an opportunity, which is more than doubtful."

"Hurry up, Bastin, hurry up!" said the unfeeling Bickley, "or you will be late for your appointment and put your would-be neophyte into a bad temper."

Then Bastin went, carrying under his arm a large Bible printed in the language of the South Sea Islands.

A little while later Yva appeared, arrayed in her wondrous robes which, being a man, it is quite impossible for me to describe. She saw us looking at these, and, after greeting us both, also Tommy, who was enraptured at her coming, asked us how the ladies of our country attired themselves.

We tried to explain, with no striking success.

"You are as stupid about such matters as were the men of the Old World," she said, shaking her head and laughing. "I thought that you had with you pictures of ladies you have known which would show me."

Now, in fact, I had in a pocket-book a photograph of my wife in evening-dress, also a miniature of her head and bust painted on ivory, a beautiful piece of work done by a master hand, which I always wore. These, after a moment's hesitation, I produced and showed to her, Bickley having gone away for a little while to see about something connected with his attempted analysis of the Life-water. She examined them with great eagerness, and as she did so I noted that her face grew tender and troubled.

"This was your wife," she said as one who states what she knows to be a fact. I nodded, and she went on:

"She was sweet and beautiful as a flower, but not so tall as I am, I think."

"No," I answered, "she lacked height; given that she would have been a lovely woman."

"I am glad you think that women should be tall," she said, glancing at her shadow. "The eyes were such as mine, were they not—in colour, I mean?"

"Yes, very like yours, only yours are larger."

"That is a beautiful way of wearing the hair. Would you be angry if I tried it? I weary of this old fashion."

"Why should I be angry?" I asked.

At this moment Bickley reappeared and she began to talk of the details of the dress, saying that it showed more of the neck than had been the custom among the women of her people, but was very pretty.

"That is because we are still barbarians," said Bickley; "at least, our women are, and therefore rely upon primitive methods of attraction, like the savages yonder."

She smiled, and, after a last, long glance, gave me back the photograph and the miniature, saying as she delivered the latter:

"I rejoice to see that you are faithful, Humphrey, and wear this picture on your heart, as well as in it."

"Then you must be a very remarkable woman," said Bickley. "Never before did I hear one of your sex rejoice because a man was faithful to somebody else."

"Has Bickley been disappointed in his love-heart, that he is so angry to us women?" asked Yva innocently of me. Then, without waiting for an answer, she inquired of him whether he had been successful in his analysis of the Life-water.

"How do you know what I was doing with the Life-water? Did Bastin tell you?" exclaimed Bickley.

"Bastin told me nothing, except that he was afraid of the descent to Nyo; that he hated Nyo when he reached it, as indeed I do, and that he thought that my father, the Lord Oro, was a devil or evil spirit from some Under-world which he called hell."

"Bastin has an open heart and an open mouth," said Bickley, "for which I respect him. Follow his example if you will, Lady Yva, and tell us who and what is the Lord Oro, and who and what are you."

"Have we not done so already? If not, I will repeat. The Lord Oro and I are two who have lived on from the old time when the world was different, and yet, I think, the same. He is a man and not a god, and I am a woman. His powers are gréat because of his knowledge, which he has gathered from his forefathers and in a life of a thousand years before he went to sleep. He can do things you cannot do. Thus, he can pass through space and take others with him, and return again. He can learn what is happening in far-off parts of the world, as he did when he told you of the war in which your country is concerned. He has terrible powers; for instance, he can kill, as he killed those savages. Also, he knows the secrets of the earth, and, if it pleases him, can change its turning so that earthquakes happen and sea becomes land, and land sea, and the places that were hot grow cold, and those that were cold grow hot."

"All of which things have happened many time in the history of the globe," said Bickley, "without the help of the Lord Oro."

"Others had knowledge before my father, and others doubtless will have knowledge after him. Even I, Yva, have some knowledge, and knowledge is strength."

"Yes," I interposed, "but such powers as you attribute to your father are not given to man."

"You mean to man as you know him, man like Bickley, who thinks that he has learned everything that was ever learned. But it is not so. Hundreds of thousands of years ago men knew more than it seems they do to-day, ten times more, as they lived ten times longer, or so you tell me."

"Men?" I said.

"Yes, men, not gods or spirits, as the uninstructed nations supposed them to be. My father is a man subject to the hopes and terrors of man. He desires power which is ambition, and when the world refused his rule, he destroyed that part of it which rebelled, which is revenge. Moreover, above all things he dreads death, which is fear. That is why he suspended life in himself and me for two hundred and fifty thousand years, as his knowledge gave him strength to do, because death was near and he thought that sleep was better than death."

"Why should he dread to die," asked Bickley, "seeing that sleep and death are the same?"

"Because his knowledge tells him that Sleep and Death are *not* the same, as you, in your foolishness, believe, for there Bastin is wiser than you. Because for all his wisdom he remains ignorant of what happens to man when the Light of Life is blown out by the breath of Fate. That is why he fears to die and why he talks with Bastin the Preacher, who says he has the secret of the future."

"And do you fear to die?" I asked.

"No, Humphrey," she answered gently. "Because I think that there is no death, and, having done no wrong, I dread no evil. I had dreams while I was asleep, O Humphrey, and it seemed to me that——"

Here she ceased and glanced at where she knew the miniature was hanging upon my breast.

"Now," she continued, after a little pause, "tell me of your world, of its history, of its languages, of what happens there, for I long to know."

So then and there, assisted by Bickley, I began the education of the Lady Yva. I do not suppose that there was ever a more apt pupil in the whole earth. To begin with, she was better acquainted with every subject on which I touched than I was myself; all she lacked was information as to its modern aspect. Her knowledge ended two hundred and fifty thousand years ago, at which date, however, it would seem that civilisation had already touched a higher water-mark than it has ever since attained. Thus, this vanished people understood astronomy, natural magnetism, the force of gravity, steam, also electricity to some subtle use of which, I gathered, the lighting of their underground city was to be attributed. They had mastered architecture and the arts, as their buildings and statues showed; they could fly through the air better than we have learned to do within the last few years.

More, they, or some of them, had learned the use of the Fourth Dimension, that is their most instructed individuals, could move *through* opposing things, as well as over them, up into them and across them. This power these possessed in a two-fold form. I mean, that they could either disintegrate their bodies at one spot and cause them to integrate again at another, or they could project what the old Egyptians called the Ka or Double, and modern Theosophists name the Astral Shape, to any distance. Moreover, this Double, or Astral Shape, while itself invisible, still, so to speak, had the use of its senses. It could see, it could hear, and it could remember, and, on returning to the body, it could avail itself of the experience thus acquired.

Thus, at least, said Yva, while Bickley contemplated her with a cold and unbelieving eye. She even went further and alleged that in certain instances, individuals of her extinct race had been able to pass through the ether and to visit other worlds in the depths of space.

"Have you ever done that?" asked Bickley.

"Once or twice I dreamed that I did," she replied quietly.

"We can all dream," he answered.

As it was my lot to make acquaintance with this strange and uncanny power at a later date, I will say no more of it now.

Telepathy, she declared, was also a developed gift among the Sons of Wisdom; indeed, they seem to have used it as we use wireless messages. Only, in their case, the sending and receiving stations were skilled and susceptible human beings who went on duty for so many hours at a time. Thus intelligence was transmitted with accuracy and despatch. Those who had this faculty were, she said, also very apt at reading the minds of others and therefore not easy to deceive.

"Is that how you know that I had been trying to analyse your Life-water?" asked Bickley.

"Yes," she answered, with her unvarying smile. "At the moment I spoke thereof you were wondering whether my father would be angry if he knew that you had taken the water in a little flask." She studied him for a moment, then added: "Now you are wondering, first, whether I did not see you take the water from the fountain and guess the purpose, and, secondly, whether perhaps Bastin did not tell me what you were doing with it when we met in the sepulchre."

"Look here," said the exasperated Bickley, "I admit that telepathy and thought-reading are possible to a certain limited extent. But supposing that you possess those powers, as I think in English, and you do not know English, how can you interpret what is passing in my mind?"

"Perhaps you have been teaching me English all this while without knowing it, Bickley. In any case, it matters little, seeing that what I read is the thought, not the language with which it is clothed. The thought comes from your mind to mine—that is, if I wish it, which is not often—and I interpret it in my own or other tongues."

"I am glad to hear it is not often, Lady Yva, since thoughts are generally considered private."

"Yes, and therefore I will read yours no more. Why should I, when they are so full of disbelief of all I tell you, and sometimes of other things about myself which I do not seek to know?"

"No wonder that, according to the story in the pictures, those Nations, whom you named Barbarians, made an end of your people, Lady Yva."

"You are mistaken, Bickley; the Lord Oro made an end of the Nations, though against my prayer," she added with a sigh.

Then Bickley departed in a rage, and did not appear again for an hour.

"He is angry," she said, looking after him; "nor do I wonder. It is hard for the very clever like Bickley, who think that they have mastered all things, to find that after all they are quite ignorant. I am sorry for him, and I like him much."

"Then you would be sorry for me also, Lady Yva?"

"Why?" she asked with a dazzling smile, "when your heart is athirst for knowledge, gaping for it like a fledgling's mouth for food, and, as it chances, though I am not very wise, I can satisfy something of your soul-hunger."

"Not very wise!" I repeated.

"No, Humphrey. I think that Bastin, who in many ways is so stupid, has more true wisdom than I have, because he can believe and accept without question. After all, the wisdom of my people is all of the universe and its wonders. What you think magic is not magic; it is only gathered knowledge and the finding out of secrets. Bickley will tell you the same, although as yet he does not believe that the mind of man can stretch so far."

"You mean that your wisdom has in it nothing of the spirit?"

"Yes, Humphrey, that is what I mean. I do not even know if there is such a thing as spirit. Our god was Fate; Bastin's god is a spirit, and I think yours also."

"Yes."

"Therefore, I wish you and Bastin to teach me of your god, as does Oro, my father. I want—oh! so much, Humphrey, to learn whether we live after death."

"You!" I exclaimed. "You who, according to the

story, have slept for two hundred and fifty thousand years! You, who have, unless I mistake, hinted that during that sleep you may have lived in other shapes! Do you doubt whether we can live after death?"

"Yes. Sleep induced by secret arts is not death, and during that sleep the *I* within might wander and inhabit other shapes, because it is forbidden to be idle. Moreover, what seems to be death may not be death, only another form of sleep from which the *I* awakes again upon the world. But at last comes the real death, when the *I* is extinguished to the world. That much I know, because my people learned it."

"You mean, you know that men and women may live again and again upon the world?"

"Yes, Humphrey, I do. For in the world there is only a certain store of life which in many forms travels on and on, till the lot of each *I* is fulfilled. Then comes the real death, and after that—what, oh!—what?"

"You must ask Bastin," I said humbly. "I cannot dare to teach of such matters."

"No, but you can and do believe, and that helps me, Humphrey, who am in tune with you. Yes, it helps me much more than do Bastin and his new religion, because such is woman's way. Now, I think Bickley will soon return, so let us talk of other matters. Tell me of the history of your people, Humphrey, that my father says are now at war."

CHAPTER XVIII

THE ACCIDENT

BICKLEY did return, having recovered his temper, since after all it was impossible for anyone to remain angry with the Lady Yva for long, and we spent a very happy time together. We instructed and she was the humble pupil.

How swift and nimble was her intelligence! In that one morning she learned all our alphabet and how to write our letters. It appeared that among her people, at any rate in their later periods, the only form of writing that was used was a highly concentrated shorthand which saved labour. They had no journals, since news which arrived telepathically or by some form of wireless was proclaimed to those who cared to listen, and on it all formed their own judgments. In the same way poems and even romances were repeated, as in Homer's day or in the time of the Norse *sagas,* by word of mouth. None of their secret knowledge was written down. Like the ritual of Freemasonry it was considered too sacred.

Moreover, when men lived for hundreds of years this was not so necessary, especially as their great fear was lest it should fall into the hands of the outside nations, whom they called Barbarians. For, be it remembered, these Sons of Wisdom were always a very small people who ruled by the weight of their intelligence and the strength of their accumulated lore. Indeed, they could scarcely be called a people; rather were they a few families, all of them more or less connected with the original ruling Dynasty which considered itself half divine. These families were waited upon by a multitude of servants or slaves drawn from the subject nations, for the most part skilled in one art or another, or perhaps, remarkable for their personal beauty. Still they remained outside the pale.

The Sons of Wisdom did not intermarry with them or teach them their learning, or even allow them to drink of their Life-water. They ruled them as men rule dogs, treating them with kindness, but no more, and as many dogs run their course and die in the lifetime of one master, so did many of these slaves in that of one of the Sons of Wisdom. Therefore, the slaves came to regard their lords not as men, but gods. They lived but three score years and ten like the rest of us, and went their way, they, whose great-great-grandfathers had served the same master and whose great-great-great-grandchildren would still serve him. What should we think of a lord who we knew was already adult in the time of William the Conqueror, and who remained still vigorous and all-powerful in that of George V? One, moreover, who commanded almost infinite knowledge to which we were denied the key? We might tremble before him and look upon him as half-divine, but should we not long to kill him and possess his knowledge and thereby prolong our own existence to his wondrous measure?

Such, said Yva, was the case with their slaves and the peoples from whence these sprang. They grew mad with jealous hate, till at length came the end we knew.

Thus we talked on for hours till the time came for us to eat. As before Yva partook of fruit and we of such meats as we had at hand. These, we noticed, disgusted her, because, as she explained, the Children of Wisdom, unless driven thereto by necessity, touched no flesh, but lived on the fruits of the earth and wine alone. Only the slaves and the Barbarians ate flesh. In these views Bickley for once agreed with her, that is, except as regards the wine, for in theory, if not in practice—he was a vegetarian.

"I will bring you more of the Life-water," she said, "and then you will grow to hate these dead things, as I do. And now farewell. My father calls me. I hear him though you do not. To-morrow I cannot come, but the day after I will come and bring you the Life-water. Nay, accompany me not, but as I see he wishes it, let Tommy go with me. I will care for him, and he is a friend in all that lonely place."

So she went, and with her Tommy, rejoicing.

"Ungrateful little devil!" said Bickley. "Here we've fed and petted him from puppyhood, or at least you have, and yet he skips off with the first stranger. I never saw him behave like that to any woman, except your poor wife."

"I know," I answered. "I cannot understand it. Hullo! here comes Bastin."

Bastin it was, dishevelled and looking much the worse for wear, also minus his Bible in the native tongue.

"Well, how have you been getting on?" said Bickley.

"I should like some tea, also anything there is to eat."

We supplied him with these necessaries, and after a while he said slowly and solemnly:

"I cannot help thinking of a childish story which Bickley told or invented one night at your house at home. I remember he had an argument with my wife, which he said put him in mind of it, I am sure I don't know why. It was about a monkey and a parrot that were left together under a sofa for a long while, where they were so quiet that everybody forgot them. Then the parrot came out with only one feather left in its tail and none at all on its body, saying, 'I've had no end of a time!' after which it dropped down and died. Do you know, I feel just like that parrot, only I don't mean to die, and I think I gave the monkey quite as good as he gave me!"

"What happened?" I asked, intensely interested.

"Oh! the Glittering Lady took me into that palace hall where Oro was sitting like a spider in a web, and left me there. I got to work at once. He was much interested in the Old Testament stories and said there were points of truth about them, although they had evidently come down to the modern writer—he called him a *modern* writer—in a legendary form. I thought his remarks impertinent and with difficulty refrained from saying so. Leaving the story of the Deluge and all that, I spoke of other matters, telling him of eternal life and Heaven and Hell, of which the poor benighted man had never heard. I pointed out especially that unless he repented, his life, by all accounts, had been so wicked, that he was certainly destined to the latter place."

"What did he say to that?" I asked.

"Do you know, I think it frightened him, if one could imagine Oro being frightened. At any rate he remarked that the truth or falsity of what I said was an urgent matter for him, as he could not expect to live more than a few hundred years longer, though perhaps he might prolong the period by another spell of sleep. Then he asked me why I thought him so wicked. I replied because he himself said that he had drowned millions of people, which showed an evil heart and intention even if it were not a fact. He thought a long while and asked what could be done in the circumstances. I replied that repentance and reparation were the only courses open to him."

"Reparation!" I exclaimed.

"Yes, reparation was what I said, though I think I made a mistake there, as you will see. As nearly as I can remember, he answered that he was beginning to repent, as from all he had learned from us, he gathered that the races which had arisen as a consequence of his action, were worse than those which he had destroyed. As regards reparation, what he had done once he could do again. He would think the matter over seriously, and see if it were possible and advisable to raise those parts of the world which had been sunk, and sink those which had been raised. If so, he thought that would make very handsome amends to the departed nations and set him quite right with any superior Power, if such a thing existed. What are you laughing at, Bickley? I don't think it a laughing matter, since such remarks do not seem to me to indicate any real change in Oro's heart, which is what I was trying to effect."

Bickley, who was convulsed with merriment, wiped his eyes and said:

"You dear old donkey, don't you see what you have done, or rather would have done if there were a word of truth in all this ridiculous story about a deluge? You would be in the way of making your precious pupil, who certainly is the most masterly old liar in the world, repeat his offence and send Europe to the bottom of the sea."

"That did occur to me, but it doesn't much matter

as I am quite certain that such a thing would never be allowed. Of course there was a real deluge once, but Oro had no more to do with it than I had. Don't you agree, Arbuthnot?"

"I think so," I answered cautiously, "but really in this place I am beginning to lose count of what is or is not possible. Also, of course, there may have been many deluges; indeed the history of the world shows that this was so; it is written in its geological strata. What was the end of it?"

"The end was that he took the South Sea Bible and, after I had explained a little about our letters, seemed to be able to read it at once. I suppose he was acquainted with the art of printing in his youth. At any rate he said that he would study it, I don't know how, unless he can read, and that in two days' time he would let me know what he thought about the matter of my religion. Then he told me to go. I said that I did not know the way and was afraid of losing myself. Thereupon he waved his hand, and I really can't say what happened."

"Did you levitate up here," asked Bickley, "like the late lamented Mr. Home at the spiritualistic séances?"

"No, I did not exactly levitate, but something or someone seemed to get a hold of me, and I was just rushed along in a most tumultuous fashion. The next thing I knew was that I was standing at the door of that sepulchre, though I have no recollection of going up in the lift, or whatever it is. I believe those beastly caves are full of ghosts, or devils, and the worst of it is that they have kept my solar-tope, which I put on this morning forgetting that it would be useless there."

"The Lady Yva's Fourth Dimension in action," I suggested, "only it wouldn't work on solar-topes."

"I don't know what you are talking about," said Bastin, "but if my hat had to be left, why not my boots and other garments? Please stop your nonsense and pass the tea. Thank goodness I haven't got to go down there to-morrow, as he seems to have had enough of me for the present, so I vote we all pay a visit to the ship. It will be a very pleasant change. I couldn't stand two days running with that old fiend, and his ghosts or devils in the cave."

Next morning accordingly, fearing no harm from the Orofenans, we took the canoe and rowed to the main island. Marama had evidently seen us coming, for he and a number of his people met us with every demonstration of delight, and escorted us to the ship. Here we found things just as we had left them, for there had been no attempt at theft or other mischief.

While we were in the cabin a fit of moral weakness seemed to overcome Bickley, the first and I may add the last from which I ever saw him suffer.

"Do you know," he said, addressing us, "I think that we should do well to try to get out of this place. Eliminating a great deal of the marvellous with which we seem to have come in touch here, it is still obvious that we find ourselves in very peculiar and unhealthy surroundings. I mean mentally unhealthy, indeed I think that if we stay here much longer we shall probably go off our heads. Now that boat on the deck remains sound and seaworthy. Why should not we provision her and take our chance? We know more or less which way to steer."

Bastin and I looked at each other. It was he who spoke first.

"Wouldn't it be rather a risky job in an open

boat?" he asked. "However, that doesn't matter much because I don't take any account of risks, knowing that I am of more value than a sparrow and that the hairs of my head are all numbered."

"They might be numbered under water as well as above it," muttered Bickley, "and I feel sure that on your own showing, you would be as valuable dead as alive."

"What I seem to feel," went on Bastin, "is that I have work to my hand here. Also, the *locum tenens* at Fulcombe no doubt runs the parish as well as I could. Indeed I consider him a better man for the place than I am. That old Oro is a tough proposition, but I do not despair of him yet, and besides him there is the Glittering Lady, a most open-minded person, whom I have not yet had any real opportunity of approaching in a spiritual sense. Then there are all these natives who cannot learn without a teacher. So on the whole I think I would rather stay where I am until Providence points out some other path."

"I am of the same opinion, if for somewhat different reasons," I said. "I do not suppose that it has often been the fortune of men to come in touch with such things as we have found upon this island. They may be illusions, but at least they are very interesting illusions. One might live ten lifetimes and find nothing else of the sort. Therefore I should like to see the end of the dream."

Bickley reflected a little, then said:

"On the whole I agree with you. Only my brain totters and I am terribly afraid of madness. I cannot believe what I seem to hear and see, and that way madness lies. It is better to die than to go mad."

"You'll do that anyway when your time comes,

Bickley, I mean decease, of course, interrupted Bastin. "And who knows, perhaps all this is an opportunity given by Providence to open your eyes, which, I must say, are singularly blind. You think you know everything there is to learn, but the fact is that like the rest of us, you know nothing at all, and good man though you are, obstinately refuse to admit the truth and to seek support elsewhere. For my part I believe that you are afraid of falling in love with that Glittering Lady and of being convinced by her that you are wrong in your most unsatisfactory conclusions."

"I am out-voted anyway," said Bickley, "and for the rest, Bastin, look after yourself and leave me alone. I will add that on the whole I think you are both right, and that it is wisest for us to stop where we are, for after all we can only die once."

"I am not so sure, Bickley. There is a thing called the second death, which is what is troubling that old scoundrel, Oro. Now I will go and look for those books."

So the idea of flight was abandoned, although I admit that even to myself it had attractions. For I felt that I was being wrapped in a net of mysteries from which I saw no escape. Yes, and of more than mysteries; I who had sworn that I would never look upon another woman, was learning to love this sweet and wondrous Yva, and of that what could be the end?

We collected all we had come to seek, and started homewards escorted by Marama and his people, including a number of young women who danced before us in a light array of flowers.

Passing our old house, we came to the grove where

the idol Oro had stood and Bastin was so nearly sacrificed. There was another idol there now which he wished to examine, but in the end did not as the natives so obviously objected. Indeed Marama told me that notwithstanding the mysterious death of the sorcerers on the Rock of Offerings, there was still a strong party in the island who would be glad to do us a mischief if any further affront were offered to their hereditary god.

He questioned us also tentatively about the apparition, for such he conceived it to be, which had appeared upon the rock and killed the sorcerers, and I answered him as I thought wisest, telling him that a terrible Power was afoot in the land, which he would do well to obey.

"Yes," he said; "the God of the Mountain of whom the tradition has come down to us from our forefathers. He is awake again; he sees, he hears and we are afraid. Plead with him for us, O Friend-from-the-Sea."

As he spoke we were passing through a little patch of thick bush. Suddenly from out of this bush, I saw a lad appear. He wore a mask upon his face, but from his shape could not have been more than thirteen or fourteen years of age. In his hand was a wooden club. He ran forward, stopped, and with a yell of hate hurled it, I think at Bastin, but it hit me. At any rate I felt a shock and remembered no more.

Dreams. Dreams. Endless dreams! What were they all about? I do not know. It seemed to me that through them continually I saw the stately figure of old Oro contemplating me gravely, as though he were making up his mind about something in which I must play a part. Then there was another figure, that of the gracious but imperial Yva, who from time to time, as I thought, leant over me and whispered in my ear words of rest and comfort. Nor was this all, since her shape had a way of changing suddenly into that of my lost wife who would speak with her voice. Or perhaps my wife would speak with Yva's voice. To my disordered sense it was as though they were one personality, having two shapes, either of which could be assumed at will. It was most strange and yet to me most blessed, since in the living I seemed to have found the dead, and in the dead the living. More, I took journeys, or rather some unknown part of me seemed to do so. One of these I remember, for its majestic character stamped itself upon my mind in such a fashion that all the waters of delirium could not wash it out nor all its winds blow away that memory.

I was travelling through space with Yva a thousand times faster than light can flash. We passed sun after sun. They drew near, they grew into enormous, flaming Glories round which circled world upon world. They became small, dwindled to points of light and disappeared.

We found footing upon some far land and passed a marvellous white city wherein were buildings with domes of crystal and alabaster, in the latter of which were set windows made of great jewels; sapphires or rubies they seemed to me. We went on up a lovely valley. To the left were hills, down which tumbled waterfalls; to the right was a river broad and deep that seemed to overflow its banks as does the Nile. Behind were high mountains on the slopes of which grew forests of glorious trees, some of them aflame with bloom, while far away up their crests stood colossal golden statues set wide apart. They looked like guardian angels watching that city and that vale. The land was lit with a light such as that of the moon, only intensified and of many colours. Indeed looking up, I saw that above us floated three moons, each of them bigger than our own at the full, and gathered that here it was night.

We came to a house set amid scented gardens and having in front of it terraces of flowers. It seemed not unlike my own house at home, but I took little note of it, because of a woman who sat upon the verandah, if I may call it so. She was clad in garments of white silk fastened about her middle with a jewelled girdle. On her neck also was a collar of jewels. I forget the colour; indeed this seemed to change continually as the light from the different moons struck when she moved, but I think its prevailing tinge was blue. In her arms this woman nursed a beauteous, sleeping child, singing happily as she rocked it to and fro. Yva went towards the woman who looked up at her step and uttered a little cry. Then for the first time I saw the woman's face. It was that of my dead wife!

As I followed in my dream, a little cloud of mist seemed to cover both my wife and Yva, and when I reached the place Yva was gone. Only my wife remained, she and the child. There she stood, solemn and sweet. While I drew near she laid down the child upon the cushioned seat from which she had risen. She stretched out her arms and flung them about me. She embraced me and I embraced her in a rapture of reunion. Then turning she lifted up the child, it was a girl, for me to kiss.

"See your daughter," she said, "and behold all that I am making ready for you where we shall dwell in a day to come."

I grew confused.

"Yva," I said. "Where is Yva who brought me here? Did she go into the house?"

"Yes," she answered happily. "Yva went into the house. Look again!"

I looked and it was Yva's face that was pressed against my own, and Yva's eyes that gazed into mine. Only she was garbed as my wife had been, and on her bosom hung the changeful necklace.

"You may not stay," she whispered, and lo! it was my wife that spoke, not Yva.

"Tell me what it means?" I implored.

"I cannot," she answered. "There are mysteries that you may not know as yet. Love Yva if you will and I shall not be jealous, for in loving Yva you love me. You cannot understand? Then know this, that the spirit has many shapes, and yet is the same spirit—sometimes. Now I who am far, yet near, bid you farewell a while."

Then all passed in a flash and the dream ended.

Such was the only one of those visions which I can recall.

I seemed to wake up as from a long and tumultuous sleep. The first thing I saw was the palm roof of our house upon the rock. I knew it was our house, for just above me was a palm leaf of which I had myself tied the stalk to the framework with a bit of coloured ribbon that I had chanced to find in my pocket. It came originally from the programme card of a dance that I had attended at Honolulu and I had kept it because I thought it might be useful. Finally I used it to secure that loose leaf. I stared at the ribbon which brought back a flood of memories, and as I was thus engaged I heard voices talking, and listened—Bickley's voice, and the Lady Yva's.

"Yes," Bickley was saying, "he will do well now, but he went near, very near."

"I knew he would not die," she answered, "because my father said so."

"There are two sorts of deaths," replied Bickley, "that of the body and that of the mind. I was afraid that even if he lived, his reason would go, but from certain indications I do not think that will happen now. He will get quite well again—though——" and he stopped.

"I am very glad to hear you say so," chimed in Bastin. "For weeks I thought that I should have to read the Burial Service over poor Arbuthnot. Indeed I was much puzzled as to the best place to bury him. Finally I found a very suitable spot round the corner there, where it isn't rock, in which one can't dig and the soil is not liable to be flooded. In fact I went so far as to clear away the bush and to mark out the grave with its foot to the east. In this climate one can't delay, you know."

Weak as I was, I smiled. This practical proceeding was so exactly like Bastin.

"Well, you wasted your labour," exclaimed Bickley.

"Yes, I am glad to say I did. But I don't think it was your operations and the rest that cured him, Bickley, although you take all the credit. I believe it was the Life-water that the Lady Yva made him drink and the stuff that Oro sent which we gave him when you weren't looking."

"Then I hope that in the future you will not interfere with my cases," said the indignant Bickley, and either the voices passed away or I went to sleep.

When I woke up again it was to find the Lady Yva seated at my side watching me.

"Forgive me, Humphrey, because I here; others gone out walking," she said slowly in English.

"Who taught you my language?" I asked, astonished.

"Bastin and Bickley, while you ill, they teach; they teach me much. Man just same now as he was hundred thousand years ago," she added enigmatically. "All think one woman beautiful when no other woman there."

"Indeed," I replied, wondering to what proceedings on the part of Bastin and Bickley she alluded. Could that self-centred pair—oh! it was impossible.

"How long have I been ill?" I asked to escape the subject which I felt to be uncomfortable.

She lifted her beautiful eyes in search of words and began to count upon her fingers.

"Two moon, one half moon, yes, ten week, counting Sabbath," she answered triumphantly.

"Ten weeks!" I exclaimed.

"Yes, Humphrey, ten whole weeks and three days you first bad, then mad. Oh!" she went on, breaking into the Orofenan tongue which she spoke so perfectly, although it was not her own. That language of hers I never learned, but I know she thought in it and only translated into Orofenan, because of the great difficulty which she had in rendering her high and refined ideas into its simpler metaphor, and the strange words which often she introduced. "Oh! you have been very ill, friend of my heart. At times I thought that you were going to die, and wept and wept. Bickley thinks that he saved you and he is very clever. But he could not have saved you; that wanted more knowledge than any of your people have; only I pray you, do not tell him so because it would hurt his pride."

"What was the matter with me then, Yva?"

"All was the matter. First, the weapon which that youth threw—he was the son of the sorcerer whom my father destroyed—crushed in the bone of your head. He is dead for his crime and may he be accursed for ever," she added in the only outbreak of rage and vindictiveness in which I ever saw her indulge.

"One must make excuses for him; his father had been killed," I said.

"Yes, that is what Bastin tells me, and it is true. Still, for that young man I can make no excuse; it was cowardly and wicked. Well, Bickley performed what he calls operation, and the Lord Oro, he came up from his house and helped him, because Bastin is no good in such things. Then he can only turn away his head and pray. I, too, helped, holding hot water and linen and jar of the stuff that made you feel like nothing, although the sight made me feel more sick than anything since I saw one I loved killed, oh, long, long ago."

"Was the operation successful?" I asked, for I did not dare to begin to thank her.

"Yes, that clever man, Bickley, lifted the bone which had been crushed in. Only then something broke in your head and you began to bleed here," and she touched what I believe is called the temporal artery. "The vein had been crushed by the blow, and gave way. Bickley worked and worked, and just in time he tied it up before you died. Oh! then I felt as though I loved Bickley, though afterwards Bastin said that I ought to have loved *him,* since it was not Bickley who stopped the bleeding, but his prayer."

"Perhaps it was both," I suggested.

"Perhaps, Humphrey, at least you were saved. Then came another trouble. You took fever. Bickley said that it was because a certain gnat had bitten you when you went down to the ship, and my father, the Lord Oro, told me that this was right. At the least you grew very weak and lost your mind, and it seemed as though you must die. Then, Humphrey, I went to the Lord Oro and kneeled before him and prayed your life, for I knew that he could cure you if he would, though Bickley's skill was at an end.

"'Daughter,' he said to me, 'not once but again and again you have set up your will against mine in the past. Why then should I trouble myself to grant this desire of yours in the present, and save a man who is nothing to me?'

"I rose to my feet and answered, 'I do not know, my Father, yet I am certain that for your own sake it will be well to do so. I am sure that of everything even you must give an account at last, great though you be, and who knows, perhaps one life which you have saved may turn the balance in your favour.'

"'Surely the priest Bastin has been talking to you,' he said.

"'He has,' I answered, 'and not he alone. Many voices have been talking to me.'"

"What did you mean by that?" I asked.

"It matters nothing what I meant, Humphrey. Be still and listen to my story. My father thought a while and answered:

"'I am jealous of this stranger. What is he but a short-lived half-barbarian such as we knew in the old days? And yet already you think more of him than you do of me, your father, the divine Oro who has lived a thousand years. At first I helped that physician to save him, but now I think I wish him dead.'

"'If you let this man die, my Father,' I answered, 'then we part. Remember that I also have of the wisdom of our people, and can use it if I will.'

"'Then save him yourself,' he said.

"'Perhaps I shall, my Father,' I answered, 'but if so it will not be here. I say that if so we part and you shall be left to rule in your majesty alone.'

"Now this frightened the Lord Oro, for he has the weakness that he hates to be alone.

"'If I do what you will, do you swear never to leave me, Yva?' he asked. 'Know that if you will not swear, the man dies.'

"'I swear,' I answered—for your sake, Humphrey—though I did not love the oath.

"Then he gave me a certain medicine to mix with the Life-water, and when you were almost gone that medicine cured you, though Bickley does not know it, as nothing else could have done. Now I have told you the truth, for your own ear only, Humphrey."

"Yva," I asked, "why did you do all this for me?"

"Humphrey, I do not know," she answered, "but I think because I must. Now sleep a while."

CHAPTER XIX

THE PROPOSALS OF BASTIN AND BICKLEY

So far as my body was concerned I grew well with great rapidity, though it was long before I got back my strength. Thus I could not walk far or endure any sustained exertion. With my mind it was otherwise. I cannot explain what had happened to it; indeed I do not know, but in a sense it seemed to have become detached and to have assumed a kind of personality of its own. At times it felt as though it were no longer an inhabitant of the body, but rather its more or less independent partner. I was perfectly clear-headed and of insanity I experienced no symptoms. Yet my mind, I use that term from lack of a better, was not entirely under my control. For one thing, at night it appeared to wander far away, though whither it went and what it saw there I could never remember.

I record this because possibly it explains certain mysterious events, if they were events and not dreams, which shortly I must set out. I spoke to Bickley about the matter. He put it by lightly, saying that it was only a result of my long and most severe illness and that I should steady down in time, especially if we could escape from that island and its unnatural atmosphere. Yet as he spoke he glanced at me shrewdly with his quick eyes, and when he turned to go away I heard him mutter something to himself about "unholy influences" and "that confounded old Oro."

The words were spoken to himself and quite beneath

his breath, and of course not meant to reach me. But one of the curious concomitants of my state was that all my senses, and especially my hearing, had become most abnormally acute. A whisper far away was now to me like a loud remark made in a room.

Bickley's reflection, for I can scarcely call it more, set me thinking. Yva had said that Oro sent me medicine which was administered to me without Bickley's knowledge, and as she believed, saved my life, or certainly my reason. What was in it? I wondered. Then there was that Life-water which Yva brought and insisted upon my drinking every day. Undoubtedly it was a marvellous tonic and did me good. But it had other effects also. Thus, as she said would be the case, after a course of it I conceived the greatest dislike, which I may add has never entirely left me, of any form of meat, also of alcohol. All I seemed to want was this water with fruit, or such native vegetables as there were. Bickley disapproved and made me eat fish occasionally, but even this revolted me, and since I gained steadily in weight, as we found out by a simple contrivance, and remained healthy in every other way, soon he allowed me to choose my own diet.

About this time Oro began to pay me frequent visits. He always came at night, and what is more I knew when he was coming, although he never gave me warning. Here I should explain that during my illness Bastin, who was so ingenious in such matters, had built another hut in which he and Bickley slept, of course when they were not watching me, leaving our old bed-chamber to myself.

Well, I would wake up and be aware that Oro was coming. Then he appeared in a silent and mysterious way, as though he had materialised in the room, for I never saw him pass the doorway. In the moonlight, or the starlight, which flowed through the entrance and the side of the hut that was only enclosed with lattice-work, I perceived him seat himself upon a certain stool, looking like a most majestic ghost with his flowing robes, long white beard, hooked nose and hawk eyes. In the day-time he much resembled the late General Booth whom I had often seen, except for certain added qualities of height and classic beauty of countenance. At night, however, he resembled no one but himself, indeed there was something mighty and godlike in his appearance, something that made one feel that he was not as are other men.

For a while he would sit and look at me. Then he began to speak in a low, vibrant voice. What did he speak of? Well, many matters. It was as though he were unburdening that hoary soul of his because it could no longer endure the grandeur of its own loneliness. Amongst sundry secret things, he told me of the past history of this world of ours, and of the mighty civilisations which for uncounted ages he and his forefathers had ruled by the strength of their will and knowledge, of the dwindling of their race and of the final destruction of its enemies, although I noticed that now he no longer said that this was his work alone. One night I asked him if he did not miss all such pomp and power.

Then suddenly he broke out, and for the first time I really learned what ambition can be when it utterly possesses the soul of man.

"Are you mad," he asked, "that you suppose that I, Oro, the King of kings, can be content to dwell solitary in a great cave with none but the shadows of the dead to serve me? Nay, I must rule again and be even greater than before, or else I too will die. Better to face the future, even if it means oblivion, than to remain thus a relic of a glorious past, still living and yet dead, like that statue of the great god Fate which you saw in the temple of my worship."

"Bastin does not think that the future means oblivion," I remarked.

"I know it. I have studied his faith and find it too humble for my taste, also too new. Shall I, Oro, creep a suppliant before any Power, and confess what Bastin is pleased to call my sins? Nay, I who am great will be the equal of all greatness, or nothing."

He paused a while, then went on:

"Bastin speaks of 'eternity.' Where and what then is this eternity which if it has no end can have had no beginning? I know the secret of the suns and their attendant worlds, and they are no more eternal than the insect which glitters for an hour. Out of shapeless, rushing gases they gathered to live their day, and into gases at last they dissolve again with all they bore."

"Yes," I answered, "but they re-form into new worlds."

"That have no part with the old. This world, too, shall melt, departing to whence it came, as your sacred writings say, and what then of those who dwelt and dwell thereon? No, Man of to-day, give me Time in which I rule and keep your dreams of an Eternity that is not, and in which you must still crawl and serve, even if it were. Yet, if I might, I confess it, I would live on for ever, but as Master not as Slave."

On another night he began to tempt me, very subtly.

"I see a spark of greatness in you, Humphrey," he said, "and it comes into my heart that you, too, might learn to rule. With Yva, the last of my blood, it is otherwise. She is the child of my age and of a race outworn; too gentle, too much all womanly. The soul that triumphs must shine like steel in the sun, and cut if need be; not merely be beauteous and shed perfume like a lily in the shade. Yet she is very wise and fair," here he looked at me, "perchance of her might come children such as were their forefathers, who again would wield the sceptre of the dominion of the earth."

I made no answer, wondering what he meant exactly and thinking it wisest to be silent.

"You are of the short-lived races," he went on, "yet very much a man, not without intelligence, and by the arts I have I can so strengthen your frame that it will endure the shocks of time for three such lives as yours, or perchance for more, and then——"

Again he paused and went on:

"The Daughter of kings likes you also, perhaps because you resemble——" here he fixed me with his piercing eyes, "a certain kinglet of base blood whom once she also liked, but whom it was my duty to destroy. Well, I must think. I must study this world of yours also and therein you may help me. Perhaps afterwards I will tell you how. Now sleep."

In another moment he was gone, but notwithstanding his powerful command, for a while I could not sleep. I understood that he was offering Yva to me, but upon what terms? That was the question. With her was to go great dominion over the kingdoms of the earth. I could not help remembering that always this has been and still is Satan's favourite bait. To me it did not particularly appeal. I had been ambitious in my time—who is not that is worth his salt? I could have wished to excel in something, literature or art, or whatever it might be, and thus to ensure the memory of my name in the world.

Of course this is a most futile desire, seeing that soon or late every name must fade out of the world like an unfixed photograph which is exposed to the sun. Even if it could endure, as the old demi-god, or demi-devil, Oro, had pointed out, very shortly, by comparison with Time's unmeasured vastness, the whole solar system will also fade. So of what use is this feeble love of fame and this vain attempt to be remembered that animates us so strongly? Moreover, the idea of enjoying mere temporal as opposed to intellectual power, appealed to me not at all. I am a student of history and I know what has been the lot of kings and the evil that, often enough, they work in their little day.

Also if I needed any further example, there was that of Oro himself. He had outlived the greatness of his House, as a royal family is called, and after some gigantic murder, if his own story was to be believed, indulged in a prolonged sleep. Now he awoke to find himself quite alone in the world, save for a daughter with whom he did not agree or sympathise. In short, he was but a kind of animated mummy inspired by one idea which I felt quite sure would be disappointed, namely, to renew his former greatness. To me he seemed as miserable a figure as one could imagine, brooding and plotting in his illuminated cave, at the end of an extended but mis-spent life.

Also I wondered what he, or rather his *ego,* had been doing during all those two hundred and fifty thousand years of sleep. Possibly if Yva's theory, as I understood it, were correct, he had re-incarnated as Attila, or Tamerlane, or Napoleon, or even as Chaka the terrible Zulu king. At any rate there he was still in the world, filled with the dread of death, but consumed now as ever by his insatiable and most useless finite ambitions.

Yva, also! Her case was his, but yet how different. In all this long night of Time she had but ripened into one of the sweetest and most gentle women that ever the world bore. She, too, was great in her way, it appeared in her every word and gesture, but where was the ferocity of her father? Where his desire to reach to splendour by treading on a blood-stained road paved with broken human hearts? It did not exist. Her nature was different although her body came of a long line of these power-loving kings. Why this profound difference of the spirit? Like everything else it was a mystery. The two were as far apart as the Poles. Everyone must have hated Oro, from the beginning, however much he feared him, but everyone who came in touch with her must have loved Yva.

Here I may break into my personal narrative to say that this, by their own confession, proved to be true of two such various persons as Bastin and Bickley.

" The truth, which I am sure it would be wrong to hide from you, Arbuthnot," said the former to me one day, " is that during your long illness I fell in love, I suppose that is the right word, with the Glittering Lady. After thinking the matter over also, I conceived that it would be proper to tell her so if only to clear the air and prevent future misunderstandings. As I remarked to her on that occasion, I had hesitated long, as I was not certain how she would fill the place of the wife of the incumbent of an English parish."

" Mothers' Meetings, and the rest," I suggested.

" Exactly so, Arbuthnot. Also there were the views

of the Bishop to be considered, who might have objected to the introduction into the diocese of a striking person who so recently had been a heathen, and to one in such strong contrast to my late beloved wife."

"I suppose you didn't consider the late Mrs. Bastin's views on the subject of re-marriage. I remember that they were strong," I remarked rather maliciously.

"No, I did not think it necessary, since the Scriptural instructions on the matter are very clear, and in another world no doubt all jealousies, even Sarah's, will be obliterated. Upon that point my conscience was quite easy. So when I found that, unlike her parent, the Lady Yva was much inclined to accept the principles of the faith in which it is my privilege to instruct her, I thought it proper to say to her that if ultimately she made up her mind to do so—of course *this* was a *sine qua non*—I should be much honoured, and as a man, not as a priest, it would make me most happy if she would take me as a husband. Of course I explained to her that I considered, under the circumstances, I could quite lawfully perform the marriage ceremony myself with you and Bickley as witnesses, even should Oro refuse to give her away. Also I told her that although after her varied experiences in the past, life at Fulcombe, if we could ever get there, might be a little monotonous, still it would not be entirely devoid of interest."

"You mean Christmas decorations and that sort of thing?"

"Yes, and choir treats and entertaining Deputations and attending other Church activities."

"Well, and what did she say, Bastin?"

"Oh! she was most kind and flattering. Indeed that hour will always remain the pleasantest of my life. I don't know how it happened, but when it was over I felt quite delighted that she had refused me. Indeed on second thoughts, I am not certain but that I shall be much happier in the capacities of a brother and teacher which she asked me to fill, than I should have been as her husband. To tell you the truth, Arbuthnot, there are moments when I am not sure whether I entirely understand the Lady Yva. It was rather like proposing to one's guardian angel."

"Yes," I said, "that's about it, old fellow. 'Guardian Angel' is not a bad name for her."

Afterwards I received the confidence of Bickley.

"Look here, Arbuthnot," he said. "I want to own up to something. I think I ought to, because of certain things I have observed, in order to prevent possible future misunderstandings."

"What's that?" I asked innocently.

"Only this. As you know, I have always been a confirmed bachelor on principle. Women introduce too many complications into life, and although it involves some sacrifice, on the whole, I have thought it best to do without them and leave the carrying on of the world to others."

"Well, what of it? Your views are not singular, Bickley."

"Only this. While you were ill the sweetness of that Lady Yva and her wonderful qualities as a nurse overcame me. I went to pieces all of a sudden. I saw in her a realisation of every ideal I had ever entertained of perfect womanhood. So to speak, my resolves of a lifetime melted like wax in the sun. Notwithstanding her queer history and the marvels with which she is mixed up, I wished to marry her. No doubt her physical loveliness was at the bottom of it, but, however that may be, there it was."

"She is beautiful," I commented; "though I daresay older than she looks."

"That is a point on which I made no inquiries, and I should advise you, when your turn comes, as no doubt it will, to follow my example. You know, Arbuthnot," he mused, "however lovely a woman may be, it would put one off if suddenly she announced that she was—let us say—a hundred and fifty years old."

"Yes," I admitted, "for nobody wants to marry the contemporary of his great-grandmother. However, she gave her age as twenty-seven years and three moons."

"And doubtless for once did not tell the truth. But, as she does not look more than twenty-five, I think that we may all agree to let it stand at that, namely, twenty-seven, plus an indefinite period of sleep. At any rate, she is a sweet and most gracious woman, apparently in the bloom of youth, and, to cut it short, I fell in love with her."

"Like Bastin," I said.

"Bastin!" exclaimed Bickley indignantly. "You don't mean to say that clerical oaf presumed—well, well, after all, I suppose that he is a man, so one mustn't be hard on him. But who could have thought that he would run so cunning, even when he knew my sentiments towards the lady? I hope she told him her mind."

"The point is, what did she tell *you*, Bickley?"

"Me? Oh, she was perfectly charming! It really was a pleasure to be refused by her, she puts one so thoroughly at one's ease." (Here, remembering Bastin and his story, I turned away my face to hide a smile.) "She said—what did she say exactly? Such a lot that it is difficult to remember. Oh! that she was not thinking of marriage. Also, that she had not yet recovered from some recent love affair which left her heart sore, since the time of her sleep did not count. Also, that her father would never consent, and that the mere idea of such a thing would excite his animosity against all of us."

"Is that all?" I asked.

"Not quite. She added that she felt wonderfully flattered and extremely honoured by what I had been so good as to say to her. She hoped, however, that I should never repeat it or even allude to the matter again, as her dearest wish was to be able to look upon me as her most intimate friend to whom she could always come for sympathy and counsel."

"What happened then?"

"Nothing, of course, except that I promised everything that she wished, and mean to stick to it, too. Naturally, I was very sore and upset, but I am getting over it, having always practised self-control."

"I am sorry for you, old fellow."

"Are you?" he asked suspiciously. "Then perhaps you have tried your luck, too?"

"No, Bickley."

His face fell a little at this denial, and he answered:

"Well, it would have been scarcely decent if you had, seeing how lately you were married. But then, so was that artful Bastin. Perhaps you will get over it—recent marriage, I mean—as he has." He hesitated a while, then went on: "Of course you will, old fellow; I know it, and, what is more, I seem to know that when your turn comes you will get a different answer. If so, it will keep her in the family as it were—and good luck to you. Only——"

"Only what?" I asked anxiously.

"To be honest, Arbuthnot, I don't think that there will be real good luck for any one of us over this woman —not in the ordinary sense, I mean. The whole business is too strange and superhuman. Is she quite a woman, and could she really marry a man as others do?"

"It is curious that you should talk like that," I said uneasily. "I thought that you had made up your mind that the whole business was either illusion or trickery—I mean, the odd side of it."

"If it is illusion, Arbuthnot, then a man cannot marry an illusion. And if it is trickery, then he will certainly be tricked. But, supposing that I am wrong, what then?"

"You mean, supposing things are as they seem to be?"

"Yes. In that event, Arbuthnot, I am sure that something will occur to prevent your being united to a woman who lived thousands of years ago. I am sorry to say it, but Fate will intervene. Remember, it is the god of her people that I suppose she worships, and, I may add, to which the whole world bows."

At his words a kind of chill fell upon me. I think he saw or divined it, for after a few remarks upon some indifferent matter, he turned and went away.

Shortly after this Yva came to sit with me. She studied me for a while and I studied her. I had reason to do so, for I observed that of late her dress had become much more modern, and on the present occasion this struck me forcibly. I do not know exactly in what the change, or changes, consisted, because I am not skilled in such matters and can only judge of a woman's garments by their general effect. At any rate, the gorgeous sweeping robes were gone, and though her attire still looked foreign and somewhat oriental, with a touch of barbaric splendour about it—it was simpler than it had been and showed more of her figure, which was delicate, yet gracious.

"You have changed your robes, Lady," I said.

"Yes, Humphrey. Bastin gave me pictures of those your women wear." (On further investigation I found that this referred to an old copy of the *Queen* newspaper, which, somehow or other, had been brought with the books from the ship.) "I have tried to copy them a little," she added doubtfully.

"How do you do it? Where do you get the material?" I asked.

"Oh!" she answered with an airy wave of her hand, "I make it—it is there."

"I don't understand," I said, but she only smiled radiantly, offering no further explanation. Then, before I could pursue the subject, she asked me suddenly:

"What has Bickley been saying to you about me?"

I fenced, answering: "I don't know. Bastin and Bickley talk of little else. You seem to have been a great deal with them while I was ill."

"Yes, a great deal. They are the nearest to you who were so sick. Is it not so?"

"I don't know," I answered again. "In my illness it seemed to me that *you* were the nearest."

"About Bastin's words I can guess," she went on. "But I ask again—what has Bickley been saying to you about me? Of the first part, let it be; tell me the rest."

I intended to evade her question, but she fixed those violet, compelling eyes upon me and I was obliged to answer.

"I believe you know as well as I do," I said; "but if you will have it, it was that you are not as other human women are, and that he who would treat you as such, must suffer; that was the gist of it."

"Some might be content to suffer for such as I," she answered with quiet sweetness. "Even Bastin and Bickley may be content to suffer in their own little ways."

"You know that is not what I meant," I interrupted angrily, for I felt that she was throwing reflections on me.

"No; you meant that you agreed with Bickley that I am not quite a woman, as you know women."

I was silent, for her words were true.

Then she blazed out into one of her flashes of splendour, like something that takes fire on an instant; like the faint and distant star which flames into sudden glory before the watcher's telescope.

"It is true that I am not as your women are—your poor, pale women, the shadows of an hour with night behind them and before. Because I am humble and patient, do you therefore suppose that I am not great? Man from the little country across the sea, I lived when the world was young, and gathered up the ancient wisdom of a greater race than yours, and when the world is old I think that I still shall live, though not in this shape or here, with all that wisdom's essence burning in my breast, and with all beauty in my eyes. Bickley does not believe although he worships. You only half believe and do not worship, because memory holds you back, and I myself do not understand. I only know though knowing so much, still I seek roads to learning, even the humble road called Bastin, that yet may lead my feet to the gate of an immortal city."

"Nor do I understand how all this can be, Yva," I said feebly, for she dazzled and overwhelmed me with her blaze of power.

"No, you do not understand. How can you, when even I cannot? Thus for two hundred and fifty thousand years I slept, and they went by as a lightning flash. One moment my father gave me the draught and I laid me down, the next I awoke with you bending over me, or so it seemed. Yet where was I through all those centuries when for me time had ceased? Tell me, Humphrey, did you dream at all while you were ill? I ask because down in that lonely cavern where I sleep a strange dream came to me one night. It was of a journey which, as I thought, you and I seemed to make together, past suns and universes to a very distant earth. It meant nothing, Humphrey. If you and I chanced to have dreamed the same thing, it was only because my dream travelled to you. It is most common, or used to be. Humphrey, Bickley is quite right, I am not altogether as your women are, and I can bring no happiness to any man, or at the least, to one who cannot wait. Therefore, perhaps you would do well to think less of me, as I have counselled Bastin and Bickley."

Then again she gazed at me with her wonderful, great eyes, and, shaking her glittering head a little, smiled and went.

But oh! that smile drew my heart after her.

CHAPTER XX

ORO AND ARBUTHNOT TRAVEL BY NIGHT

As time went on, Oro began to visit me more and more frequently, till at last scarcely a night went by that he did not appear mysteriously in my sleeping-place. The odd thing was that neither Bickley nor Bastin seemed to be aware of these nocturnal calls. Indeed, when I mentioned them on one or two occasions, they stared at me and said it was strange that he should have come and gone as they saw nothing of him.

On my speaking again of the matter, Bickley at once turned the conversation, from which I gathered that he believed me to be suffering from delusions consequent on my illness, or perhaps to have taken to dreaming. This was not wonderful since, as I learned afterwards, Bickley, after he was sure that I was asleep, made a practice of tying a thread across my doorway and of ascertaining at the dawn that it remained unbroken. But Oro was not to be caught in that way. I suppose, as it was impossible for him to pass through the lattice-work of the open side of the house, that he undid the thread and fastened it again when he left; at least, that was Bastin's explanation, or, rather, one of them. Another was that he crawled beneath it, but this I could not believe. I am quite certain that during all his prolonged existence Oro never crawled.

At any rate, he came, or seemed to come, and pumped me—I can use no other word—most energetically as to existing conditions in the world, especially those of the civilised countries, their methods of government, their social state, the physical characteristics of the various races, their religions, the exact degrees of civilisation that they had developed, their attainments in art, science and literature, their martial capacities, their laws, and I know not what besides.

I told him all I could, but did not in the least seem to satisfy his perennial thirst for information.

"I should prefer to judge for myself," he said at last.

"Why are you so anxious to learn about all these nations, Oro?" I asked, exhausted.

"Because the knowledge I gather may affect my plans for the future," he replied darkly.

"I am told, Oro, that your people acquired the power of transporting themselves from place to place."

"It is true that the lords of the Sons of Wisdom had such power, and that I have it still, O Humphrey."

"Then why do you not go to look with your own eyes?" I suggested.

"Because I should need a guide; one who could explain much in a short time," he said, contemplating me with his burning glance until I began to feel uncomfortable.

To change the subject I asked him whether he had any further information about the war, which he had told me was raging in Europe.

He answered: "Not much; only that it was going on with varying success, and would continue to do so until the nations involved therein were exhausted," or so he believed. The war did not seem greatly to interest Oro. It was, he remarked, but a small affair compared to those which he had known in the old days. Then he departed, and I went to sleep.

Next night he appeared again, and, after talking a

little on different subjects, remarked quietly that he had been thinking over what I had said as to his visiting the modern world, and intended to act upon the suggestion.

"When?" I asked.

"Now," he said. "I am going to visit this England of yours and the town you call London, and *you* will accompany me."

"It is not possible!" I exclaimed. "We have no ship."

"We can travel without a ship," said Oro.

I grew alarmed, and suggested that Bastin or Bickley would be a much better companion than I should in my present weak state.

"An empty-headed man, or one who always doubts and argues, would be useless," he replied sharply. "You shall come and you only."

I expostulated; I tried to get up and fly—which, indeed, I did do, in another sense.

But Oro fixed his eyes upon me and slowly waved his thin hand to and fro above my head.

My senses reeled. Then came a great darkness.

They returned again. Now I was standing in an icy, reeking fog, which I knew could belong to one place only—London, in December, and at my side was Oro.

"Is this the climate of your wonderful city?" he asked, or seemed to ask, in an aggrieved tone.

I replied that it was, for about three months in the year, and began to look about me.

Soon I found my bearings. In front of me were great piles of buildings, looking dim and mysterious in the fog, in which I recognised the Houses of Parliament and Westminster Abbey, for both could be seen from where we stood in front of the Westminster Bridge Station. I explained their identity to Oro.

"Good," he said. "Let us enter your Place of Talk."

"But I am not a member, and we have no passes for the Strangers' Gallery," I expostulated.

"We shall not need any," he replied contemptuously. "Lead on."

Thus adjured, I crossed the road, Oro following me. Looking round, to my horror I saw him right in the path of a motor-bus which seemed to go over him.

"There's an end to Oro," thought I to myself. "Well, at any rate, I have got home."

Next instant he was at my side quite undisturbed by the incident of the 'bus. We came to a policeman at the door and I hesitated, expecting to be challenged. But the policeman seemed absolutely indifferent to our presence, even when Oro marched past him in his flowing robes. So I followed with a like success. Then I understood that we must be invisible.

We passed to the lobby, where members were hurrying to and fro, and constituents and pressmen were gathered, and so on into the House. Oro walked up its floor and took his stand by the table, in front of the Speaker. I followed him, none saying us No.

As it chanced there was what is called a scene in progress—I think it was over Irish matters; the details are of no account. Members shouted, Ministers prevaricated and grew angry, the Speaker intervened. On the whole, it was rather a degrading spectacle. I stood, or seemed to stand, and watched it all. Oro, in his sweeping robes, which looked so incongruous in that place, stepped, or seemed to step, up to the principal personages of the Government and Opposition, whom I indicated to him, and inspected them one by one, as a naturalist might examine strange insects. Then, returning to me, he said:

"Come away; I have seen and heard enough. Who would have thought that this nation of yours was struggling for its life in war?"

We passed out of the House and somehow came to Trafalgar Square. A meeting was in progress there, convened, apparently, to advocate the rights of Labour, also those of women, also to protest against things in general, especially the threat of Conscription in the service of the country.

Here the noise was tremendous, and, the fog having lifted somewhat, we could see everything. Speakers bawled from the base of Nelson's column. Their supporters cheered, their adversaries rushed at them, and in one or two instances succeeded in pulling them down. A woman climbed up and began to scream out something which could only be heard by a few reporters gathered round her. I thought her an unpleasant-looking person, and evidently her remarks were not palatable to the majority of her auditors. There was a rush, and she was dragged from the base of one of Landseer's lions on which she stood. Her skirt was half rent off her and her bodice split down the back. Finally, she was conveyed away, kicking, biting, and scratching, by a number of police. It was a disgusting sight, and tumult ensued.

"Let us go," said Oro. "Your officers of order are good; the rest is not good."

Later we found ourselves opposite to the doors of a famous restaurant where a magnificent and gigantic commissionaire helped ladies from motor-cars, receiving in return money from the men who attended on them. We entered; it was the hour of dinner. The place sparkled with gems, and the naked backs of the women gleamed in the electric light. Course followed upon course; champagne flowed, a fine band played, everything was costly; everything was, in a sense, repellent.

"These are the wealthy citizens of a nation engaged in fighting for its life," remarked Oro to me, stroking his long beard. "It is interesting, very interesting. Let us go."

We went out and on, passing a public-house crowded with women who had left their babies in charge of children in the icy street. It was a day of Intercession for the success of England in the war. This was placarded everywhere. We entered, or, rather, Oro did, I following him, one of the churches in the Strand where an evening service was in progress. The preacher in the pulpit, a very able man, was holding forth upon the necessity for national repentance and self-denial; also of prayer. In the body of the church exactly thirty-two people, most of them elderly women, were listening to him with an air of placid acceptance.

"The priest talks well, but his hearers are not many," said Oro. "Let us go."

We came to the flaunting doors of a great music-hall and passed through them, though to others this would have been impossible, for the place was filled from floor to roof. In its promenades men were drinking and smoking, while gaudy women, painted and low-robed, leered at them. On the stage girls danced, throwing their legs above their heads. Then they vanished amidst applause, and a woman in a yellow robe, who pretended to be tipsy, sang a horrible and vulgar song full of topical allusions, which was received with screams of delight by the enormous audience.

"Here the hearers are very many, but those to whom

they listen do not talk well. Let us go," said Oro, and we went.

At a recruiting station we paused a moment to consider posters supposed to be attractive, the very sight of which sent a thrill of shame through me. I remember that the inscription under one of them was: "What will your best girl say?"

"Is that how you gather your soldiers? Later it will be otherwise," said Oro, and passed on.

We reached Blackfriars and entered a hall at the doors of which stood women in poke-bonnets, very sweet-faced, earnest-looking women. Their countenances seemed to strike Oro, and he motioned me to follow him into the hall. It was quite full of a miserable-looking congregation of perhaps a thousand people. A man in the blue and red uniform of the Salvation Army was preaching of duty to God and country, of self-denial, hope and forgiveness. He seemed a humble person, but his words were earnest, and love flowed from him. Some of his miserable congregation wept, others stared at him open-mouthed, a few, who were very weary, slept. He called them up to receive pardon, and a number, led by the sweet-faced women, came and knelt before him. He and others whispered to them, then seemed to bless them, and they rose with their faces changed.

"Let us go," said Oro. "I do not understand these rites, but at last in your great and wonderful city I have seen something that is pure and noble."

We went out. In the streets there was great excitement. People ran to and fro pointing upwards. Searchlights, like huge fingers of flame, stole across the sky; guns boomed. At last, in the glare of a searchlight, we saw a long and sinister object floating high above us and gleaming as though it were made of silver. Flashes came from it followed by terrible booming reports that grew nearer and nearer. A house collapsed with a crash just behind us.

"Ah!" said Oro, with a smile. "I know this—it is war, war as it was when the world was different and yet the same."

As he spoke, a motor-bus rumbled past. Another flash and explosion. A man, walking with his arms round the waist of a girl just ahead of us, seemed to be tossed up and to melt. The girl fell in a heap on the pavement; somehow her head and her feet had come quite close together and yet she appeared to be sitting down. The motor-bus burst into fragments and its passengers hurtled through the air, mere hideous lumps that had been men and women. The head of one of them came dancing down the pavement towards us, a cigar still stuck in the corner of its mouth.

"Yes, this is war," said Oro. "It makes me young again to see it. But does this city of yours understand?"

We watched a while. A crowd gathered. Policemen ran up, ambulances came. The place was cleared, and all that was left they carried away. A few minutes later another man passed by with his arm round the waist of another girl. Another motor-bus rumbled up, and, avoiding the hole in the roadway, travelled on, its conductor keeping a keen look-out for fares.

The street was cleared by the police; the airship continued its course, spawning bombs in the distance, and vanished. The incident was closed.

"Let us go home," said Oro. "I have seen enough of your great and wonderful city. I would rest in the quiet of Nyo and think."

The next thing that I remember was the voice of Bastin, saying:

"If you don't mind, Arbuthnot, I wish that you would get up. The Glittering Lady (he still called her that) is coming here to have a talk with me which I should prefer to be private. Excuse me for disturbing you, but you have overslept yourself; indeed, I think it must be nine o'clock, so far as I can judge by the sun, for my watch is very erratic now, ever since Bickley tried to clean it."

"I am sorry, my dear fellow," I said sleepily, "but do you know I thought I was in London—in fact, I could swear that I have been there."

"Then," interrupted Bickley, who had followed Bastin into the hut, giving me that doubtful glance with which I was now familiar, "I wish to goodness that you had brought back an evening paper with you."

A night or two later I was again suddenly awakened to feel that Oro was approaching. He appeared like a ghost in the bright moonlight, greeted me, and said:

"To-night, Humphrey, we must make another journey. I would visit the seat of the war."

"I do not wish to go," I said feebly.

"What you wish does not matter," he replied. "*I* wish that you should go, and therefore you must."

"Listen, Oro," I exclaimed. "I do not like this business; it seems dangerous to me."

"There is no danger if you are obedient, Humphrey."

"I think there is. I do not understand what happens. Do you make use of what the Lady Yva called the Fourth Dimension, so that our bodies pass over the seas and through mountains, like the vibrations of our Wireless, of which I was speaking to you?"

"No, Humphrey. That method is good and easy, but I do not use it because if I did we should be visible in the places which we visit, since there all the atoms that make a man would collect together again and be a man."

"What, then, do you do?" I asked, exasperated.

"Man, Humphrey, is not one; he is many. Thus, amongst other things he has a Double, which can see and hear, as he can in the flesh, if it is separated from the flesh."

"The old Egyptians believed that," I said.

"Did they? Doubtless they inherited the knowledge from us, the Sons of Wisdom. The cup of our learning was so full that, keep it secret as we would, from time to time some of it overflowed among the vulgar, and doubtless thus the light of our knowledge still burns feebly in the world."

I reflected to myself that whatever might be their other characteristics, the Sons of Wisdom had lost that of modesty, but I only asked how he used his Double, supposing that it existed.

"Very easily," he answered. "In sleep it can be drawn from the body and sent upon its mission by one that is its master."

"Then while you were asleep for all those thousands of years your Double must have made many journeys."

"Perhaps," he replied quietly, "and my spirit also, which is another part of me that may have dwelt in the bodies of other men. But unhappily, if so I forget, and that is why I have so much to learn and must even make use of such poor instruments as you, Humphrey."

"Then if I sleep and you distil my Double out of me, I suppose that you sleep too. In that case who distils your Double out of *you,* Lord Oro?"

He grew angry and answered:

"Ask no more questions, blind and ignorant as you are. It is your part not to examine, but to obey. Sleep now," and again he waved his hand over me.

In an instant, as it seemed, we were standing in a grey old town that I judged from its appearance must be either in northern France or Belgium. It was much shattered by bombardment; the church, for instance, was a ruin; also many of the houses had been burnt. Now, however, no firing was going on for the town had been taken. The streets were full of armed men wearing the German uniform and helmet. We passed down them and were able to see into the houses. In some of these were German soldiers engaged in looting and in other things so horrible that even the unmoved Oro turned away his head.

We came to the market-place. It was crowded with German troops, also with a great number of the inhabitants of the town, most of them elderly men and women with children, who had fallen into their power. The Germans, under the command of officers, were dragging the men from the arms of their wives and children to one side, and with rifle-butts beating back the screaming women. Among the men I noticed two or three priests who were doing their best to soothe their companions and even giving them absolution in hurried whispers.

At length the separation was effected, whereon at a hoarse word of command, a company of soldiers began to fire at the men and continued doing so until all had fallen. Then petty officers went among the slaughtered and with pistols blew out the brains of any who still moved.

"These butchers, you say, are Germans?" asked Oro of me.

"Yes," I answered, sick with horror, for though I was in the mind and not in the body, I could feel as the mind does. Had I been in the body also, I should have fainted.

"Then we need not waste time in visiting their country. It is enough; let us go on."

We passed out into the open land and came to a village. It was in the occupation of German cavalry. Two of them held a little girl of nine or ten, one by her body, the other by her right hand. An officer stood between them with a drawn sword fronting the terrified child. He was a horrible, coarse-faced man who looked to me as though he had been drinking.

"I'll teach the young devil to show us the wrong road and let those French swine escape," he shouted, and struck with the sword. The girl's right hand fell to the ground.

"War as practised by the Germans!" remarked Oro. Then he stepped, or seemed to step up to the man and whispered, or seemed to whisper, in his ear.

I do not know what tongue or what spirit speech he used, or what he said, but the bloated-faced brute turned pale. Yes, he grew sick with fear.

"I think there are spirits in this place," he said with a German oath. "I could have sworn that something told me that I was going to die. Mount!"

The Uhlans mounted and began to ride away.

"Watch," said Oro.

As he spoke out of a dark cloud appeared an aeroplane. Its pilot saw the band of Germans beneath and dropped a bomb. The aim was good, for the missile exploded in the midst of them, causing a great cloud of dust from which arose the screams of men and horses.

"Come and see," said Oro.

We were there. Out of the cloud of dust appeared one man galloping furiously. He was a young fellow who, as I noted, had turned his head away and hidden his eyes with his hand when the horror was done yonder. All the others were dead except the officer who had worked the deed. He was still living, but both his hands and one of his feet had been blown away. Presently he died, screaming to God for mercy.

We passed on and came to a barn with wide doors that swung a little in the wind, causing the rusted hinges to scream like a creature in pain. On each of these doors hung a dead man crucified. The hat of one of them lay upon the ground, and I knew from the shape of it that he was a Colonial soldier.

"Did you not tell me," said Oro after surveying them, "that these Germans are of your Christian faith?"

"Yes; and the Name of God is always on their ruler's lips."

"Ah!" he said, "I am glad that I worship Fate. Bastin the priest need trouble me no more."

"There is something behind Fate," I said, quoting Bastin himself.

"Perhaps. So indeed I have always held, but after much study I cannot understand the manner of its working. Fate is enough for me."

We went on and came to a flat country that was lined with ditches, all of them full of men, Germans on one side, English and French upon the other. A terrible bombardment shook the earth, the shells raining upon the ditches. Presently that from the English guns ceased and out of the trenches in front of them thousands of men were vomited, who ran forward through a hail of fire in which scores and hundreds fell, across an open piece of ground that was pitted with shell craters. They came to barbed wire defenses, or what remained of them, cut the wire with nippers and pulled up the posts. Then through the gaps they surged in, shouting and hurling hand grenades. They reached the German trenches, they leapt into them and from those holes arose a hellish din. Pistols were fired and everywhere bayonets flashed.

Behind them rushed a horde of little, dark-skinned men, Indians who carried great knives in their hands. Those leapt over the first trench and running on with wild yells, dived into the second, those who were left of them, and there began hacking with their knives at the defenders and the soldiers who worked the spitting maxim guns. In twenty minutes it was over; those lines of trenches were taken, and once more from either side the guns began to boom.

"War again," said Oro, "clean, honest war, such as the god I call Fate decrees for man. I have seen enough. Now I would visit those whom you call Turks. I understand they have another worship and perhaps they are nobler than these Christians."

We came to a hilly country which I recognised as Armenia, for once I travelled there, and stopped on a seashore. Here were the Turks in thousands. They were engaged in driving before them mobs of men, women and children in countless numbers. On and on they drove them till they reached the shore. There they massacred them with bayonets, with bullets, or by drowning. I remember a dreadful scene of a poor woman standing up to her waist in the water. Three children were clinging to her—but I cannot go on, really I cannot go on. In the end a Turk waded out and bayoneted her while she strove to protect the last living child with her poor body whence it sprang.

"These, I understand," said Oro, pointing to the Turkish soldiers, "worship a prophet who they say is the voice of God."

"Yes," I answered, "and therefore they massacre these who are Christians because they worship God without a prophet."

"And what do the Christians massacre each other for?"

"Power and the wealth and territories that are power. That is, the King of the Germans wishes to rule the world, but the other Nations do not desire his dominion. Therefore they fight for Liberty and Justice."

"As it was, so it is and shall be," remarked Oro, "only with this difference. In the old world some were wise, but here——" and he stopped, his eyes fixed upon the Armenian woman struggling in her death agony while the murderer drowned her child, then added: "Let us go."

Our road ran across the sea. On it we saw a ship so large that it attracted Oro's attention, and for once he expressed astonishment.

"In my day," he said, "we had no vessels of this greatness in the world. I wish to look upon it."

We landed on the deck of the ship, or rather the floating palace, and examined her. She carried many passengers, some English, some American, and I pointed out to Oro the differences between the two peoples. These were not, he remarked, very wide except that the American women wore more jewels, also that some of the American men, to whom we listened as they conversed, spoke of the greatness of their country, whereas the Englishmen, if they said anything concerning it, belittled their country.

Presently, on the surface of the sea at a little distance appeared something strange, a small and ominous object like a can on the top of a pole. A voice cried out "*Submarine!*" and everyone near rushed to look.

"If those Germans try any of their monkey tricks on us, I guess the United States will give them hell," said another voice near by.

Then from the direction of the pole with the tin can on the top of it, came something which caused a disturbance in the smooth water and bubbles to rise in its wake.

"A torpedo!" cried some.

"Shut your mouth," said the voice. "Who dare torpedo a vessel full of the citizens of the United States?"

Next came a booming crash and a flood of upthrown water, in the wash of which that speaker was carried away into the deep. Then horror! horror! horror! indescribable, as the mighty vessel went wallowing to her doom. Boats launched; boats overset; boats dragged under by her rush through the water which could not be stayed. Maddened men and women running to and fro, their eyes starting from their heads, clasping children, fastening lifebelts over their costly gowns, or appearing from their cabins, their hands filled with jewels that they sought to save. Orders cried from high places by stern-faced officers doing their duty to the last. And a little way off that thin pole with a tin can on the top of it watching its work.

Then the plunge of the enormous ship into the deep, its huge screws still whirling in the air and the boom of the bursting boilers. Lastly everything gone save a few boats floating on the quiet sea and around them dots that were the heads of struggling human beings.

"Let us go home," said Oro, "I grow tired of this war of your Christian peoples. It is no better than that of the barbarian nations of the early world. Indeed it is worse, since then we worshipped Fate and but a few of us had wisdom. Now you all claim wisdom and declare that you worship a God of Mercy."

With these words still ringing in my ears I woke up upon the Island of Orofena, filled with terror at the horrible possibilities of nightmare.

What else could it be? There was the brown and ancient cone of the extinct volcano. There were the tall palms of the main island and the lake glittering in the sunlight between. There was Bastin conducting a kind of Sunday school of Orofenans upon the point of the Rock of Offerings, as now he had obtained the leave of Oro to do. There was the mouth of the cave, and issuing from it Bickley, who by help of one of the hurricane lamps had been making an examination of the buried remains of what he supposed to be flying machines. Without doubt it was nightmare, and I would say nothing to them about it for fear of mockery.

Yet two nights later Oro came again and after the usual preliminaries, said:

"Humphrey, this night we will visit that mighty American nation, of which you have told me so much, and the other Neutral Countries.

[At this point there is a gap in Mr. Arbuthnot's MS.,

so Oro's reflections on the Neutral Nations, if any, remain unrecorded. It continues:]

On our homeward way we passed over Australia, making a detour to do so. Of the cities Oro took no account. He said that they were too large and too many, but the country interested him so much that I gathered he must have given great attention to agriculture at some time in the past. He pointed out to me that the climate was fine, and the land so fertile that with a proper system of irrigation and water-storage it could support tens of millions and feed not only itself but a great part of the outlying world.

"But where are the people?" he asked. "Outside of those huge hives," and he indicated the great cities, "I see few of them, though doubtless some of the men are fighting in this war. Well, in the days to come this must be remedied."

Over New Zealand, which he found beautiful, he shook his head for the same reason.

On another night we visited the East. China with its teeming millions interested him extremely, partly because he declared these to be the descendants of one of the barbarian nations of his own day. He made a remark to the effect that this race had always possessed points and capacities, and that he thought that with proper government and instruction their Chinese offspring would be of use in a regenerated world.

For the Japanese and all that they had done in two short generations, he went so far as to express real admiration, a very rare thing with Oro, who was by nature critical. I could see that mentally he put a white mark against their name.

India, too, really moved him. He admired the ancient

buildings at Delhi and Agra, especially the Taj Mahal. This, he declared, was reminiscent of some of the palaces that stood at Pani, the capital city of the Sons of Wisdom, before it was destroyed by the Barbarians. The English administration of the country also attracted a word of praise from him, I think because of its rather autocratic character. Indeed he went so far as to declare that, with certain modifications, it should be continued in the future, and even to intimate that he would bear the matter in mind. Democratic forms of government had no charms for Oro.

Amongst other places, we stopped at Benares and watched the funeral rites in progress upon the banks of the holy Ganges. The bearers of the dead brought the body of a woman wrapped in a red shroud that glittered with tinsel ornaments. Coming forward at a run and chanting as they ran, they placed it upon the stones for a little while, then lifted it up again and carried it down the steps to the edge of the river. Here they took water and poured it over the corpse, thus performing the rite of the baptism of death. This done, they placed its feet in the water and left it looking very small and lonely. Presently appeared a tall, white-draped woman who took her stand by the body and wailed. It was the dead one's mother. Again the bearers approached and laid the corpse upon the flaming pyre.

"These rites are ancient," said Oro. "When I ruled as King of the World they were practised in this very place. It is pleasant to me to find something that has survived the changefulness of Time. Let it continue till the end."

Here I will cease. These experiences that I have recorded are but samples, for also we visited Russia and other countries. Perhaps, too, they were not experiences at all, but only dreams consequent on my state of health. I cannot say for certain, though much of what I seemed to see fitted in very well indeed with what I learned in after days, and certainly at the time they appeared as real as though Oro and I had stood together upon those various shores.

CHAPTER XXI

LOVE'S ETERNAL ALTAR

Now of all these happenings I said very little to Bastin and Bickley. The former would not have understood them, and the latter attributed what I did tell him to mental delusions following on my illness. To Yva I did speak about them, however, imploring her to explain their origin and to tell me whether or not they were but visions of the night.

She listened to me, as I thought not without anxiety, from which I gathered that she too feared for my mind. It was not so, however, for she said:

"I am glad, O Humphrey, that your journeyings are done, since such things are not without danger. He who travels far out of the body may chance to return there no more."

"But were they journeyings, or dreams?" I asked.

She evaded a direct answer.

"I cannot say. My father has great powers. I do not know them all. It is possible that they were neither journeyings nor dreams. Mayhap he used you as the sorcerers in the old days used the magic glass, and after he had put his spell upon you, read in your mind that which passes elsewhere."

I understood her to refer to what we call clairvoyance, when the person entranced reveals secret or distant things to the entrancer. This is a more or less established phenomenon and much less marvellous than the actual transportation of the spiritual self through space. Only I never knew of an instance in which the seer, on awaking, remembered the things that he had seen, as in my case. There, however, the matter rested, or rests, for I could extract nothing more from Yva, who appeared to me to have her orders on the point.

Nor did Oro ever talk of what I had seemed to see in his company, although he continued from time to time to visit me at night. But now our conversation was of other matters. As Bastin had discovered, by some extraordinary gift he had soon learned how to read the English language, although he never spoke a single word in that tongue. Among our reference books that we brought from the yacht, was a thin paper edition of the *Encyclopædia Britannica,* which he borrowed when he discovered that it contained compressed information about the various countries of the world, also concerning almost every other matter. My belief is that within a month or so that marvellous old man not only read this stupendous work from end to end, but that he remembered everything of interest which it contained. At least, he would appear and show the fullest acquaintance with certain subjects or places, seeking further light from me concerning them, which very often I was quite unable to give him.

An accident, as it chanced, whereof I need not set out the details, caused me to discover that his remarkable knowledge was limited. Thus, at one period, he knew little about any modern topic which began with a letter later in the alphabet than, let us say, C. A few days afterwards he was acquainted with those up to F, or G; and so on till he reached Z, when he appeared to me to know everything, and returned the book. Now, indeed, he was a monument of learning, very ancient and very new, and with some Encyclopædia-garnered facts or deductions of what had happened between.

Moreover, he took to astronomical research, for more than once we saw him standing on the rock at night studying the heavens. On one of these occasions, when he had the two metal plates, of which I have spoken, in his hands, I ventured to approach and ask what he did. He replied that he was checking his calculations that he found to be quite correct, an exact period of two hundred and fifty thousand years having gone by since he laid himself down to sleep. Then, by aid of the plates, he pointed out to me certain alterations that had happened during that period in the positions of some of the stars.

For instance, he showed me one which, by help of my glasses, I recognised as Sirius, and remarked that two hundred and fifty thousand years ago it was further away and much smaller. Now it was precisely in the place and of the size which he had predicted, and he pointed to it on his prophetic map. Again he indicated a star that the night-glass told me was Capella, which, I suppose, is one of the most brilliant stars in the sky, and showed me that on the map he had made two hundred and fifty thousand years ago, it did not exist, as then it was too far north to appear thereon. Still, he observed, the passage of this vast period of time had produced but little effect upon the face of the heavens. To the human eye the majority of the stars had not moved so very far.

"And yet they travel fast, O Humphrey," he said. "Consider then how great is their journey between the time they gather and that day when, worn-out, once more they melt to vaporous gas. You think me long-lived who compared to them exist but a tiny fraction of a second, nearly all of which I have been doomed to pass in sleep. And, Humphrey, I desire to live—I, who have great plans and would shake the world. But my day draws in; a few brief centuries and I shall be gone, and—whither, whither?"

"If you lived as long as those stars, the end would be the same, Oro."

"Yes, but the life of the stars is very long, millions of millions of years; also, after death, they re-form, as other stars. But shall I re-form as another Oro? With all my wisdom, I do not know. It is known to Fate only—Fate—the master of worlds and men and the gods they worship—Fate, whom it may please to spill my gathered knowledge, to be lost in the sands of Time."

"It seems that you are great," I said, "and have lived long and learned much. Yet the end of it is that your lot is neither worse nor better than that of us creatures of an hour."

"It is so, Humphrey. Presently you will die, and within a few centuries I shall die also and be as you are. You believe that you will live again eternally. It may be so because you *do* believe, since Fate allows Faith to shape the future, if only for a little while. But in me Wisdom has destroyed Faith and therefore I must die. Even if I sleep again for tens of thousands of years, what will it help me, seeing that sleep is unconsciousness and that I shall only wake again to die, since sleep does not restore to us our youth?"

He ceased, and walked up and down the rock with a troubled mien. Then he stood in front of me and said in a triumphant voice:

"At least, while I live I will rule, and then let come what may come. I know that you do not believe, and the first victory of this new day of mine shall be to make you believe. I have great powers and you shall see them at work, and afterwards, if things go right, rule with me for a little while, perhaps, as the first of my subjects. Hearken now; in one small matter my calculations, made so long ago, have gone wrong. They showed me that at this time a day of earthquakes, such as those that again and again have rocked and split the world, would recur. But now it seems that there is an error, a tiny error of eleven hundred years, which must go by before those earthquakes come."

"Are you sure," I suggested humbly, "that there is not also an error in those star-maps you hold?"

"I am sure, Humphrey. Some day, who knows? you may return to your world of modern men who, I gather, have knowledge of the great science of astronomy. Take now these maps with which I have done, and submit them to the most learned of those men, and let them tell you whether I was right or wrong in what I wrote upon this metal two hundred and fifty thousand years ago. Whatever else is false, at least the stars in their motions can never die."

Then he handed me the maps and was gone. I have them to-day, and if ever this book is published, they will appear with it, that those who are qualified may judge of them and of the truth or otherwise of Oro's words.

From that night forward for quite a long time I saw Oro no more. Nor indeed did any of us, since for some reason of his own he forbade us to visit the underground city of Nyo. Oddly enough, however, he commanded Yva to bring down the spaniel, Tommy, to be with him from time to time. When I asked her why, she said it was because he was lonely and desired the dog's companionship. It seemed to us very strange that this super-man, who had the wisdom of ten Solomons gathered in one within his breast, should yet desire the company of a little dog. What then was the worth of learning and long life, or, indeed, of anything? Well, Solomon himself asked the question ages since, and could give no answer save that all is vanity.

I noted about this time that Yva began to grow very sad and troubled; indeed, looking at her suddenly on two or three occasions, I saw that her beautiful eyes were aswim with tears. Also, I noted that always as she grew sadder she became, in a sense, more human. In the beginning she was, as it were, far away. One could never forget that she was the child of some alien race whose eyes had looked upon the world when, by comparison, humanity was young; at times, indeed, she might have been the denizen of another planet, strayed to earth. Although she never flaunted it, one felt that her simplest word hid secret wisdom; that to her books were open in which we could not read. Moreover, as I have said, occasionally power flamed out of her, power that was beyond our ken and understanding.

Yet with all this there was nothing elfish about her, nothing uncanny. She was always kind, and, as we could feel, innately good and gentle-hearted, just a woman made half-divine by gifts and experience that others lack. She did not even make use of her wondrous beauty to madden men, as she might well have done had she been so minded. It is true that both Bastin and Bickley fell in love with her, but that was only because all with whom she had to do must love her, and then, when she told them that it might not be, it was in such a fashion that no soreness was left behind. They went on loving her, that was all, but as men love their sisters or their daughters; as we conceive that they may love in that land where there is no marrying or giving in marriage.

But now, in her sadness, she drew ever nearer to us, and especially to myself, more in tune with our age and thought. In truth, save for her royal and glittering loveliness in which there was some quality which proclaimed her of another blood, and for that reserve of hidden power which at times would look out of her eyes or break through her words, she might in most ways have been some singularly gifted and beautiful modern woman.

The time has come when I must speak of my relations with Yva and of their climax. As may have been guessed, from the first I began to love her. While the weeks went on that love grew and grew, until it utterly possessed me, although for a certain reason connected with one dead, at first I fought against it. Yet it did not develop quite in the fashion that might have been expected. There was no blazing up of passion's fire; rather was there an ever-increasing glow of the holiest affection, till at last it became a lamp by which I must guide my feet through life and death. This love of mine seemed not of earth but from the stars. As yet I had said nothing to her of it because in some way I felt that she did not wish me to do so, felt also that she was well aware of all that passed within my heart, and desired, as it were, to give it time to ripen there. Then one day there came a change, and though no glance or touch of Yva's told me so, I knew that the bars were taken down and that I might speak.

It was a night of full moon. All that afternoon she

had been talking to Bastin apart, I suppose about religion, for I saw that he had some books in his hand from which he was expounding something to her in his slow, earnest way. Then she came and sat with us while we took our evening meal. I remember that mine consisted of some of the Life-water which she had brought with her and fruit, for, as I think I have said, I had acquired her dislike to meat, also that she ate some plantains, throwing the skins for Tommy to fetch and laughing at his play. When it was over, Bastin and Bickley went away together, whether by chance or design I do not know, and she said to me suddenly:

"Humphrey, you have often asked me about the city Pani, of which a little portion of the ruins remains upon this island, the rest being buried beneath the waters. If you wish I will show you where our royal palace was before the barbarians destroyed it with their airships. The moon is very bright, and by it we can see."

I nodded, for, knowing what she meant, somehow I could not answer her, and we began the ascent of the hill. She explained to me the plan of the palace when we reached the ruins, showing me where her own apartments had been, and the rest. It was very strange to hear her quietly telling of buildings which had stood and of things that had happened over two hundred and fifty thousand years before, much as any modern lady might do of a house that had been destroyed a month ago by an earthquake or a Zeppelin bomb, while she described the details of a disaster which now frightened her no more. I think it was then that for the first time I really began to believe that in fact Yva had lived all those æons since and been as she still appeared.

We passed from the palace to the ruins of the temple, through what, as she said, had been a pleasure-garden, pointing out where a certain avenue of rare palms had grown, down which once it was her habit to walk in the cool of the day. Or, rather, there were two terraced temples, one dedicated to Fate like that in the underground city of Nyo, and the other to Love. Of the temple to Fate she told me her father had been the High Priest, and of the temple to Love she was the High Priestess.

Then it was that I understood why she had brought me here.

She led the way to a marble block covered with worn-out carvings and almost buried in the débris. This, she said, was the altar of offerings. I asked her what offerings, and she replied with a smile:

"Only wine, to signify the spirit of life, and flowers to symbolise its fragrance," and she laid her finger on a cup-like depression, still apparent in the marble, into which the wine was poured.

Indeed, I gathered that there was nothing coarse or bacchanalian about this worship of a prototype of Aphrodite; on the contrary, that it was more or less spiritual and ethereal. We sat down on the altar stone. I wondered a little that she should have done so, but she read my thought, and answered:

"Sometimes we change our faiths, Humphrey, or perhaps they grow. Also, have I not told you that sacrifices were offered on this altar?" and she sighed and smiled.

I do not know which was the sweeter, the smile or the sigh.

We looked at the water glimmering in the crater beneath us on the edge of which we sat. We looked at heaven above in which the great moon sailed royally. Then we looked into each other's eyes.

"I love you," I said.

"I know it," she answered gently. "You have loved me from the first, have you not? Even when I lay asleep in the coffin you began to love me, but until you dreamed a certain dream you would not admit it."

"Yva, what was the meaning of that dream?"

"I cannot say, Humphrey. But I tell you this. As you will learn in time, one spirit may be clothed in different garments of the flesh."

I did not understand her, but, in some strange way, her words brought to my mind those that Natalie spoke at the last, and I answered:

"Yva, when my wife lay dying she bade me seek her elsewhere, for certainly I should find her. Doubtless she meant beyond the shores of death—or perhaps she also dreamed."

She bent her head, looking at me very strangely.

"Your wife, too, may have had the gift of dreams, Humphrey. As you dream and I dream, so mayhap she dreamed. Of dreams, then, let us say no more, since I think that they have served their purpose, and all three of us understand."

Then I stretched out my arms, and next instant my head lay upon her perfumed breast. She lifted it and kissed me on the lips, saying:

"With this kiss again I give myself to you. But oh! Humphrey, do not ask too much of the god of my people, Fate," and she looked me in the eyes and sighed.

"What do you mean?" I asked, trembling.

"Many, many things. Among them, that happiness is not for mortals, and remember that though my life began long ago, I am mortal as you are, and that in eternity time makes no difference."

"And if so, Yva, what then? Do we meet but to part?"

"Who said it? Not I. Humphrey, I tell you this. Nor earth, nor heaven, nor hell have any bars through which love cannot burst its way towards re-union and completeness. Only there must be love, manifested in many shapes and at many times, but ever striving to its end, which is not of the flesh. Aye, love that has lost itself, love scorned, love defeated, love that seems false, love betrayed, love gone astray, love wandering through the worlds, love asleep and living in its sleep, love awake and yet sleeping; all love that has in it the germ of life. It matters not what form love takes. If it be true I tell you that it will win its way, and in the many that it has seemed to worship, still find the one, though perchance not here."

At her words a numb fear gripped my heart.

"Not here? Then where?" I said.

"Ask your dead wife, Humphrey. Ask the dumb stars. Ask the God you worship, for I cannot answer, save in one word—Somewhere! Man, be not afraid. Do you think that such as you and I can be lost in the aching abysms of space? I know but little, yet I tell you that we are its rulers. I tell you that we, too, are gods, if only we can aspire and belive. For the doubting and timid there is naught. For those who see with the eyes of the soul and stretch out their hands to grasp there is all. Even Bastin will tell you this."

"But," I said, "life is short. Those worlds are far away, and you are near."

She became wonderful, mysterious.

"Near I am far," she said; "and far I am near, if only this love of yours is strong enough to follow and to clasp. And, Humphrey, it needs strength, for here

I am afraid that it will bear little of such fruit as men desire to pluck."

Again terror took hold of me, and I looked at her, for I did not know what to say or ask.

"Listen," she went on. "Already my father has offered me to you in marriage, has he not, but at a price which you do not understand? Believe me, it is one that you should never pay, since the rule of the world can be too dearly bought by the slaughter of half the world. And if you would pay it, I cannot."

"But this is madness!" I exclaimed. "Your father has no powers over our earth."

"I would that I could think so, Humphrey. I tell you that he has powers and that it is his purpose to use them as he has done before. You, too, he would use, and me."

"And, if so, Yva, we are lords of ourselves. Let us take each other while we may. Bastin is a priest."

"Lords of ourselves! Why, for ought I know, at this very moment Oro watches us in his thought and laughs. Only in death, Humphrey, shall we pass beyond his reach and become lords of ourselves."

"It is monstrous!" I cried. "There is the boat, let us fly away."

"What boat can bear us out of stretch of the arm of the old god of my people, Fate, whereof Oro is the high priest? Nay, here we must wait our doom."

"Doom," I said—"doom? What then is about to happen?"

"A terrible thing, as I think, Humphrey. Or, rather, it will not happen."

"Why not, if it must?"

"Beloved," she whispered, "Bastin has expounded to me a new faith whereof the master-word is Sacrifice.

The terrible thing will not happen *because of sacrifice!* Ask me no more."

She mused a while, seated there in the moonlight upon the ancient altar of sacrifice, the veil she wore falling about her face and making her mysterious. Then she threw it back, showing her lovely eyes and glittering hair, and laughed.

"We have still an earthly hour," she said; "therefore let us forget the far, dead past and the eternities to come and be joyful in that hour. Now throw your arms about me and I will tell you strange stories of lost days, and you shall look into my eyes and learn wisdom, and you shall kiss my lips and taste of bliss—you, who were and are and shall be—you, the beloved of Yva from the beginning to the end of Time."

CHAPTER XXII

THE COMMAND

I THINK that both Bastin and Bickley, by instinct as it were, knew what had passed between Yva and myself and that she had promised herself to me. They showed this by the way in which they avoided any mention of her name. Also they began to talk of their own plans for the future as matters in which I had no part. Thus I heard them discussing the possibility of escape from the island whereof suddenly they seemed to have grown weary, and whether by any means two men (two, not three) could manage to sail and steer the lifeboat that remained upon the wreck. In short, as in all such cases, the woman had come between; also the pressure of a common loss caused them to forget their differences and to draw closer together. I who had succeeded where they both had failed, was, they seemed to think, out of their lives, so much that our ancient intimacy had ended.

This attitude hurt me, perhaps because in many respects the situation was awkward. They had, it is true, taken their failures extremely well, still the fact remained that both of them had fallen in love with the wonderful creature, woman and yet more than woman, who had bound herself to me. How then could we go on living together, I in prospective possession of the object that all had desired, and they without the pale?

Moreover, they were jealous in another and quite a different fashion because they both loved me in their own ways and were convinced that I who had hitherto loved them, henceforward should have no affection left to spare, since surely this Glittering Lady, this marvel of wisdom and physical perfections would take it all. Of course they were in error, since even if I could have been so base and selfish, this was no conduct that Yva would have wished or even suffered. Still that was their thought.

Mastering the situation I reflected a little while and then spoke straight out to them.

"My friends," I said, "as I see that you have guessed, Yva and I are affianced to each other and love each other perfectly."

"Yes, Arbuthnot," said Bastin, "we saw that in your face, and in hers as she bade us good night before she went into the cave, and we congratulate you and wish you every happiness."

"We wish you every happiness, old fellow," chimed in Bickley. He paused a while, then added, "But to be honest, I am not sure that I congratulate you."

"Why not, Bickley?"

"Not for the reason that you may suspect, Arbuthnot, I mean not because you have won where we have lost, as it was only to be expected that you would do, but on account of something totally different. I told you a while ago and repetition is useless and painful. I need only add therefore that since then my conviction has strengthened and I am sure, sorry as I am to say it, that in this matter you must prepare for disappointment and calamity. That woman, if woman she really is, will never be the wife of mortal man. Now be angry with me if you like, or laugh as you have the right to do, seeing that like Bastin and yourself, I also asked her to marry me, but something makes me speak what I believe to be the truth."

"Like Cassandra," I suggested.

"Yes, like Cassandra who was not a popular person."

At first I was inclined to resent Bickley's words—who would not have been in the circumstances? Then of a sudden there rushed in upon my mind the conviction that he spoke the truth. In this world Yva was not for me or any man. Moreover she knew it, the knowledge peeped out of every word she spoke in our passionate love scene by the lake. She was aware, and subconsciously I was aware, that we were plighting our troth, not for time but for eternity. With time we had little left to do; not for long would she wear the ring I gave her on that holy night.

Even Bastin, whose perceptions normally were not acute, felt that the situation was strained and awkward and broke in with a curious air of forced satisfaction:

"It's uncommonly lucky for you, old boy, that you happen to have a clergyman in your party, as I shall be able to marry you in a respectable fashion. Of course I can't say that the Glittering Lady is as yet absolutely converted to our faith, but I am certain that she has absorbed enough of its principles to justify me in uniting her in Christian wedlock."

"Yes," I answered, "she has absorbed its principles; she told me as much herself. Sacrifice, for instance," and as I spoke the word my eyes filled with tears.

"Sacrifice!" broke in Bickley with an angry snort, for he needed a vent to his mental disturbance. "Rubbish. Why should every religion demand sacrifice as savages do? By it alone they stand condemned."

"Because as I think, sacrifice is the law of life, at least of all life that is worth the living," I answered sadly enough. "Anyhow I believe you are right, Bickley, and that Bastin will not be troubled to marry us."

"You don't mean," broke in Bastin with a horrified air, "that you propose to dispense——"

"No, Bastin, I don't mean that. What I mean is that it comes upon me that something will prevent this marriage. Sacrifice, perhaps, though in what shape I do not know. And now good night. I am tired."

That night in the chill dead hour before the dawn Oro came again. I woke up to see him seated by my bed, majestic, and, as it seemed to me, lambent, though this may have been my imagination.

"You take strange liberties with my daughter, Barbarian, or she takes strange liberties with you, it does not matter which," he said, regarding me with his calm and terrible eyes.

"Why do you presume to call me Barbarian?" I asked, avoiding the main issue.

"For this reason, Humphrey. All men are the same. They have the same organs, the same instincts, the same desires, which in essence are but two, food and rebirth that Nature commands; though it is true that millions of years before I was born, as I have learned from the records of the Sons of Wisdom, it was said that they were half ape. Yet being the same there is between them a whole sea of difference, since some have knowledge and others none, or little. Those who have none or little, among whom you must be numbered, are Barbarians. Those who have much, among whom my daughter and I are the sole survivors, are the Instructed."

"There are nearly two thousand millions of living people in this world," I said, "and you name all of them Barbarians?"

"All, Humphrey, excepting, of course, myself and my daughter who are not known to be alive. You think that you have learned much, whereas in truth you are most ignorant. The commonest of the outer nations, when I destroyed them, knew more than your wisest know to-day."

"You are mistaken, Oro; since then we have learned something of the soul."

"Ah!" he exclaimed, "that interests me and perhaps it is true. Also, if true it is very important, as I have told you before—or was it Bastin? If a man has a soul, he lives, whereas even we Sons of Wisdom die, and in Death what is the use of Wisdom? Because you can believe, you have souls and are therefore, perhaps, heirs to life, foolish and ignorant as you are to-day. Therefore I admit you and Bastin to be my equals, though Bickley, who like myself believes nothing, is but a common chemist and doctor of disease."

"Then you bow to Faith, Oro?"

"Yes, and I think that my god Fate also bows to Faith. Perhaps, indeed, Faith shapes Fate, not Fate Faith. But whence comes that faith which even I with all my learning cannot command? Why is it denied to me and given to you and Bastin?"

"Because as Bastin would tell you, it is a gift, though one that is never granted to the proud and self-sufficient. Become humble as a child, Oro, and perchance you too may acquire faith."

"And how shall I become humble?"

"By putting away all dreams of power and its exercise, if such you have, and in repentance walking quietly to the Gates of Death," I replied.

"For you, Humphrey, who have little or none of these things, that may be easy. But for me who have much, if not all, it is otherwise. You ask me to abandon the certain for the uncertain, the known for the unknown, and from a half-god communing with the stars, to become an earthworm crawling in mud and lifting blind eyes towards the darkness of everlasting night."

"A god who must die is no god, half or whole, Oro; the earthworm that lives on is greater than he."

"Mayhap. Yet while I endure I will be as a god, so that when night comes, if come it must, I shall have played my part and left my mark upon this little world of ours. Have done!" he added with a burst of impatience. "What will you of my daughter?"

"What man has always willed of woman—herself, body and soul."

"Her soul perchance is yours, if she has one, but her body is mine to give or withhold. Yet it can be bought at a price," he added slowly.

"So she told me, Oro."

"I can guess what she told you. Did I not watch you yonder by the lake when you gave her a ring graved with the signs of Life and Everlastingness? The question is, will you pay the price?"

"Not so; the question is—what is the price?"

"This; to enter my service and henceforth do my will—without debate or cavil."

"For what reward, Oro?"

"Yva and the dominion of the earth while you shall live, neither more nor less."

"And what is your will?"

"That you shall learn in due course. On the second night from this I command the three of you to wait upon me at sundown in the buried halls of Nyo. Till then you see no more of Yva, for I do not trust her. She, too, has powers, though as yet she does not use them, and perchance she would forget her oaths, and following some new star of love, for a little while vanish with you out of my reach. Be in the sepulchre at the hour of sundown on the second day from this, all three of you, if you would continue to live upon the earth. Afterwards you shall learn my will and make your choice between Yva with majesty and her loss with death."

Then suddenly he was gone.

Next morning I told the others what had passed, and we talked the matter over. The trouble was, of course, that Bickley did not believe me. He had no faith in my alleged interviews with Oro, which he set down to delusions of a semi-mesmeric character. This was not strange, since it appeared that on the previous night he had watched the door of my sleeping-place until dawn broke, which it did long after Oro had departed, and he had not seen him either come or go, although the moon was shining brightly.

When he told me this I could only answer that all the same he had been there as, if he could speak, Tommy would have been able to certify. As it chanced the dog was sleeping with me and at the first sound of the approach of someone, woke up and growled. Then recognising Oro, he went to him, wagged his tail and curled himself up at his feet.

Bastin believed my story readily enough, saying that Oro was a peculiar person who no doubt had ways of coming and going which we did not understand. His point was, however, that he did not in the least wish to visit Nyo any more. The wonders of its underground palaces and temples had no charms for him. Also he did not think he could do any good by going, since after "sucking him as dry as an orange" with reference to religious matters "that old vampire-bat Oro had just thrown him away like the rind," and, he might add, "seemed no better for the juice he had absorbed."

"I doubt," continued Bastin, "whether St. Paul himself could have converted Oro, even if he performed miracles before him. What is the use of showing miracles to a man who could always work a bigger one himself?"

In short, Bastin's one idea, and Bickley's also for the matter of that, was to get away to the main island and thence escape by means of the boat, or in some other fashion.

I pointed out that Oro had said we must obey at the peril of our lives; indeed that he had put it even more strongly, using words to the effect that if we did not he would kill us.

"I'd take the risk," said Bickley, "since I believe that you dreamt it all, Arbuthnot. However, putting that aside, there is a natural reason why you should wish to go, and for my own part, so do I in a way. I want to see what that old fellow has up his extremely long sleeve, if there is anything there at all."

"Well, if you ask me, Bickley," I answered, "I believe it is the destruction of half the earth, or some little matter of that sort."

At this suggestion Bickley only snorted, but Bastin said cheerfully:

"I dare say. He is bad enough even for that. But as I am quite convinced that it will never be allowed, his intentions do not trouble me."

I remarked that he seemed to have carried them out once before.

"Oh! you mean the Deluge. Well, no doubt there was a deluge, but I am sure that Oro had no more to do with it than you or I, as I think I have said already. Anyhow it is impossible to leave you to descend into that hole alone. I suggest, therefore, that we should go into the sepulchre at the time which you believe Oro appointed, and see what happens. If you are not mistaken, the Glittering Lady will come there to fetch us, since it is quite certain that we cannot work the lift or whatever it is, alone. If you are mistaken we can just go back to bed as usual."

"Yes, that's the best plan," said Bickley, shortly, after which the conversation came to an end.

All that day and the next I watched and waited in vain for the coming of Yva, but no Yva appeared. I even went as far as the sepulchre, but it was as empty as were the two crystal coffins, and after waiting a while I returned. Although I did not say so to Bickley, to me it was evident that Oro, as he had said, was determined to cut off all communication between us.

The second day drew to its close. Our simple preparations were complete. They consisted mainly in making ready our hurricane lamps and packing up a little food, enough to keep us for three or four days if necessary, together with some matches and a good supply of oil, since, as Bastin put it, he was determined not to be caught like the foolish virgins in the parable.

"You see," he added, "one never knows when it might please that old wretch to turn off the incandescent gas or electric light, or whatever it is he uses to illumine his family catacombs, and then it would be awkward if we had no oil."

"For the matter of that he might steal our lamps," suggested Bickley, "in which case we should be where Moses was when the light went out."

"I have considered that possibility," answered Bastin, "and therefore, although it is a dangerous weapon to carry loaded, I am determined to take my revolver. If necessary I shall consider myself quite justified in shooting him to save our lives and those of thousands of others."

At this we both laughed; somehow the idea of Bastin trying to shoot Oro struck us as intensely ludicrous. Yet that very thing was to happen.

It was a peculiarly beautiful sunset over the southern seas. To the west the great flaming orb sank into the ocean, to the east appeared the silver circle of the full moon. To my excited fancy they were like scales hanging from the hand of a materialised spirit of calm. Over the volcano and the lake, over the island with its palm trees, over the seas beyond, this calm brooded. Save for a few travelling birds the sky was empty; no cloud disturbed its peace; the world seemed steeped in innocence and quiet.

All these things struck me, as I think they did the others, because by the action of some simultaneous thought it came to our minds that very probably we were looking on them for the last time. It is all very well to talk of the Unknown and the Infinite whereof we are assured we are the heirs, but that does not make it any easier for us to part with the Known and the Finite. The contemplation of the wonders of Eternity does not conceal the advantages of actual and existent Time. In short there is no one of us, from a sainted archbishop down to a sinful suicide, who does not regret the necessity of farewell to the pleasant light and the kindly race of men wherewith we are acquainted.

For after all, who can be quite certain of the Beyond?

It may be splendid, but it will probably be strange, and from strangeness, after a certain age, we shrink. We know that all things will be different there; that our human relationships will be utterly changed, that perhaps sex which shapes so many of them, will vanish to be replaced by something unknown, that ambitions will lose their hold of us, and that, at the best, the mere loss of hopes and fears will leave us empty. So at least we think, who seek not variation but continuance, since the spirit must differ from the body and that thought alarms our intelligence.

At least some of us think so; others, like Bickley, write down the future as a black and endless night, which after all has its consolations since, as has been wisely suggested, perhaps oblivion is better than any memories. Others again, like Bastin, would say of it with the Frenchman, *plus ça, change, plus c'est la même chose.* Yet others, like Oro, consider it as a realm of possibilities, probably unpleasant and perhaps non-existent; just this and nothing more. Only one thing is certain, that no creature which has life desires to leap into the fire and from the dross of doubts, to resolve the gold—or the lead—of certainty.

"It is time to be going," said Bastin. "In these skies the sun seems to tumble down, not to set decently as it does in England, and if we wait any longer we shall be late for our appointment in the sepulchre. I am sorry because although I don't often notice scenery, everything looks rather beautiful this evening. That star, for instance, I think it is called Venus."

"And therefore one that Arbuthnot should admire," broke in Bickley, attempting to lighten matters with a joke. "But come on and let us be rid of this fool's errand. Certainly the world is a lovely place after all, and for my part I hope that we haven't seen the last of it," he added with a sigh.

"So do I," said Bastin, "though of course, Faith teaches us that there are much better ones beyond. It is no use bothering about what they are like, but I hope that the road to them doesn't run through the hole that the old reprobate, Oro, calls Nyo."

A few minutes later we started, each of us carrying his share of the impedimenta. I think that Tommy was the only really cheerful member of the party, for he skipped about and barked, running backwards and forwards into the mouth of the cave, as though to hurry our movements.

"Really," said Bastin, "it is quite unholy to see an animal going on in that way when it knows that it is about to descend into the bowels of the earth. I suppose it must like them."

"Oh! no," commented Bickley, "it only likes what is in them—like Arbuthnot. Since that little beast came in contact with the Lady Yva, it has never been happy out of her company."

"I think that is so," said Bastin. "At any rate I have noticed that it has been moping for the last two days, as it always does when she is not present. It even seems to like Oro who gives me the creeps, perhaps because he is her father. Dogs must be very charitable animals."

By now we were in the cave marching past the wrecks of the half-buried flying-machines, which Bickley, as he remarked regretfully, had never found time thoroughly to examine. Indeed, to do so would have needed more digging than we could do without proper instruments, since the machines were big and deeply entombed in dust.

We came to the sepulchre and entered.

"Well," said Bickley, seating himself on the edge of one of the coffins and holding up his lamp to look about him, "this place seems fairly empty. No one is keeping the assignation, Arbuthnot, although the sun is well down."

As he spoke the words Yva stood before us. Whence she came we did not see, for all our backs were turned at the moment of her arrival. But there she was, calm, beautiful, radiating light.

CHAPTER XXIII

IN THE TEMPLE OF FATE

YVA glanced at me, and in her eyes I read tenderness and solicitude, also something of inquiry. It seemed to me as though she were wondering what I should do under circumstances that might, or would, arise, and in some secret fashion of which I was but half conscious, drawing an answer from my soul. Then she turned, and, smiling in her dazzling way, said:

"So, Bickley, as usual, you did not believe? Because *you* did not see him, therefore the Lord Oro, my father, never spoke with Humphrey. As though the Lord Oro could not pass you without your knowledge, or, perchance, send thoughts clothed in his own shape to work his errand."

"How do you know that I did not believe Arbuthnot's story?" Bickley asked in a rather cross voice and avoiding the direct issue. "Do you also send thoughts to work *your* errands clothed in your own shape, Lady Yva?"

"Alas! not so, though perhaps I could if I might. It is very simple, Bickley. Standing here, I heard you say that although the sun was well down there was no one to meet you as Humphrey had expected, and from those words and your voice I guessed the rest."

"Your knowledge of the English language is improving fast, Lady Yva. Also, when I spoke, you were not here."

"At least I was very near, Bickley, and these walls

are thinner than you think," she answered, contemplating what seemed to be solid rock with eyes that were full of innocence. "Oh! friend," she went on suddenly, "I wonder what there is which will cause you to believe that you do not know all; that there exist many things beyond the reach of your learning and imagination? Well, in a day or two, perhaps, even you will admit as much, and confess it to me—elsewhere," and she sighed.

"I am ready to confess now that much happens which I do not understand at present, because I have not the key to the trick," he replied.

Yva shook her head at him and smiled again. Then she motioned to all of us to stand close to her, and, stooping, lifted Tommy in her arms. Next moment that marvel happened which I have described already, and we were whirling downwards through space, to find ourselves in a very little time standing safe in the caves of Nyo, breathless with the swiftness of our descent. How and on what we descended neither I nor the others ever learned. It was and must remain one of the unexplained mysteries of our great experience.

"Whither now, Yva?" I asked, staring about me at the radiant vastness.

"The Lord Oro would speak with you, Humphrey. Follow. And I pray you all do not make him wrath, for his mood is not gentle."

So once more we proceeded down the empty streets of that underground abode which, except that it was better illuminated, reminded me of the Greek conception of Hades. We came to the sacred fountain over which stood the guardian statue of Life, pouring from the cups she held the waters of Good and Ill that mingled into one health-giving wine.

"Drink, all of you," she said; "for I think before the

sun sets again upon the earth we shall need strength, every one of us."

So we drank, and she drank herself, and once more felt the blood go dancing through our veins as though the draught had been some nectar of the gods. Then, having extinguished the lanterns which we still carried, for here they were needless, and we wished to save our oil, we followed her through the great doors into the vast hall of audience and advanced up it between the endless, empty seats. At its head, on the dais beneath the arching shell, sat Oro on his throne. As before, he wore the jewelled cap and the gorgeous, flowing robes, while the table in front of him was still strewn with sheets of metal on which he wrote with a pen, or stylus, that glittered like a diamond or his own fierce eyes. Then he lifted his head and beckoned to us to ascend the dais.

"You are here. It is well," he said, which was all his greeting. Only when Tommy ran up to him he bent down and patted the dog's head with his long, thin hand, and, as he did so, his face softened. It was evident to me that Tommy was more welcome to him than were the rest of us.

There was a long silence while, one by one, he searched us with his piercing glance. It rested on me, the last of the three of us, and from me travelled to Yva.

"I wonder why I have sent for you?" he said at length, with a mirthless laugh. "I think it must be that I may convince Bickley, the sceptic, that there are powers which he does not understand, but that I have the strength to move. Also, perhaps, that your lives may be spared for my own purposes in that which is about to happen. Hearken! My labours are finished;

my calculations are complete," and he pointed to the sheets of metal before him that were covered with cabalistic signs. "To-morrow I am about to do what once before I did and to plunge half the world in the deeps of ocean and lift again from the depths that which has been buried for a quarter of a million years."

"Which half?" asked Bickley.

"That is my secret, Physician, and the answer to it lies written here in signs you cannot read. Certain countries will vanish, others will be spared. I say that it is my secret."

"Then, Oro, if you could do what you threaten, you would drown hundreds of millions of people."

"If I could do! If I could do!" he exclaimed, glaring at Bickley. "Well, to-morrow you shall see what I can do. Oh! why do I grow angry with this fool? For the rest, yes, they must drown. What does it matter? Their end will be swift; some few minutes of terror, that is all, and in one short century every one of them would have been dead."

An expression of horror gathered on Bastin's face.

"Do you really mean to murder hundreds of millions of people?" he asked, in a thick, slow voice.

"I have said that I intend to send them to that heaven or that hell of which you are so fond of talking, Preacher, somewhat more quickly than otherwise they would have found their way thither. They have disappointed me, they have failed; therefore, let them go and make room for others who will succeed."

"Then you are a greater assassin than any that the world has bred, or than all of them put together. There is nobody as bad, even in the Book of Revelation!" shouted Bastin, in a kind of fury. "Moreover, I am not like Bickley. I know enough of you and your hellish powers to believe that what you plan, that you can do."

"I believe it also," sneered Oro. "But how comes it that the Great One whom you worship does not prevent the deed, if He exists, and it be evil?"

"He *will* prevent it!" raved Bastin. "Even now He commands me to prevent it, and I obey!" Then, drawing the revolver from his pocket, he pointed it at Oro's breast, adding: "Swear not to commit this crime, or I will kill you!"

"So the man of peace would become a man of blood," mused Oro, "and kill that *I* may not kill for the good of the world? Why, what is the matter with that toy of yours, Preacher?" and he pointed to the pistol.

Well might he ask, for as he spoke the revolver flew out of Bastin's hand. High into the air it flew, and as it went discharged itself, all the six chambers of it, in rapid succession, while Bastin stood staring at his arm and hand which he seemed unable to withdraw.

"Do you still threaten me with that outstretched hand, Preacher?" mocked Oro.

"I can't move it," said Bastin; "it seems turned to stone."

"Be thankful that you also are not turned to stone. But, because your courage pleases me, I will spare you, yes, and will advance you in my New Kingdom. What shall you be? Controller of Religions, I think, since all the qualities that a high priest should have are yours—faith, fanaticism and folly."

"It is very strange," said Bastin, "but all of a sudden my arm and hand are quite well again. I suppose it must have been 'pins and needles,' or something of that sort which made me throw away the pistol and pull the trigger when I didn't mean to do so."

Then he went to fetch that article which had fallen

beyond the dais, and quite forgot his intention of executing Oro in the interest of testing its mechanism, which proved to be destroyed. To his proposed appointment he made no illusion. If he comprehended what was meant, which I doubt, he took it as a joke.

"Hearken all of you," said Oro, lifting his head suddenly, for while Bastin recovered the revolver he had been brooding. "The great thing which I shall do to-morrow must be witnessed by you because thereby only can you come to understand my powers. Also yonder where I bring it about in the bowels of the earth, you will be safer than elsewhere, since when and perhaps before it happens, the whole world will heave and shake and tremble, and I know not what may chance, even in these caves. For this reason also, do not forget to bring the little hound with you, since him least of all of you would I see come to harm, perhaps because once, hundreds of generations ago as you reckon time, I had a dog very like to him. Your mother loved him much, Yva, and when she died, this dog died also. He lies embalmed with her on her coffin yonder in the temple, and yesterday I went to look at both of them. The beasts are wonderfully alike, which shows the everlastingness of blood."

He paused a while, lost in thought, then continued: "After the deed is done I'll speak with you and you shall choose, Strangers, whether you will die your own masters, or live on to serve me. Now there is one problem that is left to me to solve—whether I can save a certain land—do not ask which it is, Humphrey, though I see the question in your eyes—or must let it go with the rest. I only answer you that I will do my best because you love it. So farewell for a while, and,

Preacher, be advised by me and do not aim too high again."

"It doesn't matter where I aim," answered Bastin sturdily, "or whether I hit or miss, since there is something much bigger than me waiting to deal with you. The countries that you think you are going to destroy will sleep quite as well to-morrow as they do to-night, Oro."

"Much better, I think, Preacher, since by then they will have left sorrow and pain and wickedness and war far behind them."

"Where are we to go?" I asked.

"The Lady Yva will show you," he answered, waving his hand, and once more bent over his endless calculations.

Yva beckoned to us and we turned and followed her down the hall. She led us to a street near the gateway of the temple and thence into one of the houses. There was a portico to it leading to a court out of which opened rooms somewhat in the Pompeian fashion. We did not enter the rooms, for at the end of the court were a metal table and three couches also of metal, on which were spread rich-looking rugs. Whence these came I do not know and never asked, but I remember that they were very beautiful and soft as velvet.

"Here you may sleep," she said, "if sleep you can, and eat of the food that you have brought with you. To-morrow early I will call you when it is time for us to start upon our journey into the bowels of the earth."

"I don't want to go any deeper than we are," said Bastin doubtfully.

"I think that none of us want to go, Bastin," she answered with a sigh. "Yet go we must. I pray of you, anger the Lord Oro no more on this or any other matter. In your folly you tried to kill him, and as it chanced he bore it well because he loves courage. But another time he may strike back, and then, Bastin——"

"I am not afraid of him," he answered, "but I do not like tunnels. Still, perhaps it would be better to accompany you than to be left in this place alone. Now I will unpack the food."

Yva turned to go.

"I must leave you," she said, "since my father needs my help. The matter has to do with the Force that he would let loose to-morrow, and its measurements; also with the preparation of the robes that we must wear lest it should harm us in its leap."

Something in her eyes told me that she wished me to follow her, and I did so. Outside the portico where we stood in the desolate, lighted street, she halted.

"If you are not afraid," she said, "meet me at midnight by the statue of Fate in the great temple, for I would speak with you, Humphrey, where, if anywhere, we may be alone."

"I will come, Yva."

"You know the road, and the gates are open, Humphrey."

Then she gave me her hand to kiss and glided away.

I returned to the others and we ate, somewhat sparingly, for we wished to save our food in case of need, and having drunk of the Life-water, were not hungry. Also we talked a little, but by common consent avoided the subject of the morrow and what it might bring forth.

We knew that terrible things were afoot, but lacking any knowledge of what these might be, thought it useless to discuss them. Indeed we were too depressed, so much so that even Bastin and Bickley ceased from arguing. The latter was so overcome by the exhibition of Oro's powers when he caused the pistol to leap into the air and discharge itself, that he could not even pluck up courage to laugh at the failure of Bastin's efforts to do justice on the old Super-man, or rather to prevent him from attempting a colossal crime.

At length we lay down on the couches to rest, Bastin remarking that he wished he could turn off the light, also that he did not in the least regret having tried to kill Oro. Sleep seemed to come to the others quickly, but I could only doze, to wake up from time to time. Of this I was not sorry, since whenever I dropped off dreams seemed to pursue me. For the most part they were of my dead wife. She appeared to be trying to console me for some loss, but the strange thing was that sometimes she spoke with her own voice and sometimes with Yva's, and sometimes looked at me with her own eyes and sometimes with those of Yva. I remember nothing else about these dreams, which were very confused.

After one of them, the most vivid of all, I awoke and looked at my watch. It was half-past eleven, almost time for me to be starting. The other two seemed to be fast asleep. Presently I rose and crept down the court without waking them. Outside the portico, which by the way was a curious example of the survival of custom in architecture, since none was needed in that weatherless place, I turned to the right and followed the wide street to the temple enclosure. Through the pillared courts I went, my footsteps, although I walked as softly as I could, echoing loudly in that intense silence, through the great doors into the utter solitude of the vast and perfect fane.

Words cannot tell the loneliness of that place. It flowed over me like a sea and seemed to swallow up my being, so that even the wildest and most dangerous beast would have been welcome as a companion. I was as terrified as a child that wakes to find itself deserted in the dark. Also an uncanny sense of terrors to come oppressed me, till I could have cried aloud if only to hear the sound of a mortal voice. Yonder was the grim statue of Fate, the Oracle of the Kings of the Sons of Wisdom, which was believed to bow its stony head in answer to their prayers. I ran to it, eager for its terrible shelter, for on either side of it were figures of human beings. Even their cold marble was company of a sort, though alas! over all frowned Fate.

Let anyone imagine himself standing alone beneath the dome of St. Paul's; in the centre of that cathedral brilliant with mysterious light, and stretched all about it a London that had been dead and absolutely unpeopled for tens of thousands of years. If he can do this he will gather some idea of my physical state. Let him add to his mind-picture a knowledge that on the following day something was to happen not unlike the end of the world, as prognosticated by the Book of Revelation and by most astronomers, and he will have some idea of my mental perturbations. Add to the mixture a most mystic yet very real love affair and an assignation before that symbol of the cold fate which seems to sway the universes down to the tiniest detail of individual lives, and he may begin to understand what I, Humphrey Arbuthnot, experienced during my vigil in this sanctuary of a vanished race.

It seemed long before Yva came, but at last she did come. I caught sight of her far away beyond the temple gate, flitting through the unholy brightness of the pillared courts like a white moth at night and seeming quite as small. She approached; now she was as a ghost, and then drawing near, changed into a living, breathing, lovely woman. I opened my arms, and with something like a sob she sank into them and we kissed as mortals do.

"I could not come more quickly," she said. "The Lord Oro needed me, and those calculations were long and difficult. Also twice he must visit the place whither we shall go to-morrow, and that took time."

"Then it is close at hand?" I said.

"Humphrey, be not foolish. Do you not remember, who have travelled with him, that Oro can throw his soul afar and bring it back again laden with knowledge, as the feet of a bee are laden with golden dust? Well, he went and went again, and I must wait. And then the robes and shields; they must be prepared by his arts and mine. Oh! ask not what they are, there is no time to tell, and it matters nothing. Some folk are wise and some are foolish, but all which matters is that within them flows the blood of life and that life breeds love, and that love, as I believe, although Oro does not, breeds immortality. And if so, what is Time but as a grain of sand upon the shore?"

"This, Yva; it is ours, who can count on nothing else."

"Oh! Humphrey, if I thought that, no more wretched creature would breathe to-night upon this great world."

"What do you mean?" I asked, growing fearful, more at her manner and her look than at her words.

"Nothing, nothing, except that Time is so very short. A kiss, a touch, a little light and a little darkness, and it is gone. Ask my father Oro who has lived a thousand years and slept for tens of thousands, as I have, and he will say the same. It is against Time that he fights; he who, believing in nothing beyond, will inherit nothing, as Bastin says; he to whom Time has brought nothing save a passing, blood-stained greatness, and triumph ending in darkness and disaster, and hope that will surely suffer hope's eclipse, and power that must lay lown its coronet in dust."

"And what has it brought to you, Yva, beyond a fair body and a soul of strength?"

"It has brought a spirit, Humphrey. Between them the body and the soul have bred a spirit, and in the fires of tribulation from that spirit has been distilled the essence of eternal love. That is Time's gift to me, and therefore, although still he rules me here, I mock at Fate," and she waved her hand with a gesture of defiance at the stern-faced, sexless effigy which sat above us, the sword across its knees.

"Look! Look!" she went on in a swelling voice of music, pointing to the statues of the dotard and the beauteous woman. "They implore Fate, they worship Fate. *I* do not implore, *I* do not worship or ask a sign as even Oro does and as did his forefathers. *I* rise above and triumph. As Fate, the god of my people, sets his foot upon the sun, so I set my foot upon Fate, and thence, like a swimmer from a rock, leap into the waters of Immortality."

I looked at her whose presence, as happened from time to time, had grown majestic beyond that of woman; I studied her deep eyes which were full of lights, not of this world, and I grew afraid.

"What do you mean?" I asked. "Yva, you talk like one who has finished with life."

"It passes," she answered quickly. "Life passes like breath fading from a mirror. So should all talk who breathe beneath the sun."

"Yes, Yva, but if you went and left me still breathing on that mocking glass——"

"If so, what of it? Will not your breath fade also and join mine where all vapours go? Or if it were yours that faded and mine that remained for some few hours, is it not the same? I think, Humphrey, that already you have seen a beloved breath melt from the glass of life," she added, looking at me earnestly.

I bowed my head and answered:

"Yes, and therefore I am ashamed."

"Oh! why should you be ashamed, Humphrey, who are not sure but that two breaths may yet be one breath? How do you know that there is a difference between them?"

"You drive me mad, Yva. I cannot understand."

"Nor can I altogether, Humphrey. Why should I, seeing that I am no more than woman, as you are no more than man? I would always have you remember, Humphrey, that I am no spirit or sorceress, but just a woman—like her you lost."

I looked at her doubtfully and answered:

"Women do not sleep for two hundred thousand years. Women do not take dream journeys to the stars. Women do not make the dead past live again before the watcher's eyes. Their hair does not glimmer in the dusk nor do their bodies gleam, nor have they such strength of soul or eyes so wonderful, or loveliness so great."

These words appeared to distress her who, as it seemed to me, was above all things anxious to prove herself woman and no more.

"All these qualities are nothing, Humphrey," she cried. "As for the beauty, such as it is, it comes to me with my blood, and with it the glitter of my hair which is the heritage of those who for generations have drunk of the Life-water. My mother was lovelier than I, as was her mother, or so I have heard, since only the fairest were the wives of the Kings of the Children of Wisdom. For the rest, such arts as I have spring not from magic, but from knowledge which your people will acquire in days to come, that is, if Oro spares them. Surely you above all should know that I am only woman," she added very slowly and searching my face with her eyes.

"Why, Yva? During the little while that we have been together I have seen much which makes me doubt. Even Bickley the sceptic doubts also."

"I will tell you, though I am not sure that you will believe me." She glanced about her as though she were frightened lest someone should overhear her words or read her thoughts. Then she stretched out her hands and drawing my head towards her, put her lips to my ear and whispered:

"Because once you saw me *die,* as women often die —giving life for life."

"I saw *you* die?" I gasped.

She nodded, then continued to whisper in my ear, not in her own voice, but another's:

"*Go where you seem called to go, far away. Oh! the wonderful place in which you will find me, not knowing that you have found me. Good-bye for a little while; only for a little while, my own, my own!*"

I knew the voice as I knew the words, and knowing, I think that I should have fallen to the ground, had she not supported me with her strong arms.

"Who told you?" I stammered. "Was it Bickley or Bastin? They knew, though neither of them heard those holy words."

"Not Bickley nor Bastin," she answered, shaking her head, "no, nor you yourself, awake or sleeping, though once, by the lake yonder, you said to me that when a certain one lay dying, she bade you seek her elsewhere, for certainly you would find her. Humphrey, I cannot say who told me those words because I do not know. *I think they are a memory, Humphrey!*"

"That would mean that you, Yva, are the same as one who was—not called Yva."

"The same as one who was called *Natalie,* Humphrey," she replied in solemn accents. "One whom you loved and whom you lost."

"Then you think that we live again upon this earth?"

"Again and yet again, until the time comes for us to leave the earth for ever. Of this, indeed, I am sure, for that knowledge was part of the secret wisdom of my people."

"But you were not dead. You only slept."

"The sleep was a death-sleep which went by like a flash, yes, in an instant, or so it seemed. Only the shell of the body remained preserved by mortal arts, and when the returning spirit and the light of life were poured into it again, it awoke. But during this long death-sleep, that spirit may have spoken through other lips and that light may have shone through other eyes, though of these I remember nothing."

"Then that dream of our visit to a certain star may be no dream?"

"I think no dream, and you, too, have thought as much."

"In a way, yes, Yva. But I could not believe and turned from what I held to be a phantasy."

"It was natural, Humphrey, that you should not believe. Hearken! In this temple a while ago I showed you a picture of myself and of a man who loved me and whom I loved, and of his death at Oro's hands. Did you note anything about that man?"

"Bickley did," I answered. "Was he right?"

"I think that he was right, since otherwise I should not have loved you, Humphrey."

"I remember nothing of that man, Yva."

"It is probable that you would not, since you and he are very far apart, while between you and him flow wide seas of death, wherein are set islands of life; perhaps many of them. But I remember much who seem to have left him but a very little while ago."

"When you awoke in your coffin and threw your arms about me, what did you think, Yva?"

"I thought *you* were that man, Humphrey."

There was silence between us and in that silence the truth came home to me. Then there before the effigy of Fate and in the desolate, glowing temple we plighted anew our troth made holy by a past that thus so wonderfully lived again.

Of this consecrated hour I say no more. Let each picture it as he will. A glory as of heaven fell upon us and in it we dwelt a space.

"Beloved," she whispered at length in a voice that was choked as though with tears, "if it chances that we should be separated again for a little while, you will not grieve over much?"

"Knowing all I should try not to grieve, Yva,

seeing that in truth we never can be parted. But do you mean that I shall die?"

"Being mortal either of us might seem to die, Humphrey," and she bent her head as though to hide her face. "You know we go into dangers this day."

"Does Oro really purpose to destroy much of the world and has he in truth the power, Yva?"

"He does so purpose and most certainly he has the power, unless—unless some other Power should stay his hand."

"What other power, Yva?"

"Oh! perhaps that which you worship, that which is called Love. The love of man may avert the massacre of men. I hope so with all my heart. Hist! Oro comes. I feel, I know that he comes, though not in search of us who are very far from his thought to-night. Follow me. Swiftly."

She sped across the temple to where a chapel opened out of it, which was full of the statues of dead kings, for here was the entrance to their burial vault. We reached it and hid behind the base of one of these statues. By standing to our full height, without being seen we still could see between the feet of the statue that stood upon a pedestal.

Then Oro came.

CHAPTER XXIV

THE CHARIOT OF THE PIT

Oro came and of necessity alone. Yet there was that in his air as he advanced into the temple, which suggested a monarch surrounded by the pomp and panoply of a great court. He marched, his head held high, as though heralds and pursuivants went in front of him, as though nobles surrounded him and guards or regiments followed after him. Let it be admitted that he was a great figure in his gorgeous robes, with his long white beard, his hawk-like features, his tall shape and his glittering eyes, which even at that distance I could see. Indeed once or twice I thought that he glanced out of the corners of them towards the chapel where we were hid. But this I think was fancy. For as Yva said, his thoughts were set elsewhere.

He reached the statue of Fate and stood for a while contemplating it and the suppliant figures on either side, as though he were waiting for his invisible court to arrange itself. Then he doffed his jewelled cap to the effigy, and knelt before it. Yes, Oro the Ancient, the Super-man, the God, as the early peoples of the earth fancied such a being, namely, one full of wrath, revenge, jealousy, caprice and power, knelt in supplication to this image of stone which he believed to be the home of a spirit, thereby showing himself to be after all not so far removed from the savages whose idol Bastin had destroyed. More, in a clear and resonant voice which reached us even across that great space, he put up his prayer. It ran something as follows, for although I did not understand the language in which he spoke Yva translated it to me in a whisper:

"God of the Sons of Wisdom, God of the whole earth, only God to whom must bow every other Power and Dominion, to thee I, Oro the Great King, make prayer and offer sacrifice. Twenty times ten thousand years and more have gone by since I, Oro, visited this, thy temple and knelt before this, thy living effigy, yet thou, ruler of the world, dost remember the prayer I made and the sacrifice I offered. The prayer was for triumph over my enemies and the sacrifice a promise of the lives of half of those who in that day dwelt upon the earth. Thou heardest the prayer, thou didst bow thy head and accept the sacrifice. Yea, the prayer was granted and the sacrifice was made, and in it were counted the number of my foes.

"Then I slept. Through countless generations I slept on and at my side was the one child of my body that was left to me. What chanced to my spirit and to hers during that sleep, thou knowest alone, but doubtless they went forth to work thy ends.

"At the appointed time which thou didst decree, I awoke again and found in my house strangers from another land. In the company of one of those whose spirit I drew forth, I visited the peoples of the new earth, and found them even baser and more evil than those whom I had known. Therefore, since they cannot be bettered, I purpose to destroy them also, and on their wreck to rebuild a glorious empire, such as was that of the Sons of Wisdom at its prime.

"A sign! O Fate, ruler of the world, give me a sign that my desire shall be fulfilled."

He paused, stretching out his arms and staring upwards. While he waited I felt the solid rock on which I stood quiver and sway beneath my feet so that Yva and I clung to each other lest we should fall. This chanced also. The shock of the earth tremor, for such without doubt it was, threw down the figures of the ancient man and the lovely woman which knelt as though making prayers to Fate, and shook the marble sword from off its knees. As it fell Oro caught it by the hilt, and, rising, waved it in triumph.

"I thank thee, God of my people from the beginning," he cried. "Thou hast given to me, thy last servant, thine own sword and I will use it well. For these worshippers of thine who have fallen, thou shalt have others, yes, all those who dwell in the new world that is to be. My daughter and the man whom she has chosen to be the father of the kings of the earth, and with him his companions, shall be the first of the hundreds of millions that are to follow, for they shall kiss thy feet or perish. Thou shalt set thy foot upon the necks of all other gods; thou shalt rule and thou alone, and, as of old, Oro be thy minister."

Still holding the sword, he flung himself down as though in an ecstasy, and was silent.

"I read the omen otherwise," whispered Yva. "The worshippers of Fate are overthrown. His sword of power is fallen, but not into the hands that clasped it, and he totters on his throne. A greater God asserts dominion of the world and this Fate is but his instrument."

Oro rose again.

"One prayer more," he cried. "Give me life, long life, that I may execute thy decrees. By word or gesture show me a sign that I shall be satisfied with life, a year for every year that I have lived, or twain!"

He waited, staring about him, but no token came; the idol did not speak or bow its head, as Yva had told me it was wont to do in sign of accepted prayer, how, she knew not. Only I thought I heard the echo of Oro's cries run in a whisper of mockery round the soaring dome.

Once more Oro flung himself upon his knees and began to pray in a veritable agony.

"God of my forefathers, God of my lost people, I will hide naught from thee," he said. "I who fear nothing else, fear death. The priest-fool yonder with his new faith, has spoken blundering words of judgment and damnation which, though I do not believe them, yet stick in my heart like arrows. I will stamp out his faith, and with this ancient sword of thine drive back the new gods into the darkness whence they came. Yet what if some water of Truth flows through the channel of his leaden lips, and what if because I have ruled and will rule as thou didst decree, therefore, in some dim place of souls, I must bear these burdens of terror and of doom which I have bound upon the backs of others! Nay, it cannot be, for what power is there in all the universe that dares to make a slave of Oro and to afflict him with stripes?

"Yet this can be and mayhap will be, that presently I lose my path in the ways of everlasting darkness, and become strengthless and forgotten as are those who went before me, while my crown of Power shines on younger brows. Alas! I grow old, since æons of sleep have not renewed my strength. My time is short and yet I would not die as mortals must. Oh! God of my people, whom I have served so well, save me from the death I dread. For I would not die. Give me a sign; give me the ancient, sacred sign!"

So he spoke, lifting his proud and splendid head and watching the statue with wide, expectant eyes.

"Thou dost not answer," he cried again. "Wouldst thou desert me, Fate? Then beware lest I set up some new god against thee and hurl thee from thine immemorial throne. While I live I still have powers, I who am the last of thy worshippers, since it seems that my daughter turns her back on thee. I will get me to the sepulchre of the kings and take counsel with the dust of that wizard who first taught me wisdom. Even from the depths of death he must come to my call clad in a mockery of life, and comfort me. A little while yet I will wait, and it thou answer not, then Fate, soon I'll tear the sceptre from thy hand, and thou shalt join the company of dead gods." And throwing aside the sword, again Oro laid down his head upon the ground and stretched out his arms in the last abasement of supplication.

'Come," whispered Yva, "while there is yet time. Presently he will seek this place to descend to the sepulchre, and if he learns that we have read his heart and know him for a coward deserted of his outworn god, surely he will blot us out. Come, and be swift and silent."

We crept out of the chapel, Yva leading, and along the circle of the great dome till we reached the gates. Here I glanced back and perceived that Oro, looking unutterably small in that vastness, looking like a dead man, still lay outstretched before the stern-faced, unanswering Effigy which, with all his wisdom, he believed to be living and divine. Perhaps once it was, but if so its star had set for ever, like those of Amon, Jupiter and Baal, and he was its last worshipper.

Now we were safe, but still we sped on till we

reached the portico of our sleeping place. Then Yva turned and spoke.

"It is horrible," she said, "and my soul sickens. Oh, I thank the Strength which made it that I have no desire to rule the earth, and, being innocent of death, do not fear to die and cross his threshold."

"Yes, it is horrible," I answered. "Yet all men fear death."

"Not when they have found love, Humphrey, for that I think is his true name, and, with it written on his brow, he stands upon the neck of Fate who is still my father's god."

"Then he is not yours, Yva?"

"Nay. Once it was so, but now I reject him; he is no longer mine. As Oro threatens, and perchance dare do in his rage, I have broken his chain, though in another fashion. Ask me no more; perhaps one day you will learn the path I trod to freedom."

Then before I could speak, she went off:

"Rest now, for within a few hours I must come to lead you and your companions to a terrible place. Yet whatever you may see or hear, be not afraid, Humphrey, for I think that Oro's god has no power over you, strong though he was, and that Oro's plans will fail, while I, who too have knowledge, shall find strength to save the world."

Then of a sudden, once again she grew splendid, almost divine; no more a woman but as it were an angel. Some fire of pure purpose seemed to burn up in her and to shine out of her eyes. Yet she said little. Only this indeed:

"To everyone, I think, there comes the moment of opportunity when choice must be made between what is great and what is small, between self and its desires and the good of other wanderers in the way. This day that moment may draw near to you or me, and if so, surely we shall greet it well. Such is Bastin's lesson, which I have striven to learn."

Then she flung her arms about me and kissed me on the brow as a mother might, and was gone.

Strangely enough, perhaps because of my mental exhaustion, for what I had passed through seemed to overwhelm me so that I could no longer so much as think with clearness, even after all that I have described I slept like a child and awoke refreshed and well.

I looked at my watch to find that it was now eight o'clock in the morning in this horrible place where there was neither morn, nor noon, nor night, but only an eternal brightness that came I knew not whence, and never learned.

I found that I was alone, since Bickley and Bastin had gone to fill our bottles with the Life-water. Presently they returned and we ate a little; with that water to drink one did not need much food. It was a somewhat silent meal, for our circumstances were a check on talk; moreover, I thought that the others looked at me rather oddly. Perhaps they guessed something of my midnight visit to the temple, but if so they thought it wisest to say nothing. Nor did I enlighten them.

Shortly after we had finished Yva appeared. She was wonderfully quiet and gentle in her manner, calm also, and greeted all of us with much sweetness. Of our experiences during the night she said no word to me, even when we were alone. One difference I noticed about her, however; that she was clothed in garments such as I had never seen her wear before. They were close fitting, save for a flowing cape, and made of some grey material, not unlike a coarse homespun or even asbestos cloth. Still they became her very well, and when I remarked upon them, all she answered was that part of our road would be rough. Even her feet were shod with high buskins of this grey stuff.

Presently she touched Bastin on the shoulder and said that she would speak with him apart. They went together into one of the chambers of that dwelling and there remained for perhaps the half of an hour. It was towards the end of this time that in the intense silence I heard a crash from the direction of the temple, as though something heavy had fallen to the rocky floor. Bickley also heard this sound. When the two reappeared I noticed that though still quite calm, Yva looked radiant, and, if I may say so, even more human and womanly than I had ever seen her, while Bastin also seemed very happy.

"One has strange experiences in life, yes, very strange," he remarked, apparently addressing the air, which left me wondering to what particular experience he might refer. Well, I thought that I could guess.

"Friends," said Yva, "it is time for us to be going and I am your guide. You will meet the Lord Oro at the end of your journey. I pray you to bring those lamps of yours with you, since all the road is not lightened like this place."

"I should like to ask," said Bickley, "whither we go and for what object, points on which up to the present we have had no definite information."

"We go, friend Bickley, deep into the bowels of the world, far deeper, I think, than any mortal men have gone hitherto, that is, of your race."

"Then we shall perish of heat," said Bickley, "for with every thousand feet the temperature rises many degrees."

"Not so. You will pass through a zone of heat, but so swiftly that if you hold your breath you will not suffer overmuch. Then you will come to a place where a great draught blows which will keep you cool, and thence travel on to the end."

"Yes, but to what end, Lady Yva?"

"That you will see for yourselves, and with it other wondrous things."

Here some new idea seemed to strike her, and after a little hesitation she added:

"Yet why should you go? Oro has commanded it, it is true, but I think that at the last he will forget. It must be decided swiftly. There is yet time. I can place you in safety in the sepulchre of Sleep where you found us. Thence cross to the main island and sail away quickly in your boat out into the great sea, where I believe you will find succour. Know that after disobeying him, you must meet Oro no more lest it should be the worse for you. If that be your will, let us start. What say you?"

She looked at me.

"I say, Yva, that I am willing to go if you come with us. Not otherwise."

"I say," said Bickley, "that I want to see all this supernatural rubbish thoroughly exploded, and that therefore I should prefer to go on with the business."

"And I say," said Bastin, "that my most earnest desire is to be clear of the whole thing, which wearies and perplexes me more than I can tell. Only I am not going to run away, unless you think it desirable to do so too, Lady Yva. I want you to understand that I am not in the least afraid of the Lord Oro, and do not for one moment believe that he will be allowed to bring about disaster to the world, as I understand is his wicked object. Therefore on the whole I am indifferent and quite prepared to accept any decision at which the rest of you may arrive."

"Be it understood," said Yva with a little smile when Bastin had finished his sermonette, "that I must join my father in the bowels of the earth for a reason which will be made plain afterwards. Therefore, if you go we part, as I think to meet no more. Still my advice is that you should go." *

To this our only answer was to attend to the lighting of our lamps and the disposal of our small impedimenta, such as our tins of oil and water bottles. Yva noted this and laughed outright.

"Courage did not die with the Sons of Wisdom," she said.

Then we set out, Yva walking ahead of us and Tommy frisking at her side.

Our road led us through the temple. As we passed the great gates I started, for there, in the centre of that glorious building, I perceived a change. The statue of Fate was no more! It lay broken upon the pavement among those fragments of its two worshippers which I had seen shaken down some hours before.

"What does this mean?" I whispered to Yva. "I have felt no other earthquake."

"I do not know," she answered, "or if I know I may not say. Yet learn that no god can live on without a single worshipper, and, in a fashion, that idol was alive, though this you will not believe."

"How very remarkable," said Bastin, contemplating

* It is fortunate that we did not accept Yva's offer. Had we done so we should have found ourselves shut in, and perished, as shall be told.—H. A.

the ruin. "If I were superstitious, which I am not, I should say that this occurrence was an omen indicating the final fall of a false god. At any rate it is dead now, and I wonder what caused it?"

"I felt an earth tremor last night," said Bickley, "though it is odd that it should only have affected this particular statue. A thousand pities, for it was a wonderful work of art."

Then I remembered and reminded Bickley of the crash which we had heard while Yva and Bastin were absent on some secret business in the chamber.

Walking the length of the great church, if so it could be called, we came to an apse at the head of it where, had it been Christian, the altar would have stood. In this apse was a little open door through which we passed. Beyond it lay a space of rough rock that looked as though it had been partially prepared for the erection of buildings and then abandoned. All this space was lighted, however, like the rest of the City of Nyo, and in the same mysterious way. Led by Yva, we threaded our path between the rough stones, following a steep downward slope. Thus we walked for perhaps half a mile, till at length we came to the mouth of a huge pit that must, I imagine, have lain quite a thousand feet below the level of the temple.

I looked over the edge of this pit and shrank back terrified. It seemed to be bottomless. Moreover, a great wind rushed up it with a roaring sound like to that of an angry sea. Or rather there were two winds, perhaps draughts would be a better term, if I may apply it to an air movement of so fierce and terrible a nature. One of these rushed up the pit, and one rushed down. Or it may have been that the up rush alternated with the down rush. Really it is impossible to say.

"What is this place?" I asked, clinging to the others and shrinking back in alarm from its sheer edge and bottomless depth, for that this was enormous we could see by the shaft of light which flowed downwards farther than the eye could follow.

"It is a vent up and down which air passes from and to the central hollows of the earth," Yva answered. "Doubtless in the beginning through it travelled that mighty force which blew out these caves in the heated rocks, as the craftsman blows out glass."

"I understand," said Bastin. "Just like one blows out a bubble on a pipe, only on a larger scale. Well, it is very interesting, but I have seen enough of it. Also I am afraid of being blown away."

"I fear that you must see more," answered Yva with a smile, "since we are about to descend this pit."

"Do you mean that we are to go down that hole, and if so, how? I don't see any lift, or moving staircase, or anything of that sort."

"Easily and safely enough, Bastin. See."

As she spoke a great flat rock of the size of a small room appeared, borne upwards, as I suppose, by the terrific draught which roared past us on its upward course. When it reached the lip of the shaft, it hung a little while, then moved across and began to descend with such incredible swiftness that in a few seconds it had vanished from view.

"Oh!" said Bastin, with his eyes almost starting out of his head, "that's the lift, is it? Well, I tell you at once I don't like the look of the thing. It gives me the creeps. Suppose it tilted."

"It does not tilt," answered Yva, still smiling. "I tell you, Bastin, that there is naught to fear. Only yesterday, I rode this rock and returned unharmed."

"That is all very well, Lady Yva, but you may know how to balance it; also when to get on and off."

"If you are afraid, Bastin, remain here until your companions return. They, I think, will make the journey."

Bickley and I intimated that we would, though to tell the truth, if less frank we were quite as alarmed as Bastin.

"No, I'll come too. I suppose one may as well die this way as any other, and if anything were to happen to them and I were left alone, it would be worse still."

"Then be prepared," said Yva, "for presently this air-chariot of ours will return. When it appears and hangs upon the edge, step on to it and throw yourselves upon your faces and all will be well. At the foot of the shaft the motion lessens till it almost stops, and it is easy to spring, or even crawl to the firm earth."

Then she stooped down and lifted Tommy who was sniffing suspiciously at the edge of the pit, his long ears blown straight above his head, holding him beneath her left arm and under her cloak, that he might not see and be frightened.

We waited a while in silence, perhaps for five or six minutes, among the most disagreeable, I think, that I ever passed. Then far down in the brightness below appeared a black speck that seemed to grow in size as it rushed upwards.

"It comes," said Yva. "Prepare and do as I do. Do not spring, or run, lest you should go too far. Step gently on to the rock and to its centre, and there lie down. Trust in me, all of you."

"There's nothing else to do," groaned Bastin.

The great stone appeared and, as before, hung at

the edge of the pit. Yva stepped on to it quietly, as she did so, catching hold of my wrist with her disengaged hand. I followed her feeling very sick, and promptly sat down. Then came Bickley with the air of the virtuous hero of a romance walking a pirate's plank, and also sat down. Only Bastin hesitated until the stone began to move away. Then with an ejaculation of "Here goes!" he jumped over the intervening crack of space and landed in the middle of us like a sack of coal. Had I not been seated really I think he would have knocked me off the rock. As it was, with one hand he gripped me by the beard and with the other grasped Yva's robe, of neither of which would he leave go for quite a long time, although we forced him on to his face. The lantern which he held flew from his grasp and descended the shaft on its own account.

"You silly fool!" exclaimed Bickley whose perturbation showed itself in anger. "There goes one of our lamps."

"Hang the lamp!" muttered the prostrate Bastin. "We shan't want it in Heaven, or the other place either."

Now the stone which had quivered a little beneath the impact of Bastin, steadied itself again and with a slow and majestic movement sailed to the other side of the gulf. There it felt the force of gravity, or perhaps the weight of the returning air pressed on it, which I do not know. At any rate it began to fall, slowly at first, then more swiftly, and afterwards at an incredible pace, so that in a few seconds the mouth of the pit above us grew small and presently vanished quite away. I looked up at Yva who was standing composedly in the midst of our prostrate shapes. She bent down and called in my ear:

"All is well. The heat begins, but it will not endure for long."

I nodded and glanced over the edge of the stone at Bastin's lantern which was sailing alongside of us, till presently we passed it. Bastin had lit it before we started, I think in a moment of aberration, and it burned for quite a long while, showing like a star when the shaft grew darker as it did by degrees, a circumstance that testifies to the excellence of the make, which is one advertised not to go out in any wind. Not that we felt wind, or even draught, perhaps because we were travelling with it.

Then we entered the heat zone. About this there was no doubt, for the perspiration burst out all over me and the burning air scorched my lungs. Also Tommy thrust his head from beneath the cloak with his tongue hanging out and his mouth wide open.

"Hold your breaths!" cried Yva, and we obeyed until we nearly burst. At least I did, but what happened to the others I do not know.

Fortunately it was soon over and the air began to grow cool again. By now we had travelled an enormous distance, it seemed to be miles on miles, and I noticed that our terrific speed was slackening, also that the shaft grew more narrow, till at length there were only a few feet between the edge of the stone and its walls. The result of this, or so I supposed, was that the compressed air acted as a buffer, lessening our momentum, till at length the huge stone moved but very slowly.

"Be ready to follow me," cried Yva again, and we rose to our feet, that is, Bickley and I did, but poor Bastin was semi-comatose. The stone stopped and Yva sprang from it to a rock platform level with which it lay.

We followed, dragging Bastin between us. As we did so something hit me gently on the head. Is was Bastin's lamp, which I seized.

"We are safe. Sit down and rest," said Yva, leading us a few paces away.

We obeyed and presently by the dim light saw the stone begin to stir again, this time upwards. In another twenty seconds it was away on its never-ending journey.

"Does it always go on like that?" said Bastin, sitting up and staring after it.

"Tens of thousands of years ago it was journeying thus, and tens of thousands of years hence it will still be journeying, or so I think," she replied. "Why not, since the strength of the draught never changes and there is nothing to wear it except the air?"

Somehow the vision of this huge stone, first loosed and set in motion by heaven knows what agency, travelling from æon to æon up and down that shaft in obedience to some law I did not understand, impressed my imagination like a nightmare. Indeed I often dream of it to this day.

I looked about me. We were in some cavernous place that could be but dimly seen, for here the light that flowed down the shaft from the upper caves where it was mysteriously created, scarcely shone, and often indeed was entirely cut off, when the ever-journeying stone was in the narrowest parts of the passage. I could see, however, that this cavern stretched away both to right and left of us, while I felt that from the left, as we sat facing the shaft, there drew down a strong blast of fresh air which suggested that somewhere, however far away, it must open on to the upper world. For the rest its bottom and walls seemed to be smooth as though they had been planed in the past ages by the action of cosmic forces. Bickley noticed this the first and pointed it out to me. We had little time to observe, however, for presently Yva said:

"If you are rested, friends, I pray you light those lamps of yours, since we must walk a while in darkness."

We did and started, still travelling downhill. Yva walked ahead with me and Tommy who seemed somewhat depressed and clung close to our heels. The other two followed, arguing strenuously about I know not what. It was their way of working off irritation and alarms.

I asked Yva what was about to happen, for a great fear oppressed me.

"I am not sure, Beloved," she answered in a sweet and gentle voice, "who do not know all Oro's secrets, but as I think, great things. We are now deep in the bowels of the world, and presently, perhaps, you will see some of its mighty forces whereof your ignorant races have no knowledge, doing their everlasting work."

"Then how is it that we can breathe here?" I asked.

"Because this road that we are following connects with the upper air or used to do so, since once I followed it. It is a long road and the climb is steep, but at last it leads to the light of the blessed sun, nor are there any pitfalls in the path. Would that we might tread it together, Humphrey," she added with passion, "and be rid of mysteries and the gloom, or that light which is worse than gloom."

"Why not?" I asked eagerly. "Why should we not turn and flee?"

"Who can flee from my father, the Lord Oro?" she replied. "He would snare us before we had gone a mile. Moreover, if we fled, by to-morrow half the world must perish."

"And how can we save it by not flying, Yva?"

"I do not know, Humphrey, yet I think it will be saved, perchance by sacrifice. That is the keystone of your faith, is it not? Therefore if it is asked of you to save the world, you will not shrink from it, will you, Humphrey?"

"I hope not," I replied, without enthusiasm, I admit. Indeed it struck me that a business of this sort was better fitted to Bastin than to myself, or at any rate to his profession. I think she guessed my thoughts, for by the light of the lamp I saw her smile in her dazzling way. Then after a swift glance behind her, she turned and suddenly kissed me, as she did so calling down everlasting blessings on my head and on my spirit. There was something very wonderful about this benediction of Yva's and it thrilled me through and through, so that to it I could make no answer.

Next moment it was too late to retreat, for our narrowing passage turned and we found ourselves in a wondrous place. I call it wondrous because of it we could see neither the beginning nor the end, nor the roof, nor aught else save the rock on which we walked, and the side or wall that our hands touched. Nor was this because of darkness, since although it was not illuminated like the upper caverns, light of a sort was present. It was a very strange light, consisting of brilliant and intermittent flashes, or globes of blue and lambent flame which seemed to leap from nowhere into nowhere, or sometimes to hang poised in mid air.

"How odd they are," said the voice of Bastin behind me. "They remind me of those blue sparks which jump up from the wires of the tramways in London on a dark night. You know, don't you, Bickley? I mean when the conductor pulls round that long stick with an iron wheel on the top of it."

"Nobody but you could have thought of such a comparison, Bastin," answered Bickley. "Still, multiplied a thousandfold they are not unlike."

Nor indeed were they, except that each blue flash was as big as the full moon and in one place or another they were so continuous that one could have read a letter by their light. Also the effect of them was ghastly and most unnatural, terrifying, too, since even their brilliance could not reveal the extent of that gigantic hollow in the bowels of the world wherein they leapt to and fro like lightnings, or hung like huge, uncanny lanterns.

CHAPTER XXV

SACRIFICE

"The air in this place must be charged with some form of electricity, but the odd thing is that it does not seem to harm us," said Bickley in a matter-of-fact fashion as though he were determined not to be astonished.

"To me it looks more like marsh fires or St. Elmo lights, though how these can be where there is no vapour, I do not know," I answered.

As I spoke a particularly large ball of flame fell from above. It resembled a shooting star or a meteor more than anything else that I had ever seen, and made me wonder whether we were not perhaps standing beneath some inky, unseen sky.

Next moment I forgot such speculations, for in its blue light, which made him terrible and ghastly, I perceived Oro standing in front of us clad in a long cloak.

"Dear me!" said Bastin, "he looks just like the devil, doesn't he, and now I come to think of it, this isn't at all a bad imitation of hell."

"How do you know it is an imitation?" asked Bickley.

"Because whatever might be the case with *you*, Bickley, if it were, the Lady Yva and I should not be here."

Even then I could not help smiling at this repartee, but the argument went no further for Oro held up his hand and Yva bent the knee in greeting to him.

"So you have come, all of you," he said. "I thought

that perhaps there were one or two who would not find courage to ride the flying stone. I am glad that it is not so, since otherwise he who had shown himself a coward should have had no share in the rule of that new world which is to be. Therefore I chose yonder road that it might test you."

"Then if you will be so good as to choose another for us to return by, I shall be much obliged to you, Oro," said Bastin.

"How do you know that if I did it would not be more terrible, Preacher? How do you know indeed that this is not your last journey from which there is no return?"

"Of course I can't be sure of anything, Oro, but I think the question is one which you might more appropriately put to yourself. According to your own showing you are now extremely old and therefore your end is likely to come at any moment. Of course, however, if it did you would have one more journey to make, but it wouldn't be polite for me to say in what direction."

Oro heard, and his splendid, icy face was twisted with sudden rage. Remembering the scene in the temple where he had grovelled before his god, uttering agonised, unanswered prayers for added days, I understood the reason of his wrath. It was so great that I feared lest he should kill Bastin (who only a few hours before, be it remembered, had tried to kill *him*) then and there, as doubtless he could have done if he wished. Fortunately, if he felt it; the impulse passed.

"Miserable fool!" he said. "I warn you to keep a watch upon your words. Yesterday you would have slain me with your toy. To-day you stab me with your ill-omened tongue. Be fearful lest I silence it for ever."

"I am not in the least fearful, Oro, since I am sure that *you* can't hurt me at all any more than I could hurt you last night because, you see, it wasn't permitted. When the time comes for me to die, I shall go, but *you* will have nothing to do with that. To tell the truth, I am very sorry for you, as with all your greatness, your soul is of the earth, earthy, also sensual and devilish, as the Apostle said, and, I am afraid, very malignant, and you will have a great deal to answer for shortly. Yours *won't* be a happy deathbed, Oro, because, you see, you glory in your sins and don't know what repentance means."

I must add that when I heard these words I was filled with the most unbounded admiration for Bastin's fearless courage which enabled him thus to beard this super-tyrant in his den. So indeed were we all, for I read it in Yva's face and heard Bickley mutter:

"Bravo! Splendid! After all there is something in faith!"

Even Oro appreciated it with his intellect, if not with his heart, for he stared at the man and made no answer. In the language of the ring, he was quite "knocked out" and, almost humbly, changed the subject.

"We have yet a little while," he said, "before that happens which I have decreed. Come, Humphrey, that I may show you some of the marvels of this bubble blown in the bowels of the world," and he motioned to us to pick up the lanterns.

Then he led us away from the wall of the cavern, if such it was, for a distance of perhaps six or seven hundred paces. Here suddenly we came to a great groove in the rocky floor, as broad as a very wide roadway, and mayhap four feet in depth. The bottom of this groove was polished and glittered; indeed it gave us the impression of being iron, or other ore which had been welded together beneath the grinding of some immeasurable weight. Just at the spot where we struck the groove, it divided into two, for this reason.

In its centre the floor of iron, or whatever it may have been, rose, the fraction of an inch at first, but afterwards more sharply, and this at a spot where the groove had a somewhat steep downward dip which appeared to extend onwards I know not how far.

Following along this central rise for a great way, nearly a mile, I should think, we observed that it became ever more pronounced, till at length it ended in a razor-edge cliff which stretched up higher than we could see, even by the light of the electrical discharges. Standing against the edge of this cliff, we perceived that at a distance from it there were now *two* grooves of about equal width. One of these ran away into the darkness on our right as we faced the sharp edge, and at an ever-widening angle, while the other, at a similar angle, ran into the darkness to the left of the knife of cliff. That was all.

No, there were two more notable things. Neither of the grooves now lay within hundreds of yards of the cliff, perhaps a quarter of a mile, for be it remembered we had followed the rising rock between them. To put it quite clearly, it was exactly as though one line of rails had separated into two lines of rails, as often enough they do, and an observer standing on high ground between could see them both vanishing into tunnels to the right and left, but far apart.

The second notable thing was that the right-hand groove, where first we saw it at the point of separation, was not polished like the left-hand groove, although at some time or other it seemed to have been subjected to the pressure of the same terrific weight which cut its fellow out of the bed of rock or iron, as the sharp wheels of a heavily laden wagon sink ruts into a roadway.

"What does it all mean, Lord Oro?" I asked when he had led us back to the spot where the one groove began to be two grooves, that is, a mile or so away from the razor-edged cliff.

"This, Humphrey," he answered. "That which travels along yonder road, when it reaches this spot on which we stand, follows the left-hand path which is made bright with its passage. Yet, could a giant at that moment of its touching this exact spot on which I lay my hand, thrust it with sufficient strength, it would leave the left-hand road and take the right-hand road."

"And if it did, what then, Lord Oro?"

"Then within an hour or so, when it had travelled far enough upon its way, the balance of the earth would be changed, and great things would happen in the world above, as once they happened in bygone days. Now do you understand, Humphrey?"

"Good Heavens! Yes, I understand now," I answered. "But fortunately there is no such giant."

Oro broke into a mocking laugh and his grey old face lit up with a fiendish exultation, as he cried:

"Fool! I, Oro, am that giant. Once in the dead days I turned the balance of the world from the right-hand road which now is dull with disuse, to the left-hand road which glitters so brightly to your eyes, and the face of the earth was changed. Now again I will turn it from the left-hand road to the right-hand road in which for millions of years it was wont to run, and once more the face of the earth shall change, and those who are left living upon the earth, or who in the course of ages shall come to live upon the new earth, must bow down to Oro and take him and his seed to be their gods and kings."

When I heard this I was overwhelmed and could not answer. Also I remembered a certain confused picture which Yva had shown to us in the Temple of Nyo. But supported by his disbelief, Bickley asked:

"And how often does the balance of which you speak come this way, Lord Oro?"

"Once only in many years; the number is my secret, Bickley," he replied.

"Then there is every reason to hope that it will not trouble us," remarked Bickley with a suspicion of mockery in his voice.

"Do you think so, you learned Bickley?" asked Oro. "If so, I do not. Unless my skill has failed me and my calculations have gone awry, that Traveller of which I tell should presently be with us. Hearken now! What is that sound we hear?"

As he spoke there reached our ears the first, far-off murmurs of a dreadful music. I cannot describe it in words because that is impossible, but it was something like to the buzz of a thousand humming-tops such as are loved by children because of their weird song.

"Back to the wall!" cried Oro triumphantly. "The time is short!"

So back we went, Oro pausing a while behind and overtaking us with long, determined strides. Yva led us, gliding at my side and, as I thought, now and again glanced at my face with a look that was half anxious and half pitiful. Also twice she stooped and patted Tommy.

We reached the wall, though not quite at the spot

whence we had started to examine the grooved roads. At least I think this was so, since now for the first time I observed a kind of little window in its rocky face. It stood about five feet from its floor level, and was perhaps ten inches square, not more. In short, except for its shape it resembled a ship's porthole rather than a window. Its substance appeared to be talc, or some such material, and inches thick, yet through it, after Oro had cast aside some sort of covering, came a glare like that of a search-light. In fact it was a search-light so far as concerned one of its purposes.

By this window or porthole lay a pile of cloaks, also four objects which looked like Zulu battle shields cut in some unknown metal or material. Very deftly, very quietly, Yva lifted these cloaks and wrapped one of them about each of us, and while she was thus employed I noticed that they were of a substance very similar to that of the gown she wore, which I have described, but harder. Next she gave one of the metal-like shields to each of us, bidding us hold them in front of our bodies and heads, and only to look through certain slits in them in which were eye-pieces that appeared to be of the same horny stuff as the search-light window. Further, she commanded us to stand in a row with our backs against the rock wall, at certain spots which she indicated with great precision, and whatever we saw or heard on no account to move.

So there we stood, Bickley next to me, and beyond him Bastin. Then Yva took the fourth shield, as I noted a much larger one than ours, and placed herself between me and the search-light or porthole. On the other side of this was Oro who had no shield.

These arrangements took some minutes and during that time occupied all our attention. When they were completed, however, our curiosity and fear began to re-assert themselves. I looked about me and perceived that Oro had his right hand upon what seemed to be a rough stone rod, in shape not unlike that with which railway points are moved. He shouted to us to stand still and keep the shields over our faces. Then very gently he pressed upon the lever. The porthole sank the fraction of an inch, and instantly there leapt from it a most terrific blaze of lightning, which shot across the blackness in front and, as lightning does, revealed far, far away another wall, or rather cliff, like that against which we leant.

"All works well," exclaimed Oro in a satisfied voice, lifting his hand from the rod, "and the strength which I have stored will be more than enough."

Meanwhile the humming noise came nearer and grew in volume.

"I say," said Bickley, "as you know, I have been sceptical, but I don't like this business. Oro, what are you going to do?"

"Sink half the world beneath the seas," said Oro, "and raise up that which I drowned more than two thousand centuries ago. But as you do not believe that I have this power, Bickley, why do you ask such questions?"

"*I* believe that you have it, which was why I tried to shoot you yesterday," said Bastin. "For your soul's sake I beg you to desist from an attempt which I am sure will not succeed, but which will certainly involve your eternal damnation, since the failure will be no fault of yours."

Then I spoke also, saying:

"I implore you, Lord Oro, to let this business be. I do not know exactly how much or how little you can do, but I understand that your object is to slay men by millions in order to raise up another world of which you will be the absolute king, as you were of some past empire that has been destroyed, either through your agency or otherwise. No good can come of such ambitions. Like Bastin, for your soul's sake I pray you to let them be."

"What Humphrey says I repeat," said Yva. "My Father, although you know it not, you seek great evil, and from these hopes you sow you will harvest nothing save a loss of which you do not dream. Moreover, your plans will fail. Now I who am, like yourself, of the Children of Wisdom, have spoken for the first and last time, and my words are true. I pray you give them weight, my Father."

Oro heard, and grew furious.

"What!" he said. "Are you against me, every one, and my own daughter also? I would lift you up, I would make you rulers of a new world; I would destroy your vile civilisations which I have studied with my eyes, that I may build better! To you, Humphrey, I would give my only child in marriage that from you may spring a divine race of kings! And yet you are against me and set up your puny scruples as a barrier across my path of wisdom. Well, I tread them down, I go on my appointed way. But beware how you try to hold me back. If any one of you should attempt to come between me and my ends, know that I will destroy you all. Obey or die."

"Well, he has had his chance and he won't take it," said Bastin in the silence that followed. "The man must go to the devil his own way and there is nothing more to be said."

I say the silence, but it was no more silent. The

distant humming grew to a roar, the roar to a hellish hurricane of sound which presently drowned all attempts at ordinary speech.

Then bellowing like ten millions of bulls, at length far away there appeared something terrible. I can only describe its appearance as that of an attenuated mountain on fire. When it drew nearer I perceived that it was more like a ballet-dancer whirling round and round upon her toes, or rather all the ballet-dancers in the world rolled into one and then multiplied a million times in size. No, it was like a mushroom with two stalks, one above and one below, or a huge top with a point on which it spun, a swelling belly and another point above. But what a top! It must have been two thousand feet high, if it was an inch, and its circumference who could measure?

On it came, dancing, swaying and spinning at a rate inconceivable, so that it looked like a gigantic wheel of fire. Yet it was not fire that clothed it but rather some phosphorescence, since from it came no heat. Yes, a phosphorescence arranged in bands of ghastly blue and lurid red, with streaks of other colours running up between, and a kind of waving fringe of purple.

The fire-mountain thundered on with a voice like to that of avalanches or of icebergs crashing from their parent glaciers to the sea. Its terrific aspect was appalling, and its weight caused the solid rock to quiver like a leaf. Watching it, we felt as ants might feel at the advent of the crack of doom, for its mere height and girth and size overwhelmed us. We could not even speak. The last words I heard were from the mouth of Oro who screamed out:

"Behold the balance of the World, you miserable,

doubting men, and behold me change its path—turning it as the steersman turns a ship!"

Then he made certain signs to Yva, who in obedience to them approached the porthole or search-light to which she did something that I could not distinguish. The effect was to make the beam of light much stronger and sharper, also to shift it on to the point or foot of the spinning mountain and, by an aiming of the lens from time to time, to keep it there.

This went on for a while, since the dreadful thing did not travel fast notwithstanding the frightful speed of its revolutions. I should doubt indeed if it advanced more quickly than a man could walk; at any rate so it seemed to us. But we had no means of judging its real rate of progress whereof we knew as little as we did of the course it followed in the bowels of the earth. Perhaps that was spiral, from the world's deep heart upwards, and this was the highest point it reached. Or perhaps it remained stationary, but still spinning, for scores or hundreds of years in some central power-house of its own, whence, in obedience to unknown laws, from time to time it made these terrific journeys.

No one knows, unless perhaps Oro did, in which case he kept the information to himself, and no one will ever know. At any rate there it was, travelling towards us on its giant butt, the peg of the top as it were, which, hidden in a cloud of friction-born sparks that enveloped it like the cup of a curving flower of fire, whirled round and round at an infinite speed. It was on this flaming flower that the search-light played steadily, doubtless that Oro might mark and measure its monstrous progress.

"He is going to try to send the thing down the right-hand path," I shouted into Bickley's ear.

"Can't be done! Nothing can shift a travelling weight of tens of millions of tons one inch," Bickley roared back, trying to look confident.

Clearly, however, Yva thought that it could be done, for of a sudden she cast down her shield and, throwing herself upon her knees, stretched out her hands in supplication to her father. I understood, as did we all, that she was imploring him to abandon his hellish purpose. He glared at her and shook his head. Then, as she still went on praying, he struck her across the face with his hand and pushed her to her feet again. My blood boiled as I saw it and I think I should have sprung at him, had not Bickley caught hold of me, shouting, "Don't, or he will kill her and us too."

Yva lifted her shield and returned to her station, and in the blue discharges which now flashed almost continuously, and the phosphorescent glare of the advancing mountain, I saw that though her beautiful face worked beneath the pain of the blow, her eyes remained serene and purposeful. Even then I wondered—what was the purpose shining through them. Also I wondered if I was about to be called upon to make that sacrifice of which she had spoken, and if so, how. Of one thing I was determined—that if the call came it should not find me deaf. Yet all the while I was horribly afraid.

At another sign from Oro, Yva did something more to the lens—again, being alongside of her, I could not see what it was. The beam of light shifted and wandered till, far away, it fell exactly upon that spot where the rock began to rise into the ridge which separated the two grooves or roads and ended in the razor-edged cliff. Moreover I observed that Oro, who left it the last of us, had either placed something white to mark this first infinitesimal bulging of the floor of the groove, or had smeared it with chalk or shining pigment. I observed also what I had not been able to see before, that a thin white line ran across the floor, no doubt to give the precise direction of this painted rise of rock, and that the glare of the search-light now lay exactly over that line.

The monstrous, flaming gyroscope fashioned in Nature's workshop, for such without doubt it was, was drawing near, emitting as it came a tumult of sounds which, with the echoes that they caused, almost overwhelmed our senses. Poor little Tommy, already cowed, although he was a bold-natured beast, broke down entirely, and I could see from his open mouth that he was howling with terror. He stared about him, then ran to Yva and pawed at her, evidently asking to be taken into her arms. She thrust him away, almost fiercely, and made signs to me to lift him up and hold him beneath my shield. This I did, reflecting sadly that if I was to be sacrificed, Tommy must share my fate. I even thought of passing him on to Bickley, but had no time. Indeed I could not attract his attention, for Bickley was staring with all his eyes at the nightmare-like spectacle which was in progress about us. Indeed no nightmare, no wild imagination of which the mind of man is capable, could rival the aspect of its stupendous facts.

Think of them! The unmeasured space of blackness threaded by those globes of ghastly incandescence that now hung a while and now shot upwards, downwards, across, apparently without origin or end, like a stream of meteors that had gone mad. Then the travelling mountain, two thousand feet in height, or more, with its enormous saucer-like rim painted round with bands of lurid red and blue, and about its grinding foot the tulip bloom of emitted flame. Then the fierce-faced Oro at his post, his hand upon the rod, waiting, remorseless, to drown half of this great world, with the lovely Yva standing calm-eyed like a saint in hell and watching me above the edge of the shield which such a saint might bear to turn aside the fiery darts of the wicked. And lastly we three men flattened terror-stricken, against the wall.

Nightmare! Imagination! No, these pale before that scene which it was given to our human eyes to witness.

And all the while, bending, bowing towards us—away from us—making obeisance to the path in front as though in greeting, to the path behind as though in farewell; instinct with a horrible life, with a hideous and gigantic grace, that titanic Terror whirled onwards to the mark of fate.

At the moment nothing could persuade me that it was not alive and did not know its awful mission. Visions flashed across my mind. I thought of the peoples of the world sleeping in their beds, or going about their business, or engaged even in the work of war. I thought of the ships upon the seas steaming steadily towards their far-off ports. Then I thought of what presently might happen to them, of the tremors followed by convulsions, of the sudden crashing down of cities, such as we had seen in the picture Yva showed us in the Temple, of the inflow of the waters of the deep piled up in mighty waves, of the woe and desolation as of the end of the world, and of the quiet, following death. So I thought and in my heart prayed to the great Arch-Architect of the Universe to stretch out His Arm to avert this fearsome ruin of His handiwork.

Oro glared, his thin fingers tightened their grip upon the rod, his hair and long beard seemed to bristle with furious and delighted excitement. The purple-fringed rim of the Monster had long overshadowed the whited patch of rock; its grinding foot was scarce ten yards away. Oro made more signs to Yva who, beneath the shelter of her shield, again bent down and did something that I could not see. Then, as though her part were played, she rose, drew the grey hood of her cloak all about her face so that her eyes alone remained visible, took one step towards me and in the broken English we had taught her, called into my ear.

"Humphrey, God you bless! Humphrey, we meet soon. Forget not me!"

She stepped back again before I could attempt to answer, and next instant with a hideous, concentrated effort, Oro bending himself double, thrust upon the rod, as I could see from his open mouth, shouting while he thrust.

At the same moment, with a swift spring, Yva leapt immediately in front of the lens or window, so that the metallic shield with which she covered herself pressed against its substance.

Simultaneously Oro flung up his arms as though in horror.

Too late! The shutter fell and from behind it there sprang out a rush of living flame. It struck on Yva's shield and expanded to right and left. The insulated shield and garments that she wore seemed to resist it. For a fraction of time she stood there like a glowing angel, wrapped in fire.

Then she was swept outwards and upwards and at a little distance dissolved like a ghost and vanished from our sight.

Yva was ashes! Yva was gone! The sacrifice was consummated!

And not in vain! Not in vain! On her poor breast she had received the full blast of that hellish lightning flash. Yet whilst destroying, it turned away from her, seeking the free paths of the air. So it came about that its obstructed strength struck the foot of the travelling gyroscope, diffused and did not suffice to thrust it that one necessary inch on which depended the fate of half the world, or missing it altogether, passed away on either side. Even so the huge, gleaming mountain rocked and trembled. Once, twice, thrice, it bowed itself towards us as though in majestic homage to greatness passed away. For a second, too, its course was checked, and at the check the earth quaked and trembled. Yes, then the world shook, and the blue globes of fire went out, while I was thrown to the ground.

When they returned again, the flaming monster was once more sailing majestically upon its way and *down the accustomed left-hand path!*

Indeed the sacrifice was not in vain. The world shook—but Yva had saved the world!

CHAPTER XXVI

TOMMY

I LAY still a while, on my back as I had fallen, and beneath the shield-like defence which Yva had given to me. Notwithstanding the fire-resisting, metalised stuff of which it was made, I noted that it was twisted and almost burnt through. Doubtless the stored-up electricity or earth magnetism, or whatever it may have been that had leapt out of that hole, being diffused by the resistance with which it was met, had grazed me with its outer edge, and had it not been for the shield and cloak, I also should have been burned up. I wished, oh! how I wished that it had been so. Then, by now all must have finished and I should have known the truth as to what awaits us beyond the change: sleep, or dreams, or perchance the fullest life. Also I should not have learned alone.

Lying there thus, idly, as though in a half-sleep, I felt Tommy licking my face, and throwing my arm about the poor little frightened beast, I watched the great world-balance as it retreated on its eternal journey. At one time its vast projecting rim had overshadowed us and almost seemed to touch the cliff of rock against which we leant. I remember that the effect of that shining arch a thousand feet or so above our heads was wonderful. It reminded me of a canopy of blackest thunder clouds supported upon a framework of wheeling rainbows, while beneath it all the children of the devil shouted together in joy. I noted this effect only a few seconds before Yva spoke to me and leapt into the path of the flash.

Now, however, it was far away, a mere flaming wheel that became gradually smaller, and its Satanic voices were growing faint. As I have said, I watched its disappearance idly, reflecting that I should never look upon its like again; also that it was something well worth going forth to see. Then I became aware that the humming, howling din had decreased sufficiently to enable me to hear human voices without effort. Bastin was addressing Bickley—like myself they were both upon the ground.

"Her translation, as you may have noticed, Bickley, if you were not too frightened, was really very remarkable. No doubt it will have reminded you, as it did me, of that of Elijah. She had exactly the appearance of a person going up to Heaven in a vehicle of fire. The destination was certainly the same, and even the cloak she wore added a familiar touch and increased the similarity."

"At any rate it did not fall upon you," answered Bickley with something like a sob, in a voice of mingled awe and exasperation. "For goodness' sake! Bastin, stop your Biblical parallels and let us adore, yes, let us adore the divinest creature that the earth has borne!"

Never have I loved Bickley more than when I heard him utter those words.

"'Divinest' is a large term, Bickley, and one to which I hesitate to subscribe, remembering as I do certain of the prophets and the Early Fathers with all their faults, not of course to mention the Apostles. But——" here he paused, for suddenly all three of us became aware of Oro.

He also has been thrown to the ground by the strength of the prisoned forces which he gathered and loosed upon their unholy errand, but, as I rejoiced to observe, had suffered from them much more than ourselves. Doubtless this was owing to the fact that he had sprung forward in a last wild effort to save his daughter, or to prevent her from interfering with his experiment, I know not which. As a result his right cheek was much scorched, his right arm was withered and helpless, and his magnificent beard was half burnt off him. Further, very evidently he was suffering from severe shock, for he rocked upon his feet and shook like an aspen leaf. All this, however, did not interfere with the liveliness of his grief and rage.

There he stood, a towering shape, like a lightning-smitten statue, and cursed us, especially Bastin.

"My daughter has gone!" he cried, "burned up by the fiery power that is my servant. Nothing remains of her but dust, and, Priest, this is your doing. You poisoned her heart with your childish doctrines of mercy and sacrifice, and the rest, so that she threw herself into the path of the flash to save some miserable races that she had never even known."

He paused exhausted, whereon Bastin answered him with spirit:

"Yes, Oro, she being a holy woman, has gone where *you* will never follow her. Also it is your own fault since you should have listened to her entreaties instead of boxing her ears like the brute you are."

"My daughter is gone," went on Oro, recovering his strength, "and my great designs are ruined. Yet only for a while," he added, "for the world-balance will return again, if not till long after your life-spans are done."

"If you don't doctor yourself, Lord Oro," said Bickley, also rising, "I may tell you as one who understands such things, that most likely it will be after *your* life-span is done also. Although their effect may be delayed, severe shocks from burns and over-excitement are apt to prove fatal to the aged."

Oro snarled at him; no other word describes it.

"And there are other things, Physician," he said, "which are apt to prove fatal to the young. At least now you will no longer deny my power."

"I am not so sure," answered Bickley, "since it seems that there is a greater Power, namely that of a woman's love and sacrifice."

"And a greater still," interrupted Bastin, "Which put those ideas into her head."

"As for you, Humphrey," went on Oro, "I rejoice to think that you at least have lost two things that man desires above all other things—the woman you sought and the future kingship of the world."

I stood up and faced him.

"The first I have gained, although how, you do not understand, Oro," I answered. "And of the second, seeing that it would have come through you, on your conditions, I am indeed glad to be rid. I wish no power that springs from murder, and no gifts from one who answered his daughter's prayer with blows."

For a moment he seemed remorseful.

"She vexed me with her foolishness," he said. Then his rage blazed up again:

"And it was you who taught it to her," he went on. "You are guilty, all three of you, and therefore I am left with none to serve me in my age; therefore also my mighty schemes are overthrown."

"Also, Oro, if you speak truth, therefore half the

world is saved," I added quietly, "and one has left it of whom it was unworthy."

"You think that these civilisations of yours, as you are pleased to call them, are saved, do you?" he sneered. "Yet, even if Bickley were right and I should die and become powerless, I tell you that they are already damned. I have studied them in your books and seen them with my eyes, and I say that they are rotten before ever they are ripe, and that their end shall be the end of the Sons of Wisdom, to die for lack of increase. That is why I would have saved the East, because in it alone there is increase, and thence alone can rise the great last race of man which I would have given to your children for an heritage. Moreover, think not that you Westerners have done with wars. I tell you that they are but begun and that the sword shall eat you up, and what the sword spares class shall snatch from class in the struggle for supremacy and ease."

Thus he spoke with extraordinary and concentrated bitterness that I confess would have frightened me, had I been capable of fear, which at the moment I was not. Who is afraid when he has lost all?

Nor was Bastin alarmed, if for other reasons.

"I think it right to tell you, Oro," he said, "that the only future you need trouble about is your own. God Almighty will look after the western civilisations in whatever way He may think best, as you may remember He did just now. Only I am sure *you* won't be here to see how it is done."

Again fury blazed in Oro's eyes.

"At least I will look after you, you half-bred dogs, who yap out ill-omened prophecies of death into my face. Since the three of you loved my daughter whom you brought to her doom, and were by her beloved, if differently, I think it best that you should follow on her road. How? That is the question? Shall I leave you to starve in these great caves?—Nay, look not towards the road of escape which doubtless she pointed out to you, for, as Humphrey knows, I can travel swiftly and I will make sure that you find it blocked. Or shall I——" and he glanced upwards at the great globes of wandering fire, as though he purposed to summon them to be our death, as doubtless he could have done.

"I do not care what you do," I answered wearily. "Only I would beg you to strike quickly. Yet for my friends I am sorry, since it was I who led them on this quest, and for you, too, Tommy," I added, looking at the poor little hound. "You were foolish, Tommy," I went on, "when you scented out that old tyrant in his coffin, at least for your own sake."

Indeed the dog was terribly scared. He whined continually and from time to time ran a little way and then returned to us, suggesting that we should go from this horror-haunted spot. Lastly, as though he understood that it was Oro who kept us there, he went to him and jumping up, licked his hand in a beseeching fashion.

The super-man looked at the dog and as he looked the rage went out of his face and was replaced by something resembling pity.

"I do not wish the beast to die," he muttered to himself in low reflective tones, as though he thought aloud, "for of them all it alone liked and did not fear me. I might take it with me but still it would perish of grief in the loneliness of the caves. Moreover, she loved it whom I shall see no more; yes, Yva——" as he spoke the name his voice broke a little. "Yet if I suffer them to escape they will tell my story to the world and make me a laughing-stock. Well, if they do, what does it matter? None of those Western fools would believe it; thinking that they knew all; like Bickley they would mock and say that they were mad, or liars."

Again Tommy licked his hand, but more confidently, as though instinct told him something of what was passing in Oro's mind. I watched with an idle wonder, marvelling whether it were possible that this merciless being would after all spare us for the sake of the dog.

So, strange to say, it came about, for suddenly Oro looked up and said:

"Get you gone, and quickly, before my mood changes. The hound has saved you. For its sake I give you your lives, who otherwise should certainly have died. She who has gone pointed out to you, I doubt not, a road that runs to the upper air. I think that it is still open. Indeed," he added, closing his eyes for a moment, "I see that it is still open, if long and difficult. Follow it, and should you win through, take your boat and sail away as swiftly as you can. Whether you die or live I care nothing, but my hands will be clean of your blood, although yours are stained with Yva's. Begone! and my curse go with you."

Without waiting for further words we went to fetch our lanterns, water-bottles and bag of food which we had laid down at a little distance. As we approached them I looked up and saw Oro standing some way off. The light from one of the blue globes of fire which passed close above his head, shone upon him and made him ghastly. Moreover, it seemed to me as though approaching death had written its name upon his malevolent countenance.

I turned my head away, for about his aspect in those sinister surroundings there was something horrible, something menacing and repellent to man and of him I wished to see no more. Nor indeed did I, for when I glanced in that direction again Oro was gone. I suppose that he had retreated into the shadows where no light played.

We gathered up our gear, and while the others were relighting the lanterns, I walked a few paces forward to the spot where Yva had been dissolved in the devouring fire. Something caught my eye upon the rocky floor. I picked it up. It was the ring, or rather the remains of the ring that I had given her on that night when we declared our love amidst the ruins by the crater lake. She had never worn it on her hand but for her own reasons, as she told me, suspended it upon her breast beneath her robe. It was an ancient ring that I had bought in Egypt, fashioned of gold in which was set a very hard basalt or other black stone. On this was engraved the *ank* or looped cross, which was the Egyptian symbol of Life, and round it a snake, the symbol of Eternity. The gold was for the most part melted, but the stone, being so hard and protected by the shield and asbestos cloak, for such I suppose it was, had resisted the fury of the flash. Only now it was white instead of black, like a burnt onyx that had known the funeral pyre. Indeed, perhaps it was an onyx. I kissed it and hid it away, for it seemed to me to convey a greeting and with it a promise.

Then we started, a very sad and dejected trio. Leaving with a shudder that vast place where the blue lights played eternally, we came to the shaft up and down which the travelling stone pursued its endless path, and saw it arrive and depart again.

"I wonder he did not send us that way," said Bickley, pointing to it.

"I am sure I am very glad it never occurred to him," answered Bastin, "for I am certain that we could not have made the journey again without our guide, Yva."

I looked at him and he ceased. Somehow I could not bear, as yet, to hear her beloved name spoken by other lips.

Then we entered the passage that she had pointed out to us, and began a most terrible journey which. so far as we could judge, for we lost any exact count of time, took us about sixty hours. The road, it is true, was smooth and unblocked, but the ascent was fearfully steep and slippery; so much so that often we were obliged to pull each other up it and lie down to rest.

Had it not been for those large, felt-covered bottles of Life-water, I am sure we should never have won through. But this marvellous elixir, drunk a little at a time, always re-invigorated us and gave us strength to push on. Also we had some food, and fortunately our spare oil held out, for the darkness in that tunnel was complete. Tommy became so exhausted that at length we must carry him by turns. He would have died had it not been for the water; indeed I thought that he was going to die.

After our last rest and a short sleep, however, he seemed to begin to recover, and generally there was something in his manner which suggested to us that he knew himself to be not far from the surface of the earth towards which we had crawled upwards for thousands upon thousands of feet, fortunately without meeting with any zone of heat which was not bearable.

We were right, for when we had staggered forward a little further, suddenly Tommy ran ahead of us and vanished. Then we heard him barking but where we could not see, since the tunnel appeared to take a turn and continue, but this time on a downward course, while the sound of the barks came from our right. We searched with the lanterns which were now beginning to die and found a little hole almost filled with fallen pieces of rock. We scooped these away with our hands, making an aperture large enough to creep through. A few more yards and we saw light, the blessed light of the moon, and in it stood Tommy barking hoarsely. Next we heard the sound of the sea. We struggled on desperately and presently pushed our way through bushes and vegetation on to a steep declivity. Down this we rolled and scrambled, to find ourselves at last lying upon a sandy beach, whilst above us the full moon shone in the heavens.

Here, with a prayer of thankfulness, we flung ourselves down and slept.

If it had not been for Tommy and we had gone further along the tunnel, which I have little doubt stretched on beneath the sea, where, I wonder, should we have slept that night?

When we woke the sun was shining high in the heavens. Evidently there had been rain towards the dawn, though as we were lying beneath the shelter of some broad-leaved tree, from it we had suffered little inconvenience. Oh! how beautiful, after our sojourn in those unholy caves, were the sun and the sea and the sweet air and the raindrops hanging on the leaves.

We did not wake of ourselves; indeed if we had been left alone I am sure that we should have slept the clock round, for we were terribly exhausted. What woke us was the chatter of a crowd of Orofenans who were gathered at a distance from the tree and engaged in staring at us in a frightened way, also the barks of Tommy who objected to their intrusion. Among the people I recognised our old friend the chief Marama by his feather cloak, and sitting up, beckoned to him to approach. After a good deal of hesitation he came, walking delicately like Agag, and stopping from time to time to study us, as though he were not sure that we were real.

"What frightens you, Marama?" I asked him.

"You frighten us, O Friend-from-the-Sea. Whence did you and the Healer and the Bellower come and why do your faces look like those of ghosts and why is the little black beast so large-eyed and so thin? Over the lake we know you did not come, for we have watched day and night; moreover there is no canoe upon the shore. Also it would not have been possible."

"Why not?" I asked idly.

"Come and see," he answered.

Rising stiffly we emerged from beneath the tree and perceived that we were at the foot of the cliff against which the remains of the yacht had been borne by the great tempest. Indeed there it was within a couple of hundred yards of us.

Following Marama we climbed the sloping path which ran up the cliff and ascended a knoll whence we could see the lake and the cone of the volanco in its centre. At least we used to be able to see this cone, but now, at any rate with the naked eye, we could make out nothing, except a small brown spot in the midst of the waters of the lake.

"The mountain which rose up many feet in that storm which brought you to Orofena. Friend-from-the-

Sea, has now sunk till only the very top of it is to be seen," said Marama solemnly. "Even the Rock of Offerings has vanished beneath the water, and with it the house that we built for you."

"Yes," I said, affecting no surprise. "But when did that happen?"

"Five nights ago the world shook, Friend-from-the-Sea, and when the sun rose we saw that the mouth of the cave which appeared on the day of your coming, had vanished, and that the holy mountain itself had sunk deep, so that now only the crest of it is left above the water."

"Such things happen," I replied carelessly.

"Yes, Friend-from-the-Sea. Like many other marvels they happen where you and your companions are. Therefore we beg you who can arise out of the earth like spirits, to leave us at once before our island and all of us who dwell thereon are drowned beneath the ocean. Leave us before we kill you, if indeed you be men, or die at your hands if, as we think, you be evil spirits who can throw up mountains and drag them down, and create gods that slay, and move about in the bowels of the world."

"That is our intention, for our business here is done," I answered calmly. "Come now and help us to depart. But first bring us food. Bring it in plenty, for we must victual our boat."

Marama bowed and issued the necessary orders. Indeed food sufficient for our immediate needs was already there as an offering, and of it we ate with thankfulness.

Then we boarded the ship and examined the lifeboat. Thanks to our precautions it was still in very fair order and only needed some little caulking which we did with grass fibre and pitch from the stores. After this with the help of the Orofenans who worked hard in their desperate desire to be rid of us, we drew the boat into the sea, and provisioned her with stores from the ship, and with an ample supply of water. Everything being ready at last, we waited for the evening wind which always blew off shore, to start. As it was not due for half an hour or more, I walked back to the tree under which we had slept and tried to find the hole whence we had emerged from the tunnel on to the face of the cliff.

My hurried search proved useless. The declivity of the cliff was covered with tropical growth, and the heavy rain had washed away every trace of our descent, and very likely filled the hole itself with earth. At any rate, of it I could discover nothing. Then as the breeze began to blow I returned to the boat and here bade adieu to Marama, who gave me his feather cloak as a farewell gift.

"Good-bye, Friend-from-the-Sea," he said to me. "We are glad to have seen you and thank you for many things. But we do not wish to see you any more."

"Good-bye, Marama," I answered. "What you say, we echo. At least you have now no great lump upon your neck and we have rid you of your wizards. But beware of the god Oro who dwells in the mountain, for if you anger him he will sink your island beneath the sea."

"And remember all that I have taught you," shouted Bastin.

Marama shivered, though whether at the mention of the god Oro, of whose powers the Orofenans had so painful a recollection, or at the result of Bastin's teachings, I do not know. And that was the last we shall ever see of each other in this world.

The island faded behind us and, sore at heart because of all that we had found and lost again, for three days we sailed northward with a fair and steady wind. On the fourth evening by an extraordinary stroke of fortune, we fell in with an American tramp steamer, trading from the South Sea Islands to San Francisco. To the captain, who treated us very kindly, we said simply that we were a party of Englishmen whose yacht had been wrecked on a small island several hundreds of miles away, of which we knew neither the name, if it had one, nor the position.

This story was accepted without question, for such things often happen in those latitudes, and in due course we were landed at San Francisco, where we made certain depositions before the British Consul as to the loss of the yacht *Star of the South.* Then we crossed America, having obtained funds by cable, and sailed for England in a steamer flying the flag of the United States.

Of the great war which made this desirable I do not speak since it has nothing, or rather little, to do with this history. In the end we arrived safely at Liverpool, and thence travelled to our homes in Devonshire.

Thus ended the history of our dealings with Oro, the super-man who began his life more than two hundred and fifty thousand years ago, and with his daughter, Yva, whom Bastin still often calls the Glittering Lady.

CHAPTER XXVII

BASTIN DISCOVERS A RESEMBLANCE

THERE is little more to tell.

Shortly after our return Bickley, like a patriotic Englishman, volunteered for service at the front and departed in the uniform of the R.A.M.C. Before he left he took the opportunity of explaining to Bastin how much better it was in such a national emergency as existed, to belong to a profession in which a man could do something to help the bodies of his countrymen that had been broken in the common cause, than to one like his in which it was only possible to pelt them with vain words.

"You think that, do you, Bickley?" answered Bastin. "Well, I hold that it is better to heal souls than bodies, because, as even you will have learned out there in Orofena, they last so much longer."

"I am not certain that I learned anything of the sort," said Bickley, "or even that Oro was more than an ordinary old man. He said that he had lived a thousand years, but what was there to prove this except his word, which is worth nothing?"

"There was the Lady Yva's word also, which is worth a great deal, Bickley."

"Yes, but she may have meant a thousand moons. Further, as according to her own showing she was still quite young, how could she know her father's age?"

"Quite so, Bickley. But all she actually said was that she was of the same age as one of our women of twenty-seven, which may have meant two hundred and seventy for all I know. However, putting that aside you will admit that they had both slept for two hundred and fifty thousand years."

"I admit that they slept, Bastin, because I helped to awaken them, but for how long there is nothing to show, except those star maps which are probably quite inaccurate."

"They are not inaccurate," I broke in, "for I have had them checked by leading astronomers who say that they show a marvellous knowledge of the heavens as these were two hundred and fifty thousand years ago, and are to-day."

Here I should state that those two metal maps and the ring which I gave to Yva and found again after the catastrophe, were absolutely the only things connected with her or with Oro that we brought away with us. The former I would never part with, feeling their value as evidence. Therefore, when we descended to the city Nyo and the depths beneath, I took them with me wrapped in cloth in my pocket. Thus they were preserved. Everything else went when the Rock of Offerings and the cave mouth sank beneath the waters of the lake.

This may have happened either in the earth tremor, which no doubt was caused by the advance of the terrific world-balance, or when the electric power, though diffused and turned by Yva's insulated body, struck the great gyroscope's travelling foot with sufficient strength, not to shift it indeed on to the right-hand path as Oro had designed, but still to cause it to stagger and even perhaps to halt for the fraction of a second. Even this pause may have been enough to cause convulsions of the earth above; indeed, I gathered from Marama and other Orofenans that such convulsions had occurred on and around the island at what must have corresponded with that moment of the loosing of the force.

This loss of our belongings in the house of the Rock of Offerings was the more grievous because among them were some Kodak photographs which I had taken, including portraits of Oro and one of Yva that was really excellent, to say nothing of pictures of the mouth of the cave and of the ruins and crater lake above. How bitterly I regret that I did not keep these photographs in my pocket with the map-plates.

"Even if the star-maps are correct, still it proves nothing," said Bickley, "since possibly Oro's astronomical skill might have enabled him to draw that of the sky at any period, though I allow this is impossible."

"I doubt his taking so much trouble merely to deceive three wanderers who lacked the knowledge even to check them," I said. "But all this misses the point, Bickley. However long they had slept, that man and woman did arise from seeming death. They did dwell in those marvellous caves with their evidences of departed civilisations, and they did show us that fearful, world-wandering gyroscope. These things we saw."

"I admit that we saw them, Arbuthnot, and I admit that they are one and all beyond human comprehension. To that extent I am converted, and, I may add, humbled," said Bickley.

"So you ought to be," exclaimed Bastin, "seeing that you always swore that there was nothing in the world that is not capable of a perfectly natural explanation."

"Of which all these things may be capable, Bastin, if only we held the key."

"Very well, Bickley, but how do you explain what the Lady Yva did? I may tell you now what she commanded me to conceal at the time, namely, that she became a Christian; so much so that by her own will, I baptised and confirmed her on the very morning of her sacrifice. Doubtless it was this that changed her heart so much that she became willing, of course without my knowledge, to leave everything she cared for," here he looked hard at me, "and lay down her life to save the world, half of which she believed was about to be drowned by Oro. Now, considering her history and upbringing, I call this a spiritual marvel, much greater than any you now admit, and one *you* can't explain, Bickley."

"No, I cannot explain, or, at any rate, I will not try," he answered, also staring hard at me. "Whatever she believed, or did not believe, and whatever would or would not have happened, she was a great and wonderful woman whose memory I worship."

"Quite so, Bickley, and now perhaps you see my point, that what you describe as mere vain words may also be helpful to mankind; more so, indeed, than your surgical instruments and pills."

"You couldn't convert Oro, anyway," exclaimed Bickley, with irritation.

"No, Bickley; but then I have always understood that the devil is beyond conversion because he is beyond repentance. You see, I think that if that old scoundrel was not the devil himself, at any rate he was a bit of him, and, if I am right, I am not ashamed to have failed in his case."

"Even Oro was not utterly bad, Bastin," I said, reflecting on certain traits of mercy that he had shown, or that I dreamed him to have shown in the course of our mysterious midnight journeys to various parts of the earth. Also I remembered that he had loved Tommy and for his sake had spared our lives. Lastly, I do not altogether wonder that he came to certain hasty conclusions as to the value of our modern civilisations.

"I am very glad to hear it, Humphrey, since while there is a spark left the whole fire may burn up again, and I believe that to the Divine mercy there are no limits, though Oro will have a long road to travel before he finds it. And now I have something to say. It has troubled me very much that I was obliged to leave those Orofenans wandering in a kind of religious twilight."

"You couldn't help that," said Bickley, "seeing that if you had stopped, by now you would have been wandering in religious light."

"Still, I am not sure that I ought not to have stopped. I seem to have deserted a field that was open to me. However, it can't be helped, since it is certain that we could never find that island again, even if Oro has not sunk it beneath the sea, as he is quite capable of doing, to cover his tracks, so to speak. So I mean to do my best in another field by way of atonement."

"You are not going to become a missionary?" I said.

"No, but with the consent of the Bishop, who, I think, believes that my *locum* got on better in the parish than I do, as no doubt was the case, I, too, have volunteered for the Front, and been accepted as a chaplain of the 201st Division."

"Why, that's mine!" said Bickley.

"Is it? I am very glad, since now we shall be able to pursue our pleasant arguments and to do our best to open each other's minds."

"You fellows are more fortunate than I am," I remarked. "I also volunteered, but they wouldn't take me, even as a Tommy, although I misstated my age. They told me, or at least a specialist whom I saw did afterwards, that the blow I got on the head from that sorcerer's boy——"

"I know, I know!" broke in Bickley almost roughly. "Of course, things might go wrong at any time. But with care you may live to old age."

"I am sorry to hear it," I said with a sigh, "at least I think I am. Meanwhile, fortunately there is much that I can do at home; indeed a course of action has been suggested to me by an old friend who is now in authority."

Once more Bickley and Bastin in their war-stained uniforms were dining at my table and on the very night of their return from the Front, which was unexpected. Indeed Tommy nearly died of joy on hearing their voices in the hall. They, who played a worthy part in the great struggle, had much to tell me, and naturally their more recent experiences had overlaid to some extent those which we shared in the mysterious island of Orofena. Indeed we did not speak of these until, just as they were going away, Bastin paused beneath a very beautiful portrait of my late wife, the work of an artist famous for his power of bringing out the inner character, or what some might call the soul, of the sitter. He stared at it for a while in his short-sighted way, then said: "Do you know, Arbuthnot, it has sometimes occurred to me, and never more than at this moment, that although they were different in height and so on, there was a really curious physical resemblance between your late wife and the Lady Yva."

"Yes," I answered. "I think so too."

Bickley also examined the portrait very carefully, and as he did so I saw him start. Then he turned away, saying nothing.

Such is the summary of all that has been important in my life. It is, I admit, an odd story and one which suggests problems that I cannot solve. Bastin deals with such things by that acceptance which is the privilege and hall-mark of faith; Bickley disposes, or used to dispose, of them by a blank denial which carries no conviction, and least of all to himself.

What is life to most of us who, like Bickley, think ourselves learned? A round, short but still with time and to spare wherein to be dull and lonesome; a fateful treadmill to which we were condemned we know not how, but apparently through the casual passions of those who went before us and are now forgotten, causing us, as the Bible says, to be born in sin; up which we walk wearily we know not why, seeming never to make progress; off which we fall outworn we know not when or whither.

Such upon the surface it appears to be, nor in fact does our ascertained knowledge, as Bickley would sum it up, take us much further. No prophet has yet arisen who attempted to define either the origin or the reasons of life. Even the very Greatest of them Himself is quite silent on this matter. We are tempted to wonder why. Is it because life as expressed in the higher of human beings, is, or will be too vast, too multiform and too glorious for any definition which we could understand? Is it because in the end it will involve for some, if not for all, majesty on unfathomed majesty, and glory upon unimaginable glory such as at present far outpass the limits of our thought?

The experiences which I have recorded in these pages awake in my heart a hope that this may be so. Bastin is wont, like many others, to talk in a light fashion of Eternity without in the least comprehending what he means by that gigantic term. It is not too much to say that Eternity, something without beginning and without end, and involving, it would appear, an everlasting changelessness, is a state beyond human comprehension. As a matter of fact we mortals do not think in constellations, so to speak, or in æons, but by the measures of our own small earth and of our few days thereon. We cannot really conceive of an existence stretching over even one thousand years, such as that which Oro claimed and the Bible accords to a certain early race of men, omitting of course his two thousand five hundred centuries of sleep. And yet what is this but one grain in the hourglass of time, one day in the lost record of our earth, of its sisters the planets and its father the sun, to say nothing of the universes beyond?

It is because I have come in touch with a prolonged though perfectly finite existence of the sort, that I try to pass on the reflections which the fact of it awoke in me. There are other reflections connected with Yva and the marvel of her love and its various manifestations which arise also. But these I keep to myself. They concern the wonder of woman's heart, which is a microcosm of the hopes and fears and desires and despairs of this humanity of ours whereof from age to age she is the mother.

HUMPHREY ARBUTHNOT.

NOTE

BY J. R. BICKLEY, M.R.C.S.

WITHIN about six months of the date on which he wrote the last words of this history of our joint adventures, my dear friend, Humphrey Arbuthnot, died suddenly, as I had foreseen that probably he would do, from the results of the injury he received in the island of Orofena.

He left me the sole executor to his will, under which he divided his property into three parts. One third he bequeathed to me, one third (which is strictly tied up) to Bastin, and one third to be devoted, under my direction, to the advancement of Science.

His end appears to have been instantaneous, resulting from an effusion of blood upon the brain. When I was summoned I found him lying dead by the writing desk in his library at Fulcombe Priory. He had been writing at the desk, for on it was a piece of paper on which appear these words: *"I have seen her. I——"* There the writing ends, not stating whom he thought he had seen in the moments of mental disturbance or delusion which preceded his decease.

Save for certain verbal corrections, I publish this manuscript without comment as the will directs, only adding that it sets out our mutual experiences very faithfully, though Arbuthnot's deductions from them are not always my own.

I would say also that I am contemplating another visit to the South Sea Islands, where I wish to make some further investigations. I dare say, however, that these will be barren of results, as the fountain of Life-water is buried for ever, nor, as I think, will any human being stand again in the Hades-like halls of Nyo. It is probable also that it would prove impossible to rediscover the island of Orofena, if indeed that volcanic land still remains above the waters of the deep.

Now that he is a very wealthy man, Bastin talks of accompanying me for purposes quite different from my own, but on the whole I hope he will abandon this idea. I may add that when he learned of his unexpected inheritance he talked much of the "deceitfulness of riches," but that he has not as yet taken any steps to escape their golden snare. Indeed he now converses of his added "opportunities of usefulness," I gather in connection with missionary enterprise.

J. R. BICKLEY.

P.S.—I forgot to state that the spaniel Tommy died within three days of his owner. The poor little beast was present in the room at the time of Arbuthnot's passing away, and when found seemed to be suffering from shock. From that moment Tommy refused food and finally was discovered quite dead and lying by the body on Marama's feather cloak, which Arbuthnot often used as a dressing-gown. As Bastin raised some religious objections, I arranged without his knowledge that the dog's ashes should rest not far from those of the master and mistress whom it loved so well.

J. R. B.